P9-CQM-425

Truth... and Consequences

"Does the observance of a nude male in a photograph or painting arouse you strongly? . . . somewhat? . . . not at all?"

The answers to this and similar questions will be tabulated to become part of a vast, anonymous percentage in a nation-wide study of the Sex Habits of the Married American Female. But what of the woman herself, who is left with the bare ravage of her hidden desires, her unfaced failures?

What of Kathleen, who wears widowhood with a shamed relief? What of Naomi, whose restless torment drives her to seek out men? What of Sarah, who abandons children and husband for a lover?

And Paul—what about Paul, a dedicated member of the scientific team, who falls in love with one of the subjects . . . who is forced to question the integrity of his respected leader and the validity of the study itself?

This outspoken novel reveals an explosive human drama in a small suburb of California that could be Anywhere, U.S.A.—and leaves some searching questions in the readers' minds about sin, sex, and surveys.

"The author is a serious writer. . . . In this highly colored novel are some serious, searching discussions between scientists on the validity and usefulness of sex surveys . . . illuminating as they are candid. . . . It should be read."
—*N. Y. World Telegram*

World Renowned Authors from SIGNET

IRVING WALLACE

The Chapman Report

Ⓞ
A SIGNET BOOK
NEW AMERICAN LIBRARY

For information address Simon and Schuster, Inc.,
1230 Avenue of the Americas, New York, New York 10020,
publishers of the hardcover edition of this book.

 SIGNET TRADEMARK REG. U.S. PAT. OFF. AND FOREIGN COUNTRIES
REGISTERED TRADEMARK—MARCA REGISTRADA
HECHO EN CHICAGO, U.S.A.

SIGNET, SIGNET CLASSICS, MENTOR, PLUME, MERIDIAN AND NAL
BOOKS *are published by The New American Library, Inc.,*
1633 Broadway, New York, New York 10019

First Signet Printing, May, 1961

32   33   34   35   36   37   38

PRINTED IN THE UNITED STATES OF AMERICA

FOR
Sylvia

Every act of human coitus has something of the quality of a drama; it commences with some form of pursuit and may be climaxed by total intimacy, but often is not. By itself, sex cannot substitute for intimacy. . . .

—NELSON N. FOOTE
Family Study Center
University of Chicago

TO MANY WOMEN

and

A FEW MEN

IT IS POSSIBLE *that several of the many women with whom I have crossed paths in the years between puberty and the present will look into this book as they might into a mirror and, through some personal alchemy, see a reflection of themselves. To one and all, I assure them, I would have been totally incapable of capturing their beauty, habits, experiences, and elusive femininity on paper, even if I had wanted to do so. They possessed, all of them, too much complexity, as I possessed too little art, to serve as prototypes for the women in these pages.*

The women in the morality play that follows are pure fiction—creatures of the author's imagination—and if any female reader finds here the remotest resemblance to herself, or to any other human being, living or dead, I must firmly state that the resemblance is one of incredible coincidence.

I must make the same disclaimer to male readers. If, somewhere in this happy land, there is a man who feels ill-used because he believes that he inhabits these pages, let him be relieved of the notion at once. Every man in this novel, from first page to last, is the result of make-believe.

Among readers of both sexes, there may be a temptation to ascribe to Dr. Chapman and other sexologists in this novel some of the characteristics and methods of real-life sex historians like Drs. Alfred C. Kinsey, G. V. Hamilton, Robert L. Dickinson, Lewis M. Terman, and others. Those who wish to play out the fantasy, and enjoy the fun of it, may do so, but at their own risk, not mine. For their speculations will have no basis in fact. Since 1915, when the pursuit of sexual behavior by scientific investigators first began, dozens of notable men and women have honorably served this occupation. I have never met, nor even seen, one of them. Nor have I met any of their associates.

I have undertaken to use, in a work of the imagination, an occupation that is a phenomenon of our time, a time in which I grew up, an age preoccupied with sex, with surveys, with confessions, with statistics. I have invented a group of sexologists and shown them at labor. If, by wildest chance, one of them resembles in some way someone who is alive, or was alive, I will be flattered at the accidental accuracy and perception of my pen, but surprised, too, since every character in this book is a product of my working daydreams.

I leave the patient reader with the sensible words of W. Somerset Maugham: "This practice of ascribing originals for the creatures of the novelist's fancy is a very mischievous one."

IRVING WALLACE

Los Angeles, California

1

ONCE A DAY, at exactly ten minutes to nine in the morning, a long, gray sight-seeing bus, streaked with dust, lumbered up Sunset Boulevard and entered that suburb of Los Angeles known as The Briars. The uniformed guide and driver of the bus adjusted the silver microphone before his lips and resumed his soporific drone: "Ladies and gentlemen, we are now passing through The Briars . . ."

No stir of excitement resulted among the passengers, already sated by the gaudy homes of motion-picture celebrities in Beverly Hills and Bel-Air, left behind twenty minutes before. The Briars, they heard, and sensed before they heard, held no more exotic wonders than the better sections of the towns they had briefly escaped in Pennsylvania, Kansas, Georgia, and Idaho. The Briars was, to sight, the model of perfect normalcy, and, therefore, nothing to write home about.

Many of the passengers used this interlude to change their positions, massage their necks, light cigarettes, or make a remark to their neighbors as they waited for the transition to the more promising Pacific Ocean and its Malibu colony. But a few, mostly women with young faces and old hands, continued to gaze out their windows, admiring the relaxed, graceful, rural beauty of the suburb, wondering what the community was like and how it would be to become a member of its exclusive population.

Many buses like this one had passed daily through The Briars, during the several decades of its development. And always, to the transient beholder, the surface vision of placidity, retreat, and conventionality prevailed. And, indeed, the obvious buildings and guidebook statistics were comforting and familiar. For The Briars was to Los Angeles what Lake Forest is to Chicago and Scarsdale is to New York City.

Since it was a formal part of greater Los Angeles, without government autonomy of its own, the boundaries of The Briars

9

had been fixed irregularly and erratically, long before, by a combination of local business boosters, realtors, and succcessive editors of throw-away weekly newspapers. Generally, it was regarded as a subdivision of eight square miles located on either side of curving Sunset Boulevard, between Westwood to the east and the Pacific Palisades to the West.

The subdivision restrictions were such that almost all lots were oversize, and the houses, most often one-story colonial or contemporary ranch modern, were spacious and set back sixty or more feet from the wide, paved streets. Almost every house was partially obscured, and so made more tantalizing by green mounds of landscaped earth or by a ring of eucalyptus trees, by hedges of hibiscus or a high stone wall.

A single major shopping area, advertised as The Village Green, much given to quaint shop structures (the shoemaker and barber labored under a modified Moulmein pagoda) and to exotic imported commodities and overpriced domestic products, gave sustenance to the area. Other indications of social conformity were the four elementary schools, the one junior high school, and the single senior high school. Almost defensively, the people of The Briars seemed to have built too many churches: two Catholic, one Latter-day Saints, one Methodist, one Christian Science, one Presbyterian, and one Jewish synagogue. At the fringes of The Village Green stood a branch of the main post office, a dimly lighted and understocked public library (the majority in The Briars bought their own books), an American Legion hall, an Optimist Club, a Junior Chamber of Commerce building, and the brick and stone, modernized Gothic edifice belonging to The Briars' Women's Association.

Except for several streets of new apartment buildings, much addicted to heavy brass outdoor fittings and occupied largely by white-collar workers who commuted to the city, the avenues of The Briars were populated by houses owned for the most part by their possessors, instead of the local drive-in bank. The owners of these houses earned from $20,000 to $100,000 a year. Few were advanced enough in years to be retired. The Briars was a community of the relatively young or middle-aged. Although its politics were actually liberal, its outward aspect was sufficiently staid and conservative to discourage invasion by persons employed in the entertainment industries. Members of the retrenching motion-picture business rarely got farther west than the opulence of Beverly Hills, and members of the expanding television business preferred the activity and excitement of more metropolitan areas.

Local realtors estimated that there were 14,000 men, women, and children in The Briars. The pages of the slender yearly telephone directory gave the occupations of the home-owners: a clothing-store proprietor, a structural engineer, a psychiatrist, a building contractor, a research analyst, a writer, a dry cleaner, a motel owner, a university president, an advertising executive, an art dealer, a pet-shop proprietor, an attorney-at-law, an accountant, an architect, a banker, a dentist.

These were the men, and when they departed for their places of vocation, usually in the remote city, The Briars became a community of women.

From behind the windows of the daily sight-seeing bus, the passengers, predominantly female, stared with envy at those of their own sex whom they glimpsed in The Briars. There was always the slowly receding view of a blonde in Capri pants sliding into her low-slung Jaguar in a driveway, or an attractive dark-haired matron in an expensive orlon robe chatting with the head gardener from the front steps, or the well-formed wives in tight white shorts gracefully and expertly bounding about on a private tennis court, or the redhead, her hair caught in a silk scarf, behind the wheel of a Lincoln Continental, steering into a parking spot in front of the shopping arcade.

What the passengers in the sight-seeing bus did not see they invented and embellished in their own minds. They could imagine clearly how these women of The Briars lived. In the mornings, the female population of The Briars sent their young off in chartered buses to airy schools; dawdled over breakfast served by colored maids while they leafed through the latest *Vogue* or *Harper's Bazaar*; sunbathed in halters and shorts on contour lounges set on flagstoned patios; dressed leisurely in imported sweaters and skirts for luncheons with elegant friends on Wilshire Boulevard. And in the afternoons they browsed through magnificent, semi-exclusive dress shops, or relaxed in beauty salons, or attended tea or garden parties. And in the evenings, when they were not with husbands and friends in Palm Springs or Las Vegas or Sun Valley, they were in the city for an art movie, a play, a night club featuring the currently popular topical comedian. Sometimes they supervised an intimate dinner at home, or, in a silk shantung jump-suit, received guests (offering their warm cheeks to the men and cool handshakes to the wives) and drank immoderately, laughing at flirtatious sex jokes told against the dinning stereophonic

11

phonograph. The morning following, while a maid sent the husband to work and the children to school, they indulged their hangovers with late sleep and awakened at last, vaguely regretting that they had not the time to read up for the approaching evening's class in art appreciation. This was, in the eyes and minds of those on the sight-seeing bus, how the women of The Briars spent their days, and, allowing for variations of individual tastes, this was actually how they did live.

But, of course, there was more behind the façade of scarves, harlequin sun glasses, loose-fitting sweaters and snug-fitting pants, more behind the foreign sports cars and leather car coats, more behind the clipped hedges and doctored elms and large, gracious houses. Because, for the outsiders who were not part of this envied life, it could not be imagined or understood that here, too, existence was often as difficult as it was easy and that for many of the 14,000 in The Briars this was the worst of times as well as the best of times.

The secret climate of The Briars, held as private as any Masonic rite, was, for most of its women, one of empty monotony, boredom, confusion. More often than not, the natives—as the parlor joke went—were restless. The malady was American and married female, but the women of The Briars chose to believe that it was exclusively their own. Yet they rarely gave voice to it, directly, openly, because they could not fully reconcile this continued unhappy unrest with material plenty.

When the women of The Briars had been single and aspiring, they had wanted only to be married and comfortable, to wear emotional security like a favorite garment and limitations on free choice like a veil, and to dwell in a sylvan paradise such as this. Now, at last, they were married (or had been) for two or five or fifteen years, and they were comfortable, and they were regulated, and they were safe in a community admired by all, and yet, somehow, it was not enough. Inarticulate for the most, they wanted more—but exactly what they wanted they could not explain, even to themselves.

And so they lost themselves in a bewildering maze of meaningless appointments, get-togethers, charities, activities, weekend flights; and to cease thinking of what was not there, they blurred their senses with vodka, sleeping pills, tranquilizing drugs, sexual experiments. And in this way, each dread morning was possible, and life went on unchanged, and seemed a vacuum, timeless except for the occasional awareness that a gray hair had dared to appear (obliterated quickly by a bleach), that the breasts sagged ever so slightly (supported hastily by the newest uplift brassière), that the flesh on the hips was less elastic (pounded speedily firm by machine bands and Swedish hands), that the children were taller and taller (but now, at last, enemy Time triumphed, for there was no combating this fact that life was growing shorter and shorter).

At five minutes after nine in the morning, the long, gray sightseeing bus, emerging from the most scenic thoroughfare in The Briars, regained its lane on Sunset Boulevard and started down the sloping highway toward destination beach.

◇   ◇   ◇

Standing on the pocked, asphalt, circular driveway, before her broad, one-story Georgian house, Kathleen Ballard waved a last time to her four-year-old daughter, Deirdre, in the back seat of the station wagon, which was part of the daily car pool taking her to the progressive nursery school in Westwood.

After the station wagon had disappeared around the corner, Kathleen lingered a moment in the driveway. She studied the bed of yellow rose bushes nearby, particularly the row of blighted ones, reminding herself that she must consult Mr. Ito about some sort of spray treatment. She had first noticed the condition of the roses a few days before and had quickly forgotten them after they made her think of herself—how the outer bloom hid, from the casual onlooker, the deep inner sickness at the root, and nothing seemed amiss until you looked closely.

Lifting her gaze from the roses, staring across the expanse of green front lawn, through the thick foliage that protected her from all but herself, Kathleen could still see the last of the familiar gray sight-seeing bus as it moved slowly away and down the hill. She did not have her wrist watch—it was Albertine's day off, and she had slept poorly, and taken a pill at dawn, and then overslept, so that there had been barely enough time to slip into a brunch coat and dress Deirdre for school. But now she knew, by the bus, that it was after nine o'clock and that she must do what she had promised Grace Waterton the night before she would do.

Reluctantly, she started back into the front outer vestibule, moving between the graceful, fluted columns, past the tall potted cypresses, and entered the cavernous, empty, elegant house, resisting and resenting the hour that lay before her. Once in the kitchen, she turned off the stove, poured herself a

13

steaming cup of coffee, and took it unsweetened to the white formica dinette table. Setting the coffee down, she found a package of cigarettes in the cupboard above the telephone. With the cigarettes and manila folder Grace had left her in one hand, and the telephone in the other, she returned to the table.

After the first sip of warming coffee, she devoted herself briefly to the ritual of the morning's initial cigarette. Inhaling deeply, then exhaling, she felt momentarily soothed. Even her slender fingers, nicotine-stained where they held the cigarette, trembled less as she continued to smoke. After a while she crushed the half-burned cigarette in the porcelain ash tray bearing the faded legend "Imperial Hotel, Tokyo" that was still on the table where Boynton had always kept it to remind him of past glories. She wondered why she did not replace the ash tray with one that would irritate her less, but she knew that it was because she did not have the nerve.

The coffee was now merely warm, and she drank it down all at once. Thus fortified, she at last opened the manila folder. There were two sheets of paper inside the folder. On the first, neatly typewritten by Grace, were the names of a dozen members of The Women's Association and their telephone numbers. Scanning the names, Kathleen recognized everyone as a friend or acquaintance or neighbor. Despite this, she still postponed the assignment of telephoning each.

When Grace had dropped off the folder the evening before, Kathleen had immediately felt helpless before the older woman's charging and aggressive heartiness. Grace Waterton was in her late fifties. Her gray hair, set several times weekly by a male hairdresser, resembled a tin wig. She was tiny, churning, and verbose. After her children had married, she had gravitated for two years between a swami in Reseda and a psychiatrist in Beverly Hills and abandoned both for the presidency of The Women's Association, which had become her entire life. In some bank, somewhere, there was a vice-president named Mr. Grace Waterton.

Although Grace had finally intimidated Kathleen into accepting the folder, Kathleen had tried to object. She was exhausted, she pleaded, and busy. Besides, she had not seen any of the women for several months, not since the last Association meeting, and the telephone calls would necessarily be long and involved. "Nonsense," Grace had said in her strident, no-nonsense tone of voice. "This is business, and you treat it as such. Just tell each one you've got a dozen more calls to make. Besides, I think it's good for you. I don't like it, Kathleen, the way you've been holing yourself up like a hermit. It's not healthy. If you won't get out to see people, at least talk to them."

Kathleen had not wanted to tell Grace, or anyone, that it was not what had happened to Boynton that had made her a recluse—or possibly it was, but in a way and for reasons different than they realized. When she had been married, and he was home, as so often he was, she desired only to be out of the house, to be lost in the noisy chaos of companionship, though it was against all her natural instincts. But in the year and four months since she had been alone, escape was not necessary. She had reverted to, and luxuriated in, the lonely independence that she had known, and loved and hated, before marriage.

Suddenly, she had been aware that Grace was speaking again and that her visitor's voice had softened slightly. "Believe me, Kathleen, dear, we all know what an ordeal you've been through. But no one will help you if you don't help yourself. You're still young, beautiful, you've got a lovely daughter —a whole life ahead, and you've got to live it. If I thought you were really unwell, darling, I'd be the first to understand. Of course, I can get someone else to make the phone calls instead of you. But we need you. I mean, like it or not, you're still one of our most important and influential members. And you can see why I have to pick twenty of our most respected members to make these calls. I mean, it simply makes the calls carry more weight. Believe me, Kathleen, we need a full turnout, and everyone on our side—especially if the churches object to this meeting. I don't know if they will, but there's talk."

Until then, Kathleen had not, absorbed as she was in the effort to avoid an unpleasant task, fully comprehended, or even listened to, the real purpose of the meeting. When she inquired again, and Grace explained it to her briskly and proudly (yet not fully able to conceal her excitement at the daring and naughtiness of the whole affair), Kathleen had been even more disturbed. She was in no mood to join a company of women in listening to a man discuss the sexual habits of the American female, no matter how clinically. Worse—for then came the sudden realization of what the lecture would lead to —she was not prepared to disclose her private secrets to a band of strangers, to disrobe figuratively before a group of leering male voyeurs.

The whole thing was insane, ill-making, yet so great was

15

Grace's enthusiasm—"it'll make our community famous; that's why Mr. Ackerman arranged it"—that Kathleen instinctively realized any objection would not be understood and would make her sexually suspect. So she had resisted no longer and had decided to bide her time.

Now, hastily lighting another cigarette, she was confronted with the damnable folder. She removed the list of names to examine the sheet of paper beneath it. This was a mimeographed publicity story—dated the following day "for immediate press release"—and it was signed by Grace Waterton. This release, Grace had explained, would give Kathleen all of the pertinent facts when she was telephoning to notify members of the special meeting two days hence. Dragging steadily at her cigarette, Kathleen read the press release.

"On Friday morning, May 22, at ten-thirty o'clock," the mimeographed story began, "Dr. George G. Chapman, world-renowned sex authority from Reardon College in Wisconsin and author of last year's best-selling *A Sex Study of the American Bachelor*, will address a full membership meeting of The Briars' Women's Association. For two weeks following the meeting, at which Dr. Chapman will discuss the purposes of his current study of the married female, Dr. Chapman and his team of assistants, Dr. Horace Van Duesen, Mr. Cass Miller, Mr. Paul Radford, all associated with Reardon College, will interview the members of the Women's Association who are, or have been, married.

"For fourteen months, the celebrated Dr. Chapman and his team have been traveling through the United States interviewing several thousand married women of widely varied educational backgrounds who represent every economic, religious, and age group. According to Dr. Chapman, the women of The Briars will be the last that he and his associates will interview before collating their findings and publishing them next year. 'The purpose of this inquiry,' says Dr. Chapman, 'is to bring into the open what has so long been hidden, the true pattern of the sexual life of American females, so that, through statistics, we may scientifically illuminate an area of human life long kept in darkness and ignorance. It is our hope that future generations of American women may profit by our findings.'

"Mrs. Grace Waterton, president of The Briars' Women's Association, has already expressed her awareness of the honor in a telegram to Dr. Chapman and promised a one hundred per cent turnout at his briefing lecture. Subjects will offer themselves for interview on a voluntary basis, but Mrs. Waterton predicts that after hearing Dr. Chapman, and learning that the actual personal interviews are even more anonymous than those in the past conducted by such pioneer investigators as Gilbert Hamilton, Alfred Kinsey, Ernest Burgess, Paul Wallin, few of the Association's 220 married members will refuse this opportunity to contribute to scientific advancement. The Association, which has its own club house and auditorium in The Briars, was established fifteen years ago and is dedicated to social and charitable works, as well as to beautifying the western area of greater Los Angeles."

Having finished reading the release, Kathleen continued to gaze at it with distaste. Irrationally offended by the words, she asked herself: What kind of Peeping Tom is this Dr. Chapman anyway?

She had heard of him, of course. Everyone had heard of him. The sensationalism of his last book (all the women she knew had read it avidly, though Kathleen had disdained even to borrow a copy), and the progress of his current study, so-called, had enlivened the pages of newspapers and periodicals for several years and had served to bring his portrait to the covers of at least a dozen magazines. One day, she supposed, Chapman would be a freak symbol of his decade and its obsessive concern with sex, just as Emile Coué was representative of a different curiosity in the nineteen-twenties.

But what, Kathleen wondered, would make a grown, educated man want to devote his life to prying into the secret sex histories of men, women, and children? The unceasing persiflage about "scientific advancement" could serve only to disguise beneath noble purpose an unhealthy and erotic mentality, or, as bad, a coarse commercial mind determined to capitalize on the forbidden. In fairness to Dr. Chapman, Kathleen remembered reading that he kept none of his considerable earnings for himself. Nevertheless, in this culture, a well-known name was equal to any annuity and might be cashed in at any time. Besides, he probably preferred notoriety to wealth.

Maybe she was being harsh with him, Kathleen reflected. Maybe the fault was her own, that she had become prim and old-fashioned, if one could really become old-fashioned at twenty-eight. Still, her conviction was unshakable: a woman's reproductive organs belonged to herself and to herself alone, and their use and activity should be known to none beyond herself, her mate, her physician.

Frowning at the necessity of having to promote something in which she did not believe, something so obviously unpalat-

17

able and indecent, Kathleen ground out her second cigarette. She brought the typed column of names and numbers back before her, lifted the receiver, and began to dial the numerals listed after Ursula Palmer's name.

✧   ✧   ✧

Ursula Palmer was an aggressive clarifier, inquirer, pinpointer. When she asked how-are-you, she meant to know, exactly, how-you-were from morning to night, and yesterday, too. No vague generalities, no misty expositions, ever satisfied her. In the world scrutinized by her luminous, large brown eyes, all had to be tangible, known, understood.

Now, one hand still resting on the space bar and keys of her typewriter and the other holding the receiver to her ear, she continued—as she had for the last several minutes—to plague Kathleen with concrete questions about Dr. Chapman's expedition into The Briars.

"Really, Ursula," Kathleen was saying with repressed exasperation, "I don't have the slightest idea why Dr. Chapman picked us for his last sampling. I only know what's on the publicity release in front of me."

"Well, then, read it to me," said Ursula. "I just want to get all the facts straight."

Ursula could hear the distant paper rustle in Kathleen's hand, and she listened, eyes closed to concentrate better, as her caller's husky voice read the words over the telephone. When Kathleen had finished, Ursula opened her eyes. "I suppose," she said into the telephone, "that covers it. Poor Dr. Chapman. He's going to be disappointed."

"What do you mean?"

"I mean what's he going to learn from this cold bunch of biddies that he doesn't already know? I can just see him asking Teresa Harnish her favorite position. Two to one she tells him it's being the wife of an art dealer."

"I don't think we're any different from women anywhere."

"Maybe not," said Ursula doubtfully.

"Can I tell Grace you're coming to the meeting?"

"Of course. I wouldn't miss it for anything."

After she had hung up, Ursula Palmer regretted that she had irritated Kathleen, as she sensed that she had and always did. It was too bad, because she sincerely respected Kathleen and wanted her friendship. Of all the women whom she knew in The Briars, it was Kathleen alone, Ursula felt, who was her intellectual equal. Moreover, Kathleen possessed that indefinable air—that thing that made a woman a lady, a kind of well-bred repose known colloquially as class. To this, or part of this, was added the glamour of wealth. Everyone knew that Kathleen had inherited a small fortune from her father. She was independent. She did not have to work. Once, in one of her monthly features for *Houseday,* Ursula had written of the average well-off suburban wife and used the person of Kathleen as the model. She envied Kathleen her striking appearance: her shining black hair, bobbed short and smart; her provocative green eyes; the small tilted nose; the full crimson mouth—all this and the Modigliani neck set on a tall, boyish, graceful figure.

Swinging her swivel chair back to the typewriter, Ursula cast a sidelong glance at the wall mirror across her library and made a silent pledge to diet seriously again. Yet, studying herself in the glass, she knew that it was hopeless. She was not meant to look like Kathleen Ballard. She was big-boned, from cheeks and shoulders to hips, and she would always weigh one hundred and thirty-five pounds. Once a drunk at a party had told her that she resembled an overweight Charlotte Brontë. She was sure that this was because she parted her dark brown hair straight down the middle. Anyway, she liked the literary allusion. For a woman of forty-one—and a mother, she remembered (reminding herself to write Devin this weekend and wondering why she could never picture his father)—she was well preserved, and vain about her small hands and shapely calves. Besides, Harold liked her this way. And, besides, she was Sappho, not Helen of Troy, Sappho of the Muse, not of Lesbos, and what she had would last longer.

She resumed banging away at the typewriter. She had another hour before she would have to leave for the airport to meet Bertram Foster and his wife, Alma. Although, in many ways, Foster was not her ideal of a publisher—his coarseness and vulgarity often made one wince, and his interests in the more commercial aspects of *Houseday* rather than the literary were sometimes disappointing—still he had been astute enough to select Ursula from among his many free-lance contributors and to promote her to Western editor of the widely circulated family magazine.

Presently, having completed her précis, Ursula drew it from the typewriter and began to proof it. The précis was cleverly conceived, designed to cater to Foster's financial prejudices and to improve Ursula's own job. It covered her office's activi-

19

ties the first half of the year. It emphasized small economies and big accomplishments. It suggested wider authority and coverage for her department, at little extra cost, and in a way that might be enticing to potential advertisers.

"Dearest?" It was Harold's voice.

Ursula looked up as Harold Palmer came tentatively into the den carrying a breakfast tray covered with eggs, toast, coffee. "You'd better have something, or you'll get a headache."

She watched absently as Harold set her dishes on the desk before her and then poured his own coffee. Although he had prepared breakfast almost every morning of their married life, and persisted in the custom even after they had employed a live-in maid, each time he made it appear as if he were going to do it this once as a favor. He was a tall, hesitant, inarticulate man, gray-faced and concave, and two years her junior. He had the appearance of, and in fact was, an accountant.

He settled in the leather chair across from her. "Hadn't you better be getting dressed?" he inquired, nodding at her quilted long robe as he stirred his coffee.

"I've got my face on, and I'm dressed underneath. I just have to slip into a skirt."

"How long are they going to be here?"

"Two weeks, I think. They're going on to Honolulu."

"Now that's the way to live." He drank his coffee. "Maybe if I land Berrey today, we'll be going to Hawaii ourselves next year."

Ursula's mind had been elsewhere. "Who's Berret?" she asked dutifully.

"Berrey," Harold repeated with shy understanding. "He owns the Berrey Cut-Rate Drugstores. There are ten in the area. It could do a good deal for me. I met him a couple times, when I was with the old firm."

The old firm, Ursula remembered, was Keller Company in Beverly Hills, a large beehive of underpaid accountants that Harold had been with since his graduation from the university. In an uncharacteristic burst of independence, he had left them three months before to open his own office. He had taken two small clients with him—but, Ursula observed wryly, it was she who was now paying the bills.

"Well, good luck," Ursula said.

"I'll need it," Harold conceded worriedly. "I'm meeting him downtown at five. I may be a little late for dinner."

"Harold, please. You know we're taking the Fosters to Panero's. You've got to be on time."

20

"Oh, I will be. But Mr. Berrey is an important man—I can't cut him short. It means a lot."

"Foster means more. You be here."

Harold did not contest this. He rose, slowly gathered the cups and saucers, piled them on the tray, and started out, as Ursula returned to her proofing. At the door he hesitated.

"Ursula."

"Yes?" She crossed out the word *detrimental* on the page before her and wrote *harmful* above it.

"I wish you could come down to the office. It still doesn't have a stick of my own furniture. I've just been waiting for you."

"I will, soon as I can," she said impatiently. Then, looking at him with a smile, speaking in a more gentle tone, she added, "You know how busy I've been. But I'll make it."

"I thought maybe Friday—"

"Friday I'm giving that enormous luncheon for the Fosters —all the publicity people, and actors . . ." Suddenly she clapped her head. "My God, I promised Kathleen Ballard I'd go to hear Dr. Chapman Friday morning. How can I?"

"Dr. Chapman? The sex expert?"

"Yes—he's lecturing at the Association. I'll tell you all about it later. I've got to think."

Harold nodded and departed for the kitchen, where the colored maid, Hally, was defrosting the refrigerator. Ursula sat back in the swivel chair and shut her eyes. Dr. Chapman would have been a lark, but now he was a nuisance. She was a working wife, and she had no time to spare for this sex gibberish. She would simply call Kathleen or Grace and plead a previous business engagement. After all, Foster came first.

Still, she was not satisfied. She rose, found cigarette and silver holder, joined them, and thoughtfully lighted up. She realized that she had looked forward to Dr. Chapman more than she had first imagined. Crossing the room, she halted before the wall of books, located *A Sex Study of the American Bachelor*, and pulled the heavy volume from the shelf. Slowly, she leafed through it, pausing here and there to absorb a graph of statistics or a long paragraph. Just as when she had read it the first time, she was fascinated—not by any relationship the numerals might have to her, but by the bedroom doors they opened into other lives.

Even as she returned the book to the shelf, the title of the article was projected before her mind's eye. It would read: " 'The Day Dr. Chapman Interviewed Me,' by a Suburban

21

Housewife." Ursula herself, of course, would be the suburban housewife. It was perfect for *Houseday*. She would handle it lightly, humorously, teasingly, and yet with just enough provocative questions and answers to make it highly quotable. And better still, the interview with Dr. Chapman or one of his team would make a perfect conversation piece for the Fosters, reinforcing his image of her as competent and witty and yet The Eternal Feminine.

Turning it over in her head, relishing it, she could visualize Bertram Foster's happy leer as she fleshed out each detail in innumerable anecdotes of the private adventure. There was no doubt in her mind now. She must attend Dr. Chapman's lecture and then volunteer for an early interview. Once Foster knew what she was sacrificing for him and the magazine, he would permit her to make a late appearance at his luncheon. She could picture her entrance—the center of all eyes, for all would know what had delayed her—and then see herself masterfully regaling employer and celebrated guests with the inside Sex Story. She was positive Foster would be more admiring than ever. It could lead to anything. Even to New York.

◇   ◇   ◇

The bus horn honked twice, loudly, beyond the window over the kitchen sink. And then, because engine trouble had detained the bus earlier, the horn honked twice again.

"Can you hold on just a minute, Kathleen?" Sarah Goldsmith said into the telephone. "It's the school bus." Capping her hand over the mouthpiece, she called to Jerome, her nine-year-old, who was finishing his cereal, and Deborah, her six-year-old, who was munching a cookie, "Hurry up now, it's the bus, it's late enough. And don't forget your lunch boxes."

Sam Goldsmith, his mouth filed with a hot cake, dropped the business section of the morning paper and held out his arms as first Deborah kissed him and then Jerome. "Now remember what I told you when you get out there at recess," he said to Jerome. "Hold the bat away from you and high—like Musial—and then cut down into the ball. You'll see."

Jerome nodded. "I'll remember, Pop."

Both children grabbed their lunch boxes, pecked hasty kisses at Sarah's face, and headed for the front door, Jerome bounding, Deborah scrambling, until they were gone, the door slamming loudly behind them. Sarah stood on tiptoe, craning her neck to see through the high window. She watched Jerome and

Deborah race across the paved parking area before the car port and climb into the bus. When it began to grind away, she lowered herself and took her hand from the mouthpiece.

"I'm sorry, Kathleen. It's like this every morning."

"Oh, I know."

"Now, about that lecture—you say everyone's going to be there?"

"That's what Grace says."

"Well, all right. I don't want to be the one who's different. I suppose it *is* important."

"For 'scientific advancement,' to quote Dr. Chapman." Kathleen paused a moment. "Of course, it's all voluntary, Sarah. After you've heard him, you either pledge to be interviewed or you decline."

"I'll do what the majority does," said Sarah. "I read his last book. I think it's a good cause. It's just that—well, I suppose it's sort of embarrassing. Is it really anonymous?"

"That's what the press release says."

"What I mean is—I once read an article about all those surveys in a digest magazine—about their history, the way they keep their material secret—but I remember even Kinsey used to sit across from you and ask questions right to your face. And there was another one before Kinsey—I don't remember his name."

Kathleen consulted the paper before her. "Could it have been Hamilton?"

"That sounds familiar. Something like that. He used to give typed questions on cards. But you still had to answer them to his face. That would make me terribly uncomfortable."

"Yes," Kathleen agreed, almost automatically. But though she sympathized with Sarah's viewpoint, she knew that she must not accept it. "Still, I understand Dr. Chapman doesn't do it exactly that way. I don't recall what I heard about his method, except it's the most anonymous of all—you really come off the assembly line hermetically sealed, like a Vestal Virgin. I wish I could tell you exactly how, Sarah. But Grace says he's going to explain all that in the lecture."

"All right. I'll be there."

After Sarah had settled the receiver in the cradle, she glanced at Sam. She wondered if he had listened to the conversation. He was still buried deeply in the latest stock averages and apparently oblivious to all. Watching him in silence, as she did so often lately, with her right hand characteristically over her heart (where lived that secret thing), she wondered

23

if he ever saw her any more as he had seen her when they first met. She thought he might be agreeably surprised if he looked closely.

Sarah Goldsmith wore her dark hair pulled sleekly back in a bun, and though her heavy, black-rimmed spectacles gave her a rather severe aspect, her face, with the unplucked eyebrows and broad nose, was remarkably Latin and soft in early mornings, when she had not yet put her glasses on. She was thirty-five, and her deep breasts and full hips were still firm and young. She was rather proud that, unlike Sam, she had never let herself go. Even after twelve years of marriage and two children, her weight had not varied by more than five pounds.

Now, with a sigh, she moved to the table, poured a cup of tea, and sat across from her husband. She gazed past his newspaper, at his arm and the portion of his thick-jowled face visible, with detached pity. Although only four years older than she, he had become, at least in her eyes, an overweight clod. She had long forgotten her need for the safety of his solidity in their early years, and her approval of his dogged fight for their security. She remembered only that, after twelve years, he had evolved into a dull, insensitive, inanimate, sedentary fixture, an object with little interest in the world around him, its high excitements and marvelous refinements, beyond an obsessive concern for his men's clothing store, his children, his back-yard garden, and his wing chair set before the television set. Love he performed dutifully, breathing hard, once a week, on Sunday night, and never satisfying her. This she might have endured, Sarah thought, had there been some romantic air about it, or some fun at least. But it had been added to the montonous necessities of eating, sleeping, and chores to be done. Oh, he was a *good* person, of course, and *kind*, there was no doubt about that. But he was good and kind in that special flabby, sentimental, Jewish way, too quick to apologize or cry or be grateful. In a world alive, he was a sort of death.

She had once read *Madame Bovary*, and she had committed to memory several lines: "Her innermost heart was waiting for something to happen. Like shipwrecked sailors, she turned a despairing gaze over the solitude of her life, seeking some white sail in the far mists of the horizon. . . . But nothing happened to her; God had willed it so! The future was a dark corridor, with its door at the end shut fast." And afterward

24

she always thought that she knew Emma Bovary better than she knew any woman friend in The Briars.

"Nine-thirty already!" she heard Sam exclaim. He was on his feet, pushing up the knot of his tie. "If I get there late like this every morning, they'll rob me blind." He started into the living room. "The minute the help sees you are lax, they take advantage. I see it all the time." He reappeared with his flannel coat. "But who can leave when it's so comfortable at home? I like to be with my wife and children. I like my home." He stood over Sarah, tugging on his coat. "Is that a crime?"

"It's very good," said Sarah.

"Or maybe it's just that I'm getting old."

"Why do you always make yourself older than you are?" said Sarah, more sharply than she had intended.

"It bothers you? All right, I'm sweet sixteen again." He bent, and her face, eyes closed, was waiting. She felt his chapped lips on her own. "Well, I'll see you at six," he said, straightening.

"Fine."

"Tonight's what? A-ha, the fat comedian at seven. Maybe we should eat in the living room so we can watch."

"All right."

He went to the door. "You got anything special today?"

"Shopping, Jerry's dental appointment after school—a million things."

"Be good."

She sat very still, listening to his leather heels on the cement, to the creaking of the car door opening. After a moment, the sedan coughed, started, and she heard it back out the driveway and then drive off.

Quickly, she finished her tea, removed her apron, and went into the master bedroom. She stood before the Empire dresser, intent on the mirror. Her hair was fine, the checked shirtmaker becoming. Unclasping her straw handbag, she pulled out lipstick and compact. Carefully, she touched up her cheeks and then painted on her lips in subdued carmine. Again, she surveyed herself in the mirror, then turned and moved to the telephone on the stand between the twin beds.

She lifted the receiver, hastily dialed, then waited. There were three rings, and his voice was on.

"Hello?"

"It's Sarah. I'll be right over."

She hung up, breathlessly went around the bed and into the

bathroom. Pulling open the drawer beside the washbasin, she reached deep inside for the zippered blue kit. Emerging and going back to the dresser, her hand fondled the kit, feeling the rim of the large diaphragm and the small tube of vaginal jelly. She dropped the kit into her straw handbag, snatched a pink cashmere sweater from the drawer, and hastened through the house to the carport.

✦   ✦   ✦

Mary Ewing McManus—she had been married less than two years, and she knew that it pleased her father that she retained the *Ewing* whenever she signed her name—sat on the rumpled bed, long, thin legs crossed beneath her blue silk nightgown.

"I think it's just the most, Kathleen," she said into the telephone. Twenty-two and uncomplicated, and in love with her husband, Mary could still be exuberant before ten in the morning. "You write a big exclamation mark after my name. I wouldn't miss it for anything in the world."

"Fine, Mary. I wish everyone were so agreeable."

Mary was surprised. "Who wouldn't want to hear Dr. Chapman? I mean, there's always something to learn." Mary Ewing had come to Norman McManus, in marriage, a healthy, cheerful, virginal young girl. Although raised with intelligence and affection, she had been, in ways, sheltered, and everything that followed her wedding night seemed new to her. She was as curious about the pathways of sex, about exploring its mysteries and learning its techniques, as she was about attempting new cooking recipes and learning to sew. One night, in the first year, after reading a chapter of a new marriage manual, she and Norman had spent the entire night, with mad hilarity and then silent excitement, testing their various erogenous zones.

"Dr Chapman isn't exactly going to be teaching anything," Kathleen was saying. "It's really a serious study he's making."

"Oh, I know," Mary said in her important, adult voice. "It's like being part of history, in a way—as if Sigmund Freud were coming to The Briars to talk about psychiatry or Karl Marx to discuss communism. It's something to tell your children."

"Well," said Kathleen uncertainly, "I guess it is, in a way."

"How's Deirdre?"

"Fine, thanks."

"She's so pretty. I'm glad you called me. See you at the lecture."

Hanging up, Mary placed the telephone on the bedstand. She felt thrilled about the invitation, like looking forward to Sunday, and she was suddenly eager to share the news with Norman. She cocked her head, listening, but heard the beat of the shower muffled in the bathroom behind her. When he was out of the shower, she would tell him.

She uncrossed her legs and fell back on the pillow, feeling alive in every limb and happy that the day was young and the night still ahead. The sounds of the shower persisted, and she thought of Norman beneath the cold spray. She could visualize him as she saw him when they often showered together. His funny scrub haircut, and the piercing dark eyes set in the square, handsome face, and his hairy chest and flat belly, and long, muscular legs. It was still a miracle to her that he had sought her out at that sorority party, three years before, and looked at none of the more attractive girls that night or any night since.

Mary Ewing McManus had no illusion about her own beauty. Even though her tangled, boyish brown hair made her resemble Wendy in *Peter Pan*—or so Norman had remarked several times, with admiration—and even though she was a vivacious extrovert, unfamiliar with a single dark mood, she did not delude herself about her physical appearance. She was a tall, bony, athletic, long-striding girl. Her brown eyes were set too close together. Her nose, while straight, was excessively evident (in finishing school she had pinned a romantic drawing of Cleopatra over her bed when she had learned of Pascal's remark that, had Cleopatra's nose "been shorter, the whole aspect of the world would have been altered"). Her mouth was small, though her lips were full and her white teeth regular. She was flat-chested—no foam padding would hide this—and flat-bottomed. And yet, she did not feel unlovely. She had grown up the center of the household and the vast family beyond, always admired and clucked over. Her natural high spirits had made prettier girls seem pallid, and she had never lacked a boy friend. And when she had wanted a husband, Norman had appeared and supplanted childhood affection with mature love.

From the moment of their meeting, Norman had become the center of her universe. Harry Ewing had objected at first, in his soft-spoken, decent way, protesting her youth and Norman's poverty (he had just been admitted to the California

27

bar). Because she adored her father, she had listened attentively, but immediately set out to win him over. Since Harry Ewing could refuse his daughter nothing, he agreed to let her have her husband, knowing she would have him anyway. The only condition Harry set—and to this Mary and Norman quickly and gratefully acceded—was that the newlyweds move into the vacant upstairs suite of the Spanish stucco house and live under the Ewing roof until they could one day get on their feet and have their own home. Then, anxious to get his daughter's marriage on a secure financial footing, Harry Ewing went further. Just when Norman had applied to several large legal firms for jobs, and when he was seriously considering going into a partnership with his old classmate, Chris Shearer, in a poorer section of downtown Los Angeles, Harry Ewing made his son-in-law a generous offer. Harry manufactured prefabricated building parts, and his legal department had four attorneys. One was leaving, and Harry tendered the position to Norman, with a starting salary of $150 a week.

Mary was overwhelmed by her father's generosity, but Norman was less so. Somehow, he felt that he was giving up part of his independence for a dowry. Moreover, the prospect of becoming a real struggling trial attorney with Chris, in a district that needed help, seemed more challenging. But, after a brief day or two of vacillation and uncertainty, he was at last convinced that Harry's opening was one that a hundred young barristers would covet (which, indeed, they would), that his concept of attorney-at-law among depressed peoples was romantic and impractical, and that, after all, Mary deserved the best. Carried away by his wife's enthusiasm, Norman joined her father's staff.

In the year and a half since, sensing her husband's restlessness at being a desk and contract lawyer, Mary had tried to alleviate his boredom. Secretly, she had spoken to her father, imploring him to give Norman some of the courtroom work. Her father had promised that he would do so at the first opportunity. That had been several months ago. Nothing had happened since.

Now, turning on her pillows to look at the electric clock, Mary saw that it was twenty to ten. Her father would be down to breakfast already, and he would be done by ten. He would expect Norman to be ready, since they drove to the plant together every morning in Harry's Cadillac. She had decided she had better remind Norman of the time, when suddenly the shower stopped.

Quickly, Mary sat up, slid off the bed, and padded barefoot to the bathroom door.

She pressed her head to the door. "Norm?"

"Yes?"

"It's twenty to ten."

"Okay."

She remembered Kathleen's call. "Guess who called."

"What?"

"I said guess who called." She raised her voice slightly. "Kathleen Ballard just telephoned. Dr. Chapman's coming here to interview us."

"I can't hear you. Come on in. The door's open."

She turned the glass knob and went inside. The narrow bathroom was warm, and steam clung to the walls and mirror. Norman was in the center of the room, beside the bathtub, standing flat-footed on a large orange mat. His arms were lifted and his muscular back to her as he wiped face and hair with a towel. He was naked, patches of wet still on his back.

Staring at him as she shut the door softly behind her, she felt again the aching pleasure in her loins that she had known the night before. He had possessed her then, and it had been excruciating and marvelous. Now, suddenly, she heard her heart.

She tried to keep her voice casual. "I was just saying, Norm . . ."

He turned, smiling at her, and her eyes touched his lean body possessively and proudly. "Hi, darling," he said. "I thought you were going to sleep."

"Someone called," she said breathlessly. "Dr. Chapman's coming to lecture at the Women's Association Friday."

"Chapman?"

"You know, the Chapman report on sex. He's going to interview us."

"Good for you. Don't keep any secrets." He handed her the towel. "Give me a hand with my back."

He turned away as she took the towel. "Should I tell him you're the best lover in the world?"

"It won't hurt to let it get around."

She touched the curve of his spine with the towel. "You *are*, you know," she said.

"Now, how would you know?" he asked teasingly as he turned again to face her. "Or is that what you tell all your men?"

She stood very still, the towel poised ridiculously between them. "I love you, Norm," she said.

His smile was gone. He reached out and drew her to him. The towel fluttered to the tile as she clutched his bare back, her eyes tightly closed. "I want you, honey," he whispered against her hair.

"Yes," she whispered, then remembered, and tried to pull away. "No, Norm, it's late—Dad's downstairs—"

"To hell with Dad," he said, kissing her neck.

"Don't say that," she said almost inaudibly, before all speech was lost, and she could say no more. Slowly, she sank to the orange mat beside Norman; then, cradled in his arm, lowered herself to her back, hardly aware of the cool contact of tile on her shoulder blades and legs. Eyes shut, she felt the sure fingers at her gown, and the desired and beloved presence all-encompassing, and in a moment she gave herself completely to sensation, unable any longer to remember that her father was downstairs, waiting.

❖   ❖   ❖

Once, during a supper party at Ursula and Harold Palmer's, a dozen guests played the word-association game. When Ursula, who was reeling off the list of words to a male guest, came to *antiseptic*, the guest automatically replied, "Teresa Harnish." This created great hilarity and extensive parlor analysis, with no serious conclusion reached beyond general agreement as to the aptness of the association. Later, the incident was repeated to Teresa, who had not been at the party, and the moment that she could she looked up the word in her dictionary. When she learned that it meant "opposing sepsis, putrefaction, or decay," she was pleased, and made no further effort at comprehending the true meaning as it might be related to her.

Now, leaning against the shelves of her study that contained not books but exquisite representations of pre-Columbian statuary mounted on small marble bases, she listened to Kathleen reading her the details of Dr. Chapman's impending arrival. At the age of thirty-six, Teresa Harnish was the perfect picture of poise and grace. Nothing harsh or real—sweat, for instance, or dirt or germs—had ever blemished her fair complexion, or so it seemed. Each blond, wavy hair was in place. The oval face, wide eyes, patrician nose, thin lips painted full, had the perpetual look of a startled chrysanthemum. Her height and figure were medium in every respect, and her raw-silk blouse, with dipping neckline, gray Bermuda shorts, and thong sandals were unwrinkled and unscuffed. Her appearance and manner gave her an air of remote and sophisticated intellectuality, which she enjoyed and fostered. Her breadth of reading knowledge was considerable, but her depth of understanding and originality of thought did not go beneath her flawless skin. She enjoyed conversation that alluded to the classical and was barely comprehensible, and she preferred her sexual activity neat and straight. If she emerged from either experience without being jostled or confused, she was satisfied. She thought Lord Byron vulgar, Gauguin disgusting, Stendhal ridiculous, and Rembrandt grubby. She rather fancied Henry James, and Thomas Gainsborough, and admired Louise de la Vallière and (somewhat guiltily) the poor Lady Blessington. She found it one of the burdens that marriage imposed to conform to her husband's respect for such weightless abstract painters as Duchamp, Gris, and Kandinsky.

"Yes, Kathleen, I think it's perfectly clear," she said into the telephone at last, in an accent long cultivated that would have troubled a philologist (who might have located it as somewhere between Boston's Beacon Hill and London's West End). "Geoffrey and I think Dr. Chapman is a marvel, a monument to enlightenment."

Geoffrey Harnish, bent over the huge, ornately carved Medici writing table nearby, absorbed in copying several oddments from Giorgio Vasari's *Delle Vite de' più eccelenti pittori, scultori, ed architettori* (the later Italian edition published in Florence in 1878) for a Pasadena customer interested in Renaissance illuminated manuscripts, glanced up sharply at the mention of Dr. Chapman's name. Teresa cocked her head coyly, bestowing upon him a secret smile, and he lifted his bushy eyebrows with agreeable surprise. Dr. Chapman had superseded Vasari, and Geoffrey Harnish settled his small, compact frame back in the fragile chair to listen. He smoothed the side of his thinning sandy hair, stroked his magnificently shaggy, incongruous Grenadier Guard mustache, and vaguely wondered if Dr. Chapman might be induced to pen the foreword to his art catalogue advertising the forthcoming exhibit of abstract art, many of the canvases concerned with conjugality, by Boris Introsky.

Teresa had been listening, and now she was speaking to Kathleen once more. "Of course, Geoffrey and I read his last survey together—well, almost together—and we were literally overwhelmed by the *scientific* approach to sexuality. The book was absolutely Olympian, my dear. Oh, there were faults, of course. Any person with some background in sociology would see that. And many did, as you no doubt remember. I think we objected most to Dr. Chapman's handling of sex as entirely a biological fact, without relationship to other human characteristics. But then, Kathleen, we must be tolerant of this man's problems. After all, how could one tabulate the pleasures of love or, as exciting, the first confrontation of the Mona Lisa in the Louvre?"

From behind his desk, Geoffrey nodded his sage approval, but at the other end of the wire, Kathleen was unprepared, at this hour, for a discourse on Dr. Chapman's method. Squirming impatiently in her kitchen chair—why had she ever accepted this beastly task from Grace?—she did not know what to say. At last she said rather lamely, "But you say you approve of Dr. Chapman?"

"My dear, this will be a memorable experience."

"Then we can count on you?"

"Darling, I would sooner have missed Coleridge's lectures on Milton and Shakespeare at the Philosophical Society."

Kathleen felt safe to interpret this as an acceptance and made a relieved check after Teresa's name, while Teresa, at her end, observed the social amenities by suggesting a luncheon in the near future.

After Teresa had returned the receiver to its cradle, Geoffrey rose, pocketed his notes from Vasari, and accompanied his wife outside to the canary-yellow Thunderbird convertible that had recently replaced the old Citroën. She slipped behind the wheel, and Geoffrey, who did not drive ("I wouldn't permit him," Teresa often explained. "It would be unsafe. His head is always in the clouds. Imagine Goethe driving in Los Angeles"), settled himself in the passenger seat beside her.

The daily morning ride from The Briars to Geoffrey's art shop in Westwood Village, leisurely made along the curves and dips of Sunset Boulevard and then across the thoroughfare bisecting the university campus, took them fourteen minutes. They discussed Dr. Chapman not as one who was curious about their private sex life—which was regularly and efficiently performed twice weekly, after brandies, with brisk detachment, some romantic whispering, and full appreciation that the classical engagement had been sanctioned by Abèlard and Heloïse, Gustave Flaubert and Louis Colet, Archduke Rudolph and Marie Vetsera, Apollinaire and Marie Laurencin—but rather as one more cultural phenomenon in their splendid lives. It was understood, unspoken, that when Geoffrey wrote his memoirs of his years with art and artists, with Teresa's close collaboration, of course, it might be amusing to devote one digressive page or paragraph to Dr. George C. Chapman, statistician of love.

Passing the university, they were reminded of the dinner they had attended the night before, at the charming hillside bungalow maintained by Professor Eric Mawson, who taught Impressionist Art at the school (though they forgave him this as they forgave Dickens his potboilers), and his tense, elderly sister. The guest of honor had been a young visiting Dutch artist, name unpronounceable (and no matter, for Geoffrey had decided at once that he had no talent), who had infuriated one and all by his dogmatic pronouncements on the classicists, Rubens among them, whom he held in contempt. When the young Dutchman had gravely stated that Hans van Meegeren, the creative forger, was the equal of Vermeer, whom he had imitated, Geoffrey had become incensed, and rebutted with telling acidity (most effectively extolling the inimitable tones of Vermeer's edges), pausing only once to permit Teresa to deliver a well-received *bon mot*.

Geoffrey was incensed still, for classical and academic art had been his first passion, and a residue of guilt remained for having abandoned a dependable mistress for the flightier Futurists. "That young idiot—daring even to bracket Van Meegeren's name with Vermeer," he said now. "It's like saying that William Ireland was the match of Shakespeare because he invented and forged *Vortigern* under the Bard's name, and it was briefly accepted. It's astonishing what these immature dabblers will do for attention."

"I think you handled him very well, dear," said Teresa.

"Sitting duck," murmured Geoffrey with satisfaction as he located a small black *cigare* (with which a bewildered Parisian dealer supplied him monthly) and lighted it.

"Well, here we are," said Teresa.

They had drawn up on the busy side street just off Westwood Boulevard. Teresa kept the engine idling as she gazed past her husband at the two windows of the narrow but beautifully appointed shop. The Henry Moore bronze was still in one window, and the large D. H. Lawrence oil in the other. A placard, with a Dadaist border, invited interested parties to the weekly Wednesday night tea and *conversazione*.

"I'm getting tired of that Lawrence," said Teresa. "It doesn't

33

wear well. He belongs in bookstores, not in an art shop."

"As a curiosity, it served," said Geoffrey, mindful that the item had gained him a paragraph in a Sunday paper two weeks before.

"I'd much prefer that new Marinetti oil," said Teresa. Her husband had recently overpaid an Italian dealer for an obtuse representation of a locomotive painted in 1910 by Filippo Tommaso Marinetti, the father of Futurism. Teresa detested it. She regarded Futurism as Philip Wilson Steer had once regarded the works of the Post-Impressionists, remembering that he had remarked, upon visiting an early Impressionists' exhibit, "I suppose they have private incomes." Teresa had suggested the Marinetti for the window because she wanted to remind Geoffrey that she was as progressive and intellectual as he.

"Ah, the Marinetti," said Geoffrey, opening the car door. "Great minds, et cetera. I was going to display it tomorrow." He stepped out on the walk, slammed the door, and stood looking down at his wife. "What is it today? Beach?"

"Just for an hour. It sets me up for the rest of the day."

"I won't get out of here until six-thirty."

"I'll be here, dear. Please don't overwork."

After he had disappeared into the shop, Teresa guided the convertible around the block to Wilshire Boulevard, ignored several young college boys who honked at her at the San Vincente turn (disdaining their rudeness, she was inexplicably pleased), and continued on to Santa Monica. After twenty-five minutes of driving, she reached the Pacific Coast Highway, where the traffic was light at this hour, and drove steadily in the salty breeze until she reached her destination, a mile before Malibu.

Her destination was a small, rocky dirt lot that jutted precariously over the wide sand beach, aiming its blunted bow directly at the white-capped breakers. For several years now, at first occasionally, then once a week, and more recently two and three times a week, Teresa had been spending her mornings in solitude on the beach below. Although the area was public, her cove was private, unpopulated by skin divers, families on picnics, or acrobatic musclemen.

The discovery of this refuge—Constable's Cove, Geoffrey had christened it the first and only time he had seen it, after John Constable's "Weymouth Bay" in the National Gallery—had been a small miracle to Teresa. Soon after she and Geoffrey had decided that certain people were not meant to have children—cannibals of life and art—she had found mornings intolerable. Afternoons were possible—there was always enough to be done at home and at The Village Green and with her friends—and evenings were busy and social, but mornings made the night too far away. And then, on a restless drive, she had found Constable's Cove and never ceased returning there to stretch in the sand, bask in the blaze of sun, daydream, nap, or read to the steady beat of the blue waves.

Having parked and carefully drawn the hand brake, she circled the convertible, opened the trunk, and extracted blanket and a slender volume of Ernest Dowson's verse, which included an appreciative essay on the poet. Glancing behind her, Teresa saw that the sun was full, but veiled by clouds and not yet hot. She decided to forgo her umbrella.

With the book under her arm and blanket in hand, her free hand protectively held forward lest she slip, she slowly made her way down the narrow, worn defile to the warm sand. A short distance away, there was a slight indentation in the cliff, and this was Constable's Cove. Teresa trudged through the sand, laid down her volume, carefully spread her blanket, then dropped down upon it. For a moment, knees lifted high inside her arms, eyes closed to the sky, she reveled in the rays of the sun and the brushing sea wind. At last she opened her eyes, stretched out, leaning on an elbow, parted the Dowson book and began to read.

She followed the first and second verses patiently, waiting for what she knew was coming, and as she began the third verse, she smiled. Mouthing the words, she read:

> *I have forgot much, Cynara! gone with the wind,*
> *Flung roses, roses riotously with the throng,*
> *Dancing, to put thy pale, lost lilies out of mind;*
> *But I was desolate and sick of an old passion,*
> *Yea, all the time, because the dance was long:*
> *I have been faithful to thee, Cynara! in my fashion.*

She had read this long ago, and now rereading it, she instinctively saw its social and conversational value (Dowson, thank heavens, was not yet stale) and began to examine it again, to file it away in memory. As she resumed reading, a voice, not a voice but more a muted foghorn, shook her back to reality. "Comeonyadope—lead me—pass it—I'm on the twenty-yard line—heave it!"

Teresa's head snapped up from the book, and she sought the

35

source of heinous interruption. On the sand, nearer the water, perhaps fifty yards off, were four grown men where before there had been no one. Even at this distance, she could see that they were gigantic young men. Two were shoulder to shoulder, bucking and bullying each other like angry elephants, in some sort of savage play. The other two were playing catch with a football, one, squat and intent, in denims, throwing to the largest of the four, in sweat shirt and trunks, who ran churning through the exploding sand to catch it.

Frowning her displeasure, Teresa continued to observe them. Like automata, the four continued their perpetual, unvarying movements, punctuating all with incomprehensible and often profane shoutings. For a while, they seemed to gravitate closer to her, and once the largest of the four came plowing within twenty yards of her, leaping high and easily, for one so brawny, to snatch the ball from the air. When he came down, he came down to a knee, then slowly rose, panting. She could see him plainly now: his dark hair cut in the so-called butch fashion and a red, open, perfectly wrought California outdoor face, with a faded gray sweat shirt emblazoned with the legend "Rams" covering a mammoth chest, tapering down to a narrow torso indecently covered by trunks so brief that a protective cup would have served as well. His thighs were bulging, and the legs were surprisingly slim.

Catching his breath, he looked up and saw Teresa staring at him. He grinned. Annoyed, she turned away and lifted her book. After a proper interval, she glanced over her shoulder. He was making his way back to his friends, bouncing the ball up and down in one hand.

Determined to ignore this temporary invasion of Constable's Cove and its dominion, Teresa set her lips—again thin, since the paint had worn off—and reclined once more with Dowson. She reread the third verse five times, but the words blurred and made no sense. She could hear the lusty exertions nearby, and the occasional outcries, and much as she tried to think of Dowson, she thought only of Dr. Chapman. What did he ask women anyway? What did he expect to hear from them? What were the standards of satisfactory sex? But then, she reflected, Dr. Chapman would not know. He would know the quantitative pattern, but not what was best. Who was to determine what was best or right or gratifying? Suddenly, for the first time, she related Dr. Chapman's inquiry to herself, her flesh, her bed, and she felt a thrill of apprehension and danger.

She looked off. All four were in the throwing and catching game now, and after a few minutes she could see that the largest of them was also the most artful. By far the most artful.

Suddenly she stood up. She had been in the Cove only a half hour, instead of the usual hour or more, but now she wanted to be home, surrounded by the security of the statuary, and abstract oils, and rare old books, as far as possible from perspiration, and agility, and muscle. She wanted the sanctity of art, civilized, not artfulness, primitive.

With her volume in hand, she snatched up her blanket, hardly bothering to shake it out, and made her way toward the path, staring straight ahead at the small ridges of sand. At the foot of the path she paused briefly and looked off at the four barbarians. The largest was standing, hands on hips, legs spread wide, regarding her boldly (and, she thought in a flash, regarding himself, too, no doubt, as some embodiment of Hercules or Apollo). Suddenly, almost insolently, he waved to her. She shuddered, turned away, and hastened up the path to the convertible.

◇ ◇ ◇

"Yes, I understand, Kathleen," said Naomi Shields as she immersed herself deeper in the bathtub of hot water, awkwardly holding the receiver high to keep it from getting wet. "But, I repeat, I couldn't be less interested. I don't give a goddam about any Dr. Chapman, and I'm not doing a strip tease for some phony scientist."

Although Naomi, however crudely, did voice some of her own sentiments, Kathleen felt by now a certain loyalty to her assignment. "You speak as if he's a charlatan."

"Oh, I know. I've read about him—he's Jesus H. Christ—and this is going to assure all married women they can hop in the hay as often as they please and not feel guilty because everyone else does it."

"That's not it at all, Naomi." Kathleen did not know Naomi as well as the other women. They had met several times, casually, on Naomi's rare visits to the Association. But she had, from time to time, heard stories, and if they were even half true, Naomi was less than inhibited in her conduct with the opposite sex. Because Kathleen was dealing with someone unrestrained, she was trying to be overly cautious. She determined to give Naomi one more chance before writing her off. "Perhaps some of us have—have the same feelings you do about a survey like this. But I still tell myself Dr. Chapman's record and intentions are the best, and the results can do some good."

"Will it cure crippled children, or keep women from growing old, or stop husbands from being thoughtless?"

"No. But as Grace says—"

"That old bag."

"Really, Naomi, she's just trying. She says—and we know this—there's too much ignorance about sex. Anything that can shed a ray of light will be healthy, normalizing. When we were kids, children knew nothing—"

"Says you! Listen, Katie, girl, when I was twelve years—there was an uncle living with us, a lecherous bastard—my old man was a salesman, always out of town—and this uncle got me down one day, breathing wine in my face, and pulled my bloomers off—" She broke off suddenly, pained by the hated remembrance. "Oh, hell," she said, "it's none of your business. I don't know what I've been saying. I got up with a splitting headache." Her temples felt clamped in a vise, twisting tighter and tighter. The two pills she had taken just before the telephone rang had not yet had any effect.

"If you don't feel well—" began Kathleen.

"I feel the way I always feel," said Naomi. "I'll be all right. I'm always at my worst at ten o'clock."

Kathleen, a secret veteran of sorrow, felt a surge of understanding and pity, and retreated. "Naomi, this is all silly. There's nothing in the rules that says you have to be there. Dr. Chapman will have enough guinea pigs. You just duck it—"

"Thanks, Katie," said Naomi, wriggling erect in the now tepid water, "but I don't think I will duck it. I'm not resigning from the human race yet." More and more lately, she found, she would take a contrary, argumentative, angry stand about anything proposed, and then, after a while, reverse herself completely, as she knew that she would from the start. "You think I want that professor to get the wrong impression of The Briars? If he feeds himself off characters like Grace Waterton and Teresa Harnish, he'll think we've got a celibacy cult out here. It would ruin the community. I've got civic pride. No, you better count Naomi in. I want to balance the picture."

"If you're sure—"

"Honey, I'm positive. I missed out on Havelock Ellis and Krafft-Ebing because I was under-age. But I'll make Chapman —one way or another, you can bet."

After she had hung up, Naomi realized that her headache was almost gone, but a residue of indefinable depression remained. Listlessly, she slopped away at her glistening body with a wash cloth. At last, she opened the drain, and as the water gurgled out, she lifted herself to her feet and stepped out of the sunken tub.

Slowly drying before the full-length door mirror, she studied her small, near perfect figure with objective fascination. She had suffered and enjoyed a long affair with her body, an affair compounded of self-hate and self-love. Divorcing herself from all logic, more easily than she had divorced herself from her husband three years ago, she blamed this body for contributing most largely to the delinquency and mismanagement of her life. She was attractive, and she had always been attractive, as long as she could remember. Now, at thirty-one, the bouffant hair-do, dark sloe eyes, flaring little nose, and small full mouth gave promise of strange delights and eroticism. Her frame—she was only five feet one—seemed sculptured from ivory by a master craftsman. Every feature and limb was perfectly proportioned, except the breasts, which were oversized, with abnormally prodigious brown nipples that reduced men to inarticulate slaves and gave Naomi the feeling of physical superiority usually possessed only by the very young.

Discarding her soggy towel, she sprinkled talcum on her skin, gently smoothed it in, then applied perfume behind her ears and between her breasts. She walked, naked, into the dressing room that led to the bedroom, released a flowing white peignoir from its hanger, and pulled it on. Loosely knotting it at the throat, she continued to the bedroom. She surveyed what she variously named, in her mind, her mausoleum or purgatory. The farthest half of the customed bed was a mess—as if it had been through a mixmaster—the pale rose bedspread a mangled mound, and the table next to the bed accusingly told her why. The ash tray was heaped with cigarette butts, the bottle of green pills was uncapped, the fifth of gin was almost empty, and the tall glass still contained the remains of an old drink and worn lemon peel. The entire room—no windows were open, for she had an inordinate fear of prowlers—reeked of stale tobacco and nauseating drink. How much had she consumed last night? Perhaps a third of the fifth. Possibly more. She could not recall. She remembered only that the two pills—or was it three?—had not brought oblivion, and so, against all resolve, she had taken a drink, and then another, and had not stopped. She had slept like death, yet the tortured blankets and pillow pressed low between the gilded headboard and the mattress gave evidence that (for her) to sleep was still to dream.

Quickly, she raised a window to air the room, and then, because the bath had revived and cleansed her, she fled the foul air. Passing through the narrow hall, through the living room and dining room into the kitchen, she tried desperately to focus on a plan for the long day ahead. As she started the coffee on the stove, and took down cup and saucer in a hand that trembled, she thought that she might visit her parents in Burbank. She had not seen them for weeks. But the very thought of a day with that loveless, bickering pair—an old father, senile and regretful, and a stepmother spouting shrill clichés—was more than she was prepared to endure. She might telephone the wonderful child down the block, Mary Ewing McManus, and go shopping with her. But she dreaded the youngster's effervescence and energy, and knew that in the end Mary's presence would make her feel unclean. She might drive into Beverly Hills and visit those females in the rental library—though she still possessed three novels that were unread and woefully overdue—and then shop for a new sweater and skirt, since several alimony checks had piled up undeposited through neglect and inertia. But Beverly Hills seemed a million miles away, and she was in no mood to walk through streets of noisy, busy, overdressed women.

Pacing, as she waited for the coffee, she felt that frighteningly recurring feeling of being suspended in space, rootless. Her peignoir had loosened, partially exposing her body, and she covered herself and tightened the cord, more distraught than ever. She did not know what she should do, but she did know what she would not do. She would not drink. The very thought of drink seemed, at once, a crutch, until she could decide. Quickly, she turned to the maple cabinet, opened it, and studied the row of bottles. There was an untouched bottle of gin. The smell of the bedroom was still in her nostrils, and the bottle repelled her. She reached for the French brandy, and a snifter above, and went into the dining room. She poured the snifter full, brought it to her nose, inhaling the aroma (which was unaccountably bitter), and then hastily drank.

She heard the coffee pot boiling in the kitchen. She finished the snifter, hastily filled it again, and then went in for her coffee. She shut off the burner. The coffee seemed superfluous right now. She leaned against the sink and drank the brandy. The burning in her throat was hardly noticeable now, and she was beginning to feel warm at the forehead. She finished the snifter, and replenished it a second time. She sipped it slowly, determined that this should be her last. There was the young manager of that food market in The Village Green, a nice blond boy, who was always very friendly. Maybe he wanted to be serious. Maybe she should encourage him. They could go to a movie tonight. It might be the beginning of something that made sense, at last. How could she have been so foolish at that foolish school? How could she have let that mere boy, a student, take her into the back yard? Or had she taken him? It was hard to remember; it had been so horrible. He—who was he?—the boy—he was a senior anyway, and she was younger then—he, she meant her husband, was going to be in the lab until ten. Or was it nine? It was so difficult to sort it out.

She stared glassily at the snifter. It was empty. She had only been sipping it. Maybe she had spilled it. She looked down at the floor. No. She took the bottle and poured. She would sip slowly and drive to the drugstore. The man at the register was always nice. And more her type. He really liked her. Maybe he was too shy to ask for a date. Of course he was shy. The way he blushed last week when she asked for a box of sanitary napkins. Wassn't it—wasn't it—was it not funny the way things were? When she was in high school, she would almost sneak in for sanitary pads, always search and find the plain wrapped box, as if no one knew then, and it was a crime. And later, in her twenties, she would ask for the box briskly, but quickly. And now she was starting in her thirties, and she asked for the box too loudly, as if she was proud that she was still a full-blown woman.

The doorbell was ringing. Her ears were buzzing, and so she listened to be very, very sure. It was the doorbell. She stood up—when had she sat down?—and walked with studied care past the refrigerator, through the service porch, carefully unlocked the door and opened it.

"Good mornin', Ma'am." He was standing, leaning sideways, because he was carrying a large bottle of spring water on one shoulder. He was so tall he would bump his head, except he was sideways. She inclined her head to examine his sideways face. Bush of chestnut hair. Eyes too narrow. Nose too long. Lips too full. Everything too much. But he was smiling. He was friendly. He liked her. He was tall.

"Another fine day, goin' to be," he added. She was behind the door, opening it farther, as he came through and lowered the bottle to the floor.

"You're new," she said thickly.

"Takin' two routes today. Hank's down with the bug."

"Oh."

He wiped the bottle quickly, unscrewed the cap, rose to remove the old bottle from the container; then, with apparently no effort, hoisted the filled bottle high and tipped it into the tank. He watched with a certain satisfaction as the fresh water seeped, gurgling into the tank.

"There you are," he said, turning. "Now you're set up for another two weeks."

"Good service," she said. She saw that he was staring at her awkwardly, and she remembered that she had on no brassière or pants beneath her peignoir. But the folds kept the negligee from being fully transparent. So what was he staring at anyway? Maybe because he liked her. Good boy.

"Well," he said.

"Do you get paid now?"

"I believe so, Ma'am."

"All right. Come on."

She moved unsteadily into the kitchen. She heard him behind her. She started into the dining room.

"Should I wait here, Ma'am?"

She felt unaccountably annoyed. "My name's Naomi."

"Yes—"

"Follow me. I have my purse—"

She chose her footsteps slowly, and heard him behind her. They moved through the dining area, and living room, into the hall, and entered the bedroom. She glanced at him. He stood inside the door, not sure what to do with his hands. He was very tall. He smiled at her. She smiled back. She took her purse from the dresser and held it out.

"Here," she said, "take the money."

"But—"

"Whatever it is."

He went stiffly to her, took the purse, opened it, fumbled inside, and found only a five-dollar bill.

"I have change," he said. He returned the purse to her and dug into his pockets. She dropped the purse on the bed and sat down on the edge, next to the crumpled rose bedspread. She watched him as he made the change.

She crossed her legs. "I like you," she said. "What's your name?"

He looked up from the bills in his hand. Her negligee had

fallen away from her legs, and her thighs were exposed. He flushed. "Johnny," he said.

Quickly, he held out the change. She reached for it, but took his wrist instead. "Come here," she said. "That's not what I want."

She pulled him, and as she did so she got to her feet. The cord at her throat, loosened, fell away, and the peignoir was open. She saw his eyes drop, and his Adam's apple bob, and knew that he saw the brown nipples and knew that this would be a good day.

"I want you," she said, smiling crookedly.

He was all breath and fright. "I'm not allowed to, Ma'am. I'd get in trouble—"

"Don't be silly." She closed the distance between them, lifting her arms around his neck. "Now, kiss me."

He reached down to remove her, but his hands missed her ribs and came to rest on the immense breasts. He pulled his hands away as if he had touched flame.

"I'm married," he gasped. "I got kids—"

"Kiss me; love me—"

"I can't!"

Reaching behind, frantically, he tore her arms off him, then wheeled, and almost running, in great, grotesque strides, he dashed out of the room.

She stood very still, riveted almost, listening to his receding footsteps in the living room, the kitchen, and then, after a moment, from far away, the service porch door slamming.

She did not move. That'll be something to tell the boys, she thought. Filthy little prig. Probably castrated anyway. What would he know about love? Jack rabbit. She looked down at her swelling breasts. She felt sober and nauseated, and could taste the brandy high in her throat, and it was sour.

For three weeks this had not happened, and now it had almost happened. Why had it happened? What was wrong? She sank down to the bed, and then lay on it, curling her legs beneath her. She felt the tears on her face, and then her body shaking and shaking as she began to sob. Her stomach was in her throat, and she wanted to retch. She stumbled to her feet, felt her way into the bathroom, and was ill. After long minutes, pale and weakened, she returned to the kitchen. She relighted the burner, and, waiting for the coffee to heat once more, she wandered to the window. The Chinese elm was full, and birds were all about it. Somewhere beyond, a dog barked, and she could hear the children in the street. It would be hot again today. She wondered what she would do.

❖ ❖ ❖

Kathleen Ballard sat at her formica table and studied the list in the open folder. She had been sitting many minutes, content to smoke and take a break since she had telephoned Naomi Shields. She ran her eyes down the checked names. Ursula. Sarah. Mary. Teresa. Naomi. They had consumed over an hour—she knew the press release by heart now—and there were still seven more to call. Would it not have been more efficient, she asked herself, to send each member of the Association a letter informing her of Dr. Chapman's lecture? At once, she knew that, while it might have been more efficient, it would have been less effective. Sarah Goldsmith and Naomi Shields would have ignored the printed invitations. And how many more? It was only direct conversation that had forced acceptances out of both women, and perhaps out of all of them. Still, thought Kathleen, it was ridiculous and ironic that she, of all people, was being forced to sell Dr. Chapman and his voyeurs to the others. Surely not one of them, all things considered, would hear or meet him with more unwillingness.

She considered the warm telephone again. Duty was duty, and that was that. Glancing at the remainder of the list, she reached for the receiver. Her hand was poised over it, when, jarringly, it rang. Startled, she instinctively withdrew her hand. At last, after the third imperious ring, she answered the phone.

"Hello?"

"Katie, doll? It's Ted."

She was not sure if she was pleased or troubled. "Ted, how are you? When did you get in?"

"Five minutes ago. I'm still in Operations. I had to hear your voice before I got tied up with Metzgar."

"Was it fun?"

"Where I was stuck, North Africa looked like Carswell Base in Texas."

"You didn't even get to see Livingston or a Mau Mau?"

"I got to see the PX. Period. How have you been? Missed me?"

"Of course."

She had not missed him, really. When Ted had informed her, two weeks before, that he had to represent Radcone in a test flight to Africa, sponsored by Strategic Air Command, she

44

had been relieved. Ever since Boynton's death sixteen months ago, Ted Dyson had been a visitor and a friend. Ted had known Boy, as he and most of America liked to call Boynton Ballard, long before Kathleen had known him. Ted and Boynton flirted with MIGs over the Yalu, wing to wing. Immediately after, Ted had gone to work for J. R. Metzgar and Radcone Aircraft in Van Nuys, and later, following a great blare of publicity when Boynton had joined him there as a test pilot, Ted always proudly claimed part of the credit for snaring him.

After Kathleen had married Boynton, it was Ted Dyson who was retained as number one bachelor friend—to run an occasional household errand, fill in when there was a female visitor from New York, escort Kathleen to a play when Boynton was busy. It was natural that when Boynton was killed, Ted would appear as official family mourner. The entire nation, Metzgar, the President in the White House, mourned, but Ted had seniority. At first, he had appeared irregularly, out of respect for Kathleen's grief, but making her aware always that he was hovering near and need only be summoned. Then, gradually, in the sixteen months past, a subtle change had overtaken Ted Dyson. As friend of the hero, he was also heir to the hero's mantle. He was elevated to the position of Radcone's first test pilot and trouble shooter, Boynton's job. He was recipient of some of Boynton's old glory and attention. And soon, as Kathleen perceived it, he began to think himself the only male capable of possessing and satisfying Boynton's widow. He was the successor and began to conduct himself as such. His appearances were more regular. His familiarity was more aggressive. And on their last date, just before the African trip, emboldened as he was by several drinks, he kissed Kathleen good night as they stood inside the door and then somehow found her breasts with his hands. But she had moved quickly away, and he had not pursued her. It was tacitly understood, by both, that he had drunk too much. And now he was back.

". . . so that's the way I think it's going to work out," he was saying.

She had not heard a word. "That's fine, Ted," she said quickly.

"Well, anyway, I'm going to be here, and I've got a lot to tell you. When can I see you?"

"I . . . I don't know. I've been so busy—"

"So now you'll be busier."

Before she could think of what to say, she heard the noisy

45

approach of a car in the driveway. It puzzled her. "Ted, one sec, there's someone here. I'll be right back."

Rising hastily from the table, she went to the window and peered outside. A battered station wagon was moving around the circular drive to her entrance. The car was familiar, and then, as it braked to a halt, she recognized the driver. At once, she remembered. Last night, James Scoville had telephoned just as Grace Waterton came calling. In haste and confusion, she had consented to let Scoville drop by in the morning. He had said that he wanted only a few minutes. Something about straightening out several points in the fourth chapter.

Kathleen hurried back to the telephone. "Ted, I'm sorry. It's Jim Scoville. I promised to help him this morning."

"Hasn't he finished that book yet?"

"It takes time."

"Well, what about our date?"

She knew that she would have to see him. Until three weeks ago it had been painless enough, sometimes even welcome, for it gave her companionship at the movies. If Ted had only not spoiled it by making a pass at her. But he *had* been drunk. "All right," she said. "Thursday. Join Deirdre and me for dinner. We can go to a show after."

"Swell, Katie. Until then."

Scoville was rapping the brass door knocker discreetly. After a troubled glance at the list of names, Kathleen hurried to the door and admitted the writer.

"Hello, Jim," she said. "I really should have called you. I'm all tied up this morning."

"It'll only be a minute," he said in his apologetic way.

"Well, if it's only that—"

"No more. I finished chapter four, and there's just the matter of verifying some dates and straightening out a couple of inconsistencies."

"Very well." She nodded. "Let's sit down. Do you need paper?"

"No, no. I have everything."

They went to the arrangement around the Biedemeir pear wood tea table. Kathleen sat on the sofa, and Scoville lowered himself to the edge of the turquoise chair, tugging a wad of yellow paper from his sport coat pocket and finding a ball point pen which he clicked open.

"How's the book going?" asked Kathleen.

"I think I can finish in two months."

"That's fast."

46

"Yes. I guess I'm enthused. Sonia had to force me to bed at midnight last night."

Kathleen had a kind of acquaintance affection for James Scoville. He was so knocked about and unobtrusive. He gave the impression of being almost six foot—the manner of his head pulled into worn, hunched shoulders, protectively, like a tortoise, made accurate estimates of his height impossible. He had dull, ash-blond hair, a bland, freckled face that seemed Albino pink, watery eyes, and receding chin, and his clothes always appeared as if he had slept in them. It was Metzgar of Radcone Aircraft who had arranged for Scoville to do the biography of Boynton.

Metzgar was wealthy and important, but like all sedentary men who had risen through use of desk and telephone, he worshiped men of action. Although he had hired Boynton, he knew that Boynton did not work for him. Boynton was his own man and respected no channels except those direct to God. This, as well as Boynton's reckless courage (in most men, born of fear, but in Boynton's case, as Kathleen alone knew, born of insensitivity and a curious, egotistical, divine sense that he was too young and too needed to be touched by death), made Metzgar his suppliant.

When Boynton had gone down in flames, in the experimental jet, crashing and disintegrating on the baking desert near Victorville, Metzgar (and he not alone) refused to accept this evidence of his idol's mortality. To keep him alive, forever living in the dreams of others, Metzgar conceived of the biography. Promising a renowned Manhattan publisher a guaranteed purchase of five thousand copies in advance (to be distributed among customers and Air Force personnel), Metzgar made the book a reality. Then he cast about for the proper writer. He wanted no word juggler who would intrude his own personality into this testament to greatness. He wanted merely a human conveyor belt to take the product, package it, and pass it on to the public.

Screening writers that he had bought and used, he recalled James Scoville. He remembered that Scoville had produced several competent articles about Radcone, and since he remembered Scoville's work and not his face or personality, he knew that he was the man. He brought Scoville in from his beach home in Venice (once, delivering some old letters, Kathleen had visited the flimsy little house and found it pitifully underfurnished and inadequate, and had been uncomfortable in the presence of the writer's wife, a gaunt, witchlike

47

girl in gypsy clothes), and then Metzgar offered Scoville the assignment. He was to have three thousand dollars from the publisher, and three thousand more from Metzgar.

Dazzled by the largest sum he had ever known, Scoville listened to Metzgar's briefing and was prepared to write as Metzgar pleased. There was left only the formality of Kathleen's co-operation. Everything in her resisted it, but in the end, she knew that Metzgar—and the million like him—must have their monument. Two weeks of evenings before a tape recorder, along with letters and clippings, gave the writer all that he needed from Kathleen. Now he was writing like the furies, and if all went well, he would soon be able to remove wife and self to a more commodious tract bungalow in San Fernando Valley. Kathleen liked Scoville. Perhaps because he was hardly a man.

"Maybe next time we can work longer," she said regretfully. "It's just that our club—our women here—are going to be interviewed by Dr. George G. Chapman, and I'm on the committee to let them know."

Scoville lifted his head, his eyes blinking. His face betrayed minor horror. "Dr. Chapman? You mean he's going to interview *you?*"

"Why, yes, of course—all of us," said Kathleen, somewhat taken aback.

"But you can't," he blurted.

Kathleen was completely at a loss. "Why not?"

"It's not right. You're not just anybody. You're—well, you were married to Boynton Ballard. It's not—it wouldn't be proper to tell some stranger your private life with *him.*" He mouthed *him* as he might Yahveh.

Kathleen stared at Scoville and understood at once. He, too, like Metzgar, like the faceless public, had a hungry need to believe in Someone. Authentic heroes were few, because they usually lived too long. A German, Goethe probably, had once said, "Every hero becomes a bore at last," and it was true. But to be a hero and be snuffed out at the peak of burning, this promised immortality. And, somehow, because she had been hero's chattel, Kathleen must be preserved by the cult, buried in the tomb with him, sanctified. Willing or not, his purity and virtue, and the quality that was more than merely mortal must continue to reside in her. And so she perceived Scoville's pain. If she disclosed to a stranger the animal habits of the hero, the mean details of fornication, she profaned a sacred memory by

48

showing that he had been like ordinary men, with base needs and weaknesses of the flesh.

From the corner of her eye, she saw Scoville, head pulled in and bent, busily examining his blank yellow paper. She wondered what he would think if he even faintly conceived what was really in her head. For she was thinking of that slate-gray, late afternoon, sixteen months ago, when man had died and hero had been born.

She had wept, of course, and fleetingly felt leaden sorrow. But if there were a scale upon which to weigh emotion, the sorrow was no heavier than she felt at the death of a distant Hungarian in an embattled street, a Peruvian in a faraway train wreck, a child found lifeless in a Bel-Air swimming pool. The sorrow had been that which grieved over the human condition; the unfairness of the life-promise that held out so much alive and then withdrew it so quickly. This was her sorrow, and this only. But as for the man, the one whose name and child she bore, the tears she had shed were not tears of love but tears of relief. Who would understand that?

"Maybe you're right," she said to Scoville at last. "Now what were the questions you wanted to ask?"

2

THEY BRACED THEMSELVES against the lurching of the train as it scraped around a curve, and then, as it seemed to shake itself straight again and pick up speed beneath them, the iron wheels clacking rhythmically on the rails, they relaxed once more.

They had been proofing the results of the week of sampling in East St. Louis, and now they were nearing the end of a five-minute recess, smoking in silence, making sporadic, inconsequential comments, waiting to resume.

Paul Radford sucked noisily at his straight-stemmed pipe, then realized the tobacco was burned out, and began to empty the white ash into the wall tray. "Do you really think Los Angeles will wrap it up?" he asked.

Across the way, Dr. George G. Chapman looked up from the sheaf of papers in his hand. "I don't know for sure, Paul. Probably. We had a wire from that woman—Mrs. Waterton—president of the . . . the . . ." He tried to remember. There had been so many.

"The Briars' Women's Association," said Dr. Horace Van Duesen.

Dr. Chapman nodded. "Yes, that's it; she promised a hundred per cent turnout."

"It never works out that way," said Cass Miller sourly.

Dr. Chapman frowned. "It might. But let's say we get seventy per cent response—I think we've been averaging close to that—well, that would be sufficient. We can cancel the optional engagement in San Francisco. We can just call it quits on the interviews and settle down to the paper work." He forced a smile. "I guess you boys would like that?"

There was no response. Paul Radford slowly rubbed the warm bowl of his pipe. Horace Van Duesen removed his horn-rimmed spectacles, held them up to the light, put them on again. Cass Miller chewed steadily at his gum, staring down at the worn carpeting.

Dr. Chapman sighed. "All right," he said, running a hand across his flat, slick gray hair, "all right, let's get back to the proofing."

For a moment longer, his eyes held on the three younger men cramped in the gray and green train bedroom that smelled of the now familiar smell of paint and metal. He could see the boredom and inattention on their faces, but he determinedly ignored this and, once more, bent his eyes closely to the typed manuscript in his hand. It was difficult focusing on the figures in the dim yellow overhead train light.

"Now, then, we've incorporated the East St. Louis sampling. That means—according to what I have here—we've interviewed 3,107 women to date." He glanced at Paul, as he usually did. "Correct?"

"Correct," repeated Paul, consulting the yellow pages in his hand. To Paul's right, Cass and Horace also looked fixedly at the papers in their laps and tiredly nodded their agreement.

"All right," said Dr. Chapman. "Now, let's check this carefully. It'll save us a good deal of drudgery when we get home." He shifted slightly in his chair, brought the manuscript closer to his face, and began to read aloud in a low, uncritical monotone. "Question. Do you feel any sexual desire at the sight of the male genitalia? Answer. Fourteen per cent feel strong desire, thirty-nine per cent feel a slight desire, six per cent say it depends on the entire physique of the man, forty-one per cent feel nothing at all." Dr. Chapman lifted his head, pleased. "Significant," he said. "Especially when you recollect our figures on male response to female nudity in the bachelor survey. Paul, make a note on that. I want to draw the analogy when I write the final report."

Paul nodded, and dutifully jotted a sentence in the margin of his paper, even though twice before in the last month he had been requested to record the very same notation. Doing so, he wondered if Dr. Chapman was as tired as he, and Horace, and Cass. It was unlike him to be forgetful and repetitious. Perhaps the fourteen months of almost uninterrupted traveling, interviewing, recording, proofing, were taking their toll.

Dr. Chapman was reading silently ahead. "Interesting," he mused, "how close these East St. Louis figures are to the national average."

"I think it's obvious women are the same everywhere," said Cass.

Horace turned to Cass. "How do you account for those lopsided percentages in Connecticut and Pennsylvania?"

"It wasn't a regional divergence," said Cass. "Those women chased more because their husbands were commuting—and they had too much money and nothing else to do. It was social and economic."

"All right, boys," said Dr. Chapman quickly, "let's not start analyzing—"

"I saw the advance sheet on The Briars," continued Cass. "With that income level, I'll lay two to one that we are approaching the land of the round heels."

Horace held up his hands in mock surrender. "Okay, okay, Mother Shipton."

"I don't like that kind of talk," Dr. Chapman said firmly to Cass. "We're scientists, not schoolboys."

Cass bit his lip and was silent.

Dr. Chapman regarded him quietly a moment, and then relented slightly. "We're all overtired. I know that. Exhaustion creates impatience, and impatience makes objectivity go out the window. We've got to watch it. We're not to permit ourselves snap judgments and unproved generalities. We're in pursuit of facts—facts and nothing more—and I want you to remember that for the next two weeks."

Paul wondered how Cass was taking this. He glanced at him. Cass's mouth was curled in a set smile that wasn't a smile. "Sorry, teacher," he said at last.

Dr. Chapman snorted and returned to the digits before him. "Where were we?"

Paul hastily answered. "Question. Do you feel any sexual desire at the sight of the male genitalia? Answer. Et cetera, et cetera."

"Do our figures jibe on that one?" asked Dr. Chapman.

"Perfect with me," said Paul. He looked at the other two. Both Horace and Cass nodded.

"Let's go on," said Dr. Chapman. His stubby finger found his place on the page before him. He read aloud. "Question. Does observation of the unclothed male in that photograph of a nudist camp arouse you? Answer. Ten per cent are strongly aroused, twenty-seven per cent only somewhat, and sixty-three per cent not at all." He lifted his head toward Paul. "Correct?"

"Correct," said Paul.

Horace straightened, pulling his shoulders back to work

loose his stiff muscles. "You know," he said to Dr. Chapman, "that category keeps giving me more trouble than any other one. So often the answers are not clear cut."

"What do you mean?" asked Dr. Chapman.

"Well, I can give you a dozen illustrations. Do you want me to go into one?"

"If it's pertinent," said Dr. Chapman.

"When we were in Chicago last month, I asked one sample if the art photographs or paintings of nude males I showed her aroused her. Well, this woman—she must have been about thirty-five—she said that nude art never affected her one way or the other, except one statue in the Art Institute—an ancient nude Greek. Whenever she looked at it, she said, she had to go home and have her husband."

"I should think that would indicate sufficient reaction to stimuli," said Dr. Chapman. "How did you record the answer?"

"Well, I wanted to be certain that some personal association didn't make this statue an exceptional thing. I kept cross-checking, as we went along, with other questions. At last, I found out that when she was—sixteen, I think—she used to keep a magazine cut-out in a drawer, under her clothes, some male Olympic swimmer in abbreviated trunks. Whenever she took it out and looked at it, she would follow with masturbation. But besides that and the statue, no other photograph or art work ever aroused her. It makes it difficult to obtain a decisive—"

"I would have classified her in the 'strongly aroused' group."

"Yes, I did. But it's often difficult—"

"Naturally," said Dr. Chapman. "We're dealing as much with grays as blacks and whites. Human emotions don't seem to measure out mathematically—but they can, with experience and intelligence applied by the interviewer." He tugged at his right ear lobe thoughtfully. "We're not infallible. The critic and layman want us to be, but we're not. Some error has to creep in as long as women will distort because of defensive exaggeration, involuntary emotional blocks, or prudish deceit. However, Horace, I believe our system of repeated double-check questions, especially the psychological ones—those, as well as consideration of the subject's entire attitude and response, are safeguards enough. In grave doubt, you still have recourse to the Double Poll. After all, in the Double Poll, we have the benefit of the forty years Dr. Julian Gleed devoted to analyzing married couples separately and setting up for us a

53

statistical basis for discrepancy or percentage of probable error. His papers are a gold mine. Too often, we neglect them. Anyway, by now, Horace, I'm sure you know when an interview is utterly hopeless and must be discarded."

"Certainly," said Horace quickly.

"Then, that's enough. Occasional indecision about recording a reply will not affect the whole."

Paul observed that whenever any one of them questioned the method, as they had more frequently done in recent months than earlier, Dr. Chapman would make his reassuring little speech. Curiously, it was always effective. There was about Dr. Chapman an air, a quality, a Messianic authority that made what they were doing seem right and important. Paul supposed that Mohammed must have projected this in defending the Koran, and Joseph Smith in presenting the Book of Mormon. For all their trials and problems, Paul knew that his own faith in their mission, in Dr. Chapman's method, stood unshaken. He knew that Horace felt that way, too; Cass, alone, was possibly the only potential apostate. Possibly. One could never be sure of the true feelings that pulsated in Cass's complex nervous system.

Dr. Chapman had resumed the proofing. Paul focused his attention on the paper in his hand. Dr. Chapman's head was low over the manuscript as he droned the questions, answers, percentages. Does observation of those three still photographs of romantic scenes from recent movies and legitimate plays excite you or fire your imagination? Yes, strongly, six per cent. Only somewhat, twenty-four per cent. Not at all, seventy per cent. Does examination of the male physical-culture magazine you have just been leafing through make you wish your husband was another type of man? Yes, definitely, fifteen per cent. In some ways, thirty-two per cent. Not at all, fifty-three per cent. For those of you who replied that you wished your husband was in some ways a different type, please define in what ways you would like him different? Taller, more athletic, forty-seven per cent. More intelligent and understanding, twenty-four per cent. Gentler, fifteen per cent. More authoritative or masculine, thirteen per cent. Does the sex scene you have just read from the unexpurgated *Lady Chatterly's Lover* by D. H. Lawrence, the scene among "the dense fir-trees," erotically stimulate you in any way? Yes, strongly, thirty per cent. Only somewhat, twenty-one per cent. Not at all, forty-nine per cent.

Although his hand continued to move his pencil down the page, Paul's mind was inattentive, and it wandered. He stared at the top of Dr. Chapman's head. Casually he wondered, as he had numerous times before, about Dr. Chapman's personal sex life. Usually, he tried not to wonder. It was an act of *lèse-majesté*. The-Queen-has-no-legs, he told himself, was the only proper note. But the nagging curiosity persisted. Paul knew, of course, that somewhere among the thousands of discarded questionnaires in the rented storage safes of the Father Marquette National Bank in the town of Reardon, there was one that revealed Dr. Chapman's sex history. Who had questioned Dr. Chapman? Who, indeed. Who created God? Who analyzed Freud? In the beginning, there was the creator. God created God; Freud analyzed Freud; and Dr. Chapman had questioned himself.

The project had its testament and books of revelation, and even its Genesis. By now, Paul could recite it by heart. Six years ago, six years and two months to be exact, Dr. George G. Chapman had been a fifty-one-year-old professor of Primate Biology at Reardon College in southern Wisconsin. Except for a paper on the mating habits of the lemur and the marmoset, he was a scholastic nonentity. His income was a comfortable $11,440 a year. He roomed, off campus, with a younger sister who was in awe of him, with her husband, who engaged him in chess when not wearied by dentistry and golf, and with three young nephews, who regarded him as joint father.

Once, in dim memory, there had been a Mrs. Chapman. George G. Chapman had been a senior at Northwestern University when he had met her at a fraternity dance and married her. She had been the well-educated daughter of a prosperous publisher of technical books in Chicago. After the wedding, the couple had spent their brief honeymoon in Key West and Havana. (The only photograph that Paul had ever seen of her, the one reproduced so often in magazines, had been taken in Havana. The enlarged snapshot was encased behind glass in a brown leather frame on Dr. Chapman's office desk. It revealed a tall girl in a shapeless, knee-length dress of the period. Her broad brow, high-boned cheeks, thin nose, and wide mouth gave the impression of one good-natured and amused. The camera had caught her squinting into the lens, because the hot and glaring Cuban sun was in her face. Across her long legs, in a faded spidery scrawl, she had written: "To the brains in the family. Love, Lucy." The glass covering the picture, the last time Paul had seen it, was dusty.)

After four years of marriage—Dr. Chapman had obtained his first teaching assignment in Oregon, and then moved to North Carolina at higher salary—his wife had incredibly suffered a paralytic stroke. She lay in a semi-coma for six weeks, and then, one cool spring dawn, she died. Less than a year later, when Reardon College had offered him the chair of Primate Biology, Dr. Chapman moved back to the lovely Wisconsin lake country, scene of his childhood and school years. Several years after, through the bait of financial assistance, he induced his new brother-in-law to establish a dental practice in the town of Reardon, a mile from the school, and then he helped his brother-in-law and sister buy a house which he made his home.

Until his nephews came, Dr. Chapman was lost to the world of books and considered somewhat antisocial and dull by faculty wives. There was a brief flurry of interest in him after his paper on the lemur and the marmoset, but when he remained vague and lumpy at parties, this interest subsided. But soon his growing nephews, whom he looked upon as his own children, gave him a link to reality and the community of the living. More frequently, he began to speak up on the trials of fatherhood and schooling, and became conversant with Dr. Spock, and even made gentle little jokes about finding future brides for the boys among the daughters of the faculty families. Gradually, a few families accepted him into their circle of friends and found him comfortable and undemanding. Finally, there occurred the event—often likened by the press to the day Franklin flew the kite and Newton saw the apple fall—when Dr. Chapman was catapulted from faculty old shoe to national celebrity with the status of foremost politician, baseball player, matinee idol, racketeer. And it was the eldest of his nephews, Jonathan, who was the catalytic agent in Dr. Chapman's transformation.

Jonathan was in his thirteenth year, and about to enter high school, when one afternoon he overheard several men-about-the-neighborhood (he was barely their junior) discuss the act of love and procreation in a language that baffled him. He had heard similar talk before, but, being an unaggressive and childish child, he had ignored it. His interests were sports and hobby cards. But now, suddenly having discovered that the presence of the opposite sex was equally as pleasurable as soft ball, he was curious for a clearer understanding of the strange chemistry between male and female that seemed to evoke expressions of excitement among his contemporaries. Rarely shy

56

with his mother, Jonathan came out with it and asked her to enlighten him. She sent him to his father. His father, busy trying to diagnose the best approach to an impacted wisdom tooth, and feeling that an authority on the biology of primates might manage the crucial explanation better, sent him to Dr. Chapman.

Not one to equivocate—for he looked upon sexual intercourse as a phenomenon no more remarkable than any other motor activity—Dr. Chapman promptly undertook to explain the act of copulation in dry scientific terms. Fifteen minutes later, when he was done, Jonathan knew considerably more about monkeys and apes, but over human love there still remained the veil. He stammered his confusion to his uncle. Surprised, Dr. Chapman stared at his nephew, and, at last, he saw him as a boy. To Dr. Chapman's credit, he sensed at once that he was incapable of communicating on this subject more simply. He realized that this was a matter that might best be handled by men who worked with words. Dr. Chapman advised Jonathan (dryly, it is to be hoped) to practice abstinence for a few days, to check his curiosity, and to withhold further inquiry, while an effort was made to locate several good books on the subject.

Impatiently, Jonathan waited. Impatiently, Dr. Chapman searched. Lucid books giving exposition on sexual union were few and far between. There were several how-to-do books, but they were dated and poorly done. There were academic studies and surveys, such as those by Davis, Hamilton, Dickinson, and Kinsey, but they were either limited, special, and incomprehensible to the younger layman, unless popularly interpreted, or so broad and general in coverage as to be useless for any specific use. There were literary novels, but they were romantic, ill-informed, and too often erotic. And nowhere was there a single popular volume, designed for ordinary adolescents, that contained sound and thorough research into the actual sex life of under-aged human beings rather than mere speculation.

For Dr. Chapman, what had begun as a routine pseudo-fatherly task now became an obsessive scientific challenge. Lemur and marmoset were forgotten. The human mammal was the game. Several years later, when he spoke and the world listened, Dr. Chapman would explain his emotions during those trying days: "Like Columbus, I found I was on an uncharted sea. Almost every avenue of human endeavor had been lighted, but human sexual relations remained a terrifying unknown area, darkened by ignorance. Some brilliant scholars had explored the field, of course. Darwin, Freud, Dickinson, Havelock Ellis, had done heroic pioneer work. There were also other sex historians and investigators. But I felt that real factual data, understandable and valuable to the masses, did not exist, and what did exist was often spoiled by the moral and social prejudices of the authors. After I had done my first tentative probings into the love life of adolescents, I foresaw that a further series of great works devoted to specific categories of sexual behavior must be done—so that the inexperienced young and their uninformed elders might apply sexual knowledge to their own lives. And so, first with my own meager savings, then with contributions from friends, then with sums earned by commercial poll-taking in other fields, and, at last, with the full support of Reardon, I began my investigations. When I proved that scientific information was being uncovered, I finally received the backing of national private funds."

Presumably, nephew Jonathan was left to find his own way —and to await publication of *Sexual Patterns in 307 Adolescents* and *A Sex Study of the American Bachelor* several years thence.

It was in the early days of his investigations, before he had received public approval, that Dr. Chapman ran into the greatest resistance. To determine a basis for interviewing and sampling, to test the value of his questions, he needed guinea pigs. Most members of the faculty, and their wives, were shocked and disapproving. At last, Dr. Chapman was forced to resort to bribes: purchasing subjects (and erratic memories of their teen-age years), from among students and idlers in the town, at so much a head, with the same calculation that blood is bought in a hospital for transfusion. Several times, local members of the clergy called upon him and tried to warn him, as tactfully as possible, that his investigation into adolescence was sinful, useless, corrupting. In desperation, Dr. Chapman pressed his nearest and dearest into the cause— interviewing his sister, his brother-in-law, several other relatives lured to the house of infamy on their vacations. And, finally, he interviewed himself, including in his personal confessional not merely experiences up to adolescence but his entire sexual history. His first collated findings in book form, obtained with the help of one assistant interviewer, earned him cash and some ungrammatical fan mail, but no national renown. Only when he confined his results to the professional journals after his next investigation were his colleagues and the great public beyond piqued, titillated, and impressed, and soon he was an institution and a force.

Yet, Paul wondered, what were Dr. Chapman's answers when he had interviewed himself?

The train lurched around a curve. Paul fell against Horace, dropping his pencil. Hastily, guiltily, he retrieved it.

"Did you get the last figures?" Dr. Chapman was asking.

"I think you'd better repeat them," said Paul.

Dr. Chapman nodded. "This was a supplementary question for married women who stated that they had participated in extramarital relations."

"Yes," said Paul.

Dr. Chapman read aloud. "Question. We would like to know the number of men, other than your husband, with whom you have had sexual intercourse since your marriage? Answer. Fifty-eight per cent, one male partner. Twenty-two per cent, two to ten male partners. Fourteen per cent, eleven to twenty-five male partners. Six per cent, twenty-six to fifty male partners." Without looking up, he asked, "Correct?"

"Correct," said Paul.

"And I thought East St. Louis was a hick town," said Cass.

Dr. Chapman cast him a pained glance.

Cass shrugged. "Forgive me. I'm punchy."

"I can see that," said Dr. Chapman. "We should be finished in ten or fifteen minutes."

He resumed reading in a persistent monotone. Sometimes his words were lost to the relentless clackety-clacking of the train wheels. Paul listened to the lulling duet of voice and steel, and he wished that Dr. Chapman would let them travel by air. But, since only the four of them knew the intricate symbol language of the questionnaire, Dr. Chapman felt flight too dangerous to the project. Yet he would not allow them to travel separately, to insure the project's survival, because he found these sleeper jumps useful for proofing. The proofing, Paul felt, was the most tedious part of the project. After each community sampling, in the interests of accuracy, Dr. Chapman and the team separately tabulated the questionnaires and drew up percentages for the particular community, so that regional variations could be measured against the national whole. Between cities, week after week, they compared their total percentages on all questions and answers.

Still, out of this meticulous and grinding paper work would grow a report that would be a sensation. Dr. Chapman's first survey had been intended for the broad lay public. Aside from squibs in *Time* and *Newsweek*, a paragraph in Winchell and an editorial in *Scholastic*, it was received as a passing oddity and invested with no more scientific authority than a syndicated reply to a lonelyheart's letter. Dismayed though he was by this cool reception, Dr. Chapman was heartened by a lesson bitterly learned. If you had something important to tell the general public, you did not go to them; you contrived to let them come to you.

Briefly, it appeared that he would have no opportunity to apply this lesson. The wind was out of Dr. Chapman's sails, and he stood becalmed. Although his stimulated and challenged mind now teemed with new projects—especially one involving a survey of adult bachelors in America—he lacked sufficient financing to proceed. His first work, it was true, had won him a minor grant from the Department of Social Sciences at Reardon, as well as free office space in an unused college quonset hut (a relic of GI students and World War II known among undergraduates as "the TB ward") and the prestige of using the school's name on his letterheads. But, without a larger grant from some private or government source, this was not enough. And the private funds and federal agencies remained aloof.

Then, overnight, financial help had come from an unexpected quarter. An important Madison Avenue advertising executive (the father of two delinquent offspring in private schools) had read Dr. Chapman's survey of adolescents, and had admired both his findings and his interviewing techniques. Presently, with the assistance of this advertising executive's agency, and soon others, Dr. Chapman was in the survey business full-time. The money earned in grub street from three commercial surveys—one for a tobacco firm to learn why people chose the brands of cigarettes they smoked, another for a political party to learn what attributes voters preferred in the personality of a candidate for Congress, the third for a cosmetic company to learn male reactions to the color and scent of women's make-up and toiletry—adequately provided the initial backing for Dr. Chapman's second serious investigation.

By this time, Dr. Chapman had organized himself and his aides into a non-profit group called Survey Studies Center. The group possessed then, and forever after, two faces: the scientific face, beloved and publicized, and the commercial face, despised and not publicized, the latter making the former possible. Both Reardon College and Dr. Chapman continued to lend their names to the commercial section of Survey Studies Center, justifying this crass participation as other universities justified big football, but publicly their hearts belonged to the scientific section.

While the commercial section of Survey Studies Center was left to the management of a club-footed scholar with protruding thyroid eyes, Marke Hildebrand, formerly employed by Gallup and Roper, Dr. Chapman concentrated his own considerable energies on the second sex survey. Now, at last, he was able to profit from the lesson of his first failure. This second survey, on the sexual behavior of adult bachelors in the United States, was carefully slanted for a limited audience of researchers, investigators, teachers—scientists all. It was written wholly in technical language. But percentages dramatized in colored pie graphs, as Dr. Chapman shrewdly perceived, were nontechnical, and overnight the figures were adopted by newspapers and magazines, rewritten and popularized and capsulized, and spewed out to the astonished and excited public.

Dr. Chapman became a household name, a bedroom name, a springboard for jokes and leers and learned commentaries. "The Chapman Report," as the lay press referred to *A Sex Study of the American Bachelor,* became an integral part of the American scene. Within four weeks, the imposing book headed the bestseller lists of the New York *Times,* New York *Herald Tribune,* and *Publishers' Weekly.* In a short time, it had sold nearly a half a million copies. Except for a liberal fund set aside for personal expenses related to his work, Dr. Chapman retained not a single dollar of the thousands pouring in from book sales and lectures. All income was plowed back into his third serious project, *A Sex History of the American Married Female,* which, unlike the other two, was conducted in the bright glare of publicity, feverishly anticipated by millions of men and women alike.

Yes, the investigation was drudgery, Paul told himself; nevertheless, it was fun. The fun of it was being in the limelight and committed to a project that everyone considered important. Also—and this could not be discounted—it was fun being privy to secrets that the entire population panted to know about. This was the real stimulation, and not the sex. Perhaps his university colleagues would never understand this aspect of it. Wherever Dr. Chapman was entertained, there were always some assistant or associate professors (who

61

should have known better) who hinted that the stimulation came from prying into the love lives of women. But Paul knew that this was not true. He, Horace, and Cass were like three obstetricians, peering into hundreds of vaginal channels every week, unmoved, detached, occupied and preoccupied. The thousands of words of love poured into their ears had lost all meaning, and the love act had become as neuter as anatomical drawings in a biology book. Despite this, in East St. Louis, after hours, Paul had several times caught himself studying the calves of passing women—and, at last, on the final night, he had found a small, dark Italian girl, with an enormous bosom, in an expensive bar, and joined her, and an hour later, lay beside her in a hotel room that was not his own, enjoying the feast of her body, but enjoying little else.

Sitting here now, on the hard seat of the swaying train, half aware of Dr. Chapman's droning voice, Horace's thick cigarette smoke, Cass's antagnostic crossing and uncrossing of his legs, he allowed his mind to drift backward to his own commitment to the project. It seemed this moment, approaching Los Angeles, nearing The Briars and two hundred more women and the survey's end, that he had been a part of it forever. Yet, it had been only three years.

He had been thirty-two years old at the time, and had been less than a year at Reardon College. He taught "English Literature—Borrow to Beardsley," and it was his third academic job. Before that, he had edited and written for a literary quarterly in Iowa, and as the result of an outstanding series of essays on English women authors of the nineteenth century, he had been invited (higher salary and transportation) to lecture at a private girls' school in Switzerland, and later he had moved on as lecturer at a teachers' college in Illinois.

During his several years in Berne, Paul had traveled considerably, and once, on a visit to the Vatican, he had become interested in the *Index Librorum Prohibitorum*. From this grew a book, *The Censorable Fringe*, a scholarly yet lively study of authors under censorship. The subjects ranged from Tyndale and Rabelais to Cleland and Joyce. The book was published by an eastern university press, while Paul was still fulfilling his contractual obligation at the teachers' college in Illinois. It brought him some minor academic renown, and several impressive teaching offers, one from Reardon College. Although Paul had always regarded authorship as his true vocation, and the lecturing activity as something that paid the freight, he was not financially in a position to resist the Reardon bid. Too, he had another book, and needed a patron, and so, after a brief bout of indecision, he accepted the post in southern Wisconsin.

At Reardon, Paul quickly achieved popularity—first with his students, who enjoyed his irreverent comments on literary immortals, and second with the faculty wives, who were attracted to his appearance and status of bachelor. Paul was six foot tall, and a bookish slouch seemed to emphasize his height. His shock of dark hair was prematurely touched with gray—someone had remarked that it made him look as if he had a past—and his elongated, deeplined face was otherwise too regular and attractive to be called Lincolnesque. He kept a spacious three-room apartment in town, puttered at notes on a book treating Sir Richard Burton as author, played tennis every Sunday, saw the Braves in Milwaukee once a month, and occasionally took Lake Forest girls dancing in Chicago.

He had not been on the campus a month when he heard about Dr. George G. Chapman and the strange doings in the quonset hut behind the Science Building. For most of the first half year that Paul was at Reardon, Dr. Chapman and his original team were on the road, quietly pursuing their male interviews. From time to time, they would return to the five dank, partitioned rooms in the quonset hut, rooms cluttered with fireproof file cabinets and enormous safes and a photographic-electronic monstrosity, conceived and designed by Dr. Chapman to reproduce and tally questionnaires, known as the STC machine. Several times, Paul caught glimpses of Dr. Chapman in his Oxford gray suit hastening across the green lawn. He was always pointed toward the Science Building, looking neither to right nor left, always hurrying, and always carrying an overstuffed briefcase. Paul had the impression of a big man—although later, he would realize that Dr. Chapman was of medium height but gave the feeling of size. His gray hair was neatly flattened by some expensive pomade, and severely parted; his face was broad and reddish, but not flabby; his chest and stomach were an enormous barrel that hung slightly over his low belt; his legs were spindly. He seemed precariously top heavy, like a quart bottle perched on toothpicks.

It was through Dr. Horace Van Duesen that Paul finally met Dr. Chapman. Horace was a young Professor of Obstetrics and Gynecology who had been disinterested in what he had so long trained for, and had hoped to become a satistician. When the second project had sufficient endowment, but was not yet fully underway, Dr. Chapman hired spare-time associates. Horace Van Duesen was the first on his staff. Horace was thin and bony; when he rose to his feet you were sure you heard him rattle. His blinking myopic eyes were limpid, his nose beaky, his chin receding and apologetic. When Paul saw his face, he thought of Aldous Huxley on Shelley: "Not human, not a man. A mixture between a fairy and a white slug . . . No blood, no real bones and bowels. Only pulp and a white juice." It seemed that Horace was aware of his liquid countenance and tried to reinforce it with the formal, starched collars, severe navy ties, and dark suits. He was more than he appeared, however. He was rigid in his essential decency, and puritanical at the core, and devoted to the belief that the only reality, comprehension, communication, lay in numbers.

Paul was drawn to him at once, because he was good, and he was level. Too, with this man, Paul decided, there could be no misunderstandings. They were brought together in a natural way. They were both lonely—or, rather, because both were unattached, hostesses assumed that they were lonely. Soon enough, Paul learned that Horace had been married for a brief period, and that his wife had left him or he had sent her away, and that now she was in the process of divorcing him in California. There had been some kind of scandal. Paul could never get it clear, nor did he wish to, and Horace never spoke of the bruise. Several times, Paul had heard professors' wives, or their grown daughters, refer to the recent Mrs. Van Duesen with antagonism and distaste. Since this always came from women, and the antagonism was unanimous, Paul felt safe in assuming that the recent Mrs. Van Duesen had been good looking and attractive to men.

As their friendship developed—poker, ball games, movies, occasional double dates, long walks and talks about their work —Paul learned of Dr. Chapman's project, and Horace learned of Paul's published book and book in the works. One summer evening, Horace asked to read *The Censorable Fringe*. A week later, having read and enjoyed it, he reported that he had loaned it to Dr. Chapman. Two days after that, in a state of excitement, Horace caught Paul between classes, before the gymnasium, and told him that Dr. Chapman wanted to see him.

And so, at last, Paul met Dr. Chapman. Horace drove Paul to the Swedish restaurant in town where, in a leather booth across the large room, Dr. Chapman was waiting. They ate and talked. They drove back to the school, and went inside the quonset hut, and Dr. Chapman showed what he and Horace and the others were doing, and he talked. Later, deciding that a breath of air would do them good, Dr. Chapman led them on a long stroll about the darkened campus, Paul striding quickly to keep up beside him, and Horace a step behind.

It was a dizzying and stimulating night, in every way, and for Paul, it was wonderful. He found Dr. Chapman quickwitted, though humorless about his work, a man as well read as himself, and a hypnotic talker. Several times during the evening, drawing himself away from the flow of words, Paul considered Dr. Chapman and saw Dwight Moody and Billy Sunday. Not only in high-pitched, droning eloquence, but in single-mindedness, was Dr. Chapman fanatic about his calling and his mission. He spoke of the men and women who were his subjects with the same bloodless detachment that one might use when speaking of halibuts, and he spoke of sex with the same offhandedness that one might use to speak of a piece of furniture or wearing apparel.

When they crossed the campus, Paul became aware—and this awareness was confirmed in later travels—that Dr. Chapman had no sensibility or consciousness of externals. He had no interests in sights and landscapes, and he had no sensory reactions. He was not even interested in people as individual human beings, except for what they might contribute to his precious digits and codings. It was during that evening, for the first time, that Paul had casually wondered about Dr. Chapman's personal sex life. Later, Horace had informed him of the once Mrs. Chapman and repeated a rumor of some handsome, middle-aged woman in Milwaukee (only a rumor, mind you, though he did go to Milwaukee several times a month, always alone), but if true, the affair was merely an anatomical convenience.

All through that night, Paul knew what was coming, and waited, fearful that it would not come (a fear rooted in the uncertainty of his academic standing, since he was not even an instructor with a Master's degree but merely a lecturer, which sometimes made him feel he did not belong to the club), but at last it did come, and he was finally not surprised.

"It's a pity, at this point, but I'm afraid I'll have to let Dominick go," Dr. Chapman had said.

They had reached the gabled Theta Xi house, and Dr. Chapman stood at the edge of the curb, making much of lighting a new cigar.

"A good man," he continued, exhaling smoke. "But he's married a Catholic girl, and she and her whole family are pounding him for his disgraceful vocation. He wants to get back to his first work—he was in physiological chemistry when I found him—but he feels a certain loyalty to me. He was with us this past year, on the interviews throughout the country. But now he's impatient and upset, and that's no good when you're collating." Suddenly, he peered through the smoke at Paul. "You're not Catholic, are you?"

"My mother adhered to the teachings of John Calvin, my father to Bob Ingersoll," said Paul. "I have a sister in New York who is devoted to Mary Baker Eddy. I'm—well, I suppose I'm most faithful to Voltaire."

Dr. Chapman stared at the pavement a moment. "Let's walk back," he said.

They walked more slowly now, and Dr. Chapman resumed again. "There's an opening," he said. "We're preparing the presentation. It is the final stage, but it's the one we'll be judged by. I'm loaded down with assisting specialists in physiology, psychiatry, sociology, endocrinology, anthropology. At this point I need someone who knows something about literature—and a little of everything else—to help with the presentation." He glanced at Paul. "Like the man who wrote your book." It was his only concession to levity the entire evening.

And so, within a week, on a part-time basis, Paul became a member of the team. During the year that followed, the latest survey was prepared for the press. The more closely Paul worked with Dr. Chapman, the more he admired him and saw in him the traits that he always wished his father had possessed. For, in Paul's eyes, Dr. Chapman wore, like three precious stones in an idol's head, the qualities of Direction, Dedication, Confidence.

Paul's admiration for Dr. Chapman carried over into the project itself, so that sometimes it seemed that all the world beyond the college hut was a primitive and ignorant place, waiting only for the Message to give its dark age a renaissance. Dr. Chapman toiled mornings, afternoons, and from eight to midnight every evening, as well. Always, Paul was beside him. The notes on Sir Richard Burton gathered dust, the Milwaukee Braves were one rooter shy, and the Lake Forest girls sighed and cast about for more likely prospects.

When the project was done, and the book put to press, Paul felt oddly bereft. Something needed and encompassing had left his life. And, when the book was printed and released, there was the dreadful apprehension. Would it be accepted, or was all this belief and devotion a delusion? Accepted it was—as few books in all history had been accepted—by specialist and layman alike. In the hysterical excitement that followed, Paul forgot his vocation, his career, his private dreams. He wanted only to go on being a part of this new adventure.

Dr. Chapman's third survey, *A Sex History of the American Married Female*, was already in preparation when the enormous success of the second venture ensured the undertaking of the third. Paul was offered a permanent job as member of the interviewing team. His salary increase was twenty-five per cent. But even without it he would have grabbed the opportunity. He resigned as lecturer on "English Literature—Borrow to Beardsley" and became a full-time investigator of female sexuality.

After the groundwork had been laid—the studying and orientation, the planning of objectives, the sifting of questions, the corresponding with friendly college groups, church organizations, community clubs, PTAs—the itinerary of the tour was set. As to personnel, Dr. Chapman had streamlined his team. On his first survey, there had been two of them, himself and an aide; on his second survey, to cover more ground, there had been seven interviewers deploying as two task forces. But now, for the third survey, Dr. Chapman decided to reduce his commandos again, for the sake of thoroughness, mobility, economy. This time, there were four of them, and a secretary. Dr. Chapman, Horace, Paul, and a portly young psychologist named Dr. Theodore Haines comprised the team. Benita Selby, a pale, withdrawn, flaxen-haired girl of twenty-nine, and frantically efficient, was the secretary. Benita was expected to fly into each city two days before the team arrived, set up the machinery, and stay on for the paper work. The fourteen-month tour was to begin in Minnesota, move to Vermont, then zig-zag up and down the land, and across to California. One month before departure, Dr. Theodore Haines resigned. He had been offered a government job in Washington—as a result of his connection with Dr. Chapman—and it was important to him to stand independently on his own two feet. Dr. Chapman cajoled, to no avail. Haines departed—and Cass Miller took his place.

Dr. Chapman had rushed to Chicago to interview candidates, and Cass had appealed to him at once. Cass was a zoologist, in a small but highly rated Ohio college. He taught four classes, and he was working for his Ph.D. His background, so similar to Dr. Chapman's own, and his fierce intensity, which, in his haste, Dr. Chapman mistook for dedication, were appealing. After surviving twenty-four hours of Dr. Chapman's penetrating questions and a superficial check into his background, Cass became the fourth member of the team.

A week later, having settled his affairs in Ohio, Cass was at Reardon, undergoing day and night briefing. Horace thought him agreeable, but Paul was less certain. Cass was short, but solid and athletic. He was dark and handsome in a brooding sort of way, like an embodiment of Hamlet. His hair was black and wavy, his eyes narrow, his lips full. His cleanliness shone, and his clothes were impeccable. He walked with the bantam-cock strut of many small men, and there was about him the feeling of one high-strung, coiled tight. He exercised in a frenzied way, and was strong and tireless at his work. Often, he was uncommunicative, which at first deceived Paul into believing that he possessed hidden wisdom. He was given to cynicism, crudities (in the manner he spoke, for he was actually erudite), moderate drinking, and long silent walks. You have to know him well, Paul often thought, really to dislike him.

During the rigorous fourteen months past, Paul had come to know him well. Weighing all personality factors, Paul decided (to himself) that what repelled him most about Cass was his attitude toward women and sex. Since all of them were devoted day after day to studying the private sexual behavior of women, any deviation from the purely scientific attitude was glaring. Dr. Chapman was simply above ordinary off-hour sex talk and drive, and was not to be judged. Horace was apathetic, as if he had expended his last emotional investment in the wife who had divorced him. Paul imagined that Horace had a low sex quotient, and that, generally, he was a recluse in his private world of fantasy. Paul himself, based on Dr. Chapman's findings in the bachelor survey, had been about normal in his desires and activity before joining the team. Recently, however, he had sublimated his physical needs in work. He now found that he could perform efficiently for several weeks without a woman. The surfeit of sex chatter each day, the long hours of note making, the constant travel, were enervating, and alcohol and sleep became satisfactory substitutes for physical love. But then, always, finally, there was a woman's voice, legs, bust, and suddenly his emotions were engaged.

Since the members of the team labored under the closest

national scrutiny, challenged constantly by moral voices of the Mrs. Grundys, their conduct had to be above reproach. Dr. Chapman hammered this home to them time and again. Paul played it safe. He found his occasional woman in the anonymity of a crowded bar or, as frequently, through a colleague in a co-operating university, a bachelor like himself who knew someone who had a friend. There was no love in this, but there was release and relaxation. Real love (whatever that was) Paul had never known, nor would he allow himself to dwell upon it. In this way, he supposed, he was like Cass, and yet he was not like Cass at all. For, he was sure, Cass hated women. Dr. Chapman, usually astute and perceptive about those near to him, was too occupied elsewhere to have discovered this fact yet. But Paul was sure. Cass's neuroses had not been so evident earlier in the investigation, when more often his intensity was leavened with humor. But lately, in the last few months certainly, especially when Dr. Chapman was not about, Cass had more and more displayed an angry, almost savage way of discussing women. It was as if they had not evolved beyond the animals he had once dissected in zoology.

Paul knew that Cass had a compulsive need for many women, for different women, and that he picked them up in almost every city they visited, sometimes with a total disregard of his position. Was it to make himself more than he was—or to make all women less? Paul did not know. But he felt that Cass made love *at* women, not *with* them. This was the basic difference between Cass and himself. Cass loved without hope. Paul, even in his most calculated adventure, hoped for more than there was, forever seeking not sex alone but total love, and never finding it.

Dimly, he heard his name, and, momentarily groping out of the recess of daydream and past, he scrambled back to the train bedroom.

Dr. Chapman, he was aware, had been addressing him. ". . . takes care of East St. Louis."

Paul nodded solemnly. "Yes, it does." Busily, he straightened the sheaf of papers on his lap.

Dr. Chapman turned to Horace and Cass. "Well, we're going to be up bright and early. We want to be at our best at The Briars."

Horace rose and stretched. "Has there been much publicity about our coming?"

"Oh, I should think so," said Dr. Chapman.

"I hate having my picture in the papers," said Horace. "I'm not the type. I always look like I'm being confirmed."

Dr. Chapman laughed. "The price of fame," he said with satisfaction. "Well, good night."

"Good night," said Horace.

He started for the door. Paul and Cass were on their feet. They both nodded to Dr. Chapman, who was stuffing his papers into his brown calf briefcase, and followed Horace. They were in the narrow corridor, Paul in the rear, when Dr. Chapman spoke up again. "Paul, can I see you for a minute—just for a minute?"

"Of course."

Paul looked after Horace and Cass, who were already moving down the corridor, hands extended like wings, balancing against the beige metal wall and the green shades, making their way toward the lounge car.

It would be their last night like this, before heading home. Paul wanted to celebrate. "Cass," he called, "if you're going to have a nightcap—"

"You're damn right," answered Cass.

". . . . I'll join you."

He watched them continue down the rolling corridor, and then he turned back into Dr. Chapman's compartment.

⋄   ⋄   ⋄

". . . you'll be quite appalled, but without men like Ackerman, our work would be ten times harder, maybe impossible," said Dr. Chapman.

He sipped his gin and tonic, and Paul, sitting across from him, drank again of his Scotch and water.

They had been conversing like this, not exactly about their work, but around their work, for five or ten minutes. Dr. Chapman had rung for the porter, and ordered the drinks—he, too, apparently, was feeling festive—and they had just got the drinks.

Dr. Chapman had been discussing inconsequential matters—California, The Briars, some friends at UCLA, a possible vacation for all when they returned to Reardon, then California again—and this was odd, since he had so little small talk. Paul divined that this was all preliminary to *something*, and he drank and waited. Now Dr. Chapman was discussing Emil Ackerman, a wealthy Los Angeles resident, who had helped make arrangements for interviews four years before and had been responsible for the contact with The Briars' Women's Association.

"But just what does he do?" Paul asked.

"I don't know," said Dr. Chapman. "He's representative of a certain profession, unclassified, unnamed, in America, that helps make the country go. He was in manufacturing, probably still is. Enormously rich. Has homes in Bel-Air, Palm Springs, Phoenix. His avocation is politics. Maybe it's his vocation. Maybe that's how he makes his money—putting in a governor or a mayor, fooling around with tax legislation. I know he's tied in with the lobbyists in Sacramento, and he has his hand in a dozen activities. He doesn't get much publicity. He doesn't run for office. He's a sort of Harry Daugherty—or, better, Jesse W. Smith, the Harding man who had the Little Green House on K Street. Ackerman's profession is doing favors."

"Purely altruism?"

"I strongly doubt it. You cast your bread upon enough waters—and you wait—and sometimes you catch a whale. It's a profitable sport. Most office holders are not titans of integrity or intelligence. You've heard the story about President Harding. His father said to him, 'If you were a girl, Warren, you'd be in the family way all the time. You can't say No.' Well, there are hundreds like that. They can't say No when Ackerman offers to do a favor, and they can't say No when he wants repayment. Ackerman's in the business of being paid back."

"What can he get back from you?"

Dr. Chapman considered his drink. "Oh, nothing. I'm sure he expects nothing from me." He looked up and smiled. "As Cass might put it, maybe he wants some phone numbers."

"I wouldn't be surprised."

"No, seriously, I think I'm his fun. He just likes the sensation of being close to us. I imagine it gives him a certain standing among his higher-echelon friends. I mean, he can pretend to be a part of this; it's something you can't buy."

"That makes sense," said Paul. He drank slowly, still wondering where all this was leading. "How did you ever tie in with him?"

"Well, you know our operation pretty well by now," said Dr. Chapman. "There's always resistance. From the start we decided to work with social groups, instead of individuals, because individuals are scared or shy. But, bolstered by group opinion, an individual usually conforms. So our problem was

71

to reach these civic and church groups. It wasn't easy. The direct approach proved impossible. Most often, they were suspicious. Who were we? What did we really want? And so forth. So I reasoned that the only way to win their confidence was through academic and political leaders. I leaned heavily on the university connections I had. In each university city, a professor or professor emeritus or member of the board of regents would send me to a politician or the head of a club—and that would usually open the door. Of course, this time, it's easier. You have no idea what it was like on the previous surveys. But now we have public acceptance. I have a reputation. It's smart—even an honor—to be part of our effort. Anyway—"

He paused to sip his gin and tonic, licked his upper lip, then went on. "Anyway, that's how I came across Ackerman. Four years ago, we wanted three group samplings in the Los Angeles area. I knew someone at UCLA, and he knew someone in the mayor's office, and he knew Ackerman. Well, I came on ahead and met Ackerman. He's a big old goat. Used to play football at Stanford, I think. While most of his schooling hasn't rubbed off, I think he takes a pleasure in being common. But he's shrewd and smart, and he knows everyone—and, as I said, everyone owes him something. Well, he got quite a kick out of the whole thing. He made three phone calls, and we had the three groups. I sent him an autographed copy of the book, and he was like a baby. Anyway, when I knew we were coming to Los Angeles again, I wrote him, told him what I wanted. And he arranged it. Don't ask me how."

"I'm looking forward to meeting him," said Paul.

Dr. Chapman's mind seemed suddenly elsewhere. "You'll meet him," he said absently. "He'll be at the lecture, you can be sure." He gazed at Paul a moment. "Actually, there's someone else I want you to meet—someone far more important to us right now."

Here it is at last, Paul told himself. He said nothing. He drank.

"Before I go into that," Dr. Chapman was saying, "I think I had better explain something to you. It's rather important, and I know I can trust your discretion."

Paul nodded.

"Because it involves the two of us." He paused a moment, considering how he should say what he wanted to say. "I'm sure you know, without my telling you, that I have a good deal of respect and affection for you."

72

"Thank you."

"I don't waste words. So I mean what I say. I've had this thing on my mind for some time. I've been holding it off until our tour was finished. Keeping a team together is important—very important——working together, no favors, no exceptions; it has to be democratic. But there comes a time when you can't depend on three men but must choose only one. Horace has seniority. He's fine, fine. We all like him. He's dependable, a workhorse. But he has no imagination, no social gift, no flair. He's not dynamic. He reflects the face of the crowd. As for Cass, well, I'll be truthful; he won't do, simply won't do. He's misplaced in this kind of work. He hasn't the detachment of a scientist. And he's disturbed. That's been evident to me for some time. Of course, he does his work, does his work well, but I'll have to drop him after this survey is done."

Paul was mildly surprised at Dr. Chapman's perception—not his perception, really, but his all-seeing, omnipotent eye. Well, so much for Horace, and goodbye Cass. One little Indian left.

"Which brings me to you," Dr. Chapman was saying. "I've watched you closely—under every circumstance—and I'm happy to say you've never disappointed. I think you like this work—"

"Very much."

"Yes. And you're good at it. I've decided you're the one I can depend upon. You see, Paul, there's more to my work than being a scientist. I learned that very quickly. The scientist part is the most important part, but it's not enough. The world demands more. To maintain my position, I have to have a second face. It's the social face, the political face, the—how shall I put it?—this way, perhaps: it's not enough to do your work; you have to sell it, also. Do you understand?"

"I think so."

"If I were scientist alone, with no other talent, this project would not exist today—but if it did exist, it would be relegated to the library stacks; it would not survive and flourish."

Paul finished his Scotch and water. There was something about all this that was vaguely upsetting—*disappointing* would be too strong a word. Yet, it was reasonable. Dr. Chapman was always reasonable.

"I see your point," said Paul.

"I knew you would," said Dr. Chapman. "Few men have

the qualifications to head up a project like this. I happen to be one." He paused. "You happen to be another."

Paul was sure that his eyes had widened. He could not think of a thing to say. He met Dr. Chapman's gaze, and waited.

"Now, I must tell you what's been happening. But I repeat, it's strictly between us." He measured his words more carefully. "I've been approached by the Zollman Foundation—you know their importance—"

Paul bobbed his head. He knew.

". . . they can do things the Rockefeller and Ford people can't do. Well, their board of directors is very impressed with my work, my record. They've been feeling me out about expansion. They would like to underwrite a new academy to be established in the East—like starting a vast laboratory or college—along the lines of the Princeton School for Advanced Studies which would be devoted entirely to the work I have been doing. Only, it would be on a much larger scale."

Paul blinked at the enormity of it. "What an opportunity—" he began.

"Exactly," said Dr. Chapman crisply. "The work would go ahead on a scale hitherto undreamed of. I've gotten as far as discussing actual projects with them. Instead of the limited approach we now have, this academy would prepare dozens of projects, train personnel to handle them, and would send countless teams around the world. For the first time we'd be able to make comparative studies of the sexual behavior of English, French, Italian, and American women. As it is now, we're confining ourselves to the United States, while brilliant sexologists abroad, like Eustace Chesser in England, Marc Lanval in France, Jonsson in Sweden, have been conducting sex surveys quite apart from us. This should all be done by one organization. Of course, there might be problems."

"What do you mean?"

"Well, there could be obstacles abroad. Take that sex study of six hundred and ten French and Belgian women that Dr. Marc Lanval started in 1935. He was constantly hampered by the authorities. Liberal as the French are about their sexual activity, they seem to discourage inquiry into it. Lanval claims he was raided more than once by the Sureté. Nevertheless, he got his results, and so would we." Dr. Chapman reflected on this a moment before continuing. "I remember Lanval asking his French and Belgian women, 'Was your physical initiation on your wedding night a good or bad experience?' Exactly fifty and one half per cent of his women said good experience, and forty-nine and one half per cent said bad. Now, wouldn't it be interesting to have the same investigator ask the very same question of American, Spanish, German, and Russian women? That's what I mean by comparative international studies. But, as I told the Zollman people, this would be only a part of our program—"

"Only a part?" echoed Paul.

"Oh, I envision endless other studies, off-shoots of our present work—international investigations into polygamy and polyandry, into the effects of venereal disease on sex life, an examination of illegitimacy in Sweden, a survey confined to mothers and the effects of children on their love lives, other surveys concerned solely with Negroes, Catholics, Jews and similar racial or religious groups, a study on the effects of birth control on sexual pleasure, a world-wide survey of artists who have devoted themselves to writing or painting romantic scenes, and so on and on. There are no boundaries to this and no language to express the good it can do. The Zollman Foundation is thinking in terms of millions of dollars— the academy would become a wonder, a marvel, a landmark of civilization—what Pliny and Aristotle and Plato would have sold themselves into bondage to establish."

"I don't know what to say. There aren't words—"

"I expected you to appreciate it. I'm glad you do. If this academy came into being, I would be its president—its mentor." He stared off for a moment, then brought his eyes back to Paul. "You understand, I would be too busy to do what I am doing now. Our work would involve national, international welfare. It would almost be elevated to governmental level. My position would force me to be one moment in the White House, the next in Stockholm with the Nobel people, the next in Africa with Schweitzer, and so forth. I would need someone to guide the actual survey work, the sampling, the real machinery of the academy. This is the job I am offering you."

Paul felt the hot flush on his cheeks. He wanted to reach out, touch Dr. Chapman, let him know what this expression of approval meant. "I . . . I'm overwhelmed, Doctor. It's . . . I never dreamed of such a thing."

"You'd be making twice the money you're making now. And you'd have authority and a certain—how shall I say?— standing; yes, standing."

"When would this happen?"

"In a year—no more," said Dr. Chapman. "After we've put

the female survey to press. Of course—" he stood up suddenly, stepped to his coat on the hanger, and found a cigar. He bit the end, then located a match. Striking it, lighting up, he sat down—"you realize that the whole—the plan—is not a reality until we have a final vote of consent from the Zollman board of directors."

"But they know your work."

"They know more. I've submitted to them, in writing, not only a complete explanation of my methods and achievements, but a detailed outline of my plans and needs. Still, the grant would be so large, it requires study by each individual board member—and a favorable majority vote when they meet in the fall. As things stand now, I believe the majority are inclined to support the idea of an academy devoted to international sex studies. But much can happen between now and the meeting. Those men, the members of the board, they're human beings. They're intelligent, but they come from every walk of life, with every background and prejudice and susceptibility—I mean susceptibility to unfavorable criticism—they can be swayed for or against. I've seen it too many times."

Paul knew that Dr. Chapman had something specific in mind. He did not know what. "I don't think you have any reason to be worried."

"But I have, Paul, I have. I won't beat around the bush with you. I have. Here, within grasp, is the biggest thing that's ever happened in my life—and yours—fulfillment of a dream beyond dreams—and yet, some small nonsense between now and late autumn, some carping little thing, could ruin the whole plan and turn Zollman against us." He stared at Paul. "Have you ever heard of Dr. Victor Jonas?"

"Of course."

Everyone associated with Dr. Chapman was aware of Dr. Jonas, the iconoclastic, outspoken, free-lance psychologist and marriage counselor. When Dr. Chapman's second book had appeared, Dr. Jonas had reviewed it for several academic journals and had been highly critical. His rhetorical skill and imagery were such that he was often quoted in newspapers and the news magazines.

"He's our Devil's Advocate," said Dr. Chapman.

"I don't understand."

"You spend your lifetime trying to promote Sainthood for some obscure, courageous, miracle-working missionary, and then you go to the Vatican to present your case and promote your cause, and there is one appointed who is the Devil's

Advocate, who tries to demolish your cause, who tries to show that your subject does not deserve Sainthood. Often the Advocate succeeds, too. Well, Dr. Jonas is our hurdle, our opposition. He's been making a study of our work—"

"Are you sure?"

"Certainly I'm sure. I've told you, Paul, you can't hold my job and be pure scientist alone. You can't be above the battle. I have my sources. Dr. Jonas is doing this study, and I happen to know that it is antagonistic. He will publish it *before* the Zollman Foundation board meets."

"But why would he do that—I mean, undertake the whole thing?"

"Because he's been hired to do it. I don't have all the facts. It's been rather hush-hush. But there's a small, crotchety splinter group of the Zollman board, the Anthony Comstock wing, who are opposed to putting money in my academy. They have other plans for the endowment. Well, they looked around for a kindred spirit in dissent. Jonas was a natural choice. He's against us—whether out of envy or malice or because he wants headlines, I can't say—but he is, and this Zollman minority is exploiting his attitude. They've given him money, out of their private purses I am sure, to make a thorough analysis of our methods and accomplishments, and tear them to shreds. Once done and published, it could have a devastating effect—not on the public at large, but on the judgment of the Zollman board. It could very well destroy my—our—academy."

Paul was bewildered. "You mean you've known this all along, and you've done nothing?"

Dr. Chapman shrugged. "What can I do? It's not befitting that I . . . I even recognize this man—"

"Reinforce your case before the public. Hire publicists if you must."

"It wouldn't help where I want it to help. No, I've thought it out. There's only one thing to do—see Jonas—he's in Los Angeles—see him and speak to him."

"I doubt if he'd listen to reason."

"Not reason." Dr. Chapman smiled. "Cash. He's obviously a man who can be bought."

"How?"

"By bringing him into our project as a consultant, an associate, and promising him an important place in the academy. We can't beat him, so we'll absorb him. He can't criticize what he's a part of."

Paul shook his head. "A man of your stature can't go to him with a bribe."

"Bribe?" Dr. Chapman's large, open face reflected astonishment. "Why, it wouldn't be that at all. We would have real use for this man on our team. I should have stressed that at once. He could keep us from becoming complacent. He could still play Devil's Advocate, but to bolster us and improve us, for our benefit, not to our detriment."

Paul wanted to believe this. He tried to see Dr. Jonas' value if he quit the society of dragons and enlisted as a knight of the round table. He could see that Jonas' values would be considerable. "Yes," Paul said. "But no matter what your motives, it'll still look like a bribe if you go to him—"

"Oh, I wouldn't go to him. You're right, of course, Paul. I couldn't." He shook the long ash off his cigar. "No, I'm not right for it, Paul. But you are. You're just the person to do it. I hope you will." He smiled again. "It's not just me now, you see, it's both of us—we've both got everything at stake."

⬦   ⬦   ⬦

"Well, well, the heir apparent," said Cass as Paul made his way into the lounge car and joined the other two at their table.

"That was long enough," Cass added, slurring his words. "What did you and the old Roman cook up for the Ides of March?"

"A new survey," said Paul pleasantly. "We're going to interview men who interview women and find out what makes them so goddam sour."

"Big joke," said Cass, noisily downing his drink.

Paul glanced at Horace, who was morosely twisting his glass. "Cass got you down, too?"

Horace lifted his head. "I was just thinking about Los Angeles. I wish we could skip it. I don't like Los Angeles."

"And miss all that great weather?" said Paul.

"You can have it."

Paul leaned across the table and pressed the buzzer. In a moment, a white-coated colored waiter appeared. Paul ordered refills for the others and a Scotch for himself. Watching the waiter go, he saw that there were three other people in the lounge car. An elderly couple, seated side by side, were absorbed in leafing pages of their bound magazines. At the far end sat a girl, bleached blonde and rather self-conscious as she pretended to read a paperback book and occasionally sip at her drink.

Cass saw Paul looking off, and he half turned and observed the blonde. "She must have just blown in," he said. "Nice tits."

"Cut it out," said Horace. "Do you want her to hear you?"

"That's right. That's just what I want her to do." Cass grinned at Paul. "If they got 'em, they should be proud of 'em. Agreed?"

"Agreed," said Paul.

"And maybe even share the wealth." He half turned again and stared at the blonde. She crossed her legs, tugged her skirt down, and concentrated on her book.

Cass swung back and began to recount a pointless and pornographic anecdote about a blonde he had once kept in Ohio. Presently, the drinks came. Paul paid, and they all devoted themselves to the business of oblivion.

Cass finished first. "Dammit, I'd sure like to tear off a piece."

"It's the movement of the train," said Horace ponderously. "I've often observed that when people are on moving vehicles —trains, boats, airplanes—they are sexually stimulated."

"Shove it," said Cass.

"You're drunk," said Paul. "Why don't you hit the sack?"

"Not alone, I don't." He pushed his chair back. "I'm going to do some missionary work, spread the gospel of Dr. Chapman, make our little slut there a statistic—"

"Shut up," said Paul angrily.

Cass glared at him, then suddenly smiled wickedly. "Did I take His name in vain? Sorry, Apostle."

He rose and unsteadily made his way to the rear of the lounge. He picked a magazine off a chair, and then he sat down next to the girl. Stiffly, she continued to read. Slowly, Cass turned the pages of the magazine.

Paul drained his glass. "Ready for bed?" he asked Horace.

"I suppose so."

But Horace had made no move to leave. He sat staring gloomily at his drink.

Observing the downcast look on Horace's face, Paul waited, puzzled. "Anything wrong?"

Horace did not reply at once. He remained immobile, except for his hands, one absently kneading the other. At last, he pushed his spectacles higher on the bridge of his nose and squinted through them at Paul.

"Yes, I guess I am worried," he said in his professorial way that sounded oddly unemotional. "I know it's foolish of me."

Paul was at a loss. "Is it anything you want to talk about?"

"Well . . ." He hesitated on the edge of some frontier of privacy, and then, averting his eyes, he left privacy behind. "You know I was married once," he said. It was a flat declaration.

Paul played no games. "So I've heard." Although he had known Horace for three years, and known him well, and exchanged many minor confidences with him, he had never heard his friend discuss his marriage. Occasionally, Paul remembered, others had mentioned the former Mrs. Van Duesen, always in passing and obliquely, and Paul understood no more than that she had left her mark on the campus and departed its ivy walks filled with dishonors.

"My ex-wife lives in Los Angeles," Horace was saying. And then he added: "I hate her. I don't ever want to see her again."

"Who says you have to see her? Los Angeles is a big city. What the devil, Horace, you were there four years ago on the bachelor survey. She must've been there then. Yet you seem to have survived it."

"That was different," said Horace. "Four years ago she lived in Burbank. Now she lives in The Briars."

Paul frowned. He tried to think of something reassuring to say. "Are you positive she's still there?"

"She was a year ago."

"Well, I'd be damned if I'd let that bug me. The odds are all on your side. The Briars must be swarming with women. We'll only be seeing a handful."

Horace shook his head with resignation, as one awaiting the blindfold. "I don't like it, that's all. I don't like being anywhere near her. I don't trust myself thinking of what I might do if I saw her." He paused, and glanced furtively at Paul. "If you knew what had happened, you'd understand." But he compressed his lips and did not reveal what had happened.

Paul felt as useless as a good Samaritan on a foggy night. "I think you can trust yourself," he said. "Apparently you didn't do anything rash when you had the—when you broke up."

"At that time I couldn't," said Horace mysteriously. "But I've had over four years to think about what she did."

Again Paul speculated on the kind of scandal that could possibly embitter a man so unfamiliar with deep emotion as was Horace. He hoped his friend would say more, but he saw that Horace had beaten his way back across his frontier of privacy.

"Well, try to put it out of your head," Paul said lamely. But he wanted to do better than this. "If you happen to run into her, you'll manage the situation. Hello. Goodbye. But I'll bet you a week's salary you don't get within a country mile of her."

Horace had hardly listened. He wagged his head miserably. "I begged Dr. Chapman to take the San Francisco date instead of Los Angeles, but once he sets his mind ..."

Paul saw that nothing more could be done for his friend. Like so many males who lived alone, old maidishly, Horace had too much spare time to masticate small things and past things. His apprehension had grown out of proportion to probability, but no one would convince him of it.

Paul pushed his chair back and stood up. "Come on, old man. Try to sleep it off. We're lucky if we get six or seven hours, as it is. By this time tomorrow, you'll be too damn busy to worry about anything."

Horace nodded without conviction, pushed himself to his feet, and came around the table.

Waiting for Horace to precede him, Paul glanced off at Cass and the blonde. Apparently, they were already on a friendly footing. Cass had said something, and she was laughing, and she leaned nearer to him, and he patted her arm. Now he was reaching behind her to touch the buzzer, and she was saying something to him.

The movement of the train, Paul thought. Or maybe this project. *A Sex History of the American Married Female*. Was she a married female? Did she have a sex history? Question. Do you feel any sexual desire at the sight of the male genitalia? Well, do you? Answer. Fourteen per cent feel strong desire.

Paul turned away. Horace had already gone. At once Paul remembered how someone had described Horace's ex-wife. The someone had been a pinched and fussy dean. The word he had used was *hetaera*. What had he really meant? Suddenly, Paul was too tired to explore it further. He started hastily after Horace, bumping against the narrow corridor of the train.

Far ahead, a whistle shrieked. The yellow streamliner hurtled westward into the night.

3

WHEN KATHLEEN BALLARD slowed her Mercedes in the thickening traffic of The Village Green—which always increased through the morning, as women converged on the business section to shop before lunch—and then drew to a halt beside the stop sign at Romola Place, she realized that her fantasy had been no more than a fantasy and a wish, after all.

She had awakened early, in the gray dawn, before the sun was up, and lay very still, her eyes closed but mind awake, adjusting to the day ahead and knowing that this was the day.

The night before, the newspapers had been full of Dr. Chapman's arrival, and Dr. Chapman's lecture (all enlarging considerably on Grace Waterton's press release), and several ran pictures of Dr. Chapman. But even knowing that they had arrived, Kathleen lay daydreaming of a last-minute reprieve. Perhaps something would happen to Dr. Chapman; he would drop dead of a heart attack—no, that was not fair—he would be hit by a car, and survive (after a long convalescence), and his associates would agree to cancel The Briars sampling, because they had enough material already. Or maybe it would happen another way. Each woman, individually, would feel that she did not want to subject herself to this ordeal. Each would stay away, certain that she would not be missed. In this way, at the appointed hour, no one would appear. Discouraged, Dr. Chapman would cancel the lecture and take his troupe to Pasadena or San Diego.

When the sun was out at last, slanting through the white drapes, and her alarm sounded shrilly and she shut it off, she could hear Deirdre stirring in the next room. She sat up, almost believing there would be no lecture, and feeling sure that she need not bother to attend. Yet, after her toilet, and breakfast, and the brief trouble with Deirdre, she returned to her bedroom to remove her brunch coat and slip into her dressy beige sweater and skirt.

Driving through The Briars, her hope of the lecture's being canceled diminished the nearer she approached The Village Green. When she reached Romola Place and peered off to her left down the long, sloping street, hope vanished completely. As far as she could see, and even beyond the bend, the curbs were lined with parked cars. They were before the post office and the Optimist Club, and they filled the Junior Chamber of Commerce lot. She turned to look at the entrance to the two-story Women's Association building. Three women—she was not sure, but one resembled Teresa Harnish—were animatedly conversing as they went inside. Two other women arrived at the entrance from opposite directions and greeted each other.

A horn honked impatiently. Kathleen glanced up at her rear-view mirror, saw a milk truck behind her, and hastily pressed the gas pedal and swung left down Romola Place. She drove slowly, in the right lane, searching for a parking place —if she found none, she would, of course, have to miss the lecture—and then, beyond the Chamber of Commerce lot, she saw a bald man maneuver his Cadillac from the curb and roar away. Reluctantly, she made for the gaping place. She would not be missing Dr. Chapman's lecture, after all.

Walking uphill toward the Women's Association building, Kathleen's mind reached back for Deirdre. It had been one of their unhappier mornings. Deirdre was an enchantment—everyone said that she looked like Kathleen—except on those mornings when she had her spells. This morning, she had screamed and resisted dressing and, once dressed, had wet her pants, and they had to be removed and replaced. At breakfast, she would not eat, and when Olive Keegan came in the car pool auto, she would not enter it. Hating herself, Kathleen had bribed Deirdre with a package of sweet gum and a new book she had been saving for a Sunday, and, at last, the morning was placid.

These rebellions, a week of every month, left Kathleen trembling and fearfully alone. She had several times spoken to Dr. Howland, and he, always hurried and harried, had by rote reminded her that four-year-olds needed consistency of handling (". . . boundaries of behavior, they want authority, they want to know how far they can go"), and Kathleen always came away hating Boynton more for having left unfinished business, and yet knowing he would have been of no use. But maybe it was really herself. If she stopped living like a recluse

—more men coming and going, the tweedy smell of men and their bass voices—it would be different. And there *was* Ted Dyson, but he was interested only in her and not in a four-year-old—he had no talent for children—but maybe it wasn't men either; maybe it was what Deirdre wanted from her and did not get—warmth—hadn't she been told that she had no warmth?

"Kathleen!"

She was just at the entrance. She turned and saw Naomi Shields crossing the street toward her, waving. Kathleen waited. A convertible was approaching rapidly.

"Look out, Naomi," Kathleen called.

Naomi halted in mid-street, then looked off toward the vehicle, smiling, waiting for it to pass. The driver, a swarthy young man in a seersucker jacket, jammed on his brakes and skidded to a halt. Naomi, still smiling, inclined her head to the driver, and then paraded slowly across the bumpers to the curb. Kathleen watched the driver. He was regarding Naomi appreciatively. At last, with a sigh of regret it seemed (for his wife? his appointment? his lack of boldness?), he shifted the gear and drove away.

Kathleen switched her gaze to Naomi. She tried to see her as the young man had seen her, and she knew at once that Naomi would always cross streets safely in traffic. Naomi's small, compact figure exuded an almost embarrassing air of obvious sensuality. The knit dress she now wore accentuated the effect. Few women, Kathleen decided, could successfully wear knit dresses—women in their thirties, that is—and Naomi was one of the few. Her doll face, and her extraordinary breasts, Kathleen concluded, must drive men insane. Did they? Were there men? Well, Dr. Chapman would know in a few days.

Naomi was beside her. "I'm glad I caught you, Katie. I'd hate to face that zoo alone."

Kathleen looked down at her and thought there was whisky in the scent of perfume. "I'm glad you could make it," she said. She could think of nothing less banal.

"I almost didn't. I woke with a splitting headache. But I feel better now." She inspected Kathleen. "You certainly look unmussed. How do you manage at this hour?"

"Clean living, I suppose," Kathleen said, not thinking, and then she was sorry, remembering the rumors about Naomi.

But Naomi seemed not to have heard. She was staring at the entrance. "Imagine a sex lecture at ten-thirty in the morning."

"I suppose it does seem more appropriate to the evening."

"Oh, I don't mean that. I think sex is fine in the morning—after you've brushed your teeth." Suddenly, she laughed. "But who wants to listen to some old poop who's over the hill?" She took Kathleen's arm. "Well, let's join the dim bulbs and get it over with."

Inside the large, gray inner hall, there were four tables, in a row, some yards apart, and on each a placard reading "A to G," "H to M," "N to S," and "T to Z." There were three nondescript girls, shorthand types with crooked teeth, behind three of the tables, and a tall, consumptive-appearing girl with lackluster flaxen hair bending across one of the tables, whispering.

"Recruitment center," said Kathleen.

"Draft board, you mean," replied Naomi, too loudly.

Apparently, the tall girl had overheard her, for now she turned, an uncertain smile on her pale face, and came awkwardly forward.

"I'm Miss Selby, Dr. Chapman's secretary," she said. "Are you here for the lecture?"

"Somebody said something about stag films," said Naomi cheerfully.

Miss Selby appeared bewildered. At last, she forced a smile. "You've been misinformed," she said.

"I hope we're not late," said Kathleen.

"No, it'll be another five minutes," said Miss Selby. "The auditorium is almost filled."

Kathleen followed Naomi down the corridor and then followed her into the auditorium. The room, three broad windows to one side and a flag on the opposite wall, held a capacity of three hundred, and now it seemed an irregular sea of heads and colored hats. Many turned toward the door, and Kathleen smiled vaguely back at the familiar faces.

"Let's get off our feet," said Naomi.

"I promised Ursula Palmer—Ursula said she was saving a seat for me." Kathleen searched uncertainly.

From a row near the front, a hand was waving a pad. Kathleen stood on her toes. The hand belonged to Ursula. Now Ursula was removing the pad from her hand and holding up two fingers.

"I think she has a seat for you, too," said Kathleen.

"Either that or she wants to go to the bathroom," said Naomi.

They started down the center aisle, Naomi walking very erect, with her large busts high, regarding her contemporaries with arch superiority, and Kathleen, warm and self-conscious.

Ursula Palmer was in the aisle seat of the fifth row. There were two empty seats beside her. She stood up to allow Naomi and Kathleen to squeeze past her.

"Hello, Naomi, Kathleen."

They greeted her and sat down.

"Sarah Goldsmith wanted me to hold one for her, too," Ursula said, lowering herself into the seat. She looked up the aisle. "I guess she couldn't make it."

"She's probably tied up with the children," said Kathleen, thinking again of Deirdre.

"Little monsters," said Ursula, because she often forgot that she was a mother.

Naomi poked her finger at the pad and pencil in Ursula's hands. "Handy tips?" she asked teasingly.

"I may write an article," said Ursula, annoyed.

Kathleen felt a hand on her shoulder. She turned. Mary McManus was in the seat behind her, smiling. "Aren't you excited, Kathleen?" Her narrow eyes and narrow face were shining.

"Well, curious," said Kathleen.

"Hi, Mary," Naomi called. "How's Clarence Darrow?"

"You mean Norman? Oh, wonderful. Dad's giving him his first court case next week."

"Bravo," said Naomi. Then she added, "What are you doing for lunch?"

"I'm free until two. Are you?"

"It's a date," said Naomi.

Ursula held up her pad and pointed it off. "I think the curtain's about to go up."

They all turned expectantly toward the barren stage. Grace Waterton was carrying a silver pitcher and drinking glass across the rostrum. She placed them carefully on the stand there. The room was hushed. Grace retraced her steps toward the wings, then halted, and descended to the pit. She started for the center aisle when Teresa Harnish, her coral headband dominating the front row, beckoned to her. Grace moved toward Teresa, and they held a brief consultation.

"If they're talking sex," said Naomi, "there's the blind leading the blind."

Grace was making her way up the center aisle. Her hair, which appeared freshly ironed, was gray-purple, and her tiny frame seemed to peck forward. She saw Ursula and Kathleen and waved. "Any minute," she said. "He's just finishing his press conference."

As Grace continued on her way, Ursula frowned. "I didn't know he was giving a press conference," she muttered. "I should be there."

"You won't miss a thing," Kathleen said to her. "What can he tell them that's new?"

Kathleen glanced up at the barren stage again, uneasily studying the lectern and pitcher and glass and the gleaming silver head of the public-address microphone. She looked at the faces around her. Small talk and gossip had ceased. All seemed to be waiting expectantly or—did she fancy it?—fearfully. Tension seemed a solid that you could reach out and touch.

She settled back into herself: What can he tell them that's new?

◇   ◇   ◇

In the large cement dressing room, behind the velvet backdrop, Dr. George G. Chapman, wearing a dark-gray tie, white shirt, and charcoal suit, sat on the bench, arms propped back on the glass-topped table, and told the press that he was making this final appearance of the long and successful road trip an occasion on which to tell them something new.

The reaction in the cold room was immediate. Paul Radford, sitting in a pull-up chair a few feet from Dr. Chapman, could see it on every face. There were five reporters, four men and a woman, from the local dailies and the wire services, and two photographers. They were sitting or standing in a semicircle before Dr. Chapman, and somehow, all at once they seemed to be leaning closer to him. Beyond them, Emil Ackerman, a jolly, blubbery face on a fat body that spilled over his folding chair, sat with his arms folded and legs crossed. Now he unfolded his arms and uncrossed his legs. He scratched at the lapel of his tan silk suit, and then he found a gold cigarette case, and a cigarette, his eyes never leaving Dr. Chapman.

Dr. Chapman straightened on the bench and brought his hands together, lacing his fingers. He contemplated them for a moment, and then he looked up.

"Everywhere I have traveled," he said, "I have been asked to give out some summary, some trend, of our inquiry into the sexual history of the married female. Everywhere I have declined."

87

Paul shifted in his chair and stared at the maroon carpet. What Dr. Chapman was telling the press was not quite accurate, he knew. The project had been no more than six months on the road when, to climax every big-city press conference, Dr. Chapman had begun to drop a new and provocative generality gleaned from his female survey. He judged, and correctly so, that these insignificant morsels would be lapped up by the sensation-hungry press and enlarged upon under great black headlines. Thus, the project would be kept before the public, dynamic, important, and, appetites would be constantly whetted for the appearance of the forthcoming book. Dr. Chapman never discussed these casual droppings. Pure science was above catering to popularization and publicity. Perhaps he did not even design or plan them in advance. But so strong was his instinct for survival, for the project's advancement, that possibly unconsciously he had kept adding these transfusions. Never before, however, had he prefaced an announcement of something new and newsworthy so definitely.

He wants to wind up the tour on a high note, Paul told himself. Or maybe this is the beginning of a campaign to combat Dr. Jonas before the jurors of the Zollman Foundation. Until now, Paul had tried to push off the uncomfortable assignment before him. He did not want to call on Dr. Jonas with a blatant bribe. But there could be no doubt that the future of the project was at stake. That justified what he must do, and what Dr. Chapman was now doing.

"...I have declined," resumed Dr. Chapman, having disposed of his cigar stub, "because I did not feel we had gathered enough of a sampling to see any definite trends, and even after we had, I was reticent because I wanted to check and study my totals with my staff. However, now that we are in Los Angeles for our final sampling—we have carefully interviewed over three thousand American married women, divorcees, widows, to date—I feel it only fair to let the public in on one aspect of our findings, one that I know to be generally accurate, and one that will have immediate significance to married women throughout the nation."

Paul, observing the eager faces of the reporters, could conjure up a vision of the headlines expanding larger and larger, like mammoth balloons puffed round by the words Dr. Chapman was breathing.

"It became clearly evident to those of us on the team, very early, that the greatest—" Dr. Chapman paused, reconsidered, modified—"one of the greatest misunderstandings existing between the sexes is the belief that men and women are possessed of like or similar drives and emotions. While it is a fact that men and women are physiologically alike in genital responses, in location of erogenous zones, this alikeness does not carry over into needs and desires. The public seems to believe that for every man on earth who wants sexual relations, there also exists a woman who feels exactly the same way. In short, that both sexes have equal need of sexual release. While, I repeat, I am not yet prepared to present you with statistical evidence on this important point, I am quite prepared to make a general statement about it. To date, our findings explode the belief completely. To date, our findings indicate that sexual participation is less important to the American female than it is to the American male."

He paused. There was a flicker of a smile on his face as the reporters bent to their pencils. He glanced at Paul, who nodded approvingly, and then across at Ackerman, who lifted a chubby hand in brief salute.

The rangy reporter with the gray felt hat, standing behind the chairs, looked up from the folded papers in his hand. "Dr. Chapman, I want to be sure I have this right. Are you saying that, after talking to three thousand women, you believe that women aren't as interested in sex as men?"

"I'm saying something like that, based on our survey," said Dr. Chapman agreeably. Then he added quickly, "Of course, we're referring to American married women. I'm in no position to speak for the English or the French—"

"I'll speak for them!" boomed Ackerman from across the room. "When I was in Paris last year—" He paused, and grinned. "I better not, there's a lady in the room. Meet you boys down at the bar later."

Everyone laughed. The girl reporter made a mock grimace. "Aw, come on," she said to Ackerman. He shook his head.

"Our sampling includes only American married women," Dr. Chapman repeated.

"Can you tell us more about that?" the girl reporter asked. Paul noticed that though her hair had a Bohemian tousle, and her legs were long and shapely, her face was all sharp features. But the legs were fine. Her eyes were very bright. Paul bet himself that she was reporter and not voyeur, interested in story and not sex.

"I intend to," said Dr. Chapman to the girl. "Our findings on the married female are now of more value, because we have a detailed record of the unmarried male to employ as some standard of comparison. Our respective samplings indicate that the average male is more concerned, even obsessed, with sex than the average female. More often that not, the basic reason a male will marry is because he wishes to possess a woman sexually. Later, should he be disappointed, or tire of his wife—I am speaking of sex—he may divorce her, or be unfaithful, or turn to psychiatry or drink. On the other hand, the female does not marry mainly because she wishes to be possessed by a man—again, sexually. It is one of her motivations, of course, but not the basic one. In her attitude toward physical love, she is the more passive partner. She marries for security, social acceptance, conformity, children, companionship. She desires normal sexual outlets, but if they disappoint her, she will more often than not resist the extreme measures of a divorce, a lover, an analyst, a bottle. If physical love dissatisfies, she will repress it, suffer and survive the emotional ill effects, and sublimate her needs in other equally important comforts like children, home, social life, and so forth."

Dr. Chapman waited while the reporters busily scribbled. When most of them had caught up, he continued.

"Based on our findings, I suspect that men have created a fictional world of women—women who do not really exist in today's America. This is one of the many significant points I hope to bring out, and support with evidence, in *A Sex History of the American Married Female*, which we plan to release to the public next spring. Consider the mediums of entertainment and escape—I refer specifically to novels, plays, motion pictures, television. The men who are the writers in these mediums most often project heroines who hunger to receive sexual love, who cannot have enough of it, who respond erotically and without inhibition. Those are the American women of fiction. But our interviews indicate that they are not the women of fact. These women of fiction, invented by men, are performing as men think women should—or wish they would. But the women my colleagues and I have met are quite the opposite. They are real, and most of them—the majority—can take sex or leave it alone; they do not daydream about it and excite themselves as men do; they are not stimulated by nude or semi-nude men; they are not overcome by handsome, virile men. In novels and motion pictures, they are. Men seem to think they are. But it is not so. Facts are facts. It is not true."

They were all writing. The girl reporter's forehead was furrowed. She held up one hand. Dr. Chapman nodded.

"Speaking for the distaff side," she said, "if what you are

90

saying is true, Dr. Chapman, why do so many women like sex novels—I mean, those books seem to sell—and the rental libraries—doesn't that show women are interested?"

Dr. Chapman puckered his lips and studied the ceiling. "I'm glad you asked that," he said at last. "Of course, I don't have the facts. Do those books really sell? Are they mainly read by women? I don't know. But let us assume that is the case. It probably is. The answer, from my point of view, is this—and though it may sound contradictory to all I have said, it is not. Many women *are* preoccupied with sex, but in ways different than their husbands or lovers imagine. Women are attracted to romantic fiction not so much for identification or stimulation as to satisfy an irritating curiosity. First, because men place so high a premium on sexual attraction, and the rewards for possessing this attraction are so great in our society, women find that they must devote themselves to it, whether they are interested or not. Second, most American females have fallen for male propaganda. They are told, daily, that they are supposed to behave and feel the way men want them to behave and feel, yet they know they are not so behaving and feeling. It troubles them. It worries them. It gives them inferiority. And this, coupled with the whole defect in our culture—I refer to the purposeless, pointless road most women travel in their marriages, but this is another area and I will not go into it—makes women feel unfulfilled. What is wrong with them? They ask themselves this. They want to know. So they devote themselves to books, plays, movies, envying the women they read about, the women they can't be, the women who don't really exist. A large share of these wives think they are unusual, undersexed, odd. They are none of these things. They are average. They are the twenty-fifth to seventy-fifth percentile of all women. I think our survey—" he became aware of Grace Waterton in the doorway signaling to Paul. He returned his gaze to the reporters—"will dramatically prove this point. I am confident it will do much to relax tension among women in America."

"Speaking for myself," said the girl reporter, "one thing isn't clear—"

Paul was on his feet, beside Dr. Chapman, bending to him. "Pardon me, Doctor," he interrupted. "They're all assembled; they've been waiting—"

Dr. Chapman nodded, and briskly came to his feet. "I'm sorry," he said to the girl reporter and the others, "but you remember I said I would have to terminate this when the lecture could begin? These women were kind enough to appear. I don't want to keep them waiting." He smiled winningly. "Of course, you're invited to stay for my little talk. But to save you time—I know you want to file your stories—Paul Radford here has advance copies of it."

"Thanks for all of us, Dr. Chapman," the rangy reporter called after him.

"It was a pleasure," said Dr. Chapman from the door. He waited for Ackerman, and then placed his hand on the fat man's shoulder. "Why don't you find a seat, Emil? The briefing won't take more than an hour. Then we can have lunch."

They went out together. Paul picked the pile of mimeographed transcripts off the glass-topped dressing-room table and began to pass them out.

◇　◇　◇

Dr. Chapman had been speaking, in his easy, informal manner, for ten minutes, and the anxiety in the auditorium had visibly lessened. So far, the women found, there was no invasion of privacy, no shock, nothing to fear. This was an affable, *nice* man chatting with them. His personality was as reassuring as that of any elderly physician at a bedside.

Kathleen Ballard had been sitting stiffly in her seat, hardly aware of the meaning of Dr. Chapman's introductory remarks, so intent was she on resenting and rejecting him. But gradually now, her antagonism was being blunted by his friendly manner and tame speech. For the first time since he had begun, she sank back in her seat and tried to understand what he was saying.

Dr. Chapman had one elbow on the lectern, and his head intimately inclined toward the microphone as he spoke. "There was a day, not too long ago, when prudery was the fashion—you could not refer to a piano's legs, and when you wanted breast of chicken you asked for bosom of chicken, and women had no complaints between shoulders and thighs other than liver complaints. Two world wars changed all of that. Sex was brought into the open and honestly discussed. The persons responsible for this revolution were Susan B. Anthony, Sigmund Freud, Andrew J. Volstead, and General Tojo. By this, I mean that female emancipation, psychiatric airing of the libido, over-reaction to the Eighteenth Amendment, and two wars that sent American young men and women abroad to absorb the sexual mores and customs of other cultures have done much to destroy prudery.

"Yet, prudery is far from dead, and sex still remains a secret and shameful function. Although women have acquired a certain degree of freedom through employment equality, the right to divorce, the use of contraceptives, the control of venereal disease, the shift of living from rural to urban areas where activity tends to be more anonymous, though women have acquired all of these weapons of freedom, they still are not free. An unhealthy attitude toward sex persists. And too many women suffer from too little knowledge about a subject that occupies—whether they like it or not—a major and crucial part of their lives.

"Consequently, sex is the one aspect of human biology most in need of scientific inquiry. Now, pioneer steps have been made in the right direction. The misconception persists that I invented the modern sexual survey. Or that Dr. Alfred C. Kinsey did so before me. This is not so. The profession of sex investigator, historian, pollster—what will you—is relatively modern, but older than you may imagine. The real innovators in this special field of inquiry were Max Joseph Exner, who questioned 948 college students or graduates in 1915; Katherine B. Davis, who questioned 2,200 women in 1920; Gilbert V. Hamilton, who questioned 200 women and men in 1924; Robert L. Dickinson, who studied 1,000 marriages before 1931; Lewis M. Terman, who examined 792 couples in 1934; and a host of others.

"A brief review of my predecessors in the field may be enlightening and comforting. In 1915, a year dominated by the sinking of the *Lusitania,* the first transcontinental phone call made by Alexander Graham Bell, the première of *The Birth of a Nation* in this city, the jailing of Margaret Sanger by the New York Society for the Suppression of Vice, a year dominated by names such as Woodrow Wilson, Jess Willard, William Jennings Bryan—in that year there was published a thirty-nine-page pamphlet, *Problems and Principles of Sex Education,* by Max Joseph Exner. The pamphlet announced the results of what was probably the first formal sex study in our history. Exner's questionnaire went to 948 college men. They were asked, among other things, 'Have you at any time indulged in any sexual practice?' Eight out of ten replied that they had indulged in some sexual practice or another—four out of ten admitting to sexual intercourse with women, and six out of ten confessing to what was then delicately referred to as 'self-abuse.' Although Exner had conducted his poll to prove that sex education was harmful, the results of his survey had quite the opposite effect. Unwittingly, he had established a new method of acquiring information on a subject hitherto taboo.

"Five years later, in 1920, the year Sacco and Vanzetti were arrested, Harding was nominated for President, and F. Scott Fitzgerald published his first flapper novel, a woman named Katherine B. Davis undertook a courageous study of female sexual behavior which she would later publish as *Factors in the Sex Life of Twenty-Two Hundred Women*. Katherine B. Davis developed an eight-page questionnaire concerning female sexual habits from childhood to menopause, and she sent it to 10,000 members of women's clubs, as well as to college alumni. She inquired about everything from frequency of sexual desire to emotional experiences with other women. Of the 10,000 women solicited, there were 2,200 usable replies, and 1,073 of these were from married women. The compiled answers to each question were published in statistical tables. Interestingly enough—remember, this was when Mother or Grandmother was a girl—sixty-three young ladies admitted to having sexual intercourse daily, and 116 confessed that they were unhappy with their husbands.

"In 1924, Dr. Gilbert V. Hamilton, the psychiatrist, did a secret investigation of 200 women and men in New York City. He saw each subject in a private consulting room, had the subject sit in an easy chair fastened to the wall (for, in their eagerness to discuss sex, the subjects often edged the chair almost into his lap), and presented each with white cards—forty-seven cards for a woman, forty-three for a man—on which questions were listed. There were eleven questions on orgasm, five on the variations of the sexual act, eleven on intercourse, fifteen on homosexuality, and so on. Some of the questions, considering the period when they were asked, were extremely valuable. For example, Hamilton asked all women, 'If by some miracle you could press a button and find that you had never been married to your husband, would you press that button?' And again, 'Are you and your husband more or less friendly and affectionate during the first twenty-four hours after the sex act?'

"Robert L. Dickinson, the Freudian psychiatrist, published his marital findings in 1931. His questions were elaborate, and conducted under his personal supervision. Lewis M. Terman, working in California during 1934 and 1935, tested 792 couples with nine general questions.

"Now, I have said that there were a host of others doing equally useful groundwork, most of it unknown to the lay public. I speak of Ernest W. Burgess and Paul Wallin testing 1,000 engaged couples in Illinois between 1940 and 1950, and Harvey J. Locke and his associates working in Indiana and California between 1939 and 1949. I speak also of such sex investigators as Clifford Kirkpatrick working in Minnesota, Clarence W. Schroeder working in Illinois, and Judson T. Landis in Michigan.

"Of course, the great popularizer in this little-known field was Dr. Alfred C. Kinsey, of Indiana University, who died in 1956. The two surveys done under his direction were begun back in 1938. Exactly ten years later, in 1948, he reported on the sexuality of 5,300 males in his 820-page book, *Sexual Behavior in the Human Male.* Five years after that, he published a similar book about the human female, employing thirteen associates and assistants in his survey. Although he came under heavy bombardment from others in his field or allied fields, Kinsey was a pure scientist and a great one. No sexologist of the past brought more patience or knowledge to his work. Kinsey must be credited for refining interview techniques and contributing mightily to national enlightenment.

"If I may be so immodest as to mention my own already published findings, I have tried to bring this work, originated by Exner and Davis and improved by Dickinson and Kinsey, along another giant step. I have had the extreme good fortune, of course, to be able to study the efforts of those who came before me, and, where possible, I have tried to avoid the pitfalls they encountered. In my earlier samplings, I began an unusual program dealing with specifics rather than generalities. Instead of a survey on all young people, I determined to devote myself to one type—the adolescent. Instead of a survey on all types of males, I determined to concentrate on one type—the single or unmarried male. Instead of a survey on all types of females, I decided to question only one type—the married or once married female. This is a process I strongly favored, for, in this way, I was able to zero in on one type at a time, to narrow down, to pin-point, thus promising more detailed and accurate results—results that I felt would prove more useful to science and the public at large. I am convinced that this is one major contribution I have made to sex education.

"Also, if I may add this, I was the first sexologist to perfect

95

a technique of person-to-person interviews which, although subject and interviewer were in the same room, preserved complete anonymity and made honesty more possible. The details of this technique I shall describe shortly. Furthermore, I believe I have developed and perfected a new approach to interviewing that leaves no stone unturned in the quest for truth. Hamilton asked his questions in writing and took the answers orally. Kinsey asked oral questions and received oral replies. Terman asked his questions in writing and accepted the answers in writing. In all cases, the questions were direct ones about sexual behavior and feelings. I have gone further. The questions my colleagues and I ask are separated into three distinct categories, in order to determine the subject's sex performance and history, the subject's psychological attitude toward sex, and the subject's first-hand reaction to sex stimuli. Don't let any of this frighten or confuse you. It's all painless, this I promise, and certainly fascinating, and sometimes fun.

"But forgive me, I've been digressing. The point I wished to make is that, with the exception of those names that I have cited, and some I have overlooked, the subject of married sexual behavior has been handled by persons woefully uninformed or misinformed, or by persons with an ax to grind or possessed of some special dogma. Except for what married women have learned from these faulty sources, or from experiences with one or several men who are often as ill-informed as themselves, or from exaggerated gossip, or from the falsity of fiction, most married women continue through their lives burdened by medieval ignorance. As a result, their efficiency and their happiness is seriously impaired. And the subject of sex remains an under-the-table, back-room, back-street subject, suppressed and unknown and always indecent.

"My colleagues and I are dedicated to the sociological task of bringing sex into the open, and improving the lot of all women through factual knowledge. This is our crusade. This is why we are in The Briars today. To help you, and have you help us, prove that sex is a natural biological function, God given and God sanctioned, that deserves to be recognized as an act that is decent, clean, dignified, and pleasurable."

Listening, Kathleen thought, Decent, clean, dignified, and pleasurable. How are you going to prove that? By asking me? By finding out the small hells I have lived through on my back? Will that factual knowledge free those others? Will that improve the breed? You fool. You stupid science fool. What do you know about being female—a bondmaid, a receptacle, Boynton's sanctioned whore?

The hot inner flare of Kathleen's anger gave way to reason, and reason to doubt, as always: Or is it me—me, not Boynton? Could any man make me normal, give me pleasure and receive pleasure in return? Am I—no, I won't use that chilling word, I'll use another—am I cold mutton? Why that? Why ever did I think of that? I remember. The story about Oscar Wilde. His friend Ernest Dowson tried to reform him, his homosexuality, to make him normal. Dowson sent Wilde to a Dieppe brothel, and afterward Wilde said, "It was my first these ten years, and it will be the last. It was like cold mutton." I am cold mutton. But I hate it, I hate myself. I must find a man, have a man. I need one. So does poor Deirdre, but me first. She wants a father. I need a man. Maybe Ted Dyson. When am I seeing him?

✧   ✧   ✧

Ursula Palmer found that it was difficult to make notes. Several times she caught herself so absorbed in what Dr. Chapman was saying, somehow less related to the article than to herself, that she missed recording entire passages.

Now that he had paused briefly to pour himself a glass of water, and drink it, she hastily scratched across her pad: "Marriage beginnings primitive times. Groups of men mated groups women, changed partners, children in common. Church made custom law. Marriage human invention. Animals no, except maybe apes. Marriage social institution with demands, duties—mainly sexual intercourse."

She heard his voice again. She looked up and listened.

"We have our enemies, of course," said Dr. Chapman. "But it is the common lot of all probers of the truth. From the time Socrates was found guilty in Athens by 280 of his 500 jurors for telling the truth, to that more recent moment in Dayton when Scopes was found guilty of telling other truths, the leaders of enlightenment have suffered ostracism, punishment, death at the hands of the guardians of tradition, conservatism, conformity, and darkness.

"When our report on sexual patterns of the American single male first appeared, we were gratified by its overwhelming acceptance—not only by scientists and scholars, but by laymen engaged in the difficult business of life and the pursuit of happiness. But there were dissenters, of course. I'm sure you

97

remember them, the fossil-minded, who preferred the dreadful status quo of ignorance to the factuality of investigation. They were extremely vocal; they still are. They announced that our statistics were an open invitation to national promiscuity. They announced that our findings on bachelors and married women were subverting the holy state of matrimony. But fortunately the majority of American men and women, who wanted truth as much as we did, believed as we believe—that to know is better than not to know, that truth will strengthen rather than weaken morality and marriage.

"Back in 1934 and 1935, Lewis M. Terman asked 792 California women: 'Before marriage was your general attitude to sex one of disgust and aversion; indifference; interest and pleasant anticipation; or eager and passionate longing?' Thirty-four percent of these women, over one third of them, told him frankly that their attitude toward sex had been one of disgust and aversion. I think it would be safe to go even further. I would venture to guess, based on the not inconsiderable information we have obtained, that fifty to sixty per cent of all marital unions in this land suffer gravely from sexual misunderstandings. In short, five or six out of every ten women in this room are probably victims of the unnatural silence that surrounds the subject of sex. Our investigation into your lives, as into the lives of your husbands, may repair much of this damage and pain. We cannot guarantee magic—we are not in the business of magic—but I can only remind you, where there is truth there is hope."

Listening, Ursula thought, Five or six out of ten women in this room are victims. Of what? Yes, sexual misunderstandings—euphemism for mismated—but not really that, either, for if the mismated were separated to mate with others, they would still be mismated. Maybe the great man's right. It's not the principals who are wrong but their principles. Sa-ay, not bad. Maybe I'll use it. Am I one of the five or six out of ten, I mean Harold and I? We get along. Maybe not hilariously, but who does? And as for passion, we're not kids any more. But we were once. Was there passion? Hell, we have as much sex as anybody. And we have other things too. Harold's getting the Berrey account. And I've got Foster drooling. New York. What would it be like working under him? *Under* him. Ugh. What am I thinking? I'm becoming a regular Freudian flip. If only he weren't such a goddam repulsive girdle-snapper. How does Alma stand him? How does he stand her? That must be some sex life. Though a man can always get call girls, no matter how he looks. I guess she stands him because where would she be otherwise? This way, she has that moated castle in Connecticut—the gilded life. Would I make that kind of deal? What if he were demanding, wanted it two or three times a week? At least, Harold is considerate. He listens to me. And he doesn't get in the way. I mean, there's no tumult. Still, that big job in New York, that would be something. We'd be somebody. Have a place in Connecticut, too. Harold could—what in the hell could Harold do? Manage. He could manage my affairs. I'd be making big money then. Movie actresses are always doing that. Having husbands who keep busy by managing them. The role of *cavaliere servente* was an honorable one—once. Well, why not? This article could do it. It'll literally slay them. Be picked up by *Time*. Reprinted by *Reader's Digest*. I'd better keep up with these notes. What was it again? Oh, yes—five or six out of ten . . . sexual misunderstanding . . . unnatural silence surrounding . . . don't guarantee magic.

◇　◇　◇

Knowing that she was fifteen minutes late, Sarah Goldsmith considered skipping the lecture. There were a hundred things to do at home. She had been neglecting everything lately, the small things. But what impelled her to continue to Romola Place, finally, was her sense of caution. She had said that she would be there, and she might, paradoxically, be conspicuous by her absence. Also, she had told Sam that she was going. He had hardly seemed interested, yet he might remember and ask her about it. If she told him that she had skipped it, he might be curious and start asking questions. If she told him that she had attended, and lied about it, there would be no questions. But this might lead to danger. Suppose she and Sam ran into Kathleen, or any of the others, and they wondered why she had not attended—this, after telling Sam that she had. It might really arouse his suspicions. It always happened like that in those silly television mysteries. Everything was planned, foolproof, protected, and then you lied once, made some nonsensical slip, and you were caught. If you told the truth, you couldn't be caught lying.

Now, hanging back as Miss Selby softly opened the rear auditorium door, Sarah felt relieved that she had come here. Miss Selby beckoned her, and pointed off. She went to the door, saw the empty seat in the next to the last row, third off the aisle. She nodded gratefully to Miss Selby, entered the auditorium, ducked her head apologetically at Mrs. Keegan and Mrs. Joyce, slid past to the seat and filled it.

She sat very still a few moments, looking neither to right nor to left. She had better make some excuse for being late, she decided. Jerry and Debbie would be the excuse. Worrying if she were in any way disheveled, she reached back, patting her sleek hair in the always neat bun. Fred sometimes spoke of actresses who looked as if they had just got out of bed. It was a very effective look, Fred said. It was worth more than being a talented performer.

Reassured that her hair was in place, and her gray suit as well, Sarah cast about to see if she were being noticed. All faces, all eyes, were pointed toward the stage. Suddenly, she realized that she was at a lecture. Not since she had been invited by Kathleen had she even thought of why she was going or whom she would hear. Her mind was busy enough with Fred and Sam, with Fred actually. How hard and strong his body had been this morning, and how warm. With determination, she focused her attention on the stage. A strange man was speaking. She failed to grasp what he was saying, but after he paused, and began again, she was able to follow him.

"We must have your complete confidence to continue with this work and to succeed at it," said Dr. Chapman. "I believe, based on our past record, we have earned your confidence. The cornerstone of our interviewing technique—all else is built upon this foundation—is trust. We need your trust, ask it, and never once have we betrayed it. Three associates assist me in this work. They are scientists, technicians, all clinic- and laboratory-minded and trained for the task.

"For fourteen months my associates and I have questioned every type of married female—from housewife to career wife to prostitute. We have had candid interviews with secretaries, nurses, dancers, college students, waitresses, baby-sitters, mothers of large families, feminine professors, and politicians. We have talked with wives long married and just married, with widows and divorcees. We have heard and noted every conceivable type of female sexual activity—masturbation, homosexuality, heterosexuality, marital infidelity, and so forth. And, in every case, we have questioned and noted with scientific detachment. If I could choose one word to characterize our approach, I would use the word—and repeat it again and again—the word *detachment*.

"You must understand this. We are fact-finders, no more, no less. We are not in the business of appraising, commenting, or correcting. We have no emotional feelings about how you behave, about what you do. We neither praise nor condemn. And never—never do we attempt to change a subject's sexual pattern. The questions we ask are simple, and they are asked of every woman we interview. They were scientifically prepared, far in advance, and are printed on sheets of paper. Beneath each question is a blank space for the answer. The answer is always recorded as a mark or symbol, these symbols being known only by the four investigators and meaningless to anyone else. I am eager to reassure you about this. When I first established Survey Studies Center, I considered using various obsolete systems of shorthand or old military codes as means of setting down answers that were to remain secret. None of these satisfied me. Then, I began a study of dead languages and learned that at least 200 and perhaps as many as 325 artificial and so-called universal languages have been invented in the last five centuries. The most popular of these, as you may know, is Esperanto, which was invented by a Polish eye doctor in 1887. But I was seeking the least popular of these languages, one long extinct, and I found one that I felt was just right. This is the language of Solresol, conceived in 1817 and based on the seven notes of the scale. Well, I adapted Solresol to our surveys, adding various symbols to its forgotten alphabet. I have never found a human being, not even a veteran linguist or cryptographer, who could read Solresol, let alone our adaptation of it. This is the language we use to record your answers. So you know that your answers to our questions are, and will always be, confidential.

"When we leave The Briars two weeks from now, to return to Reardon College, we will have your Solresol answers with us. They will be deposited in specially rented safes of the Father Marquette National Bank off the campus. They will be removed only once, to be fed into a machine I designed, ten by twenty feet in size, known to us as the STC machine—STC standing for Solresol Translating Compiling machine. Your questionnaires will go directly into the mouth of this mechanism, the Solresol symbols will be photographed, and then, through an intricate electronic process, they will be translated into numerals for computing and totaling. Nothing is put into English until we have our totals, and then our results are published for the good of all. But, by then, each private answer has been absorbed by the whole, lost in the anonymity of the whole, and in no way can the final results ever embarrass a single person or be traced to a single individual."

Listening, Sarah thought, I suppose it is safe, the way he explains it. And it *is* for a good cause. Maybe if they'd had something like this years ago, my life would have been different. Dr. Chapman looks like a man you can trust. His eyes are friendly. Of course, what can you tell about any man until you know him? When I was immature, I liked Sam a lot; thought I did. Look how he turned out. And Fred, the first time I met Fred, he irritated me. So sure of himself and bossing everyone, yet look what he's really like. No one on earth is more decent or loving than he. There's no man like him anywhere.

Sarah stared at Dr. Chapman, seeing him, not hearing him: I suppose, for science, it would be all right to admit the truth to *him*. But why risk telling the truth to anyone? Of course, if I told a lie when I was interviewed—no, he'd find out, he's a scientist, and he'd see through it and that might get me in trouble. But why even volunteer at all? Because it would be riskier not to do it than to do it. I would be the only one, and everyone would know and begin to ask questions. Oh, hell, why is everything so simple, so complicated finally? I guess I am mixed up, because I was going to tell Fred yesterday and this morning about the lecture and interviews, and I didn't. Why didn't I? I suppose I was afraid he would object. He and that damn wife. If he were living with her, I could understand. But he's practically a bachelor. What has he got to lose if it gets out? All right, his boy, but neither of them hardly ever see the boy, and he's practically grown up, anyway. I'm the one who should be worried. But I'm not. I just don't care, I guess. In a way, I wish it were out. I'd like everyone to know. I'm so proud of Fred. There'll never be anyone else, for the rest of my life. Isn't it strange? I went with Jewish boys only. I guess the way I was raised. I always thought the others were different. That's what Mom used to say. Goyem. I'm glad Mom isn't here. I shouldn't say that. But I am, really. Maybe I shouldn't tell Dr. Chapman. Maybe he won't ask. What if someone could read the Solresol language? What if it got out? How could I face Jerry and Debbie? If they were grown up and experienced, they could understand; I could explain. But this way. No, I'll just have to wait. It's hard. How does that STC machine work? I wonder how many other women are like me? Right here. Of course, Mrs. Webb just went and left her husband. I guess she still sees that car dealer. Why doesn't she marry him? And Naomi Shields. I heard about her. But that's different. That's not love. Oh, I'm so tired of the sneaking off and worrying. I wonder how they write it in that language?

Mary Ewing McManus was disappointed. She had expected a man of Dr. Chapman's experience to be more practical. She had felt that she would listen to him and come away with something that she could use. But so far there was nothing like that at all. Only generalities. Of course, there were some interesting things she could repeat to Norman and her father at dinner. And some funny things, too. She tried to remember one of them. But she couldn't.

Mary realized that she was staring at the back of Kathleen's head. She admired Kathleen's shining black hair, and the short bob, and the cream-white neck, and wished that she could be as beautiful for Norman. Of course, Naomi was as pretty, but in a more obvious way. What distinguished Kathleen was the quiet air of sadness, of inner suffering, that surrounded her and kept all at a distance. And now, Kathleen was going to be in a book. Mary had read about the book in one of the columns. The Boynton Ballard story. It would make her love story immortal. How thrilling it was to be so near to her, to know her. Like being a part of important history. Just as listening to Dr. Chapman was a part of history.

She determined to concentrate on Dr. Chapman's lecture. Maybe he would say something useful yet. She wanted to be the best wife on earth. That was all that mattered. To make Norman happy. He seemed so moody lately, and the way he snapped at Dad after dinner last night. It was so unlike him. "Newspapers have called us pollsters," Dr. Chapman was saying. Well, that wasn't very useful. Nevertheless, Mary decided to keep listening.

"However," said Dr. Chapman, "we prefer to call ourselves investigators and statisticians of sex. We are that and nothing more. I want to repeat—I cannot repeat it too often—we are not your conscience, we are not your fathers, brothers, moral advisers. We are not here to say aye or nay to your conduct, to tell you if you are good or bad. We are here only to collect a partial history of your lives—that part of your history most often private—so that our findings will help you and all the human family."

Dr. Chapman paused, coughed, found the glass of water and swallowed a gulp. When he resumed speaking, his voice had the slightest edge of abrasive hoarseness.

"Many of you may find the idea of discussing intimate sexual details with a stranger—though he be hidden from you by a folding screen, though he be a scientist—an embarrassing idea. You will ask yourselves: How can I reveal to a stranger what I have not told any living person, not my husband, or relatives, or friends? This fear is natural to all of us. For, in some cases, if our true but hidden sexual behavior from childhood to maturity were known, it might lead to social disgrace and shame, to domestic grief and divorce. I am imploring you to put this fear aside. You are an individual, a unique entity, but your sexual behavior is anything but unique. In all my experience, I have never once heard a sex history that I have not heard repeated time and again. Requested, as you will be, to volunteer facts that you have kept hidden months, years, a lifetime, I remind you to imagine that you are speaking not to a man but to an uncritical machine, to a recording device. And to remember, also, that the findings of this machine may well improve the very life you are now living."

Listening, Mary thought, Yes, Doctor, but *how?*

◇   ◇   ◇

Although her neck ached, Teresa Harnish continued staring directly up, past the footlights, at the towering, impressive figure of Dr. Chapman above her. He was a marvel, she decided, a man infinitely more important than most men, rather a man in the image of Dr. Schweitzer, and everything he was saying was so right, so true, and would be cleansing and good for all the rest of the women in the hall. Teresa did not consider herself as part of the rest of the women in the hall. Rather, she allied her open-minded, advanced intelligence with the speaker. Dr. Chapman and she were civilizing the females of The Briars this day.

His wisdom, she had expected. It was his urbanity that charmed her. Twice, she had dipped into her small purse for the pocket-sized, white leather notebook—her Geoffrey book, she called it—in which she noted epigrams that so often came to mind, were overheard, or were read somewhere. Several times a week, usually after dinner, she would read them aloud to Geoffrey. His noble face always reflected appreciation. The two quotations she had culled from the text of Dr. Chapman's address—and already memorized for party use, if necessary—were most amusing. In the first instance, pretending to be the cracker-barrel philosopher, Dr. Chapman had quoted one Don

Herold as saying: "Women are not much, but they are the best other sex we have." Who, she wondered, was Don Herold? In the second instance, Dr. Chapman had quoted Remy de Gourmont, novelist and critic: "Of all sexual aberrations, perhaps the most peculiar is chastity." It had delighted her. How *very* French.

She looked upward again, and thought for a moment that Dr. Chapman's eyes had met her own and understood the rapport between them. She adjusted her head band. But now, once more, he was gazing out over the audience. Of course. He dared not show favoritism.

"Many of you may be wondering, 'Why does he approach us as a group? Why not preferably as individuals?' " Dr. Chapman said with a slight smile. "It would be a fair question, and it deserves reply. The approach to community groups, rather than scattered individuals, was a concept I decided upon at the outset of my bachelor survey. Of course, I foresaw that samplings of groups would save time and wasted motion. I was also aware that individuals would be less reluctant to co-operate if they were doing what everyone was doing. But the major reason for my approach to the group had a more scientific basis.

"Had I arrived in Los Angeles with my colleagues, and simply announced that I wished individuals to volunteer, I am sure I would have had as many women come forward as will eventually come forward from your organization. But, unfortunately, I would then be receiving only one type of woman —one who, on her own, was eager to discuss her sex life. This would be valuable, but it would not be representative of The Briars. For we would be recording the history of only one kind of female—one who was an exhibitionist or uninhibited or highly educated. For a fairer judgment, it would be necessary for us to know also the histories of women who were shy, fearful, fretful, withdrawn, ashamed, shocked. A cross-section of *all* married females could be obtained only by obtaining the co-operation of a large group, which would include every degree of interest and reticence. And that, my friends, is the reason I have come to your Women's Association, rather than each of you individually, for your help."

Listening, Teresa thought, How objective he is, how extremely sensible. I shall give him all the help that he needs. I shall be part of his group, although I wish I could let him know that I would have co-operated as an individual, too. Not because I am an exhibitionist. But, of course, he would perceive that at once. I would volunteer because his cause is good, and I owe it to human endeavor to help liberate my sex. I think I will even let my interviewer know this, so that he really understands me.

Suddenly, Teresa wondered, But what do they expect of me? Do they want to know how I feel or how I act? I suppose they want both. Well, Geoffrey and I are normal enough, heaven knows. We make love as people are supposed to make love, and we participate mutually and in a civilized manner. I wish they would interview Geoffrey, too. He would prove it. As to feelings, well, how does any woman feel about sexual intercourse? I want Geoffrey to be fulfilled. I'm certain he is fulfilled. He tells me that he is. Isn't that the aim and goal of love, and the role of woman? What was it that Bertrand Russell wrote? Ah, yes. "Morality in sexual relations, when it is free from superstition, consists essentially of respect for the other person, and unwillingness to use that person solely as a means of personal gratification, without regard to his or her desires." Well, amen.

I respect Geoffrey and his desires. And I'm sure that he respects me and mine. I think that's all that one should expect. If Dr. Chapman inquires, I will tell him so. There's simply too much dirtiness and vulgarity attached to sex—all that writing and talking about passion, and groaning, and biting, and being transported—who has ever been transported? Sex can be clean and orderly, and *civilized*. Ovid was a dirty old lecher. Sex can be accomplished without being ashamed of what you have done. Control and moderation, those are what count. We are not savages or animals, thank God. You do what must be done, and you keep your dignity, and your husband respects you that much more. All that reckless gossip about women losing themselves, behaving like whores—they're lying or, worse, faking.

Isn't it warm in here? I think I'll go to the beach in the morning and lie in Constable's Cove and just relax, not even read. That is, if those barbarians aren't there again. Especially that big animal. How uncouth. How insolent. Can you imagine any civilized woman allowing him to make love to her? I wonder if he has a girl? A harem, I'd venture. Cheap strumpets most likely, and maybe some dime-store clerks and wild school youngsters. I suppose it's those legs and that torso. He could be attractive, if he were a gentleman—but he'll never be one. A man like that needs a woman to help him, I mean a woman who's better than he is, to bring him up. I'm not saying me, but someone like me. I'm sure Dr. Chapman's questions will be about how one acts, not how one feels. An act is something definite. It can be recorded. Feelings are usually too mixed up.

• • •

Naomi Shields was conscious only of the dryness in her mouth. It had been almost an hour, and she was thirsty. Briefly, she considered leaving the auditorium to get a drink of water. But she realized that she was seated too far down front, and leaving would create a disturbance. Besides, she didn't want water anyway. She wanted gin. She had taken only two for breakfast, and the feeling of well-being had worn off.

She fumbled inside her purse for her cigarettes, then looked about to see if anyone else were smoking. No one was, so she supposed that it was not allowed. She closed her purse again, restlessly worrying it with her fingers. She glanced at Kathleen beside her, and at Ursula just beyond. Kathleen appeared absorbed in the lecture, and Ursula was busy with her note-taking. She envied both of them. She wished that she could become interested, engaged, absorbed, removed from herself. Most of all, she wished that she had stayed in bed this morning. Why had she come here at all? She had determined to reform, she realized, and this was part of the reformation, trying to be like others, being occupied, pursuing normal activity. If only that man wasn't so dull.

She tried to fasten on any single thing that Dr. Chapman had said. She could not recollect one. Was it that she was so damn bored with talk of sex? More and more, she had become impatient with men who ran off at the mouth about sex. That tiresome verbal seduction, that forensic love play. Christ, there was only one thing to say about sex: do you want to or don't you?

She sat erect, her breasts tightening, and stared ahead. The art of attention. That was part of pursuing normal activity. She must learn to listen. Grimly, she listened.

"Perhaps it will put your minds at ease," said Dr. Chapman, "to know the exact procedure you will face, if you volunteer. It is really quite simple and painless. As you leave this auditorium, you will find four tables in the foyer. You will go to the one bearing the initial of your surname, and sign your name and address to a volunteer pledge. By Monday morning, you will receive a post card stating the hour and the date of your interview. At the appointed time, you will come to this building and go to the upstairs corridor. There, my secretary, Miss Selby, will be waiting for you. She will lead you to one of three private offices upstairs. In the office, you will find a comfortable chair and a large screen dividing the room. Behind the screen, seated at a table, equipped only with pencil, questionnaire, and a knowledge of Solresol, will be one of the members of our team. You will not be able to see him, and he will not be able to see you.

"After you are settled down, the interviewer will ask your age, something of your background, and something of your marital situation. Then, he will ask you a series of questions. As I have already told you, these questions fall into three distinct categories. I will explain these categories to you now.

"The first category concerns only your sex performance and history. You might be asked, 'What is the frequency of your lovemaking with your husband at the present time?' or 'What was it when you were married?' Or you might be asked, 'When do you usually have intercourse with your husband, at night, in the morning, in the afternoon, in early evening?'

"The second category of questions concerns your psychological attitudes toward marital sex. You might be asked, 'If you learned tonight that your marriage was invalid because of a technicality, that you were legally free, would you want to legalize your marriage at once or to leave your spouse permanently?' Or you might be asked, 'Before your wedding, did you hope your husband would be a virgin, an experienced lover, or didn't you care?'

"The third category of questions concerns your reaction to sexual stimuli. At the proper time during the interview, you will be directed to open a leather box beside your chair, the SE box, we call it—Special Exhibits box. From it, you will be requested to remove certain artistic objects and study them. Then, you will be asked questions about your reactions to these visual stimuli. You may find yourself looking at a photograph of a nudist colony or the reproduction of an unsheathed male statue by Praxiteles and be asked, 'Are you erotically aroused by what you see, and to what extent?' Or you might find yourself reading a marked passage from an unexpurgated edition of D. H. Lawrence's classic *Lady Chatterley's Lover* and be asked, 'Does the passage you have just read excite you in any way and, if so, to what degree?'

"You may answer these three categories of questions as rapidly, as slowly, as fully, as briefly, as you desire. There may be 150 questions. Rarely more. The interview will probably take an hour and fifteen minutes. When it is terminated, you will be told so. You will then leave as you came—knowing that what you have revealed is part of a vast mass of data that will soon be fed into our STC machine, and that the total results will shed light into an area too long too dark. The entire operation is as uncomplicated as that. Neither more nor less will happen. I sincerely hope that you will volunteer for this good work—in full realization that your life, and the lives of generations to follow, will be healthier, wiser, happier, thanks to your moment of truth. You have been very kind to hear me out, and I thank you."

While joining her hands to the noisy applause all about, Naomi thought, Brother, you got me, if it'll make me healthier, wiser, happier, like hell it will. But why all that corny false modesty? Screen, dead language, safes, machines, secrecy? I've done nothing I'm ashamed of; I'm a woman, and I need it and I like it, and I bet there's thousands like me. How long did he say it would take? An hour and fifteen minutes? Brother, I could bend your fat little ear for twenty-four hours and fifteen minutes, nonstop.

"Naomi."

She turned quickly, and found Mary McManus standing over her, and realized that she alone was still seated.

"Lunch still on?" Mary asked.

"Oh, yes." Naomi hurriedly got to her feet and followed Kathleen and Ursula into the crowded aisle.

Mary was waiting, as Naomi shuffled with the throng to the next row. Mary's eyes were bright. "Wasn't it exciting?"

"Thrilling," said Naomi. "Like a first pajama party."

❖   ❖   ❖

Backstage, Dr. Chapman stood beside the water cooler, mopped his warm brow, then reached across for a paper cup and poured himself a drink. "Well, Emil," he said to Emil Ackerman, "how did I do?"

"I'm all primed to volunteer," said Ackerman, grinning. "It was even better than the speech you gave to the men a couple years ago."

Dr. Chapman smiled. "That's because this was about women. And you're a man."

"I guess I still am," agreed Ackerman.

"Well, if you think you've worked up an appetite by now—"

"I sure have," said Ackerman. "Only not for what you think."

He laughed an evil schoolboy laugh. Dr. Chapman acknowledged the joke with a slight curl of his lips, his eyes shifting quickly to observe if anyone nearby had overheard them. He did not like to be caught in situations where the pure scientist might seem mere mortal.

"Well, a good charred steak should settle you down," he said to Ackerman. Then, taking the fat man's arm, he hastily propelled him toward the stage door.

❖   ❖   ❖

When Kathleen Ballard reached the foyer, she saw that long lines had already formed at each of the four tables. Emerging from the auditorium, she had allowed herself to be separated from Ursula, Naomi, and Mary. Now the nearest door was no farther than the tables. She felt sure that she could reach the door unnoticed.

She had begun to make her way through the press of the crowd when she heard her name called loudly. She froze, then turned. Grace Waterton was elbowing toward her.

"Kathleen, you weren't leaving?"

Kathleen swallowed. She felt dozens of eyes upon her and the heat on her cheeks. "No, I—well, yes, for a moment—there's such a line, and I have so much to do; I thought I'd come back in a half hour—"

"Nonsense! You come right along with me." Grace had her hand and was tugging her toward the table at the extreme left, the one marked "A to G." There were at least twenty women in the line, and more gathering quickly at the far end. "If you have things to do, the others will understand," continued Grace in her brass voice. "Oh, Sarah—"

Sarah Goldsmith, lighting a cigarette, was at the head of the line, waiting for the stout woman ahead of her, who was bent over the table signing her name and address. Now Sarah looked up.

"Sarah, be a sport. Kathleen here has a rush appointment. Would you let her squeeze in ahead?"

Sarah Goldsmith waved her cigarette. "Hello, Kathleen. Of course; go ahead."

"I really don't like to do this," said Kathleen apologetically. She turned to protest to Grace, but Grace was already yards off, breaking into clusters of women, herding them into line.

110

Sarah had stepped back, waiting. Kathleen moved in front of her. "I was coming back," she said lamely.

"Next," called Miss Selby from the table.

Kathleen faced the table, smiled uncertainly, accepted the proffered pen, and hastily signed her name and address to the long sheet.

"Did you enjoy the lecture?" asked Miss Selby.

"Yes," said Kathleen. She felt dull and a living lie. "It was very instructive."

She quickly returned the pen, stepped away, then remembered Sarah.

"Thanks, Sarah. How's the family?"

"Status quo. Nothing fatal this week, knock wood."

"We must have lunch. I'll call you soon."

"I wish you would."

Free at last, yet less free than before (sentenced to some future terror with her name and address committed to the long sheet), Kathleen went quickly to the door and then through it.

Outside, on the sidewalk, she stood in the sun a moment, trying to remember where she had parked, and then remembering. The street ahead was happily still empty. She neither wanted to see anyone nor discuss the lecture with anyone. Slowly, she started down Romola Place.

❖   ❖   ❖

From the second-story window of The Briars' Women's Association building, Paul Radford gazed into Romola Place. There was a lone woman directly below, walking slowly down the hill. He could not see her face, but her glossy hair was dark and short, and it seemed to shine in the orange sunlight. The beige sweater and skirt appeared expensive. Paul wished he could see her face.

He shifted his pipe from one corner of his mouth to the other, drawing steadily, blowing out the blue-gray smoke, and never taking his eyes off the lone woman. She was off the sidewalk now, crossing between cars, opening the door of a Mercedes. Holding the door ajar, she settled into the front seat, one leg in and one leg out. The skirt was drawn high over the long, slender, exposed leg, and from this distance, it looked good. Then the leg was withdrawn. The door slammed.

With a sigh for all the women unmet, Paul turned back into the room. He watched Horace and Cass at the table sorting the questionnaires.

111

"Looks like the old man sold them," Paul said at last. "The lecture's over, but only a few came out."

Horace continued to work silently. But Cass seemed hopeful. "Then this is the last stop," he said. He rattled a questionnaire in his hand. "Dammit, I'm sick to the gut of these questions."

"We're illuminating a dark area," said Paul with a grin.

"Shove it," said Cass. He glared at the questionnaire. He read aloud from it in a mocking tone. " 'Since you have engaged in an extramarital affair, or affairs, can you answer the following supplementary question: During the first occasion on which you had sexual intercourse with a male other than your husband, were you the aggressor, or were you seduced, or was the mating a mutual act?' " His eyes left the page, met Paul's, and his eyes were filled with anger. "Bitches," he said finally.

"Who?" asked Paul with a frown.

"Married women," said Cass. "All of them."

And he resumed sorting the questionnaires for the married women of The Briars.

4

VILLA NEAPOLIS was the kind of motel for which Petronius might have written the advertising pamphlet. Its architect had crossed the villas of early Rome and the modern Mediterranean and the resulting hybrid structure of wood and stucco was arresting if not aesthetically commendable. The sixty apartments of Villa Neapolis, on two levels, sprawled indolently across the summit of a long hill. From an upper veranda, the view was spectacular—a patch of the blue ocean behind a moist gauze haze to the west, a woodland of green knolls rising before a university campus to the east, and, directly below, beyond the great cement circle of heated swimming pool and multicolored patio lounges, beyond the sharply descending gravel road lined with royal palms, the asphalt ribbon of Sunset Boulevard twisted through The Briars.

Emil Ackerman had made the reservations at the Villa Neapolis—a suite for Dr. Chapman, a double for Paul and Horace, a single for Cass, and a single for Miss Selby—because the motel was relatively new and patronized by passing celebrities, because the proprietor was beholden to Ackerman for some past favor and agreeable to a cut rate for two weeks, and because the location was but a mile east of The Village Green and Romola Place, where the Women's Association building stood. Dr. Chapman, usually too preoccupied to appreciate or disapprove of any transient habitation, had been impressed with the Villa Neapolis and had been effusively grateful to his political patron.

Now it was early Sunday morning, and Dr. Chapman, in sport shirt and linen slacks, sat at a white metal table beneath the shade of a large striped umbrella eating breakfast with Horace and Cass. Dr. Chapman picked thoughtfully at his eggs and bacon, Horace worked steadily at his pancakes, and Cass ignored his French toast to watch an awkward sixteen-year-old blond girl pad from the cabañas to the diving board.

"Well," said Dr. Chapman, cutting his bacon with a fork, "I'm glad we're going to wind it up here."

"I think you told me—but I'm afraid I've forgotten—how many volunteers did we get?" asked Horace.

"A most gratifying response," said Dr. Chapman. "The Association has 286 members, of which 220 are eligible for our survey. Benita has the exact figures, but I believe 201 or 202 volunteered. Assuming that seven to ten per cent, for one reason or another, do not appear, we will still have enough. I've already sent a wire canceling our tentative visit to San Francisco."

He returned to his bacon and eggs, Horace cleaned his sirupy plate with the last portion of pancake, and Cass continued to watch the sixteen-year-old blonde. She had knelt beside the pool to test the water, and then made her way to the edge of the diving board. Now she executed a graceful jackknife, cleaving the water cleanly, and a moment later she burst to the surface. Her long stroking arms brought her quickly to the ladder of the pool. She climbed out, hair stringy wet, face and limbs dripping, yellow suit clinging to her small round breasts and hips. Hastily, avoiding Cass's gaze, she tugged her skirt low.

As she trotted back to the board, Cass poked at Horace's arm and nodded off. "Look at that behind," he whispered.

Horace fished for a cigarette, "Jail bait," he murmured. "I prefer them full grown."

"Each to his own," said Cass. His eyes followed the girl. "I suppose almost every girl under seventeen or sixteen is pretty. They won't all be pretty in a few years, but they are now. Youth is beauty in itself. Every contour of the body is new. After that—" he turned back to the table and shook his head— "after that they all become used and worn. It's too bad."

Dr. Chapman had not been listening, but now he raised his head. "What's bothering you, Cass?"

"The human condition," said Cass lightly, "with accent on the female."

There was the sound of someone descending the wooden stairs, and they all turned. It was Paul Radford, in white tennis shirt and shorts, his knobby knees and bare legs accentuating his height. He greeted his colleagues, and then, almost imperceptibly, flashed a signal to Dr. Chapman, who promptly lifted himself out of the wicker chair with a grunt.

Paul and Dr. Chapman sauntered across the sunny flagstone patio, until they were out of earshot of the others. Paul halted. "I just spoke to Dr. Jonas," he said.

114

"Personally?"

"Yes. He was at home."

Dr. Chapman waited, anxiety on his face.

"It was quite brief," Paul continued. "I simply introduced myself. I told him we were finishing our survey here, that we'd be here two weeks, and—well—that I'd like to meet him."

"What did he say to that? Was he surprised?"

Paul considered. "No, not surprised. Matter of fact, I felt he was rather expecting to hear from you or from one of us; he said he knew we were in town, he'd read about it."

"He's a crafty one, that one."

"Perhaps," said Paul. "He sounded quite down-to-earth, pleasant—really friendly."

"Don't let him hoodwink you. I know all about him. You keep your guard up."

"Of course. I was extremely cautious."

"To be sure," said Dr. Chapman. "Did he want to know why you were asking to meet him?"

"Not a word. He just said he'd be delighted. I felt some kind of explanation was in order. I said, 'Dr. Jonas, we've read what you've written about Dr. Chapman's work and we've been concerned—upset about certain public comments you have made and interested and impressed by others.' I went on like that; I told him that he and the four of us were, in a sense, in the same field, with a common goal, even if our approaches were different. I thought that I might profit by talking to him, and I told him that he might find it useful to see me. He was quite affable and agreeable."

"Did he ask about me?" Dr. Chapman wanted to know.

"Not a word, until we'd made a date, and then he said, 'Of course, Radford, your boss is invited to come along, too.' "

"Your boss—is that what he said?"

"It wasn't disrespectful. His vocabulary is on the informal side."

"When are you meeting him?"

"Monday night—tomorrow—after dinner, around eight, at his place. He has a house in Cheviot Hills. I believe that's about a half hour from here."

Dr. Chapman was thinking hard, biting his lower lip. "Well, I'm glad," he said. "If he's as friendly as you say, he may be receptive to our proposition. Let me mull over the whole thing today and brief you once more after dinner tonight."

"Fine."

"Preparedness," said Dr. Chapman. "As the Good Book

says, 'Let your loins be girded about, and your lights burning.' "

Paul saw Benita Selby, carrying a large paper bag, hurriedly crossing the patio toward them. She held up the bag triumphantly. "All done," she said.

Dr. Chapman turned. "What is it?"

"I worked out the entire interview schedule," she said, "and finished the post cards." She tapped the bag. "They're all right here."

"How many cards?" asked Dr. Chapman.

"Two hundred and one, exactly."

"Let me see now," said Dr. Chapman, calculating. "There'll be three of you interviewing—I'm begging off this last time, Paul, since I want to catch up on the paper work—well now, three of you can handle six women apiece, daily, eighteen a day in all. In eleven working days, you'll have recorded 198 women—more than will show up, I warrant. Fine. That means, allowing for next Sunday off, we should be out of here two weeks from—when do the interviews start, Benita?"

"Tuesday, Doctor. They'll all have the notices tomorrow morning, and Tuesday they can start reporting."

"Plan to get us out of here two weeks from today."

"I'll make the reservations tomorrow," said Benita.

"Now, you'd better get those cards in the mail," said Dr. Chapman. "There's a post office just across from the auditorium. It's closed, but there's a box in front. There'll be several pickups this afternoon. We've rented two cars—a new Ford and a Dodge—came in an hour ago. They're in stalls forty-nine and fifty." He dug into his trouser pocket and extracted two rings of keys. "Take the Ford."

"Has it got power brakes?" asked Benita. "I get so nervous—"

"I'll drive you," said Paul. "I've got to pick up some tobacco, anyway." He took the manila bag from her. He studied it. "Well, may our last crop be our best."

"Don't you worry," said Dr. Chapman. "I had a good look at those women Friday. Most intelligent lot I've seen in months. Besides, Emil couldn't speak too highly of The Briars. Some of the finest families in the city, he said."

"I don't care if they're the finest," said Paul. "I just care about whether they're the most interesting. I'm going to be listening to sixty-six of them in eleven days."

"As the psychiatrist said, 'Who listens?' " said Benita.

"Please mail those cards," said Dr. Chapman, with the

dedicated insistence of one who had already humbled the marmoset, the lemur, and the human male.

The post-office branch that serviced The Briars furnished its mailmen with three-wheeled, gas-driven, seven-and-a-half-horsepower scooters, painted red, white, and blue, to deliver mail more efficiently to houses so widely separated by their large surrounding yards. The mailmen guided their scooters swiftly from box to box, stuffing letters into each and gunning their motors as they raced to the next stop. In this way, all the mail destined for the houses in The Briars was fully deposited in boxes before noon, and Monday was no exception.

✧   ✧   ✧

The post card addressed to Mrs. Kathleen Ballard had the following information on the back: "Your interview will take place from 4 to 5:15 at The Briars' Women's Association building, on Thursday, May 28." The information was mimeographed, except for the time, day, and date, which had been filled in by pen.

The card lay on the Biedemeir tea table in the living room with the usual Monday-morning accumulation of unimportant mail—two magazines, a department-store circular, the dairy bill, the new gasoline credit card, an invitation to a fashion show for charity, and the regular semi-monthly lavender page of trivia from an older married sister in Vermont.

Kathleen had the cup of hot coffee to her lips, and over the top of the cup she could see the heap of mail. She had glanced through it, minutes before J. Ronald Metzgar arrived, and had seen the card. She had already determined to tear the card up the moment Metzgar was gone, and if anyone phoned she would plead illness. The illness would be a lingering one and would last the entire two weeks that the doctor and his team were in The Briars. Now, aware that Metzgar was still talking, as he had been almost steadily for the past half hour, she turned her face to him and pretended comprehension.

Metzgar, she had noted long ago, had been type cast for his role in life. He looked exactly like a man who, at sixty-two, would still play tennis instead of golf, would have his third wife from society circles (each wife progressively younger and more ladylike), would be president of something terribly rich and important known as Radcone Aircraft. His wavy silver hair, rimless glasses, small, trim mustache, and smooth-shaved banker's face personified executive. He was probably just under

117

six feet, stocky rather than fat, and vain about his good health. His voice was high-pitched, and his words tumbled and overlapped in their haste, and he was said to be business shrewd and clever in a way that Kathleen had always secretly felt was obvious and overrated.

Early in the morning, Metzgar had telephoned from San Pedro to say that he would be returning to the plant in the valley and would like to look in on Kathleen about ten o'clock. He had arrived within a minute of ten o'clock, in a chauffeured black limousine now parked out in the driveway, and for a half hour he had rambled on about a recent vacation to Hawaii, labor problems, the usual incompetence resulting from too much government, and recent researches in atomic-powered aircraft. During all this, Kathleen had wondered if he were here for any special purpose, beyond a compulsive visit to the shrine.

She saw that his coffee cup was empty and interrupted. "Jay—" Boynton had always called him Jay, and she had eventually been forced to do the same—"let me get Albertine to bring some more coffee." Albertine was the thin, sinewy, crisply dressed Mulatto day worker, with gold teeth much admired by Deirdre, who appeared five times a week to make the beds, dust half the furniture, break the cups, and read in a singsong to Deirdre before bedtime.

"No, thanks, Katie. I'll be on my way in a few minutes."

"You've only just come." The amenities.

"It's wrong, I know, to rush about like this. There's always too much to do. I suppose I don't delegate enough. As Boy used to say, 'Knock it off, Jay; you only live once—enjoy it, make the peasants work for you.' And you know, when Boy said it, why, it would bring me up short. I'd take stock. I'd say to myself, He has the right philosophy. And I'd really be more sensible for a day or two. Unchain myself from the desk. I've never known another man so understanding of the real meaning and values of life."

Kathleen said nothing.

Metzgar glanced at her, and, like everyone, perhaps more than anyone, misunderstood. "I'm sorry," he said. "I guess I've always got him on my mind—always will. It's not fair to you."

She wanted to shout. But the civilizing process that had begun twenty-eight years before tightened its clamp of restraint. "It doesn't upset me any more," she said firmly. "Life goes on. Boynton was alive. Now he's dead. It's a fact. It'll happen to all of us."

118

She was sure that Metzgar did not like this. He was still smoothing his mustache with a finger, blinking down at the coffee cup. "Well, certainly, I think that's the only attitude—that's healthy," he said at last, doubt releasing each word one at a time. "As a matter of fact, there was something I wanted to discuss with you about Boy. It concerns both of us. Jim Scoville told me he saw you last week."

"Yes, briefly. He had a few last questions about the book."

"The book," said Metzgar as a priest might say Deuteronomy. "You know, Katie, we want this book to represent everything Boy stood for."

"I'm sure it will. Jim's very conscientious—and properly worshipful."

A slight flicker of disapproval winked across Metzgar's face at the levity of the last. "I feel strongly—and I know you do, too—that we must allow nothing to happen that might impair the public's image of Boy as he is remembered and as he will be truly represented in the book."

"I don't understand you."

"Jim Scoville happened to remark that you were allowing yourself to get involved in this sex survey—this Dr. Chapman thing. I'm sure Jim misunderstood you."

"Not at all," said Kathleen. "I belong to a perfectly respectable club that was selected for questioning, and I volunteered with all the rest."

"But, Katie, don't you see—you're not like all the rest; you hold a peculiar, special position in the eyes of the public. You were married to a hero. To many, it would violate the trust he left you—it would disappoint—if you allowed yourself to be forced to . . . to discuss certain matters about Boy and yourself that properly belong to only Boy and yourself."

Kathleen felt the hot twitch of her nerve fibers. "Good God, Jay, what are you trying to make me into—or Boynton? We were married, husband and wife, and we were like any other couple, despite what you may think. In the eyes of Dr. Chapman, I'm just another married—once married—woman, and Boynton was the man to whom I was married. It's all perfectly anonymous and scientific—"

"It's not right," interrupted Metzgar. "It's not fitting to your station. You just can't see how it looks to an outsider. As for the anonymity, you're too famous, and so is Boy, and it's bound to get out."

"What if it did? Every reader of your book will know I'm no longer a virgin, and Boynton was not quite a eunuch—"

119

"Really, Katie—"

"No, I mean it. We were married. We slept together. How was Deirdre born—by immaculate conception?"

"That's different. That's normal and clean. But—well, you must know this—all kinds of dirty and abnormal sex connotations are associated with Dr. Chapman's survey. His report on married women will be made public, and everyone will know you participated."

"With three or four thousand others."

"That's not the point. Please don't go through with it, Katie. It's not like you."

She saw that he was an anxious child, this tycoon, this great man, humbled still by a vision of the man he had always wanted to be. She saw that further discussion would be useless. Metzgar had not the perception, or desire even, to understand what the truth might have been, and it was simply no use with him. Now she wanted him out of the house, far away, like an old bad dream.

"Well, if you feel that fiercely about it—" she said.

"I do. It's you I'm thinking of, Katie. Call them and cancel it."

"All right, Jay. I will."

"Good girl. You're right-minded, and I knew you would see what was right." He rose to his feet, inflated with self-satisfaction. This is the way he must look and feel, she thought, after putting over one of those million-dollar deals. "You've let me go back to work with a clear head. Shall we have dinner one night soon?"

"I'd love to."

"I'll have Irene call you."

After he had driven off in his black limousine, she closed the front door, absently stared at the gold silk walls of her small entry hall, then walked restlessly into the large living room. Often, when she was disturbed, the quiet elegance of the room, so devotedly furnished, pleased and soothed her. Now, studying the long, low sofa covered with Venetian silk, the flanking turquoise Thaibok chairs, the tea table, the exquisite collection of porcelain Chinoiserie, the sliding Spanish grilled panels that hid the bar to the left of the fireplace, the three shelves of boxed Limited Editions Club books, there was little pleasure it it. The harmonious and comforting refinement of the room seemed to have no salutary effect on her jumbled brain.

At last, she went to the tea table and placed cups and saucers on the tray. Her eyes found the mail, and she took up the post card. She turned it over in her fingers without rereading it. In some curious way, it had become invested with an importance that it had not had an hour before. She had meant to rip it in half and throw it away, and possibly telephone Miss Selby and cancel out or just default by nonappearance. But by that act, she saw, she would remain imprisoned to the past. Metzgar, Scoville, the vast blur of public opinion, would remain her guardians. The three-penny post card— 4 to 5:15, Thursday, May 28—was a call to escape, to live unfettered, possessed by none but herself, to acknowledge the possibility of a future without Boynton. The card was a passport to a place of defiance and rebellion.

Firmly, she slid the card into her skirt pocket, then picked up the tray and started for the kitchen.

❖   ❖   ❖

Ursula Palmer unfastened her large leather handbag, extracted the post card, and handed it to Bertram Foster.

"There's the evidence," she said cheerfully. "I'm now a bona-fide member in low standing of Dr. Chapman's sex club."

Foster had the card in both pudgy hands, and he was reading it, moving his lips as he read. Ursula watched him closely, wondering why it took him so long when there was so little to read. His tiny, slit eyes glittered as he read. Were he any other man, Ursula thought, she would have written him off as utterly repulsive. But she quickly banished the heresy, and determined to regard him as a brilliant and wealthy cherub. His perfectly round face seemed rounder because he was almost bald. His nose was spread wide and flat, and this, with the puffed lips, made him appear gross. He was short, and hypothyroid, and the most expensive tailor in New York could make him appear neither taller nor leaner.

Now, seated—squatted really, she decided—in the pull-up chair directly across from her, in the French Provincial living room of his hotel suite, he pursed his baggy lips—a sensuous Cupid or, better, a depraved Roman senator, she decided—and looked up from the card. "Tuesday, one o'clock to two-fifteen," he said. "That's tomorrow."

"Yes."

He studied the card again; then, with seeming reluctance, as if it had been a sex offer he hated to forgo, he returned it to her. "An hour and fifteen minutes," he said. "Now, my dear,

121

what can you tell them for an hour and fifteen minutes?"

"I'm a grown woman," said Ursula, with deliberate provocation, hating this but knowing that he wanted to hear it, and that it was part of the expected game.

"You mean you've been around," said Foster with heavy pleasure.

"Don't get any wrong ideas about my past, Mr. Foster. I'm a normal married woman—"

"I've met plenty of normal women who give ideas."

"I'll bet you have."

"How long you been married?"

"Ten years, almost."

"So you had a whole lifetime before?"

"Well, yes."

It made her uncomfortable being sunk deep in the sofa, so that she had to keep pulling her dress to her knees and pressing her legs together, and he on the chair facing her, and Alma Foster off at the beauty parlor. But this was morning, she reassured herself, and men didn't make passes in the morning, and besides, the beauty parlor was probably in the hotel, and Alma would be back any minute.

"Umm, I suppose you're like most women," he was saying. "If they ask questions, there's enough to say for an hour and fifteen minutes."

He stared at her knees, and she pressed them together. "It'll make a marvelous article, Mr. Foster," she said, desperately trying to distract his gaze from her knees. "It'll make *House-day* a sell-out for that issue."

"There are always newsstand returns," he said moodily, lifting his gaze from her knees. "I was thinking about it since you told me. Maybe it could be a three-parter—"

"Oh, Mr. Foster!" She clapped her hands with delight, and in her excitement her knees parted, and his gaze dropped. She left them apart, feeling suddenly that it was unimportant, and if it made him happy, what the hell. There was so much at stake.

"Ursula, maybe I better let you in on my mind. Only the day before I left New York, I was talking to Irving Pinkert— you know who he is?"

Ursula nodded excitedly. Irving Pinkert was Foster's publishing partner. He was a silent power behind the scenes. He allowed Foster to put his name on the mastheads, and dominate the editorial content, and take the trips, but he remained overseer of the business end, which probably meant printing, advertising, distribution.

"I told Irving I had my eye on you. I was thinking of you for maybe associate editor—later, maybe something better—of *Houseday*."

"Mr. Foster, I don't know what to say."

His fat lips folded upward, pleased. To Ursula, at once, the whole concept of him was changing. He was taking on the appearance of a benevolent and wise Kris Kringle.

"Now," he was continuing, "you are far away from this, but in big companies, we have politics. The editor I want to get rid of for you—she was put in two years ago by Irving. She is no good, a lesbian. He doesn't want her no more than I do. But still, there is his pride. He put her in. He will not let her go so easy, admit he can be wrong, unless there is a special reason. My argument for you is that you have a good head, clever, a fresh injection. He doesn't disagree, but to him, you are still not proved. So it needs only something, a little thing, to push him on my side—to prove you are better. I think this sex article is exactly the medicine. It shows you are a step ahead. And it deals with something every woman and man is interested in—even Irving."

"Mr. Foster, I could kiss you!"

"Who's stopping you?"

She pushed herself to her feet and bent over him, meaning to kiss his forehead, but suddenly his lips were where his forehead had been. She felt them cushioned on her mouth, smelling of cigar and bacon, and felt his hands grip her under the armpits, one hand pressing downward and clutching at the side of her left breast. Her instinct was to pull angrily away, but he wanted this little, just as she wanted so much, and the bargain seemed eminently fair. She lingered a moment longer than she had intended, then withdrew her lips slowly, and his hand fell from her breast. She straightened and smiled down at him. "There," she said.

"That's the kind of thank-you I like," he said. "Sit down. We still have a few minutes' business before Alma drags me away."

She sat down recklessly on the sofa, her knees apart and her skirt drawn taut several inches above them. She didn't care. She saw Foster's eyes drop, and she hoped he was happy, happy as she.

"Now, my dear," he said, "my plans for you are very con-

123

crete. You do what I say, and leave Irving to me. You will be in New York by July—big office, your own, with inter-com and secretary and agents taking you to lunch—if I let them."

She laughed giddily.

"Tomorrow," he said, "you go tell your whole sex life to those men—"

"Dr Chapman."

"Yes, him. Tell him everything, hold nothing back—you understand? You tell him—well, what do they ask?"

"You mean the questions, Mr. Foster? I'm not sure, though I suppose the same as they asked the men in the last book."

"An example."

"I suppose they'll want to know about my pre-adolescent sex history, petting, premarital and marital and extramarital experiences."

He wet his lips. "Good, good; it'll make a fine article. You'll change some words—after all, we live with advertisers and churches—but for me, don't change the words. I want the facts so I can . . . can evaluate, guide you."

"What do you mean, Mr. Foster?"

"Look, my dear, you go tomorrow, and when they take notes, you take notes. Then you type up the notes, their questions, your answers—exactly—nothing left out. We will have a meeting. Tomorrow, I take Alma to Palm Springs. It's supposed to be a week, but she can stay a week. This is too important. I'll come back myself before. We'll meet right here Friday—maybe have dinner together while we work. How does that suit the future editor?"

"I think it's a marvelous idea."

"When I come back Friday I'll phone you. . . . I think that's Alma at the door." He jumped to his feet. "Write down everything. Remember—three parts."

"I won't forget, Mr. Foster."

It was only later, when Ursula had reached The Briars and was turning into her street, that she remembered the appointment with Harold. She had promised to meet him—she held up her arm and squinted at the wrist watch—ten minutes ago, to go over his new office with him and help him decorate and furnish it. Well, she'd call and explain that she'd been tied up. Then suddenly she remembered that now he wouldn't be needing the office anyway. They would be moving East. She could help him, even hire a decorator for him. That would certainly show that she was thinking of him, wouldn't it?

124

❖ ❖ ❖

Sarah Goldsmith lay on her back, eyes closed, arm limp over her forehead. Her breath still came in short gasps, and her heart hammered, and from inside her ample thighs to her feet, she was drained and spent. She felt the bed move beside her, and then she felt Fred's sturdy, hairy leg against her own, rubbing her own playfully, his toes touching her toes and curling against them. Eyes still closed, she smiled at the recollection of the minutes recently past, at the continuing, unfailing miracle of them.

"I love you," she whispered.

"You're mine," he said.

"All yours."

She opened her eyes lazily, aware of the sea-green ceiling, then looked ahead, seeing first the wide white rise of her breasts, and then the thin white cotton sheet that concealed the remainder of her empty, naked body. Against the opposite wall, the tilted mirror above the dresser revealed the cherry-wood footboard and nothing more. She turned her head on the pillow and feasted her eyes on her beloved.

He, too, lay on his back, arms on the pillow. She enjoyed again the strength of his profile. It was primitive, a throwback to the Cro-Magnon Man. The tangled dark hair, low brow, broken nose, jutting jaw, the powerful sloping shoulders, thick neck, matted chest, made a promise that was always kept. At first sight, she remembered, the caveman appearance had intrigued but deceived her. Although she had heard he was important, she could not imagine such a frame containing sensitivity and high intelligence. Later, the incongruity of his soft, melodious voice, the deeply penetrating perceptiveness of his brain, the incredible breadth of learning that embraced both Shakespeare and Tennessee Williams, had overwhelmed her.

Just past him, on the green upholstered chair, she saw a measurement of her desire and passion. The remnants of her garments had been hurriedly, unceremoniously flung in a heap —her blouse, her skirt, her brassière, her nylon panties—with only the leather jacket, the first item she had taken off, carefully hung on the back of the chair. From a pocket of the jacket she saw, protruding, a card and several envelopes. She remembered: hurrying out to the car port, she had been intercepted by the mailman for some postage due. Getting into the

125

station wagon, she had glanced at the mail, and there was the cryptic card—9 to 10:15, Thursday, May 28—and then, in her haste, for she was a half hour late, she had forgotten it. Now she wondered whatever had made her bring the mail up to Fred's apartment. Nothing, she supposed. She simply had forgotten.

She saw him stir slightly. "What are you thinking?" he asked.

She looked at him. "How much I love you. I don't know how I ever lived without you." She considered this. "Of course, I didn't live without you. I wasn't alive one cell, one breath, until I met you."

He nodded. " 'And when love speaks, the voice of all the gods/ Makes heaven drowsy with the harmony.' "

"What's that?" she asked.

"*Love's Labor's Lost,*" he said, pleased.

"Sometimes I think it's been a million years. Do you know how long, Fred?"

"A million years."

"No. Three months and two days."

He rolled over on his side, so that his chest was against her arm and his head on her shoulder. His hand found her neck and the curve of her shoulders. Slowly, gently, he massaged her.

She closed her eyes and gave herself to the sweet sensation, but gave only her body. Her mind was journeying backward— one month, two, three, three months and two days.

It had begun with an amateur production of *She Stoops to Conquer,* performed and sponsored by The Briars' Women's Association for charity. Grace Waterton, whose records showed that Sarah had appeared in college plays fifteen years before, had begged her to volunteer for the tryouts. Sarah had flatly refused. Then, Ursula Palmer, who had agreed to handle publicity for the one-night show, had prevailed upon Sarah. And she had agreed to accompany Ursula because that day had been a bad day with the children and because she was bored. But on the eve of the tryout, she had once again changed her mind. Sam, who had borne the burden of her increasing unrest, had argued with her all through dinner—it was just for fun, it might be fun, it would be good to get out of the house a few evenings a week. But she had remained adamant, until that moment after dinner when she was clearing the table and saw Sam settle his bulk before the television set. She had known then that she could not endure one more eve-

126

ning of this narcotic monotony. At once, she had telephoned Ursula, and an hour later, she had joined two dozen other women and several husbands and fiancés with acting experience in the cold auditorium of the Women's Association.

She recalled now that they had all been huddled in the first two rows waiting for him. Grace Waterton's husband knew a motion-picture producer who knew a famous director who was between pictures. The director was Fred Tauber, and since this was for a worthy charity, he was agreeable. He appeared, striding down the center aisle, trench coat thrown over his shoulders like a cape, introduced himself to Grace and then to all assembled. He apologized for being late and for being free to undertake this. It was not, he explained quickly, that he was between pictures—motion pictures didn't exist any more, no one cared about them or went to see them, and television was the current corruption, and he had plenty of television offers, but he did not wish to become the mentor of any effort dominated by a cereal or toothpaste—but what had attracted him to this was that he enjoyed the creativity of the legitimate stage, and he liked Oliver Goldsmith, and he thought that this might be enjoyable.

Sarah thought him unattractive and condescending, although his speech was oddly quiet and charming. On the stage, he summoned the aspirants eight at a time, and they sat on folding chairs and nervously read, while he paced up and down before the footlights. Sarah had ascended the stage with the second group, regretting having left the tomb of her home and the predictability of the evening, and when it was her turn, she had read for Constance Neville, who was Tony Lumpkin's cousin and Hastings' heart. Fred Tauber had not cast her a single glance, pacing all the while, as she began to read. Suddenly, he had halted, glared at her, and snapped, "I can't hear you." She swallowed, and read louder—and he continued to stare at her. Within five minutes, she had the role. That was the beginning.

Fred Tauber decided that rehearsals would take place several times a week for six weeks. Rehearsals began in the auditorium but soon moved to the large living room of Fred's apartment two blocks south of Wilshire Boulevard in Beverly Hills. After one such session, Fred invited Sarah to return alone the next evening for some intensive personal coaching. His manner was so impersonal, although he never ceased staring at her with his burning eyes, that she promised to appear.

She had put the children to bed and left Sam comfortable

before the television set, and had arrived at Fred's apartment at nine o'clock. Script in hand, he had met her at the door, more friendly than she had ever seen him. When he suggested drinks, she readily accepted. She rarely ever drank after dinner, but she was nervous and afraid, and perceived she was on the brink of some unknown place. One drink became two and four and six, and rehearsal had long before been abandoned, and she was sitting beside Fred, and she was not afraid.

It was all hazy and the first relaxed fun in weeks—no, months, years. He was telling her of his life, and of the woman from whom he was separated, the dreadful creature who would not give him a divorce, and she was telling him about Sam and wasted years and loneliness. He took her hand then, and she never remembered after if she kissed him, or he kissed her, only that they had been in each other's arms a long time, and that she held his hand tightly when they walked into the bedroom. He had undressed her, as she stood dizzily beside the bed, and then he had kissed her until she had wanted to scream. He had settled her on the bed, and she had lain there stiffly, eyes shut tightly so that she could not see and by not seeing avoid being an active participant to guilt and shame. And she had felt him beside her, caressing her, and she had clutched him at last, which had surprised her, and had wanted it done, the terrible thing, done, irrevocable and behind her. And when he had joined his body to hers, she had wanted it done swiftly as it was always with Sam, so that it was no more part of her and she part of this strange and shocking thing, and she waited for it to be done, and waited, and waited, and it wasn't done, and then suddenly, involuntarily, she was a part of it, acting as she had never acted, and feeling as she had never felt, and wanting it never done, never ended.

In the morning, in her kitchen, she avoided looking at the table where Sam and the children ate. She suffered remorse and a hangover, and had never been as excited or alive in her life. She planned to withdraw from the play, and hide the shameful episode from herself, reassuring herself constantly that it had been an accident of intoxication. By nightfall, she knew that she did not want to withdraw from the play. She began counting the hours to the next rehearsal, only dimly aware of the strange house in which she lived and the foreign persons who shared it with her.

Three nights later, in company with the group, she attended another rehearsal in Fred's apartment. She was amazed

128

that she could perform so normally, and that Fred could behave as naturally as he had always behaved. She spoke her lines automatically and wondered what he was thinking. At eleven o'clock, the rehearsal broke, and as she was getting her coat, he asked politely if she would remain behind for ten minutes to go over one speech in the first act that troubled him. She nodded dumbly, and remained behind. This time they did not drink, and hardly spoke, and this time it was not an accident. Driving home, at two in the morning, she felt as irresponsible and carefree as a dipsomaniac.

The rehearsals ended. The play went on. Lines were forgotten and props mislaid and, somehow, the final curtain fell. The applause was thunderous, and the charity was served. There could be no more nights, or few, and so the affair became a ritual of the mornings, four or five mornings a week. Her insatiability surprised, shocked, and finally delighted her. What had begun casually, with an end foreseeable—for it was impractical, purposeless, even dangerous—became a necessary habit and the absolute meaning of each day lived and each day to be lived. And yet, still, Sarah would not allow herself to believe that the affair was her entire life, her life's new direction, but rather she regarded it as a finite episode that was temporarily the only living part of her life.

His hand had ceased massaging her, and she opened her eyes. "You're a darling," she said, "my darling own."

"I hope so," he said.

"What time is it, Fred?"

"Almost noon."

"I'd better get back. One cigarette, and then I'll go. They're in my jacket. Do you mind?"

He threw aside his half of the blanket, slipped off the bed, and stretched. She stared at his solid, athletic body, and felt the glowing pride of possession. Not since the first time had she felt a single pang of guilt. It was all too satisfying and inspirited to be wrong. In all the weeks since, she had suffered only one fleeting moment of doubt colored with shame, and that was the first time she had seen him fully naked in the light—on their fourth occasion together, when he had disrobed and crossed the room toward her, and she had realized that he was not circumcised. She had never seen this before—her husband, her son, her father, were all Jewish—and now what she saw seemed shockingly alien, and in that brief moment she had suffered the sensations of mortification and depravity. But soon she was enveloped by the pain of physical

129

pleasure, and the shame was gone, and she knew that nothing like this could ever be alien.

Fred had reached her jacket on the chair. "Which pocket?" he called.

"The bottom one."

At once, she saw that this was the pocket into which she had stuffed her mail. Fred's hand was behind the letters. He pulled out the pack of cigarettes, and as he did so, the post card fell to the floor. Sarah sat up, heart pounding, and she watched him retrieve it.

He glanced at it. "Never could resist post cards," he said. He read the back, and looked up. "Who's interviewing you Thursday morning?"

"I forgot to tell you. I won't be able to see you that morning." She was thinking fast and desperately. "A woman psychiatrist is coming in from the university—child psychiatrist—she's giving free consultations all day."

"I thought your two were normal—like their mother."

"Oh, they are," she said quickly. "It's just that Debbie has been cranky lately. I guess I haven't given her the time I used to—I mean, my mind isn't on them these days."

"And won't be, if I can help it. So you have your nice long talk with that child psychiatrist."

He stuffed the card back into her jacket pocket and returned to the bed with cigarettes and matches. She lifted the blanket over her breasts, held out her hand for a cigarette, and thanked God that Fred read only the theatrical section of the daily newspapers.

❖   ❖   ❖

Mary McManus came into the dining room from the kitchen, carefully balancing the tray crowded with small glasses of orange juice and a large plate heaped with scrambled eggs and tiny crisp sausages. Since she and Norman had agreed to live with her parents, the dinette in the kitchen was found to be too small for the four of them in the morning. Now breakfast, on gay reed mats, was always served in the large dining room.

Mary lowered the tray to the table, serving first her father at the head of the table, and then Norman, and then the place where her mother sat, and finally herself. The live-in Spanish maid, Rosa, was upstairs doing the bedrooms at this hour, but even if she weren't, Mary would have insisted on serving break-

130

fast herself. It was one of the many efforts that she made to delude Norman into believing they were really in housekeeping for themselves.

Mary glanced from her father, who had taken his juice in a single gulp, to her husband, who was turning the small glass around in his fingers, staring past it absently, not yet drinking.

"Is everything all right, Norman?" she asked anxiously.

"Oh, yes—yes, fine." He drank his orange juice without interest.

"Where's your mother?" Harry Ewing wanted to know. "Her eggs will be cold."

"She went out for the mail," said Mary, finding her fork.

Eating, she shifted her eyes from Norman to her father and back again. Usually, the breakfast scene pleased her, the orderliness of it, the warmth of so many loved ones. She liked to see Norman this way, in his brown lightweight business suit, hair combed, face smooth, hands so clean. He had such a wonderful lawyer look. It made her feel proud. And then her father, in his navy-blue silk suit with the natty handkerchief, so neat and successful and every inch the executive. But Norman—for now she was looking at him again—he seemed so strange and quiet lately, especially at mealtimes. Some instinct restrained her from probing it when they were alone at night. But sooner or later, she knew, she must ask Norman—that is, if it continued.

She looked off. Her mother, wearing the pink quilted housecoat that had been a Christmas gift, appeared from the living room, busily going through the mail. Bessie Ewing was a tall, flat woman with a long mare's face and a preoccupation with the weather and her health.

"It's going to be miserably hot today," she said. "I can feel it in my bones. I wish the summer were over." When the summer was over, she'd wish for an end to winter.

"Anything in the mail?" asked Harry Ewing.

She sat down. "Nothing special." She handed her husband the mail, withholding only a post card. She turned to her daughter. "This is for you, Mary."

Mary accepted it, looked at it blankly a moment.

"Is that the appointment for the interview?" Bessie Ewing asked.

"Of course!" exclaimed Mary with a shrill squeal of delight. "I almost forgot—from Dr. Chapman—I was waiting for it." She held the card up before her husband. "Look, Norman—

tomorrow, two-thirty to three-forty-five, D-Day; by tomorrow night, I'll be part of a history book."

"Great," said Norman.

Harry Ewing had stopped sorting the mail and was staring across the table at his daughter. "What's that?" he asked. "Did you say Dr. Chapman?"

"Yes, you know—"

"I don't know," said Harry Ewing with soft patience.

"But I—no, I guess I just told Mother—I thought I'd told you. Dr. Chapman's in town, Dad—"

"I read the newspapers."

"Well, he's interviewing all the married members of the Association for his scientific work. He lectured to us, and now we're going to be interviewed. Isn't it exciting?"

Harry Ewing moved his gaze to Norman. "Does Norman know about this?"

"He's been briefing me all week," said Mary, touching her husband's arm.

Harry Ewing released the mail and sat back. His eyes rested on Norman, who felt them and looked up.

"Surely you don't approve, Norman," Harry Ewing said.

"What do you mean?"

"I mean just what I'm saying—surely, you aren't going to permit Mary to expose herself to this . . . this so-called investigation."

"I don't see anything wrong with it. I think it's a good thing. We're not in the Dark Ages."

"Are you implying that I am?" said Harry Ewing without raising his voice, though the effort was apparent.

"Really, Harry," said Bessie Ewing. "I think it's their own affair."

"Perhaps they're too immature to distinguish between right and wrong."

Mary had listened in dumb bewilderment. Her father's objection surprised her and, from long habit, impressed and unnerved her. "What can be wrong with it, Dad? It's perfectly scientific."

"That is highly questionable, I assure you," said Harry Ewing. "Dr. Chapman's methods, the value of the whole report, are suspect in the best circles. Mind you, I have no objection to older married women going. With age, you learn values, know what to accept and reject, how to handle yourself. But you were twenty-two in March, Mary."

Norman set his fork down on his plate with a clatter.

132

"When my mother was twenty-two she had three children."

Mary could almost touch the electric antagonism in the air. She rubbed the goose pimples on her arm. In two years, the only serious fight with Norman had been over children. He wanted them, at once, and many. Her father had never been more firm than in advising against them. He had told Mary, confidentially, father to daughter and only child, that she was too young, that she must learn to live in marriage first, that early years were years to be enjoyed unencumbered, that there was always time. She had never sorted out her own feelings about children. She wanted what Norman wanted. Rather, she wanted Norman to be happy with her. But she had never known her father to be unwise or to misinform her. Still, his attitude toward Dr. Chapman seemed irrational.

"Mary isn't a baby any longer," she heard Norman say in anger. "She's a grown married woman. You can't keep trying to shield her. I think this Chapman study is healthy and normal."

"I'm sorry I must disagree with you, Norman. I think it might do more harm than good."

"Well, I want her to go," said Norman doggedly.

Harry Ewing shrugged, and forced a smile. "She's your wife," he said. He consulted his watch, and pushed back his chair. "Time for work."

He rose and went into the hall for his hat. Norman glared after him, then got stiffly to his feet. He was about to start away.

"Norman," Mary called, "haven't you forgotten something?"

He returned to her, his face constricted. "Sorry," he said. He bent and kissed her briefly.

"Don't be angry," she whispered. "I want to go."

"Good," he said curtly, then pivoted and walked out.

Bessie Ewing had been peeling through the mail again, and now she unfolded a colored circular. "There's a sale at Brandon's—cotton dresses," she said.

Mary stared miserably at the card and wished that Norman would change his mind about children or that her father would change *his*. She suddenly hoped that Dr. Chapman would not question her about having children. If he did, what would she say?

❖   ❖   ❖

Teresa Harnish turned the key, let herself into the cool,

shaded living room, and removed her wrap-around sun glasses with an audible sigh of relief. It had been suffocating and blinding outside. Her arms, beneath her sleeveless white blouse, and her knees and legs, beneath her gray Bermuda shorts, were baked.

She had left Constable's Cove a half hour earlier than usual, she told herself, because even the beach offered no comfort from the relentless sun. Actually, the Cove had been lonely, and she had not been able to shed an inexplicable nervousness and irritability. It was the first time in memory that the refuge had not served her therapeutically. Certainly, the Cove itself had not disappointed. It was, this morning, as isolated and lovely as she had always known it, before the invasion of the barbarians. When she had descended the precarious decline to the sand, she fully expected to observe the four crude behemoths nearby, exercising and throwing the football. She had girded herself against them, armed with righteous anger. She was prepared to ignore them, very pointedly, and if the huge, cocksure one, with his vulgar tights and bulging thighs, approached her, as she felt he would, she would devastate him with several sharp retorts that she had polished and prepared— and that would give her peace, *if* he understood them. But, when she reached the sand, neither he nor his companions were anywhere to be seen. This had surprised her, and she told herself, Good riddance. But later, stretched on the blanket, she had turned five pages of Swinburne and two of Coventry Patmore before realizing that she had not read a word. Her mind went to the invaders, and she carried on a heated imaginary conversation with the four, with the one, and came off with banners flying.

She thought about Geoffrey's Marinetti, and the art shop, and her mornings, and wondered what it was like to be *un*intellectual like Grace Waterton, who could sublimate herself in service activity, and Sarah Goldsmith, who could make a busy and satisfying day of her children and home. Perhaps, she told herself, she had been born utterly out of her time. It happened, she was sure: one of Creation's anachronisms and inefficiencies. She could more easily envision herself as Louise Colet of Paris or Mary Wollstonecraft of London (although there was some grubbiness here that displeased) or Kitty O'Shea of Dublin, rather than Teresa Harnish of The Briars in California.

Reconsidering, she saw herself best as Marie Duplessis— offering elegance and tragedy and inspiration for the young

Dumas' lady of the camellias. But somehow the last role seemed more suited to Kathleen Ballard—what did she do with her mornings?—and then Teresa felt an insect move on the back of her hand. Hastily, she brushed it off and found herself in Constable's Cove. Ahead, the turgid water lapped exhaustedly at the wet ribbon of dark brown sand. Above, the circle of sun was a scorching lamp. Encircling her, the Cove was suddenly a geological imperfection—the rock and dirt as unappealing as any dump on an empty lot, the tangled and knotted branches and weeds parched and deformed.

If she were going to be uncomfortable and bored, she decided, she might as well be so in the cool, clean water of her sunken marble bath at home. Who was it who made a practice of letting her towering Negro manservant carry her to the bath and lower her into it? And who then received and chatted with her male circle of French and Italians while she bathed? The sculptured nude in the Villa Borghese—Canova's work—yes, Pauline Bonaparte. Extraordinary. Teresa Harnish sat up, then stood, slowly gathered her beach equipment, and started for home.

Now, in the tasteful, sparsely furnished living room, a symphony of beige and burlap and framed abstract oils, she dropped her book on the end table and became aware of Geoffrey's jacket—the navy one with the brass buttons that he had worn to the shop this morning—neatly draped on a pull-up chair.

"Geoffrey?" she called off.

"In the study!"

Puzzled, she laid her blanket and effects on the wall bench and hastened through the corridor into the study. Geoffrey was kneeling on the floor, unrolling the poster imprinted *Divan Japonais*.

"Geoffrey, are you all right?"

He glanced up. "Perfectly, my dear." He examined the poster briefly, and then rolled it up tightly.

"What are you doing home at this hour?"

He reached for another poster. "A customer from San Francisco—she just discovered Henri de Toulouse-Lautrec—"

"That's like reaching puberty at forty."

". . . and she's coming in at two. Wants everything I can show her." He unrolled another poster in his hand. It was *La Troupe de Mademoiselle Eglantine*. He pointed to the four kicking dancers. "Jane Avril, Cléopatre, Eglantine, Gazelle. Remember when we found this?" It had been on the wall of a

135

disheveled, cramped shop in the Rue de Seine ten years ago. It had cost them fifty-seven thousand francs when the franc was three hundred and eighty to one in the black market. They had always said that they had discovered Lautrec, or so it seemed in those days. Hanging his posters was an attention-getter and a snobbery. But then, there was the flood of books, and the gaudy motion picture, and soon Lautrecs were on napkins, match covers, coasters.

Geoffrey rolled up the dancers. "I'm tired of him. I'm going to unload the whole bunch. I think I should get three times what we paid." He lifted himself to his feet. "Every artist sooner or later becomes a guest who's stayed too long," he said with regret.

"I don't think people will ever tire of Da Vinci or Shakespeare. Minor artists come and go. Lautrec was a curiosity. The classicists remain."

"Don't be too sure," said Geoffrey. "Shakespeare fell into disrepute and neglect for a long period after his death. His revival is modern. He may tumble again. Even disappear."

For once, Teresa did not feel like pursuing this sort of thing further. "Maybe you're right," she said wearily. "I need a bath."

"One second." He was at the desk. "This came in the mail." He handed her the post card. "The brink of adventure," he added.

She read it. "Wednesday—ten-thirty to eleven-forty-five."

"I want a full report, play-by-play."

"Silly, what could I report that you didn't already know? You collaborated in everything I'm going to say."

"Well, now, I didn't think of that." He seemed self-satisfied, and momentarily she resented it. "The next few weeks should be exciting," he went on. "A community catharsis."

"It's healthy," she said to say something, and was at once perplexed at her indifference to the Chapman interview. But then another thought came, and grew, and she began to feel better. "You know what might be fun?" She considered it.

"What?"

"A party—a big party. We haven't had one in a month. A celebration of the new freedom. A costume affair. Something like—I have it—a come-as-the-person-you-would-like-to-have-been-when-Dr.-Chapman-interviewed-you. Wouldn't it be mad fun?"

"Marvelous, Teresa. We have a load of pay-backs to tick off, anyway."

136

For Teresa, the day was coming alive again. She moved through the room. "I can just see it. Naomi Shields as Ulysses' perfect Penelope, Sarah Goldsmith as—quick, Geoffrey, name some dreadful courtesan—"

"Hester Prynne. Harriette Wilson. Cora Pearl."

"Yes," she said excitedly, "any one of them; and the Mc-Manuses—Mary as Ninon—"

"I see. You think each woman will want to be her opposite."

"Don't you? The chaste would secretly long to be unchaste and the unchaste would prefer to appear before the good doctor as pure and maidenly."

"And you, my dear—how would you want to appear?"

Teresa saw the trap. Marie Duplessis? Intuitively, she side-stepped it. "As *myself*, darling! Isn't that cunning? But I mean it. Why would I ever want to be anything but what I am?"

⋄ ⋄ ⋄

Naomi Shields, wearing only her slip, lay curled on the unmade bed, and fitfully dozed. Gradually, the part of her that was still conscious was penetrated by the singsong bar of melody. It persisted, the same hideous music, and she opened her eyes, rolled flat on her back, and listened. At last, she realized that it was the doorbell.

She sat up. Her head felt dizzy and apart and extremely high above her body, like a toy balloon attached to a string. She knew that she had been perspiring. The cleft between her breasts felt sticky, and, except where she wore her pants, the slip clung to her. She brought the electric clock into focus. It was ten minutes before noon. She had meant to lie down a few minutes after breakfast, and it had been over two hours.

She tried to remember: yes, she had awakened at nine, fully aware of the resolve she had made after her last drink the night before. Monday, she had determined, would be a new day, a new week, a new life. Even the program had been clear in mind. Before her marriage she had gone to secretarial school for eight months. Touch typing was like dancing and a foreign language. Once learned, it was never forgotten, she hoped. Monday, she had determined, she would telephone Urusla Palmer, much as she disliked her—or, maybe better, Kathleen, who knew all those important aircraft people. She would phone one of them, both maybe, and they would help her. Why hadn't she done this long ago? It would give her life regularity and purpose, and there were always single men in an office, and maybe she would find someone wonderful. It was so *sensible*. She had carried the resolve to breakfast and seen it dissolve in the first bitter sip of coffee. Why had she taken all that vodka? She pressed her fingers to her temples, trying to remember how she got back on the bed.

The doorbell again. She swung off the bed, searched for her mules, and then forgot about them. She started for the living room, remembered that she was in her slip, and hurried back to the dressing room. Once in her white peignoir, she groped, barefooted, through the hall to the living-room door. Working the chain free, she pulled the door open, then shut her eyes and averted her face from the explosion of sunlight and the blast of hot air.

A tall, slender man, in t-shirt, faded blue denims, and leather sandals, was leaving across the lawn.

"Hi," she called out.

He halted and turned. "Hello, there."

"Were you the one ringing?"

"That's right."

He was returning, and she waited. As he drew nearer she saw that his face was ugly and striking. His chestnut-colored hair was shaggy and in need of a trim, his eyes were narrow, and deep in the sockets, his thin lips curved in a mocking smile, and there was too much jaw. He was chicken-breasted.

"Are you selling something or what?" she asked.

He reached the screen door and looked her over, top to bottom, unhurriedly and insolently. She saw now that his pale cheeks were pocked and he seemed debilitated. It was oddly attractive.

When he spoke, his lips hardly moved. She watched them, fascinated. ". . . . just down the block," he was saying.

"I'm sorry. I'm still not awake. What did you say?"

"I said I live just down the block. About five doors down. My name's Wash Dillon."

She wrinkled her forehead. The name was familiar.

"Maybe you've heard my band. We've cut some records."

"Oh, yes," she said.

"You're Mrs. Naomi Shields."

"*Miss* Shields," she said quickly.

"How could that be?" His eyes were on her bosom. "Well, anyway—" he dug back into his hip pocket and pulled out a post card—"it says here *Mrs.*"

"What is that?"

"Your mail. The mailman must have hung one on. He put

138

it in my box by mistake. It looked like some kind of interview for a job. Afraid you might not get it in time, so I came over, good neighborly like."

"Thank you." She opened the screen slightly and took the card.

"I figured nobody was home, and I was hunting for the mailbox. Where is it?"

"Next to that bush in front. It's grown over. I'll have to tell the gardener." She peered at the card and realized what it was. Her interview was on Wednesday from five-thirty to six-forty-five.

"Something important?" he asked.

She looked up. "In a way." He was very tall and curious, and she did not want him to go yet. "I guess I'm still in a daze," she said quickly. "I don't know how to thank you."

"I know how," he said. "By giving a good neighbor a good cup of coffee—for the road—it's a long block."

"All right," she said. She pushed the screen door wide, and he brushed past her into the house.

"No fuss," he said. "Where's the kitchen?"

She closed the front door, tightened the cord on her peignoir, and went into the kitchen without glancing at him. He watched her, noticing her bare feet, then followed.

She heated the coffee and busied herself laying out crackers and jam while he slumped at the dinette table, legs out, marking her every move. Self-consciously, and with an inexplicable sense of mounting turmoil, she served him and herself, and sat down across from him, sipping her tasteless coffee. She wanted vodka, but didn't dare, and kept rattling out questions to forget the vodka. But she found herself answering his questions, as often as listening to his answers to her questions.

Yes, Naomi said, she had bought the house and had been in the neighborhood three years. She knew most everyone around. Surprising that she had never seen him before. Well, Wash Dillon said, that was because he'd just come into the neighborhood a couple weeks ago. He used to live in Van Nuys, and gave up the place to go on tour with the band. Now, he had a long-term setup in Los Angeles, and he was boarding up with Mr. Agajanian, owner of the nightclub, till he could find a shack of his own. Yes, Naomi said, she knew Mrs. Agajanian—casually, that is. The Agajanians seemed very rich. Well, Wash said, anybody could become rich by screwing musicians and watering drinks and peddling to hopheads.

But, Naomi said, people like that didn't live in The Briars. Honey, Wash said, people with dough live anywhere.

He held up his coffee cup and turned it over. She brought the pot from the stove and stood awkwardly beside him, refilling it, while he smiled insolently at her bust. She poured her own cup and set the pot on the table, preferring the ring it would make to walking back to the stove in front of his eyes. Well, Naomi said, neighbors. Did his wife like The Briars? Honey, Wash said, there is no wife, not yet. Bachelorhood is best for a musician, until he is established, and now that he was established, you never could tell. What about her husband? What did he do? Well, Naomi said, she was divorced three years ago. Honey, Wash said, I just had a hunch that was so.

She held the coffee to her lips, fearful that they would betray her unaccountable agitation. She did not want to go where he was leading her—oh, she did, yes, but this was Monday, remember, and it was all going to be new and right. Desperately, she tried to divert him. How large was his band? Five-piece combination. Where were they playing? On Sunset Strip, placed called Jorrocks' Jollities. When did he perform? Every night, honey, every night.

She knew that she was running dry, and that he was waiting with that mocking smile. She was silent.

"Like I said, honey, I had a hunch you were divorced."

"You did?" Wearily, letting go.

"You can always tell when there's been no man around."

"Can you?" Goodbye Monday.

"The way a woman moves—unsettled."

"Your girl friend teach you that?" A last try.

"Sa-ay now, sharp. No, honey, my women don't move like that. My women don't move at all."

"You're pretty cocky." Goodbye job.

"Got a right to be. Never had a complaint."

"I don't like this talk!" Goddam him.

Abruptly, Naomi rose, determined to lock herself in her bedroom or have a drink first or have happen what would next happen. She started past his sprawled legs, and he reached out and took her by the waist. She tried to draw away, but his hands were big and his forearm muscular. Almost without effort, he pulled her down upon his lap. She felt him beneath her and weakly tried to free herself.

"Why did you bring that post card?" she said tearfully. "You could have—"

140

He loosened her peignoir. "I saw you a couple days ago, honey, in that sweater. Now, why would you wear a sweater like that?"

"Don't, Wash—don't, please—"

He laughed, and she shut her eyes while she fought his hands. The chimes above the kitchen door intruded.

Startled, Wash looked off, and in that moment Naomi tore free of him and staggered to her feet.

"Honey, wait now—"

"It's someone at the door," she said savagely.

"Let them be."

She saw the tear in her peignoir and hastened out of the kitchen through the dining room to the front door. She didn't care about her hair, or the tear, or anything, only that she wanted the door wide open. She yanked it open.

A skinny, sallow boy of about twelve stood against the screen. "My father came here—"

Wash appeared behind Naomi.

"Pop," the boy said, "Ma says to come home—"

Wash's smile was gone. "I'll be along. Beat it now—"

"She says I ain't to come home without you, or she'll come and get you."

Trembling, Naomi looked up at Wash. His smile was back, less mocking than brazen. "That's the way the cookie crumbles," he said. He nodded to the boy. "Okay, Johnny." He stared at Naomi again, then shrugged and started out.

"You son-of-a-bitch," she said.

He paused, turned his head, and considered her. "You look awful hungry, honey," he said. "Come over to Jorrocks' some night—if you want to be fed."

She slammed the door after him and hit the wood with her fists, and after a while, after she had ceased her sobbing, she composed herself and started back into the kitchen toward the liquor cabinet. Well, there was always Tuesday.

5

"W ELL," said Dr. Victor Jonas, emerging from the hall into the living room, "they're in bed, at last. Now we can have a little time to ourselves."

Paul Radford, who had been sitting on the sofa beside Peggy Jonas watching the opening scenes of an old movie on television, quickly pushed himself to his feet. "You've got two attractive boys there," he said to Dr. Jonas. "How old are they?"

"Thomas will be twelve in September," said Dr. Jonas, "and Matthew was just nine."

Peggy Jonas' eye left the movie a moment. "Perhaps Mr. Radford would like some coffee or tea," she said to her husband. She was a small, friendly young woman, with a frank and freckled Irish face.

"Nonsense," said Dr. Jonas. He turned to Paul. "I've something better for you out in back."

Peggy Jonas settled into the corner of the sofa. "I'll be right here, then. If you need me, make whimpering sounds."

Dr. Jonas had Paul by the arm. "Let's go," he said. "It's through the kitchen."

Paul followed his host across the dining room and kitchen. Dr. Jonas held the rear screen door open, and Paul went through it.

"Careful," said Dr. Jonas. "There are two steps."

They tramped across the wet grass toward the far side of the yard. Despite the slight drifts of fog, the moon was visible. For a moment, they walked in silence.

Paul had arrived at Dr. Jonas' modest early-American house in Cheviot Hills at ten minutes after eight. Whatever apprehension he had suffered in his drive from The Briars was swiftly dissipated by Dr. Jonas' cordial welcome. The Devil's Advocate, as Dr. Chapman had bitterly characterized him,

142

would have been completely miscast in the role of Inquisitor. He was perhaps five feet nine or ten. His rust hair, parted on the side, hung down his forehead in the Darrow manner. His gray eyes were lively and blinking, and his nose was a great hooked beak that seemed to obscure a cheerful mouth. He wore an open sport shirt, and corduroys, and he moved like a man who still had five more things to do. His pipe—which he had been smoking when he greeted Paul at the door—was an aged corncob. On anyone else, it would have been an affectation.

Dr. Jonas had been reading to his boys when Paul arrived. At once, after introducing them to Paul, he had shouted out for Peggy. Paul had insisted that he finish whatever he was reading, and immediately, without apology or self-consciousness, he had waved Paul to the large wing chair and returned to the sofa where the boys were waiting and had resumed. Paul liked that. Peggy appeared just after the story had been finished, and Paul rose to acknowledge the introduction. Then, they all sat for ten or fifteen minutes, Peggy and Dr. Jonas conversing with Paul on the science fiction just read, on comic books, the press in Los Angeles, the fog in Cheviot Hills, the beauty of The Briars, life in California versus life anywhere else, the public schools, and the Dodgers. It had all been so easy and natural that Paul felt he had been part of this family and this house for years.

Now, walking beside Dr. Jonas in the shrouded moonlight, he realized that they had arrived at a miniature bungalow located at the farthest extremity of the yard.

"My workshop," said Dr. Jonas. "I think this is why we bought the house."

He opened the door, turned up the lights, and they were inside a large single room. Paul surveyed it quickly. It was dominated by a worn oak desk piled high with loose papers and manuscripts. The armless swivel chair faced an old typewriter. A door, partially ajar, revealed a narrow lavatory. Against a wall were four file cabinets. A brick fireplace dominated another wall, and near it was a cot and then an entire wall of books.

As Dr. Jonas went to open a window, Paul, as was his habit whenever he entered a new study, strolled along the shelves and noted the book titles. He saw Dr. Chapman's book at once, and then a second copy of it. There were volumes by Freud, Adler, Jung, Alexander, Fenichel, Bergler, Dickinson, Terman, Stone, Stopes, Gorer, Hamilton, Krafft-Ebing, Lynd,

Reik, Weissenberg, Mead, Ellis, Guyon, Trilling, Kierkegaard, Riesman, Russell.

"Chartreuse, dry sherry, or cognac?" asked Dr. Jonas. He was standing beside a low table of bottles that Paul had not seen when he came in.

"Whatever you say," said Paul.

"I recommend the chartreuse highly," said Dr. Jonas.

"Perfect."

Dr. Jonas filled two liqueur glasses, set one on his desk and brought the other to the lamp table next to the plastic upholstered chair across from the desk. Paul settled in the plastic chair while Dr. Jonas filled his corncob from the walnut humidor on the desk.

"I suppose you know all about me, Mr. Radford," Dr. Jonas said suddenly.

Paul was taken aback. "Why, a little, of course—I always try to . . . to read up on someone . . . before meeting them."

"So do I." He smiled. "I even read your book."

"Oh, that—"

"You showed real promise. It's a pity you haven't written more. I presume you don't, now. One writer in the family's enough."

Paul refused to meet the allusion to Dr. Chapman head-on. "We—all of us work together on Dr. Chapman's books. I'm afraid that's enough to keep me occupied."

Dr. Jonas had the corncob smoldering. He lowered himself into the squeaking swivel chair. "You told your boss that he was also invited tonight?"

"Of course, but he couldn't make it. We start the last sampling tomorrow morning. He'll be up until midnight preparing."

"So you have to do the dirty work alone?"

Paul scowled. He was about to retort that there was no dirty work, but he knew that once he made the proposal this would make him look foolish. "I don't know what you mean," he said.

"I mean simply I can't believe you came all the way out here—to a stranger—out of mere intellectual curiosity—to pass the time of evening. I may be wrong. If so, forgive me. But that's what I mean." Observing that Paul had taken his briar from his pocket, Dr. Jonas pushed the humidor toward him. "Try my mixture."

Paul worked his way to the edge of the chair, lifted the lid of the humidor, and dipped his pipe into it.

144

"As a matter of fact," said Dr. Jonas, "I'm glad Dr. Chapman didn't come. I don't think I'd like him. And I rather think I like you."

Paul wanted to be loyal, yet was pleased with the offer of friendship. "You might be surprised. He's intelligent, decent—"

"I'm sure. But there's something else about him—I—no, forget it. What I want to say, better say, right off, is that many people who don't know me find me abrupt and disagreeable. I'm not. Understand that. I'm only frank. I may not always be right, but I am frank. When I'm in this room—the hard-think room—with my intellectual equal, I have no patience for the amenities, the social word game. That's deplorable waste. I like to get to essentials, get on with it, get the best from my opposite, and give my best, and learn and improve. That's fun. If you will tolerate that, then we will get along. This could be a valuable evening for both of us."

"Fair enough," said Paul, sinking back in the chair.

"Need a match?"

"I have one."

"Now, you know how I feel about Dr. Chapman's highly publicized surveys. I don't like them, for the most I don't. You, I assume, believe in them fervently."

"I certainly do."

"Good. The lines are drawn."

Paul recalled the emotions he had felt at Reardon, upon first reading Dr. Jonas' reviews of the bachelor survey. He had thought them short-sighted and unfair. Had Dr. Chapman's personal annoyance influenced him at the time? Dr. Chapman had loftily implied that Dr. Jonas was a gnat bothering an elephant. Of course, in all justice, Dr. Jonas' dissents were handicapped by lack of publication space. Now, however, the old emotions filtered back. Our work is so simply right, Paul thought. Why can't an intelligent man like that see it? Was he, as Dr. Chapman contended, crafty and ambitious?

"You know how I felt about the bachelor book," continued Dr. Jonas, almost uncannily, as if he were reading Paul's mind. "A few of my feelings were published. Well, I want you to know I feel even more set against the married female sampling —and the use Dr. Chapman will make of it."

"But it's still in preparation," said Paul. "How can you be critical of something you haven't read?"

Dr. Jonas' corncob had gone out, and he busied himself lighting it again. When he had it smoking, he looked up at

Paul. "There's where you are wrong. I *have* read the female findings—most of them—enough of them. As you probably know, I've been retained by a certain group connected with the Zollman Foundation in Philadelphia to analyze the female survey—both surveys, in fact. Well, your Dr. Chapman is trying to win those people over; he's been regularly sending them copies of your findings."

"It's hard to believe. The work is still in progress."

"Nevertheless, the Zollman directors are abreast of it, and so am I. They've supplied me with photostats of what you've done." He pointed off. "I have a couple hundred pages of your newest survey in the top drawer of that second cabinet. Everything, in crude form, up until two months ago. So I believe I am qualified to discuss with you your latest findings."

Paul had been totally unprepared for this, had even unconsciously counted on Dr. Jonas' lack of knowledge of their latest effort to support him, and now he was vaguely disturbed. Why had Dr. Chapman been so quick to rush their undigested efforts to critical outsiders? And why had Dr. Chapman kept this secret from him, leaving him now so vulnerable? Most probably, he supposed, Dr. Chapman had believed that Paul already knew that this must be done, that every calculated risk must be taken to sweep the day. Still, it was disquieting. Nevertheless, meeting Dr. Jonas' direct gaze now, he was determined that the unusual man behind the desk, piercing eyes, monstrous nose, foul corncob, be made to understand the basic worth of their crusade.

"Yes, I suppose you are qualified," said Paul. "What beats me, Dr. Jonas—"

"Excuse me, but would it offend you to get on a first name basis? Otherwise, it's as if the referee said, *Mister* Dempsey, this is *Mister* Tunney, who's going to try to knock your head off."

Paul laughed. "All right."

"Not that I anticipate any real Donnybrook. This *is* my study, and the word here is *gemütlichkeit*. If we're going to belabor each other, let's make it a friendly pummeling. I'm sorry I interrupted you, Paul. You were saying?"

"Okay, Victor." Paul had been prepared to make a high-level defense, but now it seemed pompous, and he tried hastily to revise and slant what he had to say to the informality of the occasion. "I read a good deal of your writings on our bachelor report. I agreed with you, still do, about a lot of minor shortcomings. But it always seemed to me you missed

146

the forest for the trees. Since the *Mayflower*, people in this country have been living in a dreary house behind a puritanical curtain. They've grown up in this cold, stark house built by John Calvin of Geneva, and the sign on the door, sternly printed by Jonathan Edwards, read, 'No frolicking.' The best parts of their lives have been lived in this dark, unlighted house, and it is unhealthy and unwholesome, and we've merely been trying to get rid of that curtain and let some light in."

"How have you done that?"

"How? By gathering data—information on a little-known subject—and we've done this on a scale never before attempted. As Dr. Chapman says, we're the fact-gatherers."

"Not enough," said Dr. Jonas placidly. "You add up your digits, and you spew them out, and you say that does good. I wonder. As someone said of another such report—I think it was Simpson in *The Humanist*—just looking up and counting stars never achieved the science of astronomy, and just collating what married women say on their sexual behavior won't give us real insight into this behavior."

"Well, I disagree with you," said Paul warmly. "We're making a giant first step. The very idea of removing sex from scrawlings on lavatory walls to frank, sensible, open discussion will do infinite good. I remember Dr. Robert Dickinson saying that the enemies of sex freedom were conception, infection, detection. True. But we've controlled most of these. Still, we are left to fight one more enemy rarely challenged—ignorance —and ignorance thrives on silence."

Dr. Jonas banged his corncob on the cork center of his circular metal ash tray. When the bowl was empty, he dipped it into the humidor again. "You are persuasive," he said. "I grant you that the final enemy is ignorance. But I believe Dr. Chapman is fighting that enemy the wrong way. He has done much good, of course, but he has done a greater amount of mischief." He ran a flaming match over the rim of the pipe and then blew the match out and dropped it into the tray. "Of course, you are dealing with married people in our society, and that makes research even more difficult. I suppose man was really meant to be polygamous, but then monogamy was imposed upon him—as were a hundred other unnatural customs and credos like turn-the-other-cheek, love-thy-neighbor, fair play, sportsmanship, and so forth. He is burdened with all sorts of pressures inconsistent with his real nature. But, by accepting this, he receives certain benefits, and so the pressures are the price for being civilized and advanced. Man sets his

147

own rules, then tries to make them work, unnatural though they may often be. Sex is one form of behavior that suffers gravely."

"I don't deny that."

"Making sex work, under these repressive circumstances, is a delicate assignment. You think it can be done by simply counting noses?"

"I don't think so and neither does Dr. Chapman. No. I'd say we're going so far, as far as we can, and others will go further."

"Yes, Paul, yes," said Dr. Jonas. "But the problem, as I see it, is this—*you* know you are going so far and no further. You understand this, but your public doesn't. The vast public has been propagandized to believe that whatever science says is so. They believe science is some mystical society, with a direct line to God, that cannot be quite understood but must be believed. Naturally, they accept Dr. Chapman's reports as the Final Word on sexual behavior. They do not know that the data are raw and uncooked. They think the findings are ready for consumption, and Dr. Chapman does not tell them otherwise. So the readers read the reports and act accordingly. Misinformation is added to ignorance, and the result is harmful."

"What makes you so positive we are disseminating misinformation?"

"Your methods. Do you want me to go into them?"

"Please do."

Paul saw that the tobacco in his own pipe had been burned to white ash. He laid the pipe aside and sipped his chartreuse. He regretted his mission. He would like to have known Dr. Jonas under other circumstances. The conversation, not unfamiliar, might have been stimulating, but now, because of what he had been asked to do, it was little more than a waiting, a prelude to a bribe. Still, he told himself, the work was not only Dr. Chapman's work but his own, his own more than Horace's or Cass's, and it must be protected.

". . . is not strictly controlled, not clinically controlled, and I think that it is wrong," Dr. Jonas was saying.

Paul gathered his wits tightly, trying to deduce what he had missed. Obviously, Dr. Jonas was discussing the interview technique.

"This business of groups volunteering does not give you truly representative subjects," Dr. Jonas continued. "The women who volunteer *want* to talk—"

148

"Is there a better technique?" Paul interrupted. "Would you prefer ringing doorbells or putting advertisements in the paper? Selecting individuals by going through the telephone directory or stopping them on street corners? Or mailing questionnaires that many will not understand or too many easily ignore? The Federal Research Committee approved of our methodological and statistical formula."

Dr. Jonas nodded. "You have had approval. And those other methods are not so accurate as the one you employ. But there are better means of finding truth than the one you use. I am certain of that. I don't want to digress into that now. I prefer to discuss your technique."

"Go ahead."

"Dr. Chapman puts so much dependence upon the representative nature of women's groups and organizations. I think that is suspect. I have a suspicion that the most representative American women do not belong to any formal groups or clubs at all. They are not joiners, and this makes them quite different from the women you interview, and you are not covering any of them. You are not even getting all the members of the organizations."

"Enough. At The Briars, there are 220 married women. Most have volunteered—201, to be exact."

"According to my information, Paul, that is exceptionally high. I believe only nine per cent—nine out of every 100 groups you sample—have volunteered one hundred per cent of their membership."

"Well, yes—"

"I contend that the women in those clubs who don't volunteer are the ones with sexual prejudices and prudery. You get the exhibitionists—I use this in the broadest sense—and the psychologically disturbed women who are eager to talk."

"We make allowances for the type."

"Not enough, Paul, not enough. I'm sure you're acquainted with the work of Abraham H. Maslow at Brandeis. He, too, made a sex study employing female volunteers. But he learned something extremely significant. Nine out of ten of the volunteers were tested and found to be high in self-esteem. They were found to be a special type of woman, aggressive and sure of themselves, and generally these were the ones who were not virgins, who were unconventional in their sex behavior, and who were masturbators. The one out of ten who scored very low in self-esteem, representative of the non-volunteering type, was unsure and inhibited, and she was

149

usually a virgin, conservative, and she did not masturbate. I feel Dr. Chapman is getting too much of the women who esteem themselves highly, and not enough of the other. Then, there's the question of memory error in the interview itself—"

Since Paul had always been troubled by the Maslow study, he decided to ignore it and seized upon the last. "I think I can speak with some personal knowledge about this. Undoubtedly, many women appear determined to withhold the truth, to omit or revise or exaggerate, but when they realize how objective we are, how eager for facts, they usually level with us."

"How can you be sure? Because of your Double Poll?"

Paul did not attempt to hide his astonishment. The Double Poll was an informal, private name given the invaluable papers Dr. Chapman had inherited from the late Dr. Julian Gleed, of Massachusetts. Dr. Gleed had been a nineteen-year-old student at Clark University in September 1909 when the controversial Dr. Sigmund Freud had appeared on his only visit to America. So taken was young Gleed by Freud's *Five Lectures on Psycho-Analysis,* especially by the fourth lecture on sexuality, that he forthwith resolved to become an analyst. Once he began his practice, Dr. Gleed found that he was most fascinated by how differently husbands and wives viewed the same events in their marriages. Soon, Dr. Gleed was making a specialty of accepting only those cases where he could treat both husband and wife, separately, on his couch. In meticulous hand, he kept voluminous records of these couples—two hundred and three married couples in all—and established a percentage of discrepancy, especially in their free association about their sexual behavior.

When Dr. Gleed published a brief summary of his findings in a psychiatric journal, one of his most avid readers was Dr. Chapman, then about to begin his bachelor survey. Dr. Chapman promptly initiated a lengthy correspondence with Dr. Gleed and soon had the old analyst's statistics and the means by which to allow for error in his own future interviews. After Dr. Gleed's death, his papers were willed to Dr. Chapman, who culled from them what more he needed. The Double Poll, as Gleed's papers were privately called, was known only to Dr. Chapman and his associates. It had never been published or publicized. It was kept as a secret measuring stick. Yet, Paul told himself incredulously, here Dr. Jonas seemed to know all about it. Paul speculated on how this was possible. At last, he concluded that Dr. Chapman had disclosed *all* his

150

procedure to the Zollman Foundation, and it had been leaked to Dr. Jonas.

"Yes, the Double Poll, among other checks," Paul heard himself say.

"I'll concede that you can allow for a certain amount of conscious lying. As a matter of fact, it's quite clever of Dr. Chapman. But how can you detect unconscious lying and allow for it?"

"Well—can you be specific?"

"A married woman comes in to see you tomorrow. You ask your set questions. She replies. She means to be honest, and she answers honestly. Or so she believes, and you believe. But memory of events in childhood or adolescence is clouded, faulty, inaccurate. Reported sexual behavior is not always true sexual behavior. Freud made that clear. You are wrestling with a woman's unconscious. She cannot deliver what is hidden from herself, what is repressed and latent. She may relate fantasies as facts, and by now believe them to be true. She may be passing along what analysts call screen memories, recent memories overlaid on old ones, so that the old ones are distorted."

"Our check questions, each differently worded, usually catch this," said Paul.

"I doubt it. She may repeat the same partially false answer a dozen times, to a dozen different questions, because she believes it to be true. Also, she may be blocking out certain events and really be convinced that they never took place. I'm simply saying that the overt, obvious, conscious reply is not enough. It doesn't say enough, and it's often not accurate."

"It's accurate often enough," said Paul doggedly. "What would you suggest? You can't put each volunteer into full analysis."

"I'd trust each one more if she was under amytal narcosis."

Paul shook his head. "My God, Victor, it's tough enough getting three thousand married women to talk sexual behavior without also demanding that they take truth serum. You'd wind up with a handful."

"Perhaps a handful would be better than three thousand," said Dr. Jonas mildly, "if you could count on what they were saying." He rose, sauntered to the window, and closed it. "You know, I've heard out hundreds of married women in my time. I used to be one of the five marriage counselors of the Conciliation Court in Los Angeles. It's a legal thing. If one of the two parties in a divorce wants a hearing, the other must,

151

under subpoena if necessary, show up and talk it out with a counselor. One year, we undertook a thousand cases—kept half of them married. I'm still in marriage counseling on a private basis."

"Do you use amytal narcosis?"

"When I have to. But infrequently. That's not the point. My colleagues and myself aren't digit-hunting like Dr. Chapman. When we take a woman's sex history, we aren't interested only in frequency of intercourse and orgasm. We're concerned with inner emotional degree and gradation more than outer physical sum and amount. That's the crux of it. That's where we most violently differ with Dr. Chapman."

Paul finished his chartreuse and watched as Dr. Jonas circled the room. He reached the desk and half sat on it. He stared down at Paul. "I was just wondering how to go on without annoying you."

"You're not annoying me a bit. I'm sold on what I'm doing. I think Dr. Chapman is a human being, but an important one, and I feel privileged to be associated with him. If I sound a little sophomoric, I'm not. I'm thirty-five, and mature in a half-assed sort of way. If I didn't believe in this, I'd clear out in two minutes. I'd go back to teaching literature or writing books—or something more useful like marriage counseling—if I considered that vocation more valuable. No, you're not annoying me at all. I've heard almost everything you're saying before, but not said as well."

"More chartreuse?"

"No, thanks. The talk is heady enough. As to your remark that we're after physical sum rather than emotional degree, I think you're way off base. That's not the point at all."

"Isn't it? I wonder." Dr. Jonas returned to his chair.

"We're in the business of statistics—not lonelyheart advice."

Dr. Jonas frowned. "By publishing for the layman, you're in both." He held a silver letter opener before his nose, regarded it fixedly, then placed it on the desk blotter. "Your Dr. Chapman is primarily a biologist. As such, he brings his special point of view to the survey. What he is interested in is numbers. I'm not. I'm a psychologist. I want to know about feelings and relationships." He found a magazine on the desk. He opened it, and Paul saw that it was *Encounter*. "I was reading an article by Geoffrey Gorer, the English anthropologist. Witty and profound. He speaks of these sex surveys, one in particular. By the standards of the interviewers he says—" Dr. Jonas sought the quotation, and then, finger on the page, read aloud—" 'Sex becomes a quite meaningless activity, save as a device for physical relaxation—something like a good sneeze, but involving the lower rather than the higher portions of the body. If tensions build up, one either takes a pinch of snuff or a mistress; it doesn't matter which.' " He lowered the magazine. "You can correct me if I'm wrong, but I am not aware that Dr. Chapman has ever used the word *love* in print or speech."

Paul said nothing.

"I'm not badgering you," said Dr. Jonas. "I miss that word. All your diagrams, graphs, tables, are devoted to the physical act—quantity, frequency, how much, how often—yet this doesn't tell these married women a damn thing about love or happiness. This is separating sex from affection, warmth, tenderness, devotion, and I don't think it should. Dr. Chapman, like so many in his field, implies that regular sexual outlet, orgasm, means happiness and health. It doesn't, believe me. So-called normal physical sex can represent love, but it can also express anxiety, fear, vanity, compulsion. I'm saying that using the physical act of sex as a unit of judgment on normality or happiness or health can be all wrong. Physical sex is one part of the whole man or whole woman. It doesn't determine character. Rather, a human being's character determines his or her sexual behavior. Terman put it best. Sexual adjustment in marriage is mostly an expression of the very same factors which enable a man or woman to adjust successfully in any human relationship. Your sex life is the slave of your over-all personality. If you are a sufficiently integrated personality, so that you get along happily in career, socially, and so forth, the odds are you'll get along sexually. If your life is an emotional mess, it may not show up in Dr. Chapman's impressive charts. A woman may have three magnificent orgasms in a week. This is fine, normal, what all must strive for, Dr. Chapman will say. But this woman may still be miserable, wanting in tender love and joy of life."

Paul had been slumping in the plastic-covered chair, long legs outstretched. Now he pulled himself upright. "I won't deny our limitations," he said. "How do you measure love? It's impossible—"

"Then why pretend that measurement of coitus and orgasm is a measurement of love?"

"Dr. Chapman doesn't say that—"

"But since he says no more, people believe it. If a large number of people show up in his digits as performing inter-

153

course three times a week, then he labels it biologically normal. But suppose my wife and I are not physically and psychologically endowed to perform three times a week. Once a week is fine for us. We read these charts and think we are abnormal, and this implies wrong and guilt and invites suffering. I just don't believe that because something is shown to be widespread that it is automatically the right thing and the healthy thing."

"You're reading only one side of the coin," said Paul. "There's another. Turn it over. Obversely, it reads—well, just the opposite of what you've been arguing—that telling everyone certain sex practices are widespread removes the shame and abnormality from them. And I say that this is helpful. It liberates millions from needless repressions and guilts."

"I'm not sure I like that kind of gamble."

"Sometimes it's necessary," said Paul. "You lock yourself up in this pretty bungalow and theorize, but we're out listening to three thousand real women with real sex histories. That's reality. That's the way the world is living. The peddlers of ignorance, of medieval morality, smear us for this. They say we are collectors and purveyors of erotic filth. You have no idea of the resistance we meet. They put Dr. Chapman with D. H. Lawrence, and Rabelais, and De Sade, and Henry Miller. But that's not the worst of it. While we're locked in battle with these roundheads, we have at our rear the special eggheads, the lint pickers and pinhead tabulators, the intellectual critics." He held up his hand. "I'm not saying you are among them, though to all intents you might as well be. But despite this, while our arms and strategy and banners may not be perfect, we go on fighting, because we know the cause, and we know we are needed. Perhaps our means to the end is wrong. Perhaps the end does not justify the means. Well— perhaps. But we are fighting, because we know someone must win a more tolerant morality and a new climate for sex—and since someone isn't doing it, now, right now, then we must."

Paul halted, breathless. Momentarily embarrassed by his outburst, he sought his pipe. Dr. Jonas smiled. "You're all right," he said.

"As I told you, I believe in this."

"Maybe I've been a little rough on you. I don't mean it personally—"

"Christ, you don't have to apologize to me."

". . . but, you see, I *don't* believe in this. When we spoke on the phone, you said we had the same goal, so let's talk.

154

Well, yes, that I believe. The same goal. You know, Paul, prattling on about tolerance and wisdom and better life used to be the province of radical or liberal boys, the very young. Now, I think it's time for the men to take over, do the boys' work. I'm sick of idealism being related to puberty. I think the business of idealism belongs to tough, sophisticated, mature grown men. I want to confine puritanism behind a small iron fence, as you do, make it a curiosity and symbol of the dead past, like Plymouth Rock. I want men and women finally free and unafraid. They must be led out of bondage to that better place. Yes, we are in full accord about that. The question is: Which road will take us swiftly and surely to that place? I have an idea, and I don't think it is Dr. Chapman's road."

Paul was suddenly conscious of his assignment. "But we're going in the same direction. That's the important thing. I'm sure Dr. Chapman would appreciate your criticisms—"

"I doubt it."

"The survey is his entire life. He's always trying to improve it. He's a pure scientist." Paul hesitated, aware of the skepticism in Dr. Jonas' face. "You don't believe me?"

"Well—"

"You seem unreasonably hostile to him."

"Because, in my opinion, he is not a pure scientist. He is as much, if not more, a publicist and politician. Those strains degrade the breed, the purity."

Fleetingly, Paul remembered the conversation on the train, when Dr. Chapman had defended the Scientist as Politician. He considered paraphrasing Dr. Chapman's explanation of the necessity, but then he thought better of it.

"I think," Dr. Jonas was saying, "you make the mistake, Paul, of mixing your own identity with Dr. Chapman's. You are devoted to truth. And you can see how I might be useful. But Dr. Chapman, I am sure, is not you, far from you."

"We're not that unlike."

"You may not want to be, but I have a hunch you are. However, that's neither here nor there."

"But it is. I'd very much like to get you together with Dr. Chapman. Let you see for yourself."

Dr. Jonas eyed Paul curiously. "Is that why you are here?"

"Not exactly," Paul said too quickly.

Dr. Jonas studied the blotter on his desk a moment. His fingers fiddled with a small clay ash tray in the shape of a sombrero. When he looked up, his voice was gentle. "Well, before we find out *exactly* why you are here, you might want to hear me out a few more minutes. I have a little more to say about your survey. My sense of completeness would be frustrated if I did not finish. I would keep thinking at night what I should have told you."

"By all means," said Paul, relieved.

"From the outset of your investigation, I noticed, Dr. Chapman, like several others before him, seemed to choose the orgasm as his unit of measurement. At first, I saw nothing wrong with that. It was something to start with. And, as you have remarked, how can one measure love? All right, then—the orgasm—but what alarmed me, what I now deplore, is the ill usage of his findings in the bachelor survey, and the dangers inherent in publishing the married female survey. Of course, Dr. Chapman is a biologist, so I can understand his affection for sub-human animals. I was not surprised when he quoted Edward Elkan, writing in that Bombay sexology journal, as stating that no female animals, except some bony fish and the swan, ever have orgasms. Nor was I surprised when Dr. Chapman reported that the average male primate indulges in sex as a reflex action, that he has his orgasm seventeen seconds after intromission, just long enough for the species to survive. But when he related this latter information to the revelation that the average single male interviewed reaches orgasm in one hundred and nineteen seconds—less than two minutes—I was disturbed."

"Why should you be? It's a fact."

"Your fact. Others have different facts. Dickinson found the average to be closer to five minutes; Kinsey found the average to be between two and three minutes. But let's say it *is* a fact. I don't object to that. What I object to is that by implication Dr. Chapman condones the fact—says brief duration of intercourse is right and good, because it is widespread and therefore normal. I'm not sure it is right and good—I speak of marital relations—and neither are most psychiatrists sure it is right and good. What is natural and easiest for the male as an animal may not be suitable to the condition of marriage that he has invented. I wouldn't be surprised if many men took this as license to abandon control."

"I can't believe that, Victor, not while women—and this I have heard from them—relate potency and virility to prolonged intercourse. And don't forget Hamilton's findings. He asked his women, 'Do you believe that your husband's orgasms occur too quickly for your own pleasure?' and forty-eight per cent answered yes, in one form or another. Most men sense this or understand it."

"Well, maybe. Mind you, I'm not saying rapid ejaculation is always wrong. An excited, erotic response can be good, if it does not stem from hostility. And often, of course, a female may be pathologically retarded in her response, and then there is no need for the male to indulge in unnatural masochism. But generally, this is not the case. And I think Dr. Chapman's use of his figures on male orgasm have been harmful. Furthermore, I don't like the way he separates orgasm from emotion. In your tables, each orgasm represents a single numeral, no more, no less, no different from any other. But don't tell me an orgasm with a streetwalker is the very same as orgasm with a pretty virgin you have married. Or that orgasm attained in harried seconds on a public stairway is the same as one attained during a leisurely vacation in a mountain hide-out. Even worse, to Dr. Chapman, that numeral on orgasm is the end of the sexual relationship."

"Isn't it?"

"For the male, technically, yes. But you've just been talking to some thousands of females. For many of them, it may not be an end but a beginning. What about procreation—pregnancy, childbirth, motherhood?"

"You're right, of course," said Paul. "I'm sure Dr. Chapman understands that. It'll be clear when the new work is written."

"I see no evidence of it in what I've read to date. You may think, Paul, I've drifted far afield. But I don't believe so. You throw a lot of cold figures out to men and women who are deeply concerned. They read them, or misread them, or are misled by what they read, and they're no higher from hell than when they started. I was going over Dr. Chapman's female pie graphs last night, and I was appalled at some of the master's sketchy and dogmatic comments to the Zollman people. In graph after graph, he seemed to be saying that women who enjoy orgasms frequently are certain to have happy marriages, as if that was all there was to love. I'm more inclined to plump with Dr. Edmund Bergler and Dr. William S. Kroger. Remember what they wrote? 'If a woman typically experiences orgasm in a series of clandestine relationships, but is cold in marriage, her orgasm is not proof of health but of neurosis.' There are a hundred authorities who believe orgasms are not so closely related to marital success as Dr. Chapman would suppose. I really worry that Dr. Chapman's undigested nonsense can do infinite damage."

157

"I think it's a pity you saw this new material before Dr. Chapman could study and edit it."

Dr. Jonas pinched the point of his hooked nose. "I only read it because Dr. Chapman saw fit to submit it to the Zollman Foundation. And that's one more point I wish to make. Do you mind?"

"Please—"

"Your boss is too impatient, too much the man in a hurry. Fretfulness, haste, may be estimable qualities in a promoter, but they work to the detriment of a scientist. Don't think me pompous or stuffy about this. I'm really concerned. If you must excuse or qualify what you have written, then don't submit it to be read. I'm referring not only to the latest findings he gave the Zollman directors but the books he has and will submit to his profession and the lay public. And even his pronouncements in the press—I read that big interview he gave when he arrived here—all about men and women having different attitudes toward the sexual act. It's taken him a long time to learn what Lord Byron knew by instinct in 1819— 'Man's love is of man's life a thing apart/'Tis woman's whole existence.'"

"Which Madame de Staël discovered a quarter of a century before Byron," Paul could not resist saying. "'Love is the whole history of a woman's life; it is only an episode in man's.' Perfectly true. But few people ever believed what Byron or Madame de Staël wrote. Now, Dr. Chapman is proving it statistically. Why shouldn't he tell the press about it? It'll certainly give more mutual understanding of love to married couples."

"Will it? The mere statistics of it—that men and women are different? I think not. Because it doesn't tell the whole truth. And either Dr. Chapman knows this and won't face it, or he simply doesn't know it—and in either case, he shouldn't go to the public with it yet. This very fact that men and women are different proves a serious error in the survey itself. Dr. Chapman's graphs show how many times a woman has sexually complied to her mate's demands, but the graphs don't show how she *felt* about complying. Which is a truer fact about a woman's love—that she agreed to copulate with her husband last night? Or that she felt a certain way about doing it before, during, and after? Remember this, Paul, a man must have desire to become one of Dr. Chapman's statistics, but a woman may become a statistic without any desire at all. More often than not, I believe, a woman will want her husband because he has been sweet and thoughtful and devoted to her the entire day, and the night's physical act of love becomes a culmination of all the other facets of love throughout the day. I think it is this, rather than an aching and demanding sexual organ, that puts a female happily into bed. With a man, it is quite the opposite. He is in bed largely because of his organ. I'm only saying Dr. Chapman's splashy interview did not explain this important difference."

"He pointed out plainly that woman's needs differ from man's," Paul interrupted doggedly.

"Not enough. He's only saying that men and women face each other on two different levels. That's disheartening to know, when you leave it that way. But if your statistics also included women's feelings and requirements—and he then told them to the press—it might do a lot of good. But here again, he's not interested in the essential, only in numbers that can be translated into headlines. If he were not so rushed to win publicity and money—"

"He doesn't keep a red cent of his earnings."

"I know that," Dr. Jonas said brusquely. "I mean money for his damn project—and I'm not sure this is all so selfless—anyway, if he weren't so rushed, he could get into his investigations with more depth. The whole atmosphere of superficiality is distressing."

"One has to set boundaries."

"Yes, Paul, but as long as you've opened the can of peas partially, open it completely, so that someone may profit by its contents. I'm not trying to harass you with generalities. I know exactly what I mean. Take this married female survey you're winding up. I want more information. And what I want is pertinent. The woman you interview—is she sterile or not? How many children does she have? If she had premarital intercourse, was she ever pregnant? If so, how did this affect her eventual marriage? This woman—was she an only child? If not, did she have an older brother or sister? What are her feelings toward the size of the male genital? What are her feelings toward intimacy during the period of menstruation? Does she prefer twin beds to a double bed? Do contraceptives restrain her response? Is she thinking of a divorce? Has she been in analysis? If she had premarital intercourse, and married her partner, did she do so because coitus was satisfactory, or in spite of the fact that it wasn't or didn't matter?" Abruptly, he stopped. "I could go on for an hour. I won't. The point is, a few of these questions should have been considered."

"How do you know they weren't?"

"I don't. I assume—based on what I perceive of Dr. Chapman's character, ambitions, aims, and previous charts." He stared at Paul a moment. "You still think Dr. Chapman would like to talk to me?"

"I know that he would."

"Why?" Before Paul could speak, Dr. Jonas spread his hands as a baseball umpire does in calling a safe play. "No prepared platitudes, Paul—and no double-talk about how the great white father always wants to improve. Just tell me the real reason he would want to see me—and why he sent you here?"

Paul felt his cheeks tighten and their color change. He sat unmoving, trying to determine his reply. Should he play Dr. Chapman's game of pretense? Surely, Dr. Jonas would find it obvious. Or should he cast aside pretense and frankly state the truth? Possibly, Dr. Jonas would be antagonized. In either instance, Paul realized, Dr. Jonas' reaction would be negative.

Through the evening, he was now aware, he had been carefully watching to detect that one crack in his host's armor. In every man, there was this crack, sometimes hardly visible, but there nonetheless. Once detected, it could often be opened wider and breached, no matter what the initial resistance, by a concerted attack on insecurity or aspiration. But Paul had been unable to find the crack in his host's integrity. Perhaps there was none. This possibility was disquieting. For all the man's bull-headed, wrong-headed opposition, Paul wanted his respect. Usually, he did not care. But this time it mattered. To repeat the contrived story would involve a calculated risk. It might reveal the crack, and Dr. Chapman would win, and he, Paul, would gain. More likely, it would reveal nothing and serve only to earn Dr. Jonas' contempt. Paul wanted neither the victory nor the defeat.

Dr. Jonas, arms crossed on his chest, corncob smoking, balanced on his swivel chair, waiting.

Paul stirred. "I'll tell you what he wanted me to talk to you about. He wants you on his team as a consultant, under contract, at half more than you're earning today."

Dr. Jonas' voice was hardly audible. "The Zollman Foundation?"

"Yes."

"He wants to buy me out?"

Paul hesitated. "Yes."

"Why are you telling me this?"

Paul shrugged. "Because if you can be bought out, you will be. And if you can't be, I've retained your friendship."

Dr. Jonas continued to teeter on the swivel chair. The only sound in the room was the squeak of its unoiled spring. That, and for Paul, his own heart. He watched and waited. The crack. Would it show?

There was a knock on the door.

Dr. Jonas looked off. "Yes?"

The door opened slightly, and Peggy's freckled face poked into the room. She glanced from one to the other. "No cuts or bruises? No knockdowns?"

"No," said Dr. Jonas.

"Well, now, you've both had enough. I've got a snack on the table. Victor, you bring your guest in before he faints from undernourishment."

"All right, dear."

Peggy's head disappeared. Dr. Jonas rose to his feet, and Paul stood up. They went through the bungalow door into the yard. The fog was thicker now. Great flaxen curls of vapor obscured the moon. The wet yard was dark except for the light from the kitchen door. Both men entered the corridor of yellow light on the grass.

Dr. Jonas took Paul's arm. Paul turned his head, and he saw that Dr. Jonas was smiling. "Let's put it this way, Paul," he said. "Let's say, you've retained my friendship."

Efficiently, Peggy Jonas cleared the dining-room table of the plates and the large platter that still held a third of the warm pizza pie. Paul and Dr. Jonas ate their Danish rolls and drank their coffee.

Not once during the time at the table had Paul or Dr. Jonas returned to their discussion of the survey. The conversation had been inconsequential and pleasant. Peggy, with a wonderful gift for mimicry, had synopsized the old motion picture that she had seen on television. Dr. Jonas spoke of the bull fights the entire family had recently witnessed in Tia Juana, and each of them had a theory about the cult that had adopted the sport in the United States, agreeing only that there was a certain snobbery involved, like proudly parading the first name of some slob of a bartender. Paul spoke of a vacation that he had once enjoyed, during the period when he had taught at the private girls' school in Berne, with the remarkable Basques in and about San Sebastián.

When the coffee was served, Dr. Jonas asked Paul if he ever intended to write again—the only allusion to any part of their talk in the rear bungalow—and Paul told him of the Sir Richard Burton literary biography begun some years before and abandoned for the collaboration on *A Sex Study of the American Bachelor*.

Now, as Peggy went into the kitchen, Dr. Jonas said, "I wonder if you've heard any rumors about the new clinic a group of us are opening in Santa Monica?"

"No, I haven't."

"Quite interesting," said Dr. Jonas. "What I'm telling you is confidential, until the project is announced shortly. The building is under construction right now, a beautiful spot overlooking the ocean. It's going to be used to mend sickly and broken marriages, just as the Menninger Clinic treats mental health."

Paul was intrigued. "What will you do there?"

"Well, I'm going to head it up. We'll have a large staff of psychiatrically oriented marriage counselers. We'll circularize the entire country, eventually. Minimum fees for help, treatment, care. It's nonprofit. We have endowments. Then, besides the actual face-to-face work, we will undertake a broad program of education." He smiled. "This is the road I'm taking—to the goal we talked about."

"It sounds too good to be true—for what it is. When do you kick off?"

"In about four months. When the building is ready. We have our staff almost organized. There are still a few key openings." He glanced keenly at Paul. "You made me an offer. Now I'd like to return the favor. Only this isn't to buy you out. It's to reform you. More important, we can use you."

"I'm damn flattered—really."

"Are you interested?" Dr. Jonas waited, then added, "And you'd still find time for travel—and Sir Richard Burton."

Paul entertained the vision briefly: solid and useful man's work on the island of Southern California, and with time to go off and write. Yet, much as he liked the vision and the person who was creating it, the stigma of treason and traitor was stamped across the fancy. This was the rival camp. He was treating with his leader's enemy, a benevolent and enlightened enemy, but an enemy. Moreover, Dr. Chapman had conjured up a vision also: the shining academy in the East, devoted to sexual behavior, international in scope, bathed in wealth and fame, and himself the second in command. Dr. Chapman had not failed him yet, and he would not fail Dr. Chapman now.

"As I said, Victor, I'm flattered," he heard himself saying.

162

"But I just couldn't. Dr. Chapman has been a good friend, and generous. I'm devoted to him. More important, I believe in him."

Dr. Jonas nodded. "Okay. My loss. Let's not worry it."

Paul consulted his watch. "I didn't know it was this late. Five more minutes and you'll be charging me rent." He pushed away from the table. "I've got to be on deck at nine tomorrow morning."

"How long will this last sample run?"

"About two weeks."

Dr. Jonas pursed his lips. "I sometimes think about those interviews of yours—"

"In what way?"

"Publication of the report is the ultimate harm—I mean, the permissive effect your data has, the sudden undermining of long-taught ideas about right and wrong, making wrong things right, because they prevail. That's the ultimate harm. But those interviews tomorrow—" He shook his head slowly. "It's all extremely clinical, like an X-ray technician busily at work."

"Not quite. Those women come in to see you. Sick or well, most have everything in order, properly in place, properly repressed, properly forgotten, and they function. And then you start hammering those questions. Each is a shaft, hurtled into a dark place, churning, overturning, impaling a fear. All order disappears. Like atoms triggered and bumping in wild chaos. You've started an uncontrolled chain of unwholesome and noxious forces. And you don't follow through, stay with the subjects, help them put everything in place again, in an orderly if different fashion. You set off the chain reaction and then let the women go, and I sometimes wonder, Go where, to what? What are they like afterward, what becomes of them?"

Paul was on his feet. "I'm sure it's not so bad as all that."

"I hope not," said Dr. Jonas without conviction.

And what bothered Paul most, that one moment, was that he was without conviction either.

6

IT HAD BEEN a long morning, Dr. Chapman reflected as he chewed the last of the corned-beef sandwich and sipped the lukewarm coffee in the paper cup.

He sat at the head of the polished table, in the upstairs conference room of The Briars' Women's Association, and Paul and Horace sat to his right, and Cass to his left, all finishing the sandwiches Benita had brought in for them.

Dr. Chapman watched Paul, who was reading the sports page of a Los Angeles morning paper as he ate, and he wondered exactly what had transpired between Paul and Dr. Victor Jonas.

Dr. Chapman had waited up an hour past his usual bedtime, the night before, to hear from Paul, but near midnight, dozing off in the motel chair, he had finally given up and gone to bed. In the morning, they were all together before breakfast, and he had not wished to question Paul in front of the others. Going to their cars, he had touched Paul's elbow, and they had fallen behind and were momentarily alone. He had inquired, in an undertone, about Dr. Jonas, and Paul had shaken his head and said he did not think there was much hope there. Benita, arms filled with folders, had dashed in and interrupted, and Paul had promised to give a full account after dinner.

They had arrived at the Association building around half past eight. The rooms, prepared the day before, were ready, and between ten minutes to nine and nine o'clock when the first three women arrived, Paul, Horace, and Cass had been in their respective sound-proof offices, waiting.

The results of the morning's sampling were beside Dr. Chapman's paper plate. Six lengthy questionnaires with the Solresol answers penciled in, so that each page appeared to have been sprinkled with alphabet soup and shorthand symbols. Crumpling his napkin, Dr. Chapman dropped it on his plate and

164

picked up the half-dozen sheets. The completeness of them, the solidity of these sex histories, always reassured him. They gave him a feeling of accomplishment, of going ahead, of adding to the world's knowledge. Often, at moments like this, the word *immortality* danced inside his head, and that gave him pleasure and, at last, displeasure (for his life was dedicated to the common weal, and personal vanity was too petty), and always he pushed it from his mind.

He scanned the top questionnaire and went slowly through the others, interpreting the foreign language known only to the four. The answers were the customary ones, although here and there a reply arrested his attention. After several minutes, Dr. Chapman placed the questionnaire beside his plate again. "Very good," he said. "No discards." He glanced at his watch. It was seven minutes before one o'clock. "Well, gentlemen, back to your stations. The women'll be here any minute."

Wearily, Cass rubbed his forehead. "Damn migraine," he complained.

"Less than two weeks to go," said Horace. "Just think of those poor analysts."

Paul pushed back his chair. "It hasn't been so bad. We may even miss it when we're done."

"Speak for wourself," said Cass. "I wasn't built for life in a gynecocracy."

They started for the door.

Somewhat winded, Ursula Palmer reached the top of the staircase. She leaned against the wall to catch her breath. Her gold wrist watch told her it was a minute before one o'clock.

All the way from her house to Romola Place she had been thinking of Bertram Foster's exciting offer. Fantasy had crowded fantasy: *Time*—"the miracle drug that has revived *Houseday* and doubled its circulation is California-born Ursula Palmer, a classical beauty with a salary of $100,000 annually"; *Vogue*—"U. Palmer, far and away the woman of the year"; Winchell—"Ursula P., hear tell, has taken over a palatial Bucks manse"; Mike Wallace—"and next week we have a real treat for you"; *New Yorker's* Talk of the Town—"decided to drop in on the cocktail party, and we had to push through layers of celebrities paying homage to the sacred object, Truman Capote, Jean Kerr, John Houston, Dean Acheson, Cole Porter, Leland Hayward, Fanny Holtzmann, the Duchess of Windsor, to find at last, behind her desk, champagne goblet in hand, that striking, brittle female publisher who . . ." Not until Ursula entered the cool Association building did she remind herself that it had not happened yet, but that it would and could if she kept her eyes and ears open and recorded the story properly.

Now, composing herself, she felt a guilt pang at not having told Harold of Foster's offer. She had instinctively avoided revealing the news, because it might create a scene. Occasionally, and in no predictable manner, Harold would redden in anger and stiffen and be disagreeable. His infrequent obeisance to Manhood. She could face such a scene, should it occur, and win, but she wanted no showdown over something that was not yet a reality. Once this interview was over, and she gave Foster her notes, she was sure that it would be settled. Foster's childish eagerness to see the unadorned notes irked her only briefly. It was little enough, she decided. Look at all those famous actresses. At one time or another, they had been forced to display more than notes of their sex lives.

The thought of notes reminded her of her job. She opened her purse, took out the small pad—two pages already filled with "a suburban housewife's" feeling on the morning of The Interview—and then located the pencil. Hastily, she wrote: "Wore lace silk blouse, powder-blue skirt, because felt consciously feminine, like schoolgirl first date; left house twenty minutes nine, arrived minute early; thoughts: never talked sex anyone except husband, not even all him, can I tell to stranger —knees weak as mounted steps." Her knees weren't weak, of course, and her thoughts had not been about the interview but rather about the result of it, but these notes were what *Houseday* readers would expect.

She tucked pad and pencil back into her purse, briskly turned the corner, and proceeded up the corridor. Ahead she could see a pale, angular girl, in a gray suit, waiting behind a desk that had been moved into the corridor.

Ursula reached the desk. "How do you do. Am I late?"

Benita Selby shook her head. "No, the other two women arrived just before you." She inspected an open ledger. "You're Mrs. Ursula Palmer?"

"Yes."

"You'll be in office C, at the end of the hall. The interviewer is ready for you."

Benita Selby placed an ink check after Ursula's name and rose. She started to the rear with Ursula following closely.

"What's the interviewer's name?" asked Ursula.

Benita seemed surprised. No one had ever asked *that* before. "Why, Dr. Horace Van Duesen."

166

"What's his background?"

"He's eminently qualified, I assure you."

"I'm certain of that."

"He's been with Dr. Chapman almost from the beginning. He was on the bachelor survey, too."

"What was his specialty before that?"

"Professor of Obstetrics and Gynecology at Reardon College."

"Good God, deliver me," said Ursula, but Benita did not see the joke.

They had reached the office. Benita opened the door, and Ursula went inside. Ursula remembered the small room, painted aquamarine. It was here that the Association mimeographed its monthly bulletin. A large folding screen, almost six feet in height, its five panels or leaves open, divided much of the room, hiding what was behind. Ursula observed the screen closely. The upper half of each panel, inside the wooden frame, was made up of basket-woven cane, and the lower half of solid walnut. The panels were joined, top to buttom, by piano hinges, obviously to obscure any view through the cracks.

"Your own screen?" Ursula asked Benita.

"Yes. They were designed by Dr. Chapman and custom made for maximum concealment. Dr. Chapman studied choir screens, Georgian screens, even Chinese imperial jade screens, before he decided upon this. He's very thorough, you know."

Ursula nodded, and inspected the dark-brown leather pull-up chair, with wooden arms, that faced the screen, and the table with ceramic ash tray beside it.

"Right here," said Benita, indicating the chair.

Ursula settled herself in the chair, purse in her lap. As she did so, she noticed for the first time a square leather box, small and maroon, at her feet.

She nudged it with a sandal. "What's this?"

"The SE box," said Benita. "Special Exhibits."

At once, Ursula remembered Dr. Chapman's reference to it during the lecture. He had said that there was a category of questions to which the subject replied after reacting to exhibits from the mysterious box. "Oh, well," said Ursula, "as long as nothing jumps out and makes a pass—"

"I assure you—" said Benita, distressed, but then she saw that Ursula had been joking, and she smiled foolishly. Anxious to avoid any further exchange, she went to the screen. "Mrs. Palmer is here, Dr. Van Duesen."

"How do you do, Mrs. Palmer," said the disembodied precise voice from behind the screen.

"Hello, there," replied Ursula cheerfully. She looked up at Benita and whispered, "What's he got back there?"

"He's seated at a card table with several pencils and a questionnaire. Nothing more."

"No special brainwashing equipment?"

"Really, Mrs. Palmer, it's all quite simple."

"May I smoke?"

"Of course," said Benita, and then she added more loudly, "Well, I'll leave you two now."

She went out the door, shutting it softly behind her.

"Just make yourself comfortable," said Horace's voice. "Whenever you're ready—"

"In a few seconds. I'm trying to find a cigarette." She found one in her purse, lighted it, then took out her pad and pencil and held them ready. "Okay," she said, "I'm as ready as I'll ever be."

"Very well," said Horace's voice. "Try to answer all the questions to the best of your ability, and as accurately as possible. Take time to think. And, of course, say as much as you wish to say. If something is not clear to me, I'll let you know. If a question is not clear to you, let me know. And be assured, please, that the answers I mark are put down in Solresol and will be seen by no one except Dr. Chapman and his associates."

"I have a poor memory," she lied, "so you'll have to give me a little time." She had to allow for her note-taking. Quickly, she began to jot down her interviewer's name and background and some of his last speech.

"Of course," said Horace's voice.

"Fire away, Gridley."

There was a moment's silence. Then, evenly, without accenting word or phrase, Horace's voice resumed.

"Your age, please?"

"Must I? Forty-one."

"Your educational background?"

"High school. Two years of junior college. I went no further because I wanted to write. I'm a writer and editor."

"Place of birth?"

"Sioux City, Iowa."

"How long have you lived in California?"

"We moved here when I was three."

"What is your current religious affiliation?"

"Episcopalian."

168

"Would you characterize yourself as a regular churchgoer, an irregular one, or one who seldom or never attends?"

"Umm . . . I'd say—make it irregular."

"Irregular?"

"Yes."

"Fine. Now then, your marital status?"

"Meaning what?"

"Are you presently married?"

"Oh, yes."

"Were you married before?"

"Yes. Once. For three months."

"What was your first husband's occupation?"

"He wrote advertising copy when I met him. He intended to become president of the company. He became unemployed instead. He drank, slept, and read want ads through our entire marriage."

"Children?"

"One. Devin. He's all I got out of my first marriage. He's nineteen now. Studying engineering at Purdue in Indiana."

"Oh, yes . . . Have you had children by your present husband?"

"No."

"How long have you been married to this husband?"

"Sixteen years."

"His occupation?"

"Accountant. He just opened his own firm."

"And you say you're a writer and editor? Are you active now?"

"Very much so. I represent a New York magazine out here." She was writing down his questions. Her own answers, she could fill in later.

"Now—" said the voice.

"Would you hold it a moment?"

"Certainly."

She caught up on her notes. "All right."

"We'll begin with a series of questions on your pre-adolescent period. These may be the most difficult for you to remember. You can have all the time you require."

Ursula waited impatiently. Who gives a damn about pre-adolescence? Not Foster, not the public, and not herself. Ursula wanted to skip all preliminaries, reach the provocative part of it, the part that guaranteed a cover line.

"Can you recollect at what age you first masturbated to orgasm?"

Ursula frowned. *This* is for *Houseday?* "Who ever did a thing like that?" she said with forced lightness.

"It's usual in pre-adolescence, between three and thirteen, and not unusual after."

This was ridiculous, even offensive, and at once she remembered *when*. Perhaps it had not been the first time, but it was the time she remembered clearly. There had been company that night, the resonant older voices from the living room, a thin wafer of light shining through the slit of door into her bedroom, and she wide awake in her new polka-dot flannel nightgown. "I was just trying to recall it," she said at last. "I must have been seven or eight—no, make it eight."

"Can you describe the method?"

The half-forgotten memory, now high-lighted by the stark frame of maturity, repelled her. How could this immature trivia be of any use to anyone? Nevertheless, the disembodied voice had disembodied ears, and they were waiting. In a firm, businesslike tone of voice, she described what she had done at eight.

The questions on pre-adolescent behavior went on in this vein for ten minutes, and Ursula found it difficult to hide her impatience. All of this was a waste of precious time, in terms of *Houseday's* million readers, and Ursula's answers became testier and testier. At last, having revealed that she had menstruated at twelve, she was relieved to graduate to premarital petting. She had too few pages of notes, but now she was sure that she would make up the lack.

"How would you define petting?" she heard Horace ask.

This was interesting—it would fascinate mothers *and* daughters who read *Houseday*—and she considered it. "Why, I suppose everything that might arouse you, short of actually doing anything final."

"Yes, but perhaps I had better be more exact."

He defined the component parts of petting. For Ursula, who had never seriously thought about these acts before—at least, not that she could definitely recall—the explicit vocabulary of science made it seem vulgar and unlovely. Nevertheless, she recorded the discussion. Foster must be served. The public, also. Anyway, her typewriter would make it more palatable, sand it down, buff it, varnish it, until the little word Galateas would be acceptable in any family living room.

He was inquiring if she had ever achieved satisfaction through petting.

"You mean the first time?"

"Yes."

"In high school, when I was a senior. I suppose you want to know how old I was? Seventeen. Does that mean I was retarded?"

No comment from the screen on her jocularity. Instead: "What was the method?"

That damn method, again. Curtly, she explained.

"Where was this done?" he asked.

"In his car. We parked in the hills, and got in the back seat. I thought I loved him, but then I changed my mind and—well, we just petted."

There was note-taking on both sides of the screen, and then the questions and answers continued, and, at last, they reached the subject of premarital intimacy.

"Three partners," she was saying.

"Where did these take place?"

"The first two in their apartments. And with the last one in motels."

"Were any one of these the men you finally married?"

"The second affair—he became my first husband."

"But no premarital experience with your present husband?"

"God, no. Harold wouldn't think of doing a thing like that before. The first affair was a college kid, when I was in school. Then—well, my other husband, the one who wrote copy—we were in the same office—it was my first job. The last one was after I had to go back to work—I was his secretary—for a short time."

"Did you reach orgasm on any of these occasions? If so—"

"No," she interrupted.

"During these intimacies, were you partially clothed or in the nude?"

"Nude."

"When did these intimacies most frequently occur—morning, afternoon, evening, night?"

"Well, I suppose you'd call it evening."

"Most often, was an artificial means used to prevent conception?"

"Yes."

"Did your partner use a contraceptive, or did you, or did both of you? Or did your partner practice Noyes' theory of male continence?"

"The men always used contraceptives."

"Now, returning to the actual act, in regard to method—"

Ursula's upper lip was damp: heaven protect the poor working girl. And then she realized that her fingers were gripping

171

the pencil so hard that they seemed bloodless, and that she had not made a single note in five minutes. Desperately, she tried to relax, to remember, to write.

". . . name the one of these most frequently employed by you?"

She named one in a voice strangely not her own. She wrote and, writing, wondered what Bertram Foster would think.

◇ ◇ ◇

When Ursula Palmer emerged into the sunlight of Romola Place at twenty minutes after two, she felt slightly let down and concerned, as she so often felt after sex and almost never after writing. The feeling was something that she could not precisely define. It seemed that there was more to be said that had not been said, though exactly what she could not imagine. The questions had covered every possible experience, and she had replied to all honestly. Yet, now, there was a hangover of an insoluble business uncompleted, and it was bothersome, for she was not sure if it involved the questions about sexual behavior or the behavior itself. The good part of it, of course, was the notes. Toward the end, she had been professional and put everything to paper, and already she could see that—with discretion and imagination—it would write well.

Her original intent had been to hurry home after the interview and transcribe the entire adventure while it was fully alive in her mind. But, at the moment, standing before the building entrance, she suddenly had no desire to relive the interview so quickly. It could wait until evening or tomorrow morning. She felt the need to be outside, among people, and not alone with the notes.

Remembering that she was almost out of stamps, she decided to cross the street to the post office and buy a roll. After that, she would see. There were a dozen household chores she had neglected since Foster's arrival. She crossed the street and was about to climb the concrete steps to the post office when she saw Kathleen Ballard appear at the top of the stairs and descend.

She waited. "Hello, Kathleen."

"Why, Ursula—"

"I was just across the street—delivering a rich and entertaining discourse on What Every Young Girl Gets to Know."

Puzzled, Kathleen looked across the street, then back at

172

Ursula, and then her eyes widened. "You mean you've had your interview already?"

"I had it," said Ursula dryly.

"Oh, I'm dying to hear everything. I don't mean anything private, but what goes on, what they ask—"

"You've come to the right party. You are speaking to a veteran of the Chapman cabal rites."

"They're interviewing me Thursday afternoon. Is it awful?"

Ursula did not want to discuss it, yet she did not want to lose Kathleen. "Let's find someplace to sit," she said. "Do you have time?"

"Deirdre's in dancing class. But I don't have to pick her up until three-thirty."

"Well, then, I'll give you the Palmer Abridged Version, skipping lightly over adolescent sex play and sundries, and concentrating mainly on coitus—yes, my dear, that's the word this season; learn to love it—coitus, marital, extramarital, and sort of marital."

"You mean they actually make you—" Kathleen's eagerness had given way to anxiety.

"They make you do nothing," said Ursula crisply. "We're all volunteers. Remember? Like Major Reed's yellow fever guinea pigs. All right, let's walk over to The Crystal Room. According to my prescription, this should be taken with something on the stomach."

❖   ❖   ❖

Those healthy, dull young women, Cass Miller thought. Slouching beside the card table, one leg crossed over the other, his pencil found the question he had just asked. "Have you ever engaged in premarital intimacies?" His pencil hooked the cypher into the blank square, and the cypher meant, to four of them, "No." This, of course ruled out the next dozen questions.

These young women were all of a type, Cass decided, as he gloomily stared at the long sheet. Coast to coast, it was the same. In the East, the type was small and keen or horsey and well mannered, with dark bangs and big bosoms and legs that were good for lacrosse. They had been to Bennington and Barnard and would marry Ivy League boys, who would later drink too much at lunch, and they merged into Perfect Hostess, Tennis Anyone, Bermuda, and Normal Outlook. In the West the type was well dressed, tall and thin, with tangled boyish hair more sun-bleached than blond, and flat breasts and bony spines and bottoms. They had been to Stanford and Switzerland and would marry intense young professional men, and they merged into Conjugal Partnership, Golf Lessons, Santa Barbara, and Outdoor Living.

He had caught one of the latter. Cass's eyes scanned what was already written. Mrs. Mary Ewing McManus. Twenty-two. University of Southern California. Born in Los Angeles. Lutheran. Regular churchgoer. Presently married. First husband. Two years. Husband an attorney. Housewife.

His gaze continued down the page. Pre-adolescent heterosexual play. Routine. Premarital petting confined to kissing and brief breast contact. Usual. Petting always halted early. And finally, now, premarital intercourse—never. Dull. Dull as dishwater.

Cass knew that the rest was predictable. Nevertheless, the Great White Father and the STC machine must be served. He looked up at the cane folding screen, with little interest in Mrs. Mary Ewing McManus behind it, and resumed in the tired voice that she mistook for scientific objectivity. "Next, we have a series of questions on marital coitus—in short, the sex history of your marriage. What is the frequency of your lovemaking at the present time?"

"Well . . ."

"I know it varies. But can you strike an average per week or month?"

"My husband and I make love on the average of three times a week," said Mary clearly and proudly.

Cass detected the pride. Sardonically amused, he moved his pencil across the page. Children of this class, perhaps the young in general, were always proud of their frequency ratio, their vigor, their tireless acrobatics, as if they had discovered sex and planted a flag upon it and owned it exclusively. In twenty years, it would be once a week, if that, and she would wonder why her husband always had to work late nights, and she would take to heavier make-up and thinner dresses and a querulous note and wish that her husband's new young business partner would be more attentive to her.

"Do you engage in petting before intercourse?" asked Cass.

"Oh, yes."

"Can you describe what you do?"

"I . . . I don't know—I mean, it's hard to explain."

Nevertheless, hesitantly, but with Cass's encouragement, she described the preliminaries of love. Left breathless at the

174

daring discussion of it, she was relieved that further necessity for exposition was done.

But no sooner had Mary relaxed than she was intimidated by a new series of queries on the act of marital love itself.

"I don't know exactly," she found herself saying. "A couple of times we timed it, just for fun."

"Well, how long did it take?"

"Once, three or four minutes, and then five minutes—about five minutes—and, the other time, the last I looked, it was almost ten minutes, but then I forgot to look again—maybe it was eleven or twelve minutes."

"Can you guess at an average?"

"Five minutes."

Steadily, Cass translated to symbols the mingled shy and boastful details of young love.

Often, in his mind, he mocked the naïveté of her worldliness, and several times he suffered the emotion of grudging envy.

"During the act of love, does it arouse you to watch your husband?" he asked.

"I don't watch."

"But when you do?"

"It makes me happy, yes."

Automatically, Cass recorded the replies, glancing down the remainder of the page and estimating that it would be fifteen minutes more and that they would be done at three-forty-five. He wondered if he could hurry it. He had the pressure and throb over his right temple, the usual prelude to migraine, and he wanted to lie down for ten minutes before the next interview at four o'clock. Well, what was left? The series of questions on extramarital experiences. Then the short second category on psychological attitudes. And, finally, the third category on reactions to sex stimuli. He was tempted to omit most of what remained. He could accurately forecast her answers. Several times recently he had been so tempted. But again, as before, remembering Dr. Chapman's persistent warning that all standard questions be read fully, he repressed the notion. Instead, for variety, he decided to skip to the third category and return to the rest later.

He found the place on the page.

"Do you see the maroon box at your feet?"

"Yes."

"Open it. Take out the first photograph on top. Study it for a moment."

He heard her fumble with the lid, then remove the photograph. He heard her strained silence.

"What do you see? I want to be sure you have the right one."

"It's a . . . a picture of a classical statue—Greek, I suppose."

"A nude adult male and rather handsome," added Cass. "Is that right?"

"Yes."

"The Hermes of Praxiteles. Now to the question. Does observation of the nude male in that photograph arouse you at all?" Inevitably, the statistical summary to date came to mind. "Four per cent are strongly aroused, eleven per cent only somewhat, and eighty-five per cent not at all." Her answer would be no.

"No," said Mary through the screen.

But Cass had already marked the answer before hearing it, and, stifling a yawn with the back of his hand, wishing he were free to take something for his head, he moved the pencil point down to the next question.

⋄ ⋄ ⋄

When Mary McManus arrived at the parking lot, hardly aware of walking the block from the Association building, she found the new Nash Rambler that was her father's anniversary gift and settled herself behind the wheel. She made no effort to turn the ignition key. She sat, holding the wheel with both hands, trying to sort out her emotions.

As in her attendance of Dr. Chapman's lecture, which had disappointed, she had expected something practical and useful for herself from the interview, and now realized that again she was disappointed. The past hour and five minutes had been far different from what she had anticipated. Her two years of marriage to Norman, in every respect normal if one believed those marriage manuals, had convinced her that she was sexually sophisticated. But now she saw that her father had been right (as ever). The interview, with questions bold, intimidating, and generally startling, had been an unexpected ordeal.

Yet, reviewing it, she could not find a single inquiry that had been either improper or salacious. Nor had she been interrogated about a single matter that she had not, at some time, personally experienced or heard about or read about. Until this afternoon, the act of love had been the most natural thing

176

on earth. But the persistent and detailed questions about every aspect of it—foreplay, position, those proddings about the climax—behavior she had never before dwelt upon—seemed to inflate the natural act beyond previous proportions.

Now, thinking it through, beyond the spinning bewilderment, she began to see that her sexual life with Norman—how much she adored him! how special he was!—was not merely one more gift of growing up, one more activity appended to the threesome that had so long been father, mother, daughter, the Ewing family. Rather, it was an act of serious importance that stood alone and concerned only the husband and wife, the McManus family. It seemed to be the one pleasure that was peculiarly her own, that could not be superimposed upon her previous existence. For the first time, she understood that the intimacy she shared and enjoyed with Norman, suddenly so complicated and unique, had no relationship to the old family or the old way but was part of a new family and a new way that cleaved her sharply from the recent past.

Until this moment, nothing else had been entirely her own. The steering wheel beneath her hands, the miniature sedan that coolly enclosed her, were cords binding her to the safe, dependent, ancient life, as did her features, her blood, her memories. When Norman had wanted to purchase the used Buick on payments, her father had ridiculed the idea and generously surprised them with the new Nash. Her father had given Norman a ready-made career, future unlimited, and saved him and both of them the inevitable struggle that would have resulted had Norman plunged headlong into that romantic partnership with Chris Shearer. And the whole mature concept of remaining unburdened by children, until they were older, saner, more secure, had been the fruits of her father's wisdom. Yes, everything, it seemed, was tied to what she had been, was still part of, except the answers she had given to questions in that room of the Association building.

She reached for the dashboard and turned the key. The motor caught at once and hummed quietly. Even before the interview she had planned to visit her father afterward. She had felt guilty and unhappy in siding with Norman against him, in rebelling against his proved judgment by submitting to the interview. She had felt that the least she could do would be to heal the hurt. After the interview, she had told herself earlier, she would casually drop in on him at the plant, as she had so often before, and then father and daughter would chat of many things, in the old familiar way, not mentioning the interview but both tacitly understanding that she owed something to Norman's authority although still (as evident) her father's daughter.

But when she wheeled the small sedan out of the lot and drove down Romola Place to Sunset Boulevard, she knew that part of her plan, the most essential part, had been changed.

Inexplicably, her need was for Norman this moment, not for her father. She must find Norman, her poor darling, and go into his arms, and tell him how much she loved him.

She steered off the Sunset ramp onto the freeway, proceeding in the slow lane, behind trucks, until the freeway merged with Sepulveda. Riding south, past the International Airport, she presently made out the towering sign in the distance that read *Ewing Manufacturing Company*. After parking in the executive section, she hastened, in long strides, toward the imposing entrance and left behind the sticky outer air for the chilled interior of the plant's main corridor.

She was hurrying up the corridor toward Norman's office, in the wing behind her father's suite, when she saw Miss Damerel emerge from the ladies' room. Miss Damerel, whose hair was iron gray and severely shingled, whose suits were iron gray and sharply cut, was Harry Ewing's private secretary and had been such for more than twenty years.

"Why, Mary," Miss Damerel called out, "it's so nice you could drop by. Your father will be pleased to see you."

For a split second, Mary's step faltered, the stimulus of an elder's voice imposing upon her Pavlov's conditioned reflex, and then, with an effort of will greater than she realized that she possessed, she nodded and blindly hurried on. She knew that Miss Damerel was watching her, surprised and disapproving. She also knew that Miss Damerel would tell her father. But today Mary McManus did not care. She did not care at all.

❖   ❖   ❖

At night, Villa Neapolis was illuminated by rows of blue and yellow lights shining from the roofs of the terraces on two levels, and by four hooded white floodlights projected from steel poles at the corners of the swimming pool. Seen at a distance, because the motel was on a hill against an arch of blue-black sky, the dots of colored light appeared to be a galaxy of artificial stars in a man-made firmament. But up near, from the vantage point of the pool, the effect was quite different. It was like setting up housekeeping under a mammoth Christmas tree, Paul Radford decided, as he came out of the shadowed dining room into the blaze of rainbow colors.

He had been preceded into the patio by Benita Selby, who had changed for dinner and was wearing a lilac Orlon sweater, new, over a sleeveless pale blue dress, old, and he was followed by Dr. Chapman, lighting his cigar, and Horace and Cass.

By mutual agreement, they had dined late, meeting at eight-thirty and eating at two tables joined together and lighted by four candles. The first day of interviewing had been, as it usually was in every new community, completely enervating, and this, combined with a constant sensibility of Dr. Chapman's dictum that the day's interviews not be gossiped about in his presence, reduced sociability to sporadic small talk and prolonged gaps of silence.

Once they were in the patio again, Cass wondered aloud if the two rented automobiles were spoken for. Benita said that she had to catch up on her journal and then write a letter. This same letter she wrote five nights a week to her invalid mother in Beloit, Wisconsin. Horace thought that he might want one of the cars. There was a movie in Westwood that he wished to see. Dr. Chapman told Cass that he could have the other car, since he and Paul were going to finish some work.

After Horace and Cass had gone off to the garages, and Benita had returned to her room, Dr. Chapman led Paul to a pair of wicker chairs near the hibiscus bushes at the far end of the pool. The patio was relatively quiet now, except for the two couples playing a vocal game of gin rummy behind the diving board. But now they were far enough away so that the card players' groans and hilarity were indistinct.

Dr. Chapman loosened his leather belt, rolling his cigar from one corner of his mouth to the other, and Paul filled his briar pipe and lighted it.

"Well, I've been waiting to hear about you and Victor Jonas," said Dr. Chapman. "All I got from you this morning was that there wasn't much hope." He searched Paul's face. "Does that mean some hope or no hope?"

"No hope," said Paul flatly and unmistakably.

Dr. Chapman grunted. "I see," he said. He stared down at the flagstone, thinking. At last, he said, "Tell me what happened."

Paul told him the events of the previous evening concisely and bluntly. He described Dr. Jonas, his wife, his sons, his house. He repeated parts of the early conversation in the rear

179

bungalow, the parts where Dr. Jonas had deduced that Paul had been sent to do Dr. Chapman's "dirty work," and where Paul had defended Dr. Chapman's honesty, omitting only Dr. Jonas' remark that he was glad Paul had come alone. Then Paul related how he had been taken fully off guard by Dr. Jonas' knowledge of the work in progress.

Dr. Chapman's head lifted up and his eyes narrowed. "How can he know what we're doing?"

"That's exactly what I asked him. He said you were filing carbons of your female findings with the Zollman Foundation—"

Paul halted, and waited for an explanation. Dr. Chapman met his gaze frankly. "Yes, that's true. They're meeting before our report will be ready, and I decided it would be in our favor to keep them up to scratch."

"But the work's not ready—it's raw."

"They're not children. There are scientists in the Foundation. They know how to read and project unfinished data. I'm sure it'll serve us."

"Then it's serving Jonas, too. The minority group at Zollman who hired him—they sent him photostats—"

"Bastards," said Dr. Chapman. "They'll do anything." He was livid. Paul could not remember ever seeing him this way before.

"I suppose all is fair—"

"The hell it is," said Dr. Chapman. "What did he say about the new material?"

"He was very frank about that and about the bachelor survey. He put all his cards on the table—or most of them."

"Like what?"

Paul summarized Dr. Jonas' objections, recounting all that he could now recall, except Dr. Jonas' remarks that Dr. Chapman was too much a politician and publicist to be a pure scientist. When Paul had finished, he saw that Dr. Chapman was chewing his cold cigar bitterly.

"I hope you didn't take all this lying down," said Dr. Chapman.

"It was give and take. He hits hard, but I counter-punched. He never conceded that we were right, but I think he knows now that we are sincere."

"Well, it's more than I can say about that bloodsucker. There's a whole tribe of them in this country—every country —ineffectual mental cripples, without imagination or guts, werewolfs lying in wait to pick up the leavings or lap up the

180

blood of the pioneers, innovators, scientists with vision who march ahead of the pack. They have nothing to build, so they tear down. It's their way to stay alive. What has Jonas ever done except scavenge?"

Paul did not disagree with Dr. Chapman. He had accurately characterized a certain breed of scientist, the calumniators who lay in wait and prey upon the investigators. But, despite his respect for his mentor's insight, Paul secretly did not feel Dr. Jonas was one of these. There was that new marriage-counseling clinic that was going up in Santa Monica. Dr. Jonas had even offered him a job. He knew that he could not mention the job, but he was tempted to mention the clinic, until he remembered that it had been told to him in confidence.

"He insists that he has the same goal that we have," said Paul obliquely.

"Blasphemy, if I ever heard it," said Dr. Chapman. "I hope you called him on that."

"No, I didn't. There was no reason to call him a liar. I think he means what he says—that we have a common goal—but different approaches."

"What constructive approach has that sniping pygmy got?"

"He's been in marriage counseling for years—"

"Paul, are you out of your mind? That's microscopic, individual work, the work of a country doctor, no more, no less. Beside him, all like him, our program and accomplishments are Herculean. We're out to help *everyone*, the nation, the wide world, and we're doing it at great sacrifice, and we'll do more, far more, if a minor Judas like Jonas doesn't ambush us when our backs are turned." He studied Paul closely a moment. "He hasn't sold you a bill of goods, has he?"

Paul laughed. "Christ, no. He was impressive, certainly—he's smart and overwhelming—but I know what I believe in, what I stand for, and nothing was said that would make me repudiate it."

Dr. Chapman seemed relieved. "I've always counted on your good sense." He threw the wet stub of his cigar into the hibiscus bushes, pulled a fresh cigar from his lapel pocket, bit the end and lighted it.

"I think what I'm trying to get across," said Paul, "is that Jonas may not be on the side of the angels, but he's decent enough. No one is simply black or white."

Dr. Chapman exhaled a stream of smoke. "When you're at war, everyone is either black or white. Equivocate, and you're dead. You can't fight with one arm tied behind your back. If

181

you're not on the side of the angels, then you're in league with the devil."

"Maybe so." Paul's interest in the argument was dwindling.

"How did you present our offer?" asked Dr. Chapman.

"Straightforwardly," said Paul. "There are no child's games with this man. I said that you thought he might be useful to us, and that he could have a job as a consultant. I put it just like that. No adornment."

"What did he say?"

"He said you wanted to buy him out—and that he wasn't selling. That was it, in effect."

Dr. Chapman tilted back in the wicker chair, blowing clouds toward the sky. At last, he straightened with a thump. "Well, I can see we're not dealing with an ordinary adversary."

"No, we're not."

"He'll rough us up in his critique to the Zollman people."

"I have no doubt of that."

"Well, I can't get the Mafia after him or anything like that. I'll have to fight him myself, fact for fact." He stared at Paul. His voice was soft and controlled again. "I'll lick him, you know."

Paul knew that he would. "Yes," he said.

"Type up a complete record of your meeting with Jonas. Every word of criticism of our survey. I want it as soon as possible. Start tonight."

"All right. I'm not sure I remember it all—"

"Whatever you do remember. Right after we get out of The Briars, we're going to whip the report into shape in half the time I'd originally planned, ship it to the Zollman directors before they meet. Then I'm going to write an overall paper anticipating and refuting all of Jonas' objections. As a matter of fact, Paul, I'm beginning to think that you accomplished more by learning his line of attack than by winning him over to us."

Paul felt no elation at the compliment. Instead, he felt a twinge of sadness at having acquired and delivered the enemy's battle plans. Of course, he had to remind himself, the battle plans were not secret, and Dr. Chapman's enemy was also his enemy.

"Yes," Dr. Chapman was saying complacently, "this may work out better than either of us planned. I'll be able to thoroughly discredit and demolish him." He rose heavily to his feet. "Nothing on earth's going to stop me. Thanks, Paul. Work hard. Good night."

182

He walked toward the Christmas tree of lights. Paul remained seated, looking after him. For a moment, the figure of the pure scientist was bathed in a halo of white light. And then, the next, he was streaked by the garish colors of blue and yellow, and, in that last moment before disappearing inside, he seemed less pure than earlier.

7

At EIGHT FORTY-FIVE the following morning, which was Wednesday morning and the beginning of the second day of interviewing in The Briars, Paul Radford sat at the table in the conference room of the Association building and sorted questionnaires. Through the open window, he could see the top of the post office, and above it, the sky leaden and overcast. There was the slightest breeze in the air, nipping and teasing the limp flag across the way.

When the door opened, Paul looked up hopefully, expecting Dr. Chapman. It was Cass.

"Hi-di-ho," Cass called out cheerfully, going directly to his papers. "Earthquake weather, according to the gasoline station attendant."

"Ignore false prophets," said Paul. He peered through the window. "It's not humid enough."

"How do you know?"

"I was around here for a year during the war. We had two quakes. It was always humid."

Cass began separating his papers. "Were the quakes bad?"

"The effect of two stiff vodkas. In the first one, a lot of crockery was displaced. In the second, we got a shimmy, but some village just over the border in Mexico fell down."

"Always Mexico," said Cass. "Where's the third musketeer?"

"Horace? In bed. He's sick. But he'll survive."

Cass was surprised. "I thought germs were afraid of him."

"Maybe they are. This was demon rum."

"I don't believe it."

"I know, but that's it. I hit the sack at one, and the next thing I knew, someone was bumping over the furniture. He smelled like a distillery. I got him to bed, but he threw up twice during the night. I finally settled him down with a sleeping pill. This morning, his face still looked off-center, like a Picasso, so I let him be."

"What happened to our cub scout?"

"Haven't the faintest idea. Don't mention it to Dr. Chapman."

"Are you kidding?"

Paul stood up and moved to the open window, searching the empty street. "I couldn't find Dr. Chapman this morning. He'll have to spell Horace."

Impatiently, Paul crossed to the door and poked his head into the corridor. He saw Dr. Chapman at Benita's desk going over the ledger with her. With relief, Paul went to join them.

"Doctor—"

Dr. Chapman lifted a hand and waved two fingers in greeting. Paul had seen several Popes, in newsreels and on television, make the same gesture of acknowledgment. "Morning, Paul. Did you work last night?"

Paul nodded. "Half done . . . I'm afraid you'll have to pinch-hit for Horace today. He's under the weather."

Dr. Chapman's concern was immediate. "What's the matter?"

"A virus, I'm sure. Twenty-four-hour variety."

"Did you call in someone?"

"I had the corner pharmacy send pills. I read it's all over the city. He'll be on his feet tomorrow."

Dr. Chapman shook his head. "I hope so. . . . All right. I'd better get ready."

He hurried off to the conference room. Paul lingered behind, then faced Benita. "Honey, call Horace, first chance. Tell him the word for today is virus, and he can take it easy. Say that Dr. Chapman's taking his place."

"Will do." Benita smiled her pale smile. "You forget my room's next to yours."

"Then you know."

"It's so unlike him. What happened?"

"He said he was going to the movies. I guess they spiked the popcorn. . . . Here come the girls. On your toes."

❖   ❖   ❖

At ten minutes to eleven, Dr. Chapman had been on his second interview of the morning for twenty minutes. His elbow on the card table, his chin propped on a fist, he continued to ask his questions in a dry monotone and record the answers with automatic precision. Usually he enjoyed these sessions, this fruitful adding to the storehouse of knowledge, but this morning, his mind was on Dr. Victor Jonas. Only half his mind received what he must inscribe. The other half wrote and rewrote the remarkable paper that would render his enemy impotent.

He had just finished jotting down a Solresol answer and was preparing to pose another question—he would not deign to ennoble all of Jonas' ridiculous charges by refuting each, he finally decided, but would take the offensive from the start —when the woman's voice on the other side of the screen interrupted him.

"May *I* ask a question?" inquired Teresa Harnish.

"Why, of course. If there's something you don't understand—"

"No, it's not that. I may be all wrong, but I think I recognize your voice. May I ask—am I being interviewed by Dr. George G. Chapman?"

"Yes indeed."

"I'm deeply honored. I simply had to know. My husband and I read your first two books, and we look forward to this one. We venerate your work. I wanted to be sure it was you. Had I gone to an analyst in Vienna at the turn of the century, I would have wanted to know if he were Sigmund Freud. I hope you understand?"

Dr. Chapman's full mind was turned toward the screen and the remarkably intelligent woman, with the well-bred accent, behind it. "You're very kind," he said.

"This is a memorable moment for me."

"Most generous. Actually, Mrs. —" he sought her name on the appointment card, and found it— "Harnish, Mrs. Harnish, I handle my interviews no differently from my associates."

"Forgive me my prejudice, but I feel I know you, and I simply feel you have more understanding."

"I try my best." He was pleased. Yes, remarkable young lady. He examined the sheet. Thirty-six. Vassar. Kansas City. Christian Science. ("All reality is in God and His creation, harmonious and eternal," Dr. Chapman remembered. "That which He creates is good, and He makes all that is made. Therefore the only reality of sin, sickness or death is the awful fact that unrealities seem real to human, erring belief, until God strips off their disguise. They are not true, because they are not of God." It seemed odd now that he had once read Mrs. Eddy. It was shortly after Lucy's death, he remembered.

Well . . .) Irregular churchgoer. Married. First husband. Ten years. Art dealer. Part-time assistant to husband. "Shall we proceed?" he asked.

"Please, Dr. Chapman."

"To return to the series of questions on premarital love-making. You stated that you had one partner before you married at twenty-six."

"Yes. But two if you wish to count my husband. After we were engaged, the marriage was delayed a year, due to family circumstances. His mother was ill, and it took all of Geoffrey's money and time. But, of course, we were adult about our relationship. Sexual union seemed quite proper. Shortly after Geoffrey's mother passed away, and he had money to open the shop, we had our wedding in Kansas City. It was quite the social event of the season, but the difficult part was, all that trying week, pretending to play the blushing bride. My parents are very rigid and formal about these matters. About Geoffrey and me—before we were married—do you wish the details?"

Dr. Chapman wet his lips. The caution sign went up in his head. Mrs. Harnish was being too easy, too liberated, too knowing. From long experience, Dr. Chapman knew that female frankness must be automatically met with wariness and a degree of distrust. Frankness was unnatural under the circumstances, he always found. It was the quick disguise that disarmed and deceived laymen.

"You mentioned two partners," he said. "Let's talk about the first."

"I'd rather draw a veil over that," she said lightly.

"You mean literally?"

"Of course not, Dr. Chapman. I'm joking. I was just out of Vassar and considering going into the theater—as a scenic designer, of course. But to my mind, Broadway is so overrated. The theaters are dreary, and those grubby, over-aged actors, and all the mutual admiration and to-do about mediocrity. I simply wasn't going to tramp those alleys. But during that dark age, I met an older man, a poet. He had been published, and he really did know everyone. I was impressed. The whole Greenwich Village thing was new to me, and I decided to marry him and have a salon. So when the time came, I allowed him to make love to me."

"You allowed him?"

Quickly, Teresa rephrased it. "I wanted him to. We made love together."

187

"How often on the average—each week?"

"Once a week, for two months."

"Where did this take place?"

"In his walk-up. I considered it very romantic then."

"Did you achieve satisfaction?"

There was a brief silence. At last, her voice filtered through the screen. "I don't think so. He always drank before, and—well, it wasn't actually much fun. I finally left him because I learned he never bathed, and he had paid for the publication of his own verse."

Dr. Chapman pressed on. He shortened his questions, to save time, but conversely her answers became longer. To keep within the allotted schedule, he combined questions. Her answers grew even longer. This was not unfamilar to Dr. Chapman. A great number of women, not ordinarily verbose, became so in the interviews—as defense against their habits, as camouflage for their embarrassment and shyness.

Questions and answers emerged from premarital intimacy into marital coitus. Mrs. Harnish's replies were more thoughtful now, and gradually more concise. Mrs. Harnish still offered herself to cohabitation twice a week. Petting and play were disposed of in a minute or two. The position favored, as in a quarter of all cases, was side by side. Mr. Harnish was valuable to Mrs. Harnish for never more than three minutes, but he gallantly accommodated her afterward. Mrs. Harnish insisted that she found relations with Mr. Harnish pleasurable, although Dr. Chapman perceived that a better word may have been *endurable*.

"Mrs. Harnish, when you make love with your husband, are you partially clothed or in the nude?"

"Well, not all nude."

"You are either nude or not nude." Dr. Chapman tried to keep the asperity out of his tone.

"I wear a nightgown."

"Do you remove it?"

"No."

"Then you are partially clothed." Dr. Chapman filled in his Solresol symbol, then resumed. "At what time of the day do you usually make love—morning, afternoon, evening, night?"

"At bedtime."

"When is that?"

"Sometime after ten."

"That would be night."

Dr. Chapman made his note and recommenced his questioning. As they went on, he detected that Mrs. Harnish's voice was lower, her accent more uncertain, and her replies considerably curtailed. They reached the world of extramarital coitus, and there Mrs. Harnish had never visited.

"Well now, that brings us to the final question of this series. You have never engaged in an extramarital relationship. Do you feel yourself capable of doing so in the future? Please answer—yes or maybe or no."

"No."

Dr. Chapman stared at the screen. A hunter on the veldt could smell the animal, feel the danger in his bones. It was an instinct born of a thousand safaris.

He tried the question another way. "You can't conceive of committing infidelity, you say. Do you ever think about it at all—merely think about it?"

"I told you no, Doctor."

"Have you ever, while petting or performing the sex act with your husband, wished or dreamed that he was another man? I mean, either a specific man you have known or met or just another man in general?"

"I have no such wishes or dreams, Doctor."

Still the scent, the rustle in the bush, but now he lowered his rifle. The over-vigor of her replies could denote distaste and shock, as well as defensiveness. He weighed the possibilities, scanning her questionnaire as he did so, and finally concluded that this young woman, an intelligent young woman, knew her mind and would keep her matrimonial bargain.

"Very well, Mrs. Harnish. Let's go on."

❧   ❧   ❧

It was not a day for the beach or for dispelling gloom. Teresa knew this as she raced the convertible over the Pacific Coast Highway toward Constable's Cove. Here, the inky clouds seemed to hang nearer the choppy water, and the raw wind from the ocean stung and hurt. The highway ahead and the uninviting beach to the left littered with rocks and seaweed were desolate. These were the moors on a moonless night, gale swept, and this was the journey from Wuthering Heights to Thrushcross Grange. I know you, Ellis Bell, because this morning, I am you.

The interview was to have been a conversation piece, especially once that she knew Dr. Chapman himself was her interrogator. But this moment she felt less interested in

189

what would make a conversation piece and what would not. Even her wonderful costume party, each woman requested to come-as-the-person-you-would-like-to-have-been-when-Dr.-Chapman-interviewed-you, failed to excite her. Since the party was on such short notice, she had decided to invite the guests by telephone. Half the calls had been made. She planned to make the remaining calls at noon, after the interview, but here it was noon, and she was driven to—no, driving to—the beach. Why? To think. About what? I don't know. Meaning? Meaning, I don't know. What did you most often think about, Ellis Bell?

In ten minutes, she was there. She gathered together her effects. After the interview, she had stopped by the house to change into Bermuda shorts, and then change again into the brief tennis shorts she had worn in Balboa last year, and found her beige corduroy coat, blanket, and barely remembered to snatch up a book on the way out.

She trod the path down to Constable's Cove, spread the blanket on the hard sand, and sat down. It was cold, and she was glad for the corduroy jacket. She had not inspected the surrounding beach yet, and now she did, and was not surprised when she saw the four of them, two against two, playing some kind of wildly athletic game of tag with a football.

For endless minutes, she held the open book in her lap, not even bothering to discover the title, and continuing frankly to observe their play or, rather, *his* play. And what came to mind were those irrelevant questions about love play and foreplay. Why would a man of Dr. Chapman's stature waste time on such nonessentials? That is, if they were nonessentials. She supposed that he knew best. Inexplicably, it saddened her.

She looked off again. He was bigger than she had remembered. Possibly, it was because he was not now in those indecent trunks but wearing jersey sweat pants, full length, such as she had once seen the cadets wear when she had attended a track and field meet at the Point. He was bare from the waist up, and enormous.

She waited and waited, and at last the play shifted nearer, and, like the first time, he came plowing through the sand toward her, glancing over his shoulder, with the football spiraling high in the air toward him. At once, she saw that the ball would overshoot him and descend upon her. As ball and man loomed, she screamed a warning, ducked low, covering her eyes. She heard the plop of the ball in the sand, and the skidding leather, and realized that she was still intact. She opened her eyes.

He was standing over her, grinning down at her, wheezing hard. "Sorry, lady."

The *lady* made her feel shamefully old, and she sat up, her chest out and corduroy jacket open. He was boyish and young, but not that young, and his square face was Slav and unshaved. Six feet four, she decided.

"That Jackie's got lotta speed but no control. We'll watch out next time."

"It's all right." She could not think of a single clever thing to say. Then she added: "I wasn't scared."

He strode off to the football and picked it up with one massive hand. He half turned. "Won't happen again."

"I don't mind," she said quickly. "It's fun watching. Is it football?"

"Touch ball. Keeps you in trim." He looked at her legs indifferently. "Ain't you cold like that?"

"A little. I thought the sun might come out."

"Naw, not today. Well—" he threw a salute—"don't take any wooden nickels."

He was about to leave. Some desperation in her reached to hold him. "Do you—are you a real football player?"

He waited. "Pro ball. Rams. Still a second-stringer, but watch my smoke this year."

"I'd like to. What name should I watch for?"

"Ed Krasowski," he said. "Right end."

She smiled. "I'll remember that." She waited to tell him her name, but he did not inquire.

"S'long, lady." He waded off through the sand, working his shoulders so that the supple muscles of his back rippled, and finally he heaved the ball toward his companions. In a moment, he had joined them. Apparently, he had said something funny, for now they all laughed.

She watched tensely. He was resuming the foreplay— dammit, no—the play; he was resuming the play. She shivered, and pulled her jacket tight, and continued to watch. After a while, the four of them tired of the sport and walked off, and it was then that Teresa got up and went home.

❖   ❖   ❖

The clock on the wall, its long minute hand jumping forward with a loud tick every sixty seconds, read eleven minutes to six, and, at last, Naomi Shields began to recapture her earlier mood. She felt gay and reckless once more. She had come to the interview in the white sweater that showed off her figure so well (although, disappointingly, there was no one to appreciate her, except the thin-lipped wallflower in the hall) and the form-fitting jet black skirt, and fortified by four undiluted straight Scotches, prepared to prove to herself and the others that she was no different from any other woman in The Briars.

The silly cane and walnut screen had been an immediate annoyance. In her manic mood, which was exhibitionistic and seductive, she had wanted to be admired openly and had looked forward to observing her male interviewer's face as she shocked and excited him, and reduced him finally to sexual suppliant. These feelings in Naomi were especially heightened when she heard Paul Radford's voice, which she decided was sexy and promising.

But his opening questions had made her thoughtful and dampened her disposition. She did not like telling him that she was already thirty-one, and that she had been brought up in strict Catholicism, against which she had revolted, and that she had not even finished high school. And then, worse, all those dreary details, distasteful even, of her pre-adolescent and adolescent years. Why was anyone ever *that* young? When she read biographies or long novels, or at least when she used to, she had always made it a point to skip the early sections about growing up. Now, thank God, her own early years were behind her, and the man had announced that they would discuss premarital coitus. Why *coitus*, after all that pompous prattle about frankness and bringing it into the open? Why not plain fucking? That's what it was, anyway. That's what it was, and she could tell them. My God, she was drunk.

She realized that an unlighted cigarette was dangling from her lips. She fumbled for a match, and then became aware of the sexy voice addressing her again. She applied the light to her cigarette, coughed, shook the match out, and dropped it to the floor. She narrowed her eyes and tried to listen.

". . . that period from puberty to marriage. Did you ever engage in premarital coitus?"

"I certainly did."

"How many partners did you have—one? two to ten? eleven to twenty-five? or more?"

"More."

"Can you estimate how many?"

192

"It's hard to remember."

"Maybe I can help. After puberty, at what age did you first engage in love-making?"

"Thirteen—no, fourteen—I was just fourteen."

"And the last time, before you were married?"

"The week before the wedding." She remembered. She had wanted satin pumps for the wedding. The shoe clerk with the Hapsburg jaw. He wouldn't take his hand off her leg. Should she explain? "I had to," she said. "My husband wouldn't until it was official."

"You were twenty-five then?"

"Just about."

"That leaves eleven premarital years—"

"About fifty," she said suddenly.

"What?"

"About fifty men. Mostly after I was twenty-one." She smiled, trying to picture his face behind the screen, and blew a smoke ring and felt superior.

There was a momentary silence. Then Paul spoke again. "In these affairs—I must ask this—did you accept favors?"

"What does that mean?" she asked.

"Well, cash gifts—"

"Hey now! Wait a minute, mister. If you're inferring that I was a prostitute—"

"I'm inferring nothing. I'm merely inquiring for the record."

"Well, you put this in your little black book. And get it right. Nobody ever touched me unless I wanted it, and I did it for love—do you understand?—because I wanted to, and no other reason."

"Of course. Please don't misunderstand—"

"See that *you* don't misunderstand."

"Shall we go on?"

She felt angry and dizzy, and glared at the screen. The nerve of the man.

"Where did these affairs usually take place?" Paul asked.

"Everywhere. Who remembers?"

"But most often?"

"Wherever I lived. I've been on my own since I was a kid."

"Did you achieve satisfaction on any of these occasions?"

"What's your guess?"

His guess was negative, but her answer was an insistent affirmative. Her capabilities, Naomi argued indignantly, were the match of any man alive.

There were several more questions, and then Paul stated

193

that they would next cover the marital relationship. With trembling hand, Naomi lighted a fresh cigarette off the stub of the old, and waited.

"You were married only once?"

"Thank God."

"For how long?"

"Six years."

"Are you divorced?"

"Almost three years ago."

"Have you had any relations with your former husband since?"

"I haven't even seen him."

Paul began to probe her life with her husband. Her replies to his inquiries were alternatingly flippant and hostile.

Once, having made some slighting remark about her husband, she seemed to regret it and was anxious to amend her pronouncement. "Don't get me wrong," she said, remembering the better times and hating to be harsh and spoil her best memories. "He was sweet. He wasn't so bad as I've made out. We had our moments."

Naomi's humor returned gradually in the next ten minutes, as Paul continued to examine her married life. By the time he reached the subject of extramarital relationships, she was in the best of spirits. The dizziness had departed, and she was beginning to feel at ease, except for the lack of a drink.

"You were married six years," said Paul. "Did you ever engage in extramarital petting—petting only?"

"Most women do. I'm no different."

"Can you recount—"

She did so, lustily.

When she was finished, Paul inquired about her actual affairs. "Did you have any with male partners other than your husband?"

This had been the beginning of the trouble. "Look," she said suddenly, "maybe I can save us both time. I'll tell you straight out, and we can get it over with. He was a great guy. I mean it. But he couldn't satisfy me. I just wasn't happy. Maybe I never will be. I meant to be faithful, and I tried—I really tried. But you're not a woman. You don't know what it's like to need love and not have it, at least not have what you need. So I cheated. Not at all the first year. But I got nervous as a cat, and I was afraid I'd come apart. So I knew I had to do what I did. But I was careful. I didn't want to spoil what

194

we had. I really wanted him—but I wanted everyone else, too. Do you understand?"

"I think so."

"I was discreet. I'd go downtown and find someone in the movie or in a bar or go shopping in the next city. I know you like statistics. I'll try to give you a few. For five years, after the first year, there was a man every—no, let me put it right —the first few years, I wouldn't do it more than once a month."

"With the same partner or different partners?"

"Different ones, of course—always—they never even knew my name. I couldn't risk getting involved. But it kept getting worse. Pretty soon I had nothing else on my mind. I thought I'd go insane. It became two, and then three a month. Finally, every week. Once someone—a friend's wife—saw me in another city with a man and that scared me witless, and then I was away so much—well, my husband became suspicious. No, that's not right. He trusted me. He became curious. So, for a while, I determined to stop going out. But I couldn't stay home. Just sit waiting for him. I was out of my mind. So when I got really desperate, I'd try strangers in the neighborhood. It wasn't easy. And it made me jumpy. Anyway, there was a school kid—not a kid exactly—he was twenty, and whenever I ran into him, I could see he was wild about me. Always staring at my bust. Well, I liked him a little, and he looked virile, and I began thinking that if I could get to trust him and have him when I needed him, maybe that would be enough and safer all around. One night, I knew my husband would be working—he had some hush-hush spare-time job— so I went out and found the boy and invited him over for the evening. Well, my husband went out about seven, and this boy showed up right after—he'd been watching from the street— and I remember, it was one of my bad nights. I simply couldn't wait. The minute he came in, I told him that I wasn't interested in conversation or tea or necking. I wish you could have seen his face, poor baby. He was afraid to use the house, so I took him out on the back lawn, and we just lay on the grass. It was wet and mad and wonderful. He was a good boy. I came when he did, and we just stayed there like two beat animals, and then, suddenly, someone turned on the back-yard lights, and it was my husband. The kid ran off, and there I was. I wanted my husband to beat me, to kill me. I was so ashamed. But he just stood there crying. That was the worst part. I tried to get him to kill me. I told him about some of the others, not all, just some. And all he did was cry. Then he walked out, and I never saw him again. So I came to California and got the divorce—my old man was living here, but his wife's a bitch, and I couldn't stay with them. I had some money from my mother, so I bought a house in The Briars. I figured here I'd meet a decent guy. I sure did, and how. I met plenty. All married. You want to know my record for the last three years? Twice a week, maybe. I'm able to keep it down to that by drinking. You'd be surprised how it helps. I mean, if you drink enough. Anyway—" she halted, breathless a moment, and squinted at the screen, wondering what he was thinking—"I don't care what you think," she said. "You want the truth. I'm not ashamed. We're all built differently. I bet you think I'm an old bag. Well, I'm not. Get rid of that lousy screen, and you'll see. Men think it shows on women, but it doesn't. Anyway, it's healthy if it's natural, and it's natural for me. Of course—" she halted again and decided that she wanted his good opinion—"I guess you'll want to know for your survey that I've reformed. I haven't done it once in three weeks. That's the truth, too. And it wasn't so hard to do, either. Like smoking. I once stopped for a month. You get withdrawal pains, sure, but if you make up your mind, you can do anything. You believe that, don't you?"

"Yes, I do." Paul's voice was low.

"I'm going to get a job. I've made up my mind. I have an appointment right after I leave here. That'll keep me busy until I get married. If I just find the right man—I mean somebody who matches me—I'll be all right; you'll see."

"I sincerely hope so."

She fell back against the chair and closed her eyes, and finally she opened them. She felt better all around. "Well, you've got to admit, I've fattened up the batting average for The Briars. . . . Any more questions?"

❖   ❖   ❖

There was still the last of Tuesday's daylight left, and Naomi's frame of mind since departing the Association building was one of unnatural excitement. The experience had been curiously stimulating and it had, in a way she did not understand, sanctioned her past conduct. Celibacy and continence seemed the lesser virtues.

Once she arrived at the boulevard stop light and turned west, Naomi knew that she would not keep the eight-o'clock appointment with Kathleen Ballard. Filled with high resolve at noon, she had telephoned Kathleen, and after exchanging gossip about mutual friends and recounting a Dr. Chapman joke that was current, she had asked to see Kathleen. Naomi had frankly told Kathleen that she wanted a favor of her—that is, if Kathleen was still on good terms with J. Ronald Metzgar of Radcone. Kathleen had said that she was, and hoped that she could be of help. They agreed to meet at Kathleen's house immediately after dinner.

Naomi made one brief stop. She parked in the lot beside Dr. Schultz's Twenty-Four-Hour Pet Hospital and asked the night attendant to release Colonel, her five-year-old cocker spaniel. Naomi had acquired Colonel as a pup, because he was the only cocker she had ever seen who did not have sad eyes. Several months before, she had put him up at the pet hospital because feeding him, cleaning him, walking him, had become too much of a chore. But today she wanted him back. While the attendant went to fetch Colonel, Naomi scribbled a check. When Colonel was brought forward, tail wagging uncontrollably at the sight of her, she felt ashamed at having neglected him so long.

With Colonel on the seat beside her, lapping gratefully at her free hand, Naomi drove hastily home. She left the car in the garage, led Colonel into the house, and gave him some milk. While he was occupied, she hastened to the bathroom, freshened her make-up, returned to the kitchen, poured a double Scotch, and, not bothering with ice, she drank it down grimacing, and then felt warm and eager again.

She found the red leash, hooked it to Colonel's collar, and started for the front door with him.

"I'm going to take you for a walk, poopsie," she said.

Outside, it was dark at last, and the street lights were on. Wrapping the leash around her hand, she held Colonel in restraint as she crossed the lawn to the street. There were no sidewalks in The Briars, despite the annual petitions from parents with children, and Naomi walked close to the curbing, past the hedges of her nearest neighbor, and continued down the block.

Approaching the fifth house from her own, the Agajanian house, she slowed. The plan that had formulated in her mind, during the latter portion of the interview, was that she would stroll past the Agajanian house, and that Wash Dillon would be outside and see her, or that he would see her and come outside. And if that didn't happen on the way going, she would

197

stop on the way back and ring the doorbell. If Wash answered, she would say that she wanted to see him after dinner. He would understand and find a way. If Mrs. Dillon answered, or more likely one of the Agajanians, she would say that she was a neighbor and that she wished Mr. Dillon to appraise the value of a rare record collection she had taken on approval.

She had arrived before the white colonial. Beyond the row of birch trees, she could see that the lights were on. Someone was at home. She looked about the front lawn. No one was in sight. Lest somebody detect her from the window, she continued her stroll with Colonel. Nearing the driveway, she heard the *pat-pat-pat* of a leather ball on the cement. In the illumination of the garage lights, a skinny boy was dribbling a basketball and trying to hit the hoop attached to the top of the garage.

This was Wash Dillon's son, she remembered, and his name was Johnny. She wondered what she should do, but then there seemed no choice. She must see Wash tonight. "Johnny," she called.

He turned, startled.

"It's Mrs. Shields."

He came toward her curiously, and then he recognized her. "Oh, hello."

"Is your father home?"

"Naw. He left us last night."

"What do you mean?"

"He took all his things. He had a fight with Ma and hit her. I don't think he's coming back."

"Where is he?"

"I don't know. 'Course, he's still at Jorrocks' Jollities. That's Mr. Agajanian's nightclub."

"I know. . . . Well, I'm sorry, Johnny."

"Makes no diff. He's never home anyway. Sa-ay, that's a nice dog."

"Yes. Good night, Johnny."

"Good night, Miss."

There was no point in going further. Naomi tugged at the leash and started back.

In the kitchen again, she pulled off her coat, threw it on a dinette chair, and opened the cupboard. There were still three cans of dog food. She opened one, emptied it into a deep dish, lured Colonel into the service porch, and then closed the kitchen door on him. He would eat and sleep. The question was—would she?

The electric clock on the oven said seven twenty-two. She wasn't hungry, except for Wash. She knew that there was still time to have something and drive over to Kathleen's. But she had no desire to see Kathleen or talk about a job. Dammit, she didn't want some dreary old job. She wanted a home with someone in it—someone.

The bottle of Scotch, half filled, was beside the sink, and there was the glass. She had to think things out. She poured three shots, until the amber liquid almost came to the top of the glass, and she drank. She leaned back against the sink and drank steadily. The fluid invaded her limbs and chest and encircled her groin. The feeling was not of warmth but of heat.

She evoked the image of Wash Dillon as she had seen him the day before yesterday, standing at the front door with the post card. It was not his shaggy hair, or death head with the face all pocked, or insolent smile, or great length of body, that she saw, but instead a towering phallus that moved at her through the mesh of door screen.

She wondered, do other women have such obscene visions? They must. Purity was the civilized Lie. Behind it, hid Desire and Lust. In his lecture, Dr. Chapman had said that there was nothing unique any woman could tell him, that most women did everything, thought everything, only never admitted it to anyone except to him, and that nothing you felt was truly unique. Was that what he had said exactly? She could not remember now.

She finished the drink and tipped the bottle toward the glass again. Her hand was unsteady and some of the liquor splashed on the sink. Holding the filled glass, she felt the searing flame across her body. The pain of the fiery torture must be quenched. For a single second, she considered trying to reach the nightclub and seek out Wash. But then the searing flame was gone, and in its wake lay a charred wasteland of agony.

She stared at the blurred glass in her hand and knew that no human being, not Wash, not anyone, could halt the agony or save what had already been devastated. There was only one course left, one measure that would end this malady that had invaded flesh and spirit. She set the glass on the sink and staggered out of the kitchen. In her passage to the bedroom, she tried to snap on the hall light but missed the switch, and finally had to return to get the light on. Blindly, she felt her way in the darkened bedroom.

With a jerky motion, she drew the drapes together. The final privacy, she thought. She moved to the foot of the bed and methodically disrobed. The clothes, she had decided, were part of the pain, and now she wanted nothing on her skin. She kicked off her shoes. She pulled the sweater upward over her head and cast it aside. She fumbled behind, managed to unhook her nylon lace brassière, slid the straps down her arms, and dropped it. She unzippered her skirt and let it fall, and then removed the garter belt. Groping for the edge of the bed, she found it, and sat, and quickly rolled off her stockings.

Finally, she was naked, and now she knew that it had not been the clothes at all that were part of the pain, but her skin, her excruciating, blazing skin. Rising, she was not sorry she had undressed. After all, after all, she had come into the world this way, and this was fitting.

She found the bathroom, and the light switch, and the medicine chest. Bottles and small boxes spilled before her hand, until she had the white container so desperately needed. Uncapping it, she shook a heap of sleeping tablets into her palm. Her desire for Nirvana, the nothingness where hurt and sorrow and guilt and regret were banished, exceeded any desire she had ever felt for a man. By twos and threes, she threw the pills into her mouth and then remembered that she required water. The glass, the water. She swallowed, swallowed. Wash it down, Wash it, Wash.

Oh, Wash. His was a better hell, a better dying.

Instantly, she wanted life to bargain with, and trade for dying.

Not yet corpsehood.

Her arm floated to the medicine chest door. Inside it, long ago, she had pasted the chart labeled *Counterdoses* as the practical ally in supporting a woman's prerogative. Overdose sleeping medicines ... two tablespoons Epsom salt in two glasses of water ... emetic soap and warm water ... Epsom ... soap ... Wash, wait, please, please wait ...

Once, later, she awakened. The luminous dial of the bedside clock told her it was after midnight. The hot agony had fled, and her skin was cool. She reached toward the pillow, finding the top of the spread and blanket, and tore them free. With one last effort, she climbed beneath the blanket, conscious for a moment of the softness and snugness, and then she was asleep again.

◇   ◇   ◇

It was after midnight when Paul Radford said good night

to Dr. Chapman and made his way to the room he shared with Horace Van Duesen in the Villa Neapolis.

He was surprised to find the big lamp on, and Horace in pajamas, propped up in bed, reading a paperback novel.

"I thought you'd be dead to the world by now," said Paul.

"I slept all day. I'm trying to get myself tired."

Paul pulled off his tie and unbuttoned his shirt. "Boy, I am bushed."

"Where were you?"

"There was a seminar at a place called the Wilshire Ebell, out toward the city. Some of the university people and a couple of analysts on the husband's role in modern marriage. Dr. Chapman had promised to be there a long time ago, and he wanted me along for the drive. The interviews ran late, and we had to eat on the run. What a day."

Paul laid out his pajamas and began to undress.

Horace put down the book. "Paul, I appreciate the way you covered for me today."

"Merely an investment. Expect you to do the same for me, when the time comes, and the way I feel, it will."

"I shouldn't have got so drunk."

"We've been gypsying around too long."

"How was it today?"

"Oh, the usual." He tied the cord of his pajama pants and pulled on the tops. "I can't imagine what would surprise me any more. Though, I must admit, it's never prosaic. The last one I had today was really a dilly—an out and out nympho."

"You mean actually?"

"No question. I never saw her, but Benita said she was a doll. It was really a session. I was sorry as hell for her. Fifty partners before she was married and once a week after, besides her husband, until he caught her at it."

He clamped the clothes hanger on his trousers and hung them up.

"You mean her husband caught her with another man?" Horace asked.

"In the back yard, of all places, with some boy. The husband walked out on her cold—can't say I blame him, except that she's so obviously ill and needs help. She came to California and kept right on with it, even worse, though she's trying to get herself in hand now, but she won't."

Horace had been listening intently. Suddenly, he asked, "What was her name?"

Paul, who had started for the bathroom, halted. "Name?

201

I don't think I—wait, yes—Shields—Naomi Shields." He wondered at the strange convulsed look on Horace's face. "Do you know the lady?"

"That was no lady," said Horace quietly, "that was my wife."

8

ALTHOUGH THEY HAD slept no more than four hours, Paul and Horace, by unspoken agreement, had risen at daybreak to avoid the others. After dressing for their third day of interviews, they had waited briefly outside the dining room of the Villa Neapolis until the doors were opened at seven-thirty. During the next half hour, except for several transient couples hastily eating their breakfasts in order to get on the road before the heavy traffic, they were alone.

By eight o'clock, they had left the dining room without seeing Dr. Chapman, Cass, or Benita, and, relieved, they had made their way to the garage. The sun simmered in the cloudless sky like an oversized egg yolk frying. The moist grass on either side of the path was warming and would soon be dry, and Paul decided that it would be as hot as it had been on Monday. He lowered the canvas top on the Ford convertible, secured it, and then settled behind the wheel next to Horace.

He eased the car backward out of the stall, and finally, gear in low and foot teasing the brake, he guided the vehicle slowly down the steep private road that led to Sunset Boulevard.

At the stop sign, he glanced at Horace. "We're a bit early. Like to take a short drive first?"

"Whatever you say."

Paul wheeled the Ford east on Sunset Boulevard, and then proceeded at thirty-five miles an hour, slowing once as they approached the university campus (the ROTC boys were drilling smartly on the green), and accelerating again as he headed in the general direction of Beverly Hills. The speed of the open car generated a breeze, where there had been none, and the air brushed them as gently as a woman's hand. At the Bel-Air gate, on impulse, Paul turned sharply left.

"Have you ever been in here?" he asked.

"I don't think so," said Horace.

"You'd remember if you had. It's exactly like a drive in the suburbs behind Honolulu."

They were on Bellagio Road, a smoothly rising, curving, asphalt roller coaster. The thick ivy and bushes bursting through the wire fences, the miles of blue and red bougainvillaea and red and purple fuchsia, hid all signs of habitation. The Monterey pine trees and sycamores guarding the road were aged and massive, and gave an impression of estate and belonging, such as the self-conscious, imported date palms of Beverly Hills had never been able to imply. Paul remembered his parents and thought of how they would have looked at these trees and then talked of the Old Country. The occasional mail boxes, usually wooden and quaint, were topped by names finely wrought in iron, several of the names celebrated. In a way, the mail boxes spoiled it, for they reminded the intruder that there was human life here, not wild life, and that the sensation of forest primeval was false.

Paul turned from the windshield to Horace, meaning to comment on the landscape, but he saw that Horace was completely oblivious to the surroundings. Horace sat slumped low, as if in a trance, arms crossed loosely on his chest, eyes staring blankly at the dashboard.

Paul had no choice but to recall the black morning that had begun after midnight. After Paul's disclosure of the interview with Naomi, Horace had remained on the bed, his face numbed as if by stroke, smoking incessantly, while he related the story of his marriage.

There was, that year before Dr. Chapman, a convention of gynecologists in Madison (Horace remembered), and Horace went up from Reardon to read a paper. The convention tried to accommodate guests in every way, and among the available conveniences offered was a secretarial pool. The girl assigned to Horace announced herself as Naomi Shields. Until he met Naomi, Horace had recognized the female as only a biological necessity, an exercise quite apart from important workaday routine. He had always been certain that he was fated to live and die a bachelor.

Naomi was something that he had never imagined a woman could be: lively, interested, beautiful, responsive. Also, and this soon proved a decisive factor, she was a young woman widely desired and sought after. The fact that she had eyes for Horace alone, gave him a special status among his colleagues, and a prideful satisfaction that he had never before felt. He began to endow Naomi with a value that superseded love.

204

("Of course, I speak from hindsight," he had conceded to Paul.) From the first, Naomi was prepared to give herself wholly to Horace, wholly and unconditionally, and it took every resource of Horace's Catholic upbringing to restrain him from taking advantage of the love-struck girl. As it was, they were engaged merely five months ("Hardly enough to know each other," he had told Paul) before he brought her down to Reardon and made her Naomi Van Duesen.

From the earliest days, he enjoyed the idea of marriage. It gave him membership in a popular social group that he had not realized existed, and for the first time in his life he possessed a feeling of belonging to something more cosmopolitan, more enjoyable, more fulfilling than the faculty staff of Reardon College. The countless accessories of the nuptial state were what pleased the most: the pineapple duckling prepared at home, the frayed shirt collars turned at last, the collaborative shopping for refrigerator and blue parakeet, the addressing of Christmas cards, the continuing envy of male friends, the casino and scrabble and double acrostics together, the brassière behind the bathroom door and the stockings drying over the tub and the toothpaste uncapped, the dividing of the Sunday paper, the buttons magically reappearing on pajamas and shirts.

But there was a price for these pleasures, these sanctioned intimacies, and it came due too often on the double bed.

His sexual needs, Horace had frankly admitted to Paul, were always less than average, as far as he could guess in those less literate pre-Chapman days. In the beginning, Naomi's tireless appetite thrilled him, made him swell with masculinity. But after a few months, there was no settling down, and her ceaseless passion became not a pleasure but a duty that mocked him. Almost every night, she expected him, and what had been love soon became labor of love. The shadow of the dread double bed darkened each born day. Only the emergence of Dr. Chapman saved him. Dr. Chapman became a rescue as effective as any ever staged by the cavalry or Marines. When Dr. Chapman took him on as a spare-time aide and demanded night work, Horace co-operated in the secret project with a fervor that Chapman mistook for scientific enthusiasm. As a result, there was friction with Naomi, but soon enough she was made to understand that twice weekly would have to be their norm. Eventually, her agitation decreased, and toward the end, it disappeared altogether. Not until the terrible denouement in the back yard and the scene afterward, did Horace realize to what degree she had reorganized her life, and at what cost she had made the adjustment.

He severed the rotten thing from his life in one clean stroke. The house was vacated; the furniture sold. Every memento, every gift, every photograph save one (a softly diffused portrait of her in profile, taken in the second year of their marriage), was liquidated. Even the single last link of communication, the alimony payment, Horace reduced to the impersonal. On the third day of every month, an attorney in Reardon, Wisconsin, mailed the check to an attorney in Burbank, California.

During the busy, arduous months of the bachelor survey, Horace managed to dedicate himself to the work and succeeded fairly well in erasing Naomi from his mind. But with the undertaking of the married female survey, this often became difficult—for, too frequently, a voice behind the screen reminded him of her voice, and more and more often the reply to his extramarital-activities question sounded intentionally sadistic as it came from behind the screen.

Horace dreaded The Briars from the moment the trip had been arranged. He had not minded being in Los Angeles during the male survey, but a sampling of married females made the proximity to Naomi unbearable. Perhaps, as he thought all along, he feared that he would see her again; or perhaps he feared that he would not. He could not define the true reason for his apprehension, but it painfully existed all the same. And then, Monday night, he *had* seen her. He had gone to the movie in Westwood and found a place three seats in from the center aisle. About twenty minutes into the main feature, a young woman came up the aisle, and she was Naomi. She did not see him and continued toward the lobby, but he saw her, and was deeply shaken, and later got extremely drunk.

In discussing Naomi's interview with Paul, Horace had been disturbed by the inevitability (at least in his own mind) of Naomi's presence among the two hundred volunteers. It was, he thought, as if some bad fate had attached itself to him and would not let him go. Paul, however, had regarded her appearance as less unusual. After all, more than three thousand women had been interviewed. The percentages were against it, as Paul had predicted earlier on the train, yet it was not so surprising that one of them might prove to be someone a member of the team would know, especially since she dwelled in the small community being sampled. Paul reminded Horace of the earlier incident in Indianapolis when he himself realized that he was questioning a married woman whom he had dated several times in school. Those things happened; they just happened. They were not allowed to happen too often in art, banished as straining credulity, but in real life they happened all too often. No, it was not the coincidence of it that had bothered Paul, but, as he told Horace, the odd fact that Naomi would offer herself to a survey of which her husband was a part. Surely she knew. Horace thought not. In the latter period of their marriage, she had not known for whom he was working spare time, since Dr. Chapman's second survey had not yet been officially announced. As to reading about his new profession afterward, that too was unlikely. Even when she read books, and those only early in their marriage, she had never had the patience for newspapers or magazines. It was hardly likely that she had changed. And if, occasionally, she glanced at a newspaper—well, Paul knew very well that the stories usually went on and on about Dr. Chapman but rarely mentioned even the names of the members of the team. Furthermore, it was unlikely that Naomi had ever revealed her married name to anyone in The Briars, so the other women would have no way of relating the Van Duesen on the Chapman team to her. No, as far as Horace could see, that part of it made sense.

Thus they had gone on talking until three in the morning, Horace doing most of the talking and Paul trying to placate and reassure him.

Remembering all of this now, in the early sun, as he drove the Ford through Bel-Air, Paul tried to discover in what way the memory of it still troubled him. His natural sorrow for a good friend, of course. But that was too simple. There was something more selfish. It was, he supposed, that all of this related directly to his bachelor state. It was possibly one more brick on the wall slowly rising that kept him from a woman, any woman, he might marry. On each brick, there was a digit, and one day this digit barrier would be too high and formidable to surmount. Naomi had been but a reflection of hundreds of other women whose intimate lives he had probed —the nameless numerals—telling him in the language of science that all there was to love and marriage was x number of means of petting, x number of positions, x number of orgasms. And perhaps, honestly, this was all that there was to it. If so, it made of marriage a bleak resort. Rather than that, he would prefer monastic isolation. Or was there more? What of the good, solid unions he had known, and the romantic fancies he had so long held? What of tenderness and things in common and procreation? Get thee behind me, Victor Jonas.

Paul swung his convertible to the extreme right of the narrow road, to allow an oncoming delivery truck to pass, and then he looked at Horace again. He felt a swell of compassion for his battered friend.

"Feeling any better, Horace?"

Horace removed his stare from the glove compartment and blinked at Paul. "I'll be all right. . . . It was damn kind of you to let me bend your ear the way I did last night."

"Don't be silly."

"You know what I was just sitting here thinking? I was thinking why I really got so plastered Monday night."

"Well, you saw her——"

"Yes, but it wasn't just seeing her. What happened was I saw her for an instant—it was the first time since that night—and that instant I knew I loved her as much as ever. It just grabbed me by the gut. It was awful, because I'm a reserved person, and there was no control in this. There she was, a dirty thing, and I loved her. After she was gone, I didn't care about what I did or said. I just wanted to see her. I didn't tell you this last night—I was ashamed—but I jumped out of my seat and went up the aisle after her like a crazy goon. She wasn't in the lobby or outside, and I went up and down the block, and other blocks, searching for her. I didn't find her. I decided to look her up in the telephone book and go see her. She was in the telephone book, all right. Then I was scared—there was a whole stranger I didn't know much about, the one on the grass with that kid—and I decided I'd better have a drink first. There were no bars around that part of Westwood. I asked someone in the street, and he said it was because of the university. Did you know that? So I drove to another section near some place called Pico and found a place and got stiff. I was in no condition to see her, and I was lucky even to get back to the motel. But I can't get it out of my mind, how I behaved. I thought she was done and dead, and I had it tucked away in an old compartment, forgotten, and then the resurrection, and what's left of me is in little pieces. I must be out of my mind. How can you love a whore?"

Paul kept his eyes on the road. "She's not a whore," he said slowly. "She's a woman who was your wife, and she's ill and needs help. And you love her."

"I do. But it would be a hundred hells."

"Maybe it would. Yes, I suppose it would." He read a metal road sign, and the arrow pointed left for Sunset Boulevard. "Well, it's almost curtain time. We'd better get back to The Briars."

❖   ❖   ❖

Cass Miller stiffened in his chair as he heard Sarah Goldsmith's answer to his question, and he glared at the screen with hatred. The bitch, he thought, the filthy, cheating bitch.

He had said, "Now there will be a series of questions on extramarital relationships." He had asked, "Have you ever engaged in coitus with a man or men other than your husband?" So certain had he been of her reply that he had marked the Solresol symbol for "Never" without waiting to hear her reply.

She had answered, "Once."

Cass could not believe his ears. "I'm sorry. Did you say you have had one man, other than your husband, since you've been married?"

She had answered nervously, "Yes, one."

Cass had found it difficult to keep the disapproval out of his voice. "When . . . when did this take place?" There must be extenuating circumstances. Long ago, certainly, when she was foolish, immature, drunk.

She had answered, "Right now."

The bitch. His head throbbed. Angrily, he erased what he had written, tearing a hole in the page as he did so.

She had made a fool of him, and he despised her. Usually, he was prepared for this, and on guard, but her appearance and her prior history had deceived him.

The interview had been scheduled for nine in the morning, and Cass had overslept and been late. Crossing to his office, from the conference room, he saw her being led in his direction by Benita. He saw that her sleek hair was in an old-fashioned bun in back, and that she wore proper glasses, and a neat, conservative, plaid dress. The glasses, the flat shoes, the maturity of her figure, the whole aspect of progressive, decent housewife, were what fooled him, but mainly the glasses.

After he had settled behind the screen, and she was ready—this Sarah Goldsmith—her history confirmed his respected opinion of her. Her answers were matter-of-fact, sensible. She was thirty-five, married twelve years. Her husband wasn't

209

exactly a ball of fire, Cass had noted during the questioning, but probably this was exactly right for her. Married twelve years, two children, synagogue during the high holidays. A good wife and mother.

"When did this take place?" he had asked about her infidelity.

"Right now," she had answered.

Lousy bitch. He should have guessed. These were the worst, these doers of laundry, and bakers of bread, and dusters of furniture. The gingham harlots.

As he recorded the answer correctly now on the questionnaire, the old sore opened and festered, and the pain of it shot to his head.

His mother, what he remembered of her, had worn her hair in a bun, except that morning—morning!—he had returned home unexpectedly when he was not supposed to, having escaped the school grounds at recess over some imagined wrong, and he had raced home to seek her comfort. Her hair loose on her shoulders, he remembered, and those big mother's breasts, and the obscenity of her position with the skinny man who was not his father. Thinking of her, he could forever remember only that picture of her, and despise her until he was nauseated—that old woman on the bed with another man, that old woman who was a mother.

Once, long after, when he was in college and still haunted by it, he had checked to find out the year his mother was born, and what his own age had been, so that he could fasten on the exact year it had happened. From this he was astonished to learn that his mother had been twenty-nine when it had happened. This was incredible to him. For him the worst of it had always been that she was an old woman who was a mother, and now he had proved she was a young woman then, and had been an old woman only when he was grown (that long after summer when she was passing through town and had shamelessly visited his father on business). Yet, somehow, the facts had never changed it in his mind: she had been old when he had been young, and a mother, and a bawd—an immoral, base, dissolute bawd, fiendish and faithless to him in her obscenity.

On the other side of the screen, Sarah shifted fretfully in her chair, worrying the handkerchief in her hand. The interviewer had been silent so long a time. Had she said the wrong thing? No, Dr. Chapman had said that they wanted the plain facts. No one would see them, ever. The crazy secret language, the bank safes, the STC machine. Nevertheless, her anxiety mounted. Why hadn't she consulted Fred Tauber first? What if it got out, by accident? What would happen to them? She wished, more than anything in the world, that she had not mentioned the affair. Why had she consented to this? Why had she told the truth? Was it because she was proud of the secret bursting inside her, the pregnancy of a new freedom, and she wanted to speak it aloud to someone, anyone?

She heard his voice. It seemed uncommonly harsh. "Please pardon the delay," he was saying. "We have optional questions for every different circumstance. Since you've told me your extramarital affair is an act of the present day, I had to find the correct set of questions. Now if you are ready—"

She was suddenly scared. "I don't know," she blurted, "maybe I shouldn't—"

The male voice beyond the cane screen was instantly suave and solicitous. "Please don't be frightened, Ma'am. I know this is important to you, and honesty is difficult under the circumstances. But our interests are purely scientific. Nothing else. To us—to me—you are anonymous, a woman who had volunteered to help this good work. When you are done, in a very short time, other women will take your place in this room, and some will reveal facts that are, for them, as difficult or more difficult to discuss. At the end of the day, all of you will be so many illegible scrawls on so many sheets of paper. You must have absolutely no fear."

The words were comforting, and Sarah nodded dumbly. "All right."

"We'll get this over with quickly. This man you spoke of—how long has this been going on?"

"Three months."

"On the average, can you recall how many times you have performed the sex act with him per month?"

"Per month?"

"Well, per week, if that's easier."

She hesitated. How would the truth make her appear? Would it be degrading or normal and attractive? She thought of Fred, of herself awakened and renewed, and decided that she was proud. "Four times a week," she said.

"Four times a week," he repeated. His voice was oddly muffled. "Is your partner single or married?"

"He's . . . he's married." But there must be no misunderstanding. She was no home-wrecker. "I'd better explain," she added hastily. "He's married but separated. His wife won't give him a divorce."

"I see."

His question had unsettled her. Of course Fred wanted a divorce. He had told her so many times. It was simply that his wife was being difficult. Otherwise, why would he be living separately?

"Can you enumerate one or more reasons for becoming involved in an extramarital affair?"

"I really can't say."

"Perhaps I can clarify the question." Cass began to recount the various reasons why married women often became adulteresses. ("When the subject is unable to give a direct reply," Dr. Chapman always maintained in his briefings, "it is useful to give them examples of answers made to the question by other women.") Cass had finished his fifth possible reason when Sarah interrupted.

"Yes, that one," she said.

"Which? The last?"

"Yes."

You weren't satisfied with your husband?"

She shivered. Why wasn't *he* satisfied with one answer? Why did he keep on like this? How could she tell him? How would he know? Did he know Sam? Had he lived with him for twelve years? Could he understand the corrosive monotony of each new month and year? Could he understand that but one life was given each woman, a single dowry to use as best she could, and if it were wasted, futilely wasted, there would be no other? "No, I wasn't," she said at last. "Something was missing. This just happened. I didn't look for it. It happened."

"During the first occasion on which you had sexual intercourse with this other man, were you the aggressor, or were you seduced by him, or was the mating a mutual act?"

How could she answer this truthfully when she herself did not know? But she must be fair to Fred, at all costs. He was no heartless and practiced Don Juan. Yet, neither was she a . . . a wicked Jezebel. She decided that the middle course was the most honest. "I suppose it was mutual," she said.

"Do you believe yourself to be equally passionate, more passionate, or less passionate than your husband?"

"My husband?" she repeated, surprised that they had returned to Sam.

"Yes."

"Oh, more passionate."

"And how would you compare yourself to the . . . the man who is not your husband."

"We're the same, I guess."

"Very well. Now another multiple-choice question. To the best of your knowledge, would you say that your husband knows of your current love affair? You may reply: he knows because he was told, he knows because he found out, he probably suspects, he does not know. Which would you say?"

"He does not know," said Sarah flatly.

At the card table, Cass scratched in the answer. Does not know. Does not know. Anger welled high in his throat. This was the worst kind, the Pretending Esther, dressing the children, writing for samples, collecting green stamps, enacting motherly-wifely devotion, playing at typical housewife, cuckolding and humiliating—four times a week. He remembered The Book of his youth on the chiffonier. "Such is the way of an adulterous woman; she eateth and wipeth her mouth and saith I have done no wickedness."

He passed his hand over his head and regarded the next questions. He would cut them short. He could not bear much more of this.

He resumed the cross-examination. Each reply fell upon him like a blow. He compared her voluptuous gluttony with her husband's asceticism. Cass's heart went out to her husband, poor overworked, exhausted fool, trying only to please someone who would not be pleased.

For the husband, for himself, for Dr. Chapman, for the husband most of all, Cass wanted to know the extent of her perfidy. "How long do you both engage in the coital act?"

"It takes longer now."

"How much longer?"

Haltingly, she discussed the duration and longevity of evil.

Cass's forehead was perspiring, and he abandoned the chronology of the questionnaire completely. "Does the sight of your partner arouse you?"

"No."

"Not at all?"

"Not much."

"What does arouse you?"

There was a silence.

"Something must arouse you," said Cass impatiently. "What is it? You can tell me."

Her answer was barely discernible. "Sexual intercourse," she said.

"Simply that?"

"Going on and on," she said.

His pencil was poised over the sheet. He tried to visualize her as he had glimpsed her in the corridor. The hair in a tight bun, the ample female hips. And then he pictured her as he had really seen her: hair loose on her shoulders and massive naked thighs—that old woman on the bed with another man. . . .

⋄ ⋄ ⋄

It was ten thirty-five, twenty minutes since she had left the Association building, when Sarah Goldsmith turned her station wagon south off Wilshire and drove the two blocks to Fred's apartment. She had told him that she would not be able to see him this morning, but after the interview, she had a sudden urge to be with him. Usually, she was careful, but this morning she allowed herself the caprice.

The interview had had a singular effect on her thinking. It had helped sort matters out. By articulating the history of her marriage and the history of her affair, she was able to see her choice more clearly. Until then, the question of choice had not come up. But now she saw Sam—and herself—factually. And Fred—and herself—truly.

She parked beneath the elms, crossed the quiet street, and went into the apartment building. In this wing there were only two tenants. A peroxide blonde of indeterminate years, and countless Siamese cats, who lived on the ground floor, and Fred, whose apartment was at the top of the stairs. Entering the cool foyer, and then starting up the stairs, Sarah was surprised to see a woman descending toward her.

Sarah's heart hammered. The woman could be emerging from only one apartment. For a moment, she loomed above. She was attired in an immaculate piqué tennis outfit, a woman in her early forties, with gray-black hair meticulously waved, and sharp, regular, aristocratic features, and a long straight figure. She came downward, step by step, eyes unwaveringly on Sarah, and then, passing, staring straight ahead. Sarah had held aside, to make room, and now she resumed her climb. At the top of the stairs, Sarah glanced below. The tall woman was at the door, gazing up at her. Their eyes met briefly. Sarah's fingers tightened. The woman went out the door.

Confused, Sarah rushed to Fred's apartment and rapped on the door. She waited. In a moment, the door opened and Fred,

214

in tennis jersey and shorts, was before her. She hurried to get inside.

"Sarah! What the devil are you doing here? I thought—"

"I had to see you. I finished early, and I wanted to." She gestured fretfully. "Who was that woman?"

"You mean you met her?"

"I certainly did. Shouldn't I have?"

"Oh, stop that. Don't be silly. It doesn't matter—only I've begged you to telephone first."

"Why? Who was she?"

"My wife."

"Your wife?" She had guessed it, but it was difficult to reconcile that juiceless, older woman with Fred's youthful vigor. "Does she do this often?"

"Do what? There's nothing. I told you we have nothing to do with each other. We have some community property. Once or twice a month she drops by to discuss business. Today she wanted to do it at the Beverly Hills Tennis Club."

"But what was she doing up *here*?"

"We hadn't finished talking. And she was thirsty."

"For water?"

"Sarah—"

She felt the tautness give, and she was free of it. "I'm sorry," she said miserably. "Please, Fred, don't be angry with me."

She went to him, head on his shoulder, arms encircling his chest.

"I'm not angry," he said. "Only try not to do this again, Sarah. I've nothing to hide. There's no one but you. But sometimes I'm out, or some friend is here, or today—she—"

"I won't, Fred, not again. I just wanted to see you."

He stroked her sleek hair. "That's good of you. I appreciate it. I want to see you as often as possible. What happened this morning? How was the child psychiatrist?"

"Psychiatrist?" She had momentarily forgotten her fiction, and then she remembered it. "Fine—very helpful. I . . . I learned a good deal."

"Have you had breakfast yet?"

"That's not what I want."

He held her off. "What do you want?"

"I want to know you love me."

He drew her to him again, and spoke gently, lucidly, as one addresses a small child. "Of course I love you. But let's not ever spoil it by being rash. I want this to go on forever. The main thing to remember is—we must both be sensible."

She gazed up at him. "Why?" she asked.

It was something she had never asked him—or herself—before.

◇　◇　◇

Long after, Paul Radford would still relive the interview that took place between the hour of four and five-fifteen that tropical Thursday afternoon.

What had first intrigued him about her was the soft, low-keyed voice that filtered through the obstructing screen. There was a throaty quality about the voice that conjured up an association of words: reposeful . . . sophisticated . . . ladylike . . . chaise longue . . . lace . . . boudoir . . . ardor . . . infinity. Someday, when they had the Zollman Foundation grant and their fabulous sex center, he would suggest to Dr. Chapman that a paper be prepared correlating feminine desirability to vocal timbre.

He wondered if the reality of her matched the promise of her voice. Again he thought, as he had several times before, that the dividing screen was an artificial nuisance, more inhibiting than encouraging.

Before him lay her history, through adolescence and the pre-marital stage. Except for certain puritanical overtones, and a tendency toward restraint, her life performance was not remarkable. Most of her early behavior was widespread and therefore, by their standard, eminently normal.

"Before we embark on a series of questions about the marital sex act," he said, "perhaps you'd like a brief break—smoke a cigarette?"

"If you please."

"Matter of fact, I'll have a pipe, if it won't annoy you?"

"Not at all."

He heard the unclasping of her purse, and he extracted his pipe and filled and lighted it. He lifted the questionnaire from the table and reviewed the beginnings of their interview, as he had several times before.

Her name was Kathleen Ballard. Her age was twenty-eight. She had been born in Richmond, Virginia, and removed to San Francisco when she was twelve—this would account for the slight Southern slur, attractive, on some of her words—and she had been educated at Roanoke College and the University of Richmond, and spent a short time at the Sorbonne, explained by the fact that her late father was high-ranking regular army. Like Paul himself, she was Presbyterian by heredity and indifferent by choice. She had recently joined a church in The Briars, but only so that her daughter might have Sunday-school activity. Her marital status was that of widow. Her husband of three years had been a jet test pilot and had met with a fatal accident over a year ago.

Paul had undergone a curious emotional conflict when he had heard the fate of her husband. His first reaction, spontaneous and uncivilized, was one of relief. Why relief? Because, he told himself, a woman like this must not be owned by any man and reduced to a commonplace chattel taken for granted. And besides, if she were free, it made his fantasies less immature. At once, the old dependable guilt overtook him. And for the feeling of relief he substituted the more acceptable and sanctimonious attitude of pity.

Now, drawing contentedly on his pipe, preparing to ask the series of questions on marital coitus, he suddenly related her last name to the test pilot recently dead. Ballard. And then it came to him that this might be the widow of the renowned Boy Ballard, a legendary figure whose name had so flamboyantly filled the front pages for several years. Of course, this was the great Boy Ballard's widow, and immediately Paul Radford felt embarrassed for his fantasies. He felt like a chimney sweep in the presence of Her Majesty. But another glance at the questionnaire reassured him. She *was* a woman.

He set the sheet on the table before him, settled his pipe in the ceramic tray, and cleared his throat. "Well, the pause that refreshes. If you're ready, I am."

"Yes, I'm ready."

"These questions will concern just the three years you were married. To begin with, what was the frequency of sexual intercourse with your husband?"

On the other side of the screen, Kathleen Ballard, in a cool, sleeveless, ice-blue linen dress, sat rigid and erect in the chair. She had just ground out the butt of her cigarette, but now she sought another in her purse.

"Let me think . . . " she said.

It was the moment that she had dreaded all these last days, but she was prepared. Meeting Ursula Palmer before the post office, Tuesday morning, had been fortunate. They had taken tea at The Crystal Room, and Ursula, with her keen reportorial mind, had explained the entire experience. In her car afterward Kathleen had located a pencil in her glove compartment,

217

and, writing on the back of a pink garage receipt, she had jotted down as many of the Chapman questions as she could remember, especially those concerning marital life. As a result, she had been ten minutes late picking up Deirdre at dancing class. But that night, and the night after, she had kept the notes before her in the kitchen, and then in the bathroom and bedroom, thinking about the questions that she would be asked and thinking about her life with Boy.

Now, holding a newly lighted cigarette between faintly nicotine-scarred fingers, she wondered if Jim Scoville, official biographer, and J. Ronald Metzgar, keeper of the shrine, had been right, and she had been wrong. It was too late now for remorse. She was face to face with it—with that surprisingly kind and thoughtful person concealed behind that sensible screen—and there was no turning back. Besides, she was prepared.

"I'm sorry," she said, "but could you ask that question again, please?"

"The frequency of—"

"Oh, yes. Three times a week," she blurted.

"Would that be the average?"

"More or less, when he was home. He was away a good deal."

"Did you engage in petting before—"

She was ready for that one, too. "Yes, of course."

"Could you describe—"

Hastily, she described it.

"How much time, on the average, did you devote to petting?"

She suffered a moment of panic. Ursula had left that one out. Or had she forgotten to note it? No, Ursula would forget nothing. Odd. She was so thorough. Maybe Ursula had not been asked the question. Why not? And why now? How much time, on the average? How could that be answered? What should it be? An hour? Too fanciful. Too pat. "Fifty minutes," she said.

Coolly, so she thought it must appear, she went on and on, with no hesitancy, with full confidence, from magnificent performances to incredible satisfactions, always the paragon of enlightened womanhood.

She had replied to a crucial question. There was a momentary silence, and she watched the screen and wondered if he approved.

"Now, as I have it here," said Paul, "you and your husband

were intimate three times weekly, with fifty minutes devoted to petting and an hour devoted to love. Do I have it right?"

The cigarette almost burned her finger, and she hastily rubbed it in the tray. Nerve filaments quivered tautly beneath her skin, and it was difficult to swallow. "Yes," she said loudly. Too loudly, she decided. "It's difficult ... to remember exactly."

More questions, too carefully worded, she thought. She wondered.

More answers, too recklessly given, he thought. He wondered.

"To what degree did you enjoy intimate relations with your mate—very much, somewhat, not very much, not at all?"

"I always enjoyed it very much. Isn't that normal?"

❖   ❖   ❖

At ten minutes after five, Paul Radford noisily pushed back his chair to indicate clearly that the interview had been terminated. "Well, that gives us everything we need. Thank you very much."

"It was painless. Thank you."

He listened intently, and heard her remove the purse from the end table, heard the clack of her high-heeled pumps on the floor, heard the door open and close, and at last he was alone with the coded sex history of Kathleen Ballard, Widow.

Scowling, he took up the sheet, rose, and started around the screen. Twenty minutes stretched between now and the next scheduled interview. He decided that he needed a cup of black coffee in the conference room. Going past the screen into the forbidden female place, he halted a moment to contemplate the empty chair, recently vacated, and the ash tray with the remains of six or seven cigarettes. And then he saw on the floor, beneath the end table, a dark-green wallet.

He moved to the table, kneeled, and picked up the wallet. It was plainly feminine, and because no one else had been in the chair this morning, he knew who its owner must be. Unsnapping it, he pondered how she could have left it behind. Then he recollected when it must have happened. During the first minutes of the interview, he had heard her drop her purse. She had requested a moment to retrieve the scattered contents. Apparently she had overlooked the wallet.

Studying the billfold, now open, and knowing its owner, he justified his next action by telling himself that he had to be positive it was her own. The wallet contained a five-dollar bill, two singles, a Diners' book, and several gasoline credit cards. Opening the flap to the celluloid inserts, he found a driver's license, and then her photograph, or, rather, her photograph with a small girl child. This, he knew, was what he had been hunting for from the beginning.

He stared at the formal, wallet-sized picture, obviously the contact print for an enlargement. He was not surprised one bit. She was almost exactly what he had imagined. Prettier, perhaps, with a loveliness that held him breathless. For long seconds, he studied the marvelous face, the dark hair bobbed short, the Oriental eyes, the tip of the nose, and the sensuous mouth.

Quickly, he closed the wallet and snapped it tight. He would give it to Benita to return.

He slipped the wallet into his pocket, and there was the questionnaire still in his hand. The questionnaire, he thought, less real, less true than the face with lips like a thread of scarlet.

For a moment, he peered down at the sheet of paper in his hand. And then, in a single abrupt motion, half exasperation, half disappointment, he tore the sheet in two.

Why had she lied?

In the corridor, he saw Benita behind the desk writing a letter.

"Any coffee?" he asked.

"On the hot plate," she said.

He nodded and went on. He did not give her the wallet.

⋄   ⋄   ⋄

Kathleen Ballard stood before the Spanish grille panel of her bar, which she had slid back earlier, and now she dropped fresh ice cubes in the two glasses, uncomfortably aware of Ted Dyson's eyes upon her. Pouring the Scotch across the ice—she really shouldn't have another drink, she knew—she was sorry that she had worn this black sheath. It left her shoulders bare and clung tightly to her thighs, and was too short. If it made her feel unclad, what was it making him feel?

Slowly, she stirred the drinks, forgetting that there was no water in them and that they need not be stirred. Yet, she had selected the dress with care, and earlier she had driven Deirdre over to the Keegans for the night, and, after the dinner was under control, she had dismissed Albertine two hours early and said that she would serve the meal herself. What had possessed her?

It was the interview, of course. She had faced the fact of it and the lie of it, these last hours since. The ordeal had been sick-making, with all those dreadful, ruthless questions, and, worse, she had misled the poor, earnest man like some psychotic liar. But it had been necessary to go through with the interview, to resolve a stand she had taken toward her past, and it had been equally necessary to prevaricate, if she were to live with that past. But the point was, and this she knew short minutes after the interview, she did not want to live with her past or make false terms with it. She wanted to start anew; she wanted to be *normal*. The questions had fashioned her goal: in a year or two from now, if she were asked them again, she wanted to be free enough, sufficiently liberated and unashamed, to answer each and all honestly. This had been her mood and temper driving home, and dressing, and waiting for Ted Dyson. Perhaps he was not her ultimate man, but he was a man, and she had not known one for a year, nearer two, perhaps ever. Lord, she was twenty-eight, and still not yet a woman.

Now, the two drinks in her hands, she left the bar and saw that Ted had, indeed, been watching her. He sat sprawled indolently on the low silk sofa, exuding cockiness, and she did not like it. In fact, there was the frightening feeling inside her that she did not like him at all. Although there was a sulky virility about him, there was also something angry, jittery, unwholesome, that reminded you of male carhops and juvenile hopheads you saw in the morning paper. Yet, he was an old friend, and he respected her, and his membership card reminded you that he was of the elite who often dwelled in the news.

She set her drink on the tea table and then went around the table to the sofa. She held out his glass.

"Hi, oasis," he said thickly.

Bending toward him, she could smell the liquor on his breath. He had been drinking before he arrived, that she knew, and this was the fourth she had served him.

He accepted the drink with his left hand and suddenly grabbed her wrist with his right.

"Come on, Katie—sit down beside me."

"Not now, Ted. I've got the dinner—"

"To hell with the dinner. Let's talk."

221

Her stance was awkward, bent forward, her wrist clamped in his hard hand.

"All right," she said. "For a minute."

He released her, and she sank into the sofa. As she did so, the narrow skirt slid above her knees. Frantically, she tried to pull it down, but then saw that he was grinning at her, and that this was a ridiculous prudery. She settled back and found that his arm was behind her and his drink, somehow, on the table.

He drew her to him, and, with reluctance, she permitted it. "Cozy," he said. "You fit nicely."

"I hope so," she said, but felt his hand close on her arm and heard her heart quicken. "You wanted to talk," she added.

"Not much. Just a little." He focused on her woozily, and she did not like his face so close. "What gives with you, honey?" he asked.

"What do you mean?"

"Maybe you got a secret life I don't know—but the way you been, it's not normal."

That word again. It struck her like a spear.

"Who says I'm not normal?" she wanted to know angrily.

"Now, don't get sore. I just mean the way you act. Like one minute you want to be friendly, and then the next you don't. You torching for Boy?"

"You know better than that."

"Last time I was here, I wanted to stay, worst way. You brushed me."

"You were drunk."

"Not that drunk. You mean, if I weren't drunk you could love me?"

"People don't talk about that."

His eyes were strange. "Maybe that's what's wrong—I talk too much."

"I didn't mean that."

"Or maybe Boy's in the way, and we ought to kill him off for good tonight."

She felt his breath on her cheek. "Right now," he whispered.

He drew her roughly to him and pressed her head into the cup of his arm with his free hand, and put his lips on hers.

It was inevitable, she knew. It was what she had planned and dreaded. Now it was here. It was normal, and maybe if she didn't think, didn't think, let go and floated, let go to his lips and hands, maybe then she would soon be normal, too. His lips were wet and bitter, and he was breathing into her, and feebly she tried to respond, pressing her mouth to his, reaching to touch his neck.

For a moment, their mouths were apart. "Good girl—good," he muttered. He kissed her again, and she received it, eyes shut, feeling herself being maneuvered against his chest, feeling his hand on her back searching for and finding the zipper. "My girl—good girl," she heard in her ear, and wanted to fight, and still did not, but knew that he was pulling her down on the sofa, and that her dress was loose, and that he was stretched beside her.

She moaned, hating herself for hating this, and he mistook the sound for passion. Excitedly, he fumbled at the bodice of her black dress.

"Ted," she said, "Ted—"

"Easy, honey—in a minute."

She tried to wriggle away from him. "No, Ted—don't—"

"I want you, honey—I want you—"

"Ted, listen—"

But he wouldn't listen. She reached for his wrists, and held them, pushing them from her with all her strength.

"Honey, you need me—"

"I don't! Now, stop it!"

Astonished by her vehemence, he relaxed his assault and stared down at her, not moving.

"You were begging for it all night," he said viciously. "What's got into you?"

"Not you or anybody!"

He showed his teeth. "That's good whore talk."

Confidently, he reached for her loose dress again, and she slapped him stingingly. He recoiled, falling backward, gripping the tea table to keep from dropping to the floor. He straightened himself, and by then she was sitting up, closing her dress.

"What kind of creep are you," he said savagely, "leading a man on—"

"I didn't mind kissing, but when you try to treat me like one of your cheap call girls—"

"You mean only call girls give out? What's with you, anyway?"

"There's nothing with me!" She felt the edge of hysteria in her voice, and she wanted to cry.

"I'll say there's nothing. Boy, oh, boy—nothing at all; frigid as an icicle."

Her voice broke. "Get out!"

"You're damn right I will." He stood up, patting his hair.

"Honey, you're going to have to phone mighty soon if you want me or anyone for a return engagement—because if it's later, you're going to be a pitiful dried-up bag."

"Goddam you, get out!"

"Sure, sure." He shook his head and started toward the door. "I've heard of frigidity, but I never had a date with a deep freeze." He opened the door and turned. "Poor old Boynton. Now I can understand; I don't blame him for shacking up with all those other babes!"

"You bastard—"

She had the heavy glass ash tray in her hand, but before she could throw it, he was out the door and gone.

✧   ✧   ✧

She had sat on the sofa, legs curled under her, for a long time, chain smoking and staring into space. She had reviewed this night, a hundred other nights, her entire life, and never had she felt more helpless.

At last, as the disaster receded and the grinding process of remembrance wearied, she got to her feet, made her way into the kitchen, and turned off the oven. She had no stomach for food and decided to prepare for bed and read until she was sleepy.

Mechanically, she had begun to sort the food that might be salvaged and put it in the freezer when the doorbell sounded. For a moment, she was gripped by the fear that it might be Ted, abject and apologetic. She hesitated. The clock read twenty after eight. Then something told her that it would not be Ted, now or ever.

She went to the entry hall, snapped on the front lights, and opened the door.

A tall man, strange to her, holding a green wallet, stood diffidently behind the welcome mat.

He smiled. "I hate to break in on you like this, Mrs. Ballard, but we know each other, even though we haven't met."

"I'm afraid I don't know you," she said impatiently.

"I'm Paul Radford. I'm one of Dr. Chapman's associates."

"Dr. Chapman? I don't understand."

"I know this is irregular, but—"

Suddenly, the expression on her face showed amazement, and then indignation. "We know each other? You mean—were you the one who interviewed me this morning?"

He nodded. "Yes. This isn't customary, of course, but I was

224

afraid you'd need your wallet. I found it on the floor after you left."

He opened the screen and handed it to her. Coloring, she hesitated, then took it. Avoiding his eyes, she busied herself opening it. "Yes, it's mine," she said finally. "I suppose I should thank you, but I won't."

The apologetic smile left his face. "You're annoyed?"

"Don't you think I have the right to be?" she said heatedly. "I only went through with that stupid interview because I was told it was the right thing and because I was assured it would be anonymous. Now, the first thing I know, I have the interviewer in my house."

"Well, not quite. If you'll let me explain. It's still perfectly anonymous. I haven't the least memory of—"

"I think it's absolutely wrong. Your conduct is inconsiderate, unforgivable—the effrontery of it. I can't tell you how much it distresses me. Having you here staring at me, after all you've heard—it makes me feel unclean."

For a moment, taken aback by the cold anger in the lovely face, Paul was tempted to tell her that he knew nothing about her from the interview, except that she had lied. Instead, trying to understand that all of this was a part of what had happened at the interview, too, he said, "I'm sorry I've upset you. I can't tell you how sorry."

"Why did you come here then?"

He hesitated, considering what he would like to say and what he should say. Suddenly, he didn't care. "I saw your picture in the wallet," he said. "I guess I had to know if you really existed. I can't explain it any more than that. It was wrong, and I hope you can forgive me. Good night."

He turned on his heel and walked swiftly, in long, uneven strides, down the circular driveway.

Kathleen did not move from the doorway. She watched him until he had disappeared into the night and her anger had turned into shame.

She had once looked up the word *frigid*. It meant wanting in warmth or ardor. It meant more, too. To her, it was the ugliest word in the English language.

After a while, she shut the door. She went into the bathroom and took a sleeping pill. At least, she did not dream.

9

BENITA SELBY'S JOURNAL. Friday, May 29: " . . . my table in the corridor of The Briars' Women's Association. Right now it is ten after ten in the morning. I can't believe this will soon be over. I view the end with mixed emotions. On the one hand, I will miss the excitement. On the other, I will be relieved, for it has been an arduous fourteen months. This is our fourth day of interviewing here, and that means we have nine days more, seven of which will be devoted to work. I had a long letter from Mom this morning. Her arthritis is worse. Everyone seems to be on edge. I drove in with Dr. Chapman, who is the one exception. He is always nice, but Cass was awful. He could be so attractive if he weren't so sarcastic. He wasn't friendly this morning. He had a headache, and I told him it was smog. He made some taunting remark about my journal, and I told him if it weren't for journals where would we be. I pointed out Philip Hone, Samuel Pepys, the Goncourt Brothers, Stendhal, and André Gide. That silenced him, except Dr. Chapman said he hoped I was being discreet, for we have enemies, and I reassured him. More and more, I feel this journal will be a wonderful record of a historic period in modern science. By that I mean, it will serve to humanize Dr. Chapman, if this is ever read.

"When we arrived, Horace and Paul were already here. Horace was a million miles away, as usual, and Paul was definitely upset about something. Usually, Paul is good-natured, but everyone must be allowed an off day. I signed the first three women in at nine, and they are there now. There were two telephone calls. The first was the publicity director of a movie studio inviting Dr. Chapman to lunch in honor of a picture being made about unmarried teen-age mothers, to which he said no because it was undignified but told them he would be willing to address the producers' guild on sex and censorship, to which they agreed—oh, this sentence, when will it stop?—anyway, it will be arranged. The second call was from a young lady requesting me to give Paul a message. She said she would like to meet him for lunch at The Crystal Room at a time convenient to him. I told her twelve sharp was the best time. She said to call if he could not make it. She had a beautiful voice, like Margaret Sullavan and others. Her name is Mrs. Ballard. What would Paul be seeing a married woman for??? . . ."

◇   ◇   ◇

When Paul arrived at The Crystal Room, he saw that she was seated alone in a mauve booth, beneath a glittering chandelier, smoking and toying with a match folder. For a moment, he stood inside the entrance behind a group of new arrivals watching her. His first judgment had not been wrong. She was exquisite. The anger of the night before had given way to curiosity, to that, and to a sense of adventure as well.

He advanced toward her booth.

"Good afternoon, Mrs. Ballard," he said.

She lifted her head quickly. "Hello." She seemed relieved. "I was positive you'd stand me up. I wouldn't blame you if you had."

"Surely you didn't believe I would." He sat down across from her.

"Anyway, I'm glad you came."

He smiled. "I'd have made book that I wouldn't see you again."

She flushed. "You understand, I don't usually call strange men and make dates—"

He was about to tease her but saw that she was too anxious.

". . . but when I awoke this morning, I realized how horridly I had behaved last night. I kept worrying—that poor man, what must he think of me—"

"He thought you were a determined wallet-loser, and you hated to have it back."

"That was what troubled me most," she said. "You had only tried to do me a favor."

"That's not quite true, Mrs. Ballard."

She stopped, and gazed at him, and he was aware of her silken lashes and Oriental eyes. "I don't understand," she said.

"I was doing myself a favor. You see, you were right last night. I won't let you torment yourself. It was unethical of me,

227

an investigator, to seek out a subject. Normally, I would have behaved with propriety. I would have turned the wallet over to Miss Selby—our secretary—and she would have telephoned you, and you would have come by and picked it up. It would have all been very correct and sterile, untouched by human hands. But it so happened that I had to open your wallet to learn who owned it. I saw your picture. I had to see you. Those are the facts. So it is you, not I who deserves the apology."

She furrowed her brow, averted her gaze, and stared down at the silver service. She thought, What is he saying? Why is he telling me this? Then she remembered. He interviewed me, and during the interview he heard all those lascivious details, and he thinks I'm sex mad, a push-over.

He frowned, observing her. He had believed that she would take his frankness for flirtatious fun, but now he saw that he had troubled her. He thought, What is she imagining? Does she think I'm trying—my God, that idiotic interview—she must think I'm using it to—

An elderly waiter, in red and blue uniform with brass buttons, was standing over them. "May I get you something from the bar before lunch?"

Paul looked from the waiter to Kathleen. "Will you join me?"

"I believe I will. Martini."

"Make that two, and very dry," Paul told the waiter, who wrote the order and was gone.

Paul turned his attention back to Kathleen. "Mrs. Ballard," he said quickly. "I think you may have misunderstood me, and it's offended you—"

"No."

"If you imagine, even for a second, that anything relating to the interview had anything to do with my calling upon you —well, I assure you, that is not so. To be perfectly honest, there have been so many interviews, I find it impossible to sort them out. I wouldn't remember if you're the nymphomaniac, the lesbian, or the lush."

She smiled at last. "The lush," she said.

"Of course. I should have spotted it—the blotched cheek, trembling hand, the slight stagger in your voice—and the cluster of diamonds spelling AA."

"Where did you say you lived—Baker Street?"

For a short time, the colloquy remained suspended at that level, formal, inoffensive, unengaged, but brought down to the two of them, finally, face to face, by the appearance of the Martinis.

"Well," he said, lifting his drink toward her, "to you—for making another day possible."

She imitated the gesture. They sipped.

"This is strong," she said.

"Frightened by an olive at an early age."

She laughed.

Both were suddenly aware that they had nothing to say to each other—or else everything. She knew nothing of him, personally, and wondered if it would be bold to ask, and he knew more of her, and knew he could not ask.

"Were you always in this kind of work?" she wanted to know.

"No; just a few years. I used to be a teacher—and writer of sorts."

"What made you give it up?"

"I'm tempted to be flippant. If I were, I'd say an interest in sex and money. My downfall. But that's not so, really. I think I was flattered by the opportunity to work under Dr. Chapman, to be on the inside of something so important. I suppose, in some secret place, I still think of myself as a writer—there's no such thing as an ex-writer—and I like to believe all this will one day be useful. When I'm old and tottering about Monte Carlo on a small pension." He paused and considered what he would say next. "There's another thing I've never articulated. Until now, I'd guess it's been subconscious. But it's poking to the surface. I think I always felt that by being in this work, finding out about others, I'd find out something about myself."

"Have you ever been interviewed—the way you interview others?"

"No. All the sampling on the bachelor survey was finished when I came in. One of my colleagues was interviewed by Dr. Chapman and, of course, the doctor interviewed himself."

"Is that possible?"

"I would say it's impossible—except for Dr. Chapman. He's a remarkable man."

"I thought his lecture was impressive."

"It always is. He's adept at that sort of thing. No, I meant as a human being. He's solid and single-minded. Dedicated. It's good to be around a man like that when everything around you seems uncertain, unsolved, flying off in every direction. He's been a fine example."

"I'm surprised you would need one," said Kathleen. "You seem . . . sure of yourself—I mean that in a nice way."

Paul smiled. "Façade," he said, "like everyone. Inside, there are too many corridors and turnings, and we're all apt to get lost sometime."

"Yes," she said solemnly.

"What I was trying to say before was—well, here I am—thirty-five, a bachelor. It surprises me; it was not what I had always dreamed—"

"Perhaps you've never been in love."

"I'm sure I have, several times, in different ways. At each age, you are in love in a different way. It's like spinning a roulette wheel. If you're lucky enough to land on the right number, you have the right way, you win. Anyway, I thought that sitting behind that screen, listening, learning, might make me a lucky one. I'm not sure now. It sorts out a lot of things, but the deeper confusion isn't touched." He finished his drink. "Maybe you're right, though. Maybe I've never been in love. Maybe I've been afraid." Thoughtfully, he rotated his empty glass.

"I didn't know that happened to men."

"Of course it does. Even to men who are married."

"You know, I never thought of that."

He continued to turn the empty glass in his hand. "I've been talking too much."

"Only fair," she said. "You've had the advantage of learning all about me."

"That was business. This is pleasure."

"You mean you don't enjoy all that vicarious sex talk with assorted women?"

He saw that she was chiding him, but he remained serious. "It's meaningless after a while. The vicarious part. I enjoy it as a . . . an investigator. It's gratifying to see the statistics develop. But as a person—" He shook his head. "There's an inevitable sadness about everyone."

She stared at her drink. "Does that include me?"

"And me." He studied her sweet, melancholy face. "Your husband—I was wondering—was he the Ballard who was so famous?"

"Yes."

"I've often thought about the widows of famous men. Presidents' widows, for instance. It must be different from having just a man removed. It must be like a planet gone, a planet

230

thickly peopled and buzzing with activity, suddenly taken away."

He waited. Her face was noncommittal.

She thought. Not like a planet removed, but like an army of occupation gone home at last.

"Something like that," she said.

"Have you adjusted to being alone?"

"You have to be very interested in yourself to adjust to being alone. I'm not sure that I am."

He had some stake in her that he did not understand, and he could not know enough. "How do you spend your time now? What do you do?"

"I do what most women do, not just widows, married ones, too." She paused. "I wait."

"For someone?"

"For something . . . for life to explain itself to me."

The waiter had returned. Suddenly, they both realized that the restaurant was filled. Kathleen ordered carefully, selecting what she thought he would expect her to like—a bouillabaisse and toasted French bread. Paul ordered exactly what she had ordered, because he wanted her to know he liked what she liked. As the waiter marked the order, Paul decided that later, when they were leaving, he would ask to see her again. He wondered if she would say yes.

♦   ♦   ♦

Benita Selby's journal. Saturday, May 30: ". . . eating together at the other end of the conference room, and talking about Cass. When Cass didn't appear at breakfast, Dr. Chapman found him ill with an upset stomach. Dr. Chapman thought it sounded like ptomaine and insisted on Cass resting. He has taken over Cass's interviews today. I had a short letter from Mom. She wants to change doctors because she feels Dr. Rubinfeer doesn't give her enough time and charges too much, and he hasn't improved the arthritis one bit. I wrote her this morning not to make any move until I get home. You start out being taken care of by your mother and always wind up taking care of her. Although, the poor thing is absolutely crippled. Mr. Borden Bush just telephoned from the network to confirm the lunch with Dr. Chapman for Monday. Mr. Bush said to remind Dr. Chapman to bring a list of the questions he wants to be asked when he appears with the panel on 'The Hot Seat.' The television show will be coast to coast a week from tomorrow. It was arranged in New York three months ago, to celebrate the end of Dr. Chapman's female survey. I'm most excited, though Dr. Chapman seems to take it in stride. There are still fifteen minutes before we resume. I think I'll read the new *Houseday* and find out what it's like being an artificial-insemination baby and why that actress gave up career and drugs for God."

✦ ✦ ✦

Ursula Palmer kneeled before the magazine rack in the hotel lobby, removed the dozen remaining copies of the latest *Houseday* from behind a rival periodical that partially covered it, and placed *Houseday* in a prominent position on top. This habit of rearranging *Houseday* was a task of long standing, one she had assumed the day that she had been hired by Bertram Foster. It comforted her to do this, for she felt that every copy of *her* magazine sold was one more guarantee of her future.

Rising, she glanced about to see if she had been noticed, but there were only several groups of men in the lobby, wearing the celluloid lapel buttons that indicated another convention had occupied the city. She looked toward the elevators, nervously waiting for Foster, but the elevators were all still airborne.

She wandered restlessly through the spacious lobby, wondering what she would tell him, and then stood beside a huge potted rubber plant, trying to think it out. Her original date with Foster had been for last night, when he was to have driven in from Palm Springs, to see her alone and read her notes. When she realized that she would not have the notes, she had telephoned him in Palm Springs to explain the delay. Alma had answered the phone. Ursula had asked Alma Foster if she were having a good time, had learned she was not having a good time, and Ursula had then inquired for Mr. Foster. He was on the golf course, it turned out, and then he had some special business in Los Angeles. "That's just it," Ursula had blurted, "he mustn't come—I'm not ready for him yet. I hope you can catch him." There had been a forbidding silence, and Ursula had realized her blunder. "Don't worry," Alma had said tightly. "I'll catch him." Ursula had tried desperately to repair the unmeasurable damage. "It's about a series of articles, Mrs. Foster. Would you tell him I don't have the notes ready yet. I'll call him when I do."

That tactical error had been committed early yesterday morning. Early this morning, the telephone had rung, and it was Foster, and it was not long distance. "Alma and I are back in the hotel," he said—stiffly, Ursula thought. "I have only some garbled message from her about your not being ready. I think you better come and explain it straight. I'll be in around noon."

She sat in the chair beside the potted rubber plant and weighed truth against white lie. Could she tell him that the notes on her interview were only one third typed? Could she tell him that she got stuck every time she tried to go on with them, reading and re-reading them, thinking about the past and about her life with Harold? Could she explain that she was up against the first writing block in her entire career? Would he understand? How could he, if she didn't? Wouldn't it be better to shift the blame to Harold—the flu was all over the place, she had read—and keep herself efficient and uncomplicated?

"Well, here you are." It was Foster speaking, as he waddled toward her, and she literally leaped to her feet.

"Oh, Mr. Foster—I'm sorry if I inconvenienced you. I hope you didn't come into town because of me."

He emitted a deep nasal snort. "I did. And Alma did, too."

"I'm sorry."

"Never mind that. With me, life never is a picnic. I want to know only one thing—what did you tell her on the phone?"

"It was nothing. I told her I had to speak to you, and she said you were playing golf and then going to Los Angeles, and I said that's what I was calling about, that the work we were to go over had been delayed, and that you should not come in until I phoned you back." She showed her bewilderment. "I don't see anything wrong."

"Naturally. Because you're not Alma. I said I had special business. I didn't say with who. The minute she found out— a-ha—anyone in skirts is poison—she began following me like a guilty conscience. So what's the use? Here we are." He studied her, his tiny eyes even tinier. "What's this about no notes? You went in and gave them your whole sex life, didn't you?"

"Oh, yes, Mr. Foster."

"More than an hour, wasn't it?" She nodded. He lifted his shoulders. "So—where's the notes?"

"I have them, but—" She saw that a group of men nearby, attracted undoubtedly by Foster's loud reference to sex, were

233

watching them. She felt uncomfortable. "May we sit down for a minute? I'll explain."

"Suits me." He took her arm, walked across the thickly carpeted lobby to a love seat near the window. "Right here."

They both sat. "I took complete notes at the interview," she went on hastily. "Every question, every one of my answers. It was very thorough."

"It was, eh? You blushed?"

"Believe me, I felt like it. But I told the truth, the whole truth—"

"So help you God?"

"Oh, yes. But I had them down in a sort of shorthand I use. I started transcribing them for you, and suddenly Harold was sick last Monday night—a hundred and two fever—and I've had my hands full with him ever since. But he's better today. I can get on it soon."

"You couldn't hire someone to dictate to?"

"Mr. Foster, I wouldn't let anyone on earth hear or see these notes—except you. Why, it'd be like undressing in front of a stranger."

"I suppose." His eyes were bright again and his fat lips moist. "So I have only a week more here. Give me a date."

"What's today? Saturday. I'll still be busy nursing Harold tomorrow, but I'll start Monday and work right through. I should have them by next Wednesday or Thursday. I'd say Thursday, to be absolutely certain."

"No sooner?"

"I'll try, but—"

"All right; we'll make it definite—definite Thursday night, here in my room. I'll work out something with Alma. You come at seven and plan to have drinks and dinner and put in a long session." He looked at her a moment. "I hope it's good."

"It will be."

"I already called Irving Pinkert and told him the whole thing about the three-parter. He's impressed, like I promised. So see that it's juicy."

"I hope it is, Mr. Foster. I'm not Madame Du Barry."

He placed his pudgy hand on her knee and rubbed it. "All women are Madame Du Barry," he said sententiously, and Ursula nodded, half believing it, and thought of New York.

But, soon after, driving westward on Wilshire Boulevard, her preoccupation with New York dimmed as the distance she put between Foster and herself grew. New York was winning every battle but the last one, and the last one was Harold. He was finally fixed fully in her mind, and when she reached Roxbury Drive in Beverly Hills, she turned off toward his new office, determined to surprise him by settling the decoration of his suite once and for all.

The white building, with its colonnades, was one of the few in the block that housed neither analysts nor internists. The black directory with white lettering, beside the elevator, was populated by public-relations counsels, business managers, and several enigmatic corporations. Not having visited the building since the week Harold had moved in, Ursula had forgotten the floor. She found Harold sandwiched between an importer and a talent agency, and took the self-service elevator to the second floor.

The office was the third from the elevator. On the frosted glass—impressively, she had to admit—was the black lettering: "Harold Palmer and Co., Certified Public Accountants." The "Co.," she knew, was merely a sop to proper status. Harold would have preferred "Ltd." had he not felt it too ostentatious. Except for a tax student who came in to help two months of the year, Harold's operation was one-man.

Feeling all benevolence, like those massive clubwomen who delivered baskets to the hundred most needy each Christmas day, Ursula opened the door and went into the reception room of "Harold Palmer and Co." What met her eye stunned her. When last she had visited the office, the once she had done so, there had been a sagging maroon sofa, a faded slip-covered chair, and a nightmarish Orozco reproduction askew on the wall, all furnished by the landlord until his tenant could become settled. But now, by some magical transformation, the landlord's pieces had disappeared, and what replaced them might have graced an interior decorator's window on Robertson Boulevard. The room sparkled with youth and newness and lightness, like a Scandinavian starlet devoted to outdoor living. The two low-slung sofas, the chairs, and desk, were Danish modern, the wood bleached walnut and the fabric gray print. A single deep red rose, in a long-necked Swedish-glass vase, stood on the coffee table between copies of *Réalité* and *Verve*. On the walls were fragile lithographs, signed in pencil, by Dufy, Matisse, and Degas. Ursula stood speechless. Whatever had happened proved but one thing—here, at least, she was expendable.

Still in small shock, she crossed to the private office door and rapped sharply.

"Yes?"

"It's Ursula."

"Come in!"

Ursula opened the door and went in. The first sight that met her eyes was the young lady's behind, large, ungirdled, wanton, disgusting. The young lady was bent across Harold's desk, lifting the lid from the carton of coffee on a tray that also contained wrapped sandwiches smelling of hot beef and gravy.

Harold appeared less gray and concave than usual. He waved his arm. "Hi!" He seemed as pleased and afraid as a schoolboy caught smoking. "This is a surprise."

"I'll bet," said Ursula frostily.

The young lady, unhurried by the intrusion, straightened at last, and her buttocks were no less large. She turned slowly, smiling. Her healthy, polished-apple face, like the light-walnut modern furniture in the office, assaulted Ursula with its unused freshness. Her hair was straw yellow, and braided too cutely, and her blue eyes were startled saucers. Her mammary development, beneath the lemon sweater, was indecent, and Ursula was pleased to see that she had thick legs. She looked like a hundred Helgas, a prize Aryan cow, and one of the Hitler *Yugend* in white middy blouse and navy skirt doing gymnastics in a Nuremberg stadium.

". . . my secretary, Marelda Zigner," the hateful goat was saying. "This is Mrs. Palmer."

"How do you do, Mrs. Palmer," said Marelda Zigner, offering two vivid dimples. Her accent was faintly Teutonic, and Ursula knew that she would not let go of it for years. Marelda turned back to the goat. "Is the lunch enough, Mr. Palmer?"

"Fine, Marelda, fine. You better go out and have yours."

"I will, please." She smiled at Ursula. "Excuse me."

Ursula's eyes followed the swaying mammaries out of the office, and Ursula glared at the goat.

"Who in the hell was *that?*" asked Ursula.

"My new secretary," Harold appeared surprised. "I told you about her last week."

"Don't tell me she also types?"

"Marelda's worth any three I ever had. Those German girls are remarkable—meticulous, neat, efficient—"

"And size forty-two."

"What?"

"Never mind." She waved her hand at the furniture. "When did all this happen?"

"The furniture? Delivered yesterday. You were so busy,

236

with the Fosters here and all, and it was making me nervous, especially since I landed the Berrey account. I didn't want him to come up here and think I was a bum—so Marelda and I went out—"

"Marelda?"

"Yes. It was my good fortune that she'd taken a course in interior decoration at a school in Stuttgart—"

"So she fixed you up all Nordic? Well, we'll see—"

"I thought you'd like it, Ursula. I've had a dozen compliments this morning."

"It's utterly incongruous. It doesn't go with you. It looks like a honeymoon cottage, not a dignified business office."

Harold's left eye jumped nervously. "I kept waiting for you." He indicated one of the sandwiches. "Will you have something?"

"I'm not hungry." She scanned the furniture again. "This must have cost a fortune."

"Not really. You know those Germans. Very frugal. And . . . and now that I have Berrey—well, we don't have to draw on your savings."

"So now you feel independent."

Harold stared at her quietly. "Don't you want me to?"

She felt nervous and confused. "Of course I do. I just don't want you to act foolishly. Well, I'd better be going."

"What made you come by? It's the first time—"

"The second time. I just wanted to see how my husband spends his day. Like any wife. Is that wrong?"

"No. I'm pleased."

She had reached the door. Some instinct, long dormant, came alive. She turned, and tried to smile. "I almost forgot, Harold—I'm going shopping; is there anything special you'd like for dinner?"

The novelty of the question, the importance it gave to his reply and to himself, disconcerted him. "I . . . I haven't thought."

"Never mind. I'll dream up something good." She pointed to his tray. "Eat before it gets cold. And chew it well. You know your stomach. I'll see you later."

She opened the door and went out, very erect, bosom high, so that Marelda would know the formidable nature of the democratic opposition.

Benita's Selby's journal. Sunday, May 31: "I'm sitting by the pool of the Villa Neapolis. I finished a five-page letter to Mom. I felt guilty about my abrupt note of yesterday, and I know what these letters mean to her. She has only a son and a daughter to hear from, not counting her sisters, and Howie hasn't time to write, so if I don't who will? I told her we are all expecting a short vacation when we get back, and then I will find out about a specialist and take her to Chicago for X rays and examination. It's very hot by the pool, but the heat is not like the Midwest but drier. You don't perspire as much. There are half a dozen people in the pool. I have on the halter and shorts I bought in Milwaukee, and sun lotion all over. There's a young man across the pool sitting and reading, and a couple of times I caught him looking at me. I must look a sight with this lotion. Dr. Chapman is at the umbrella table behind me with Cass and Horace. Cass is feeling better today. Dr. Chapman is still talking about Dr. Jonas. At breakfast, he saw an article and architect's drawing about an enormous new marriage-counseling clinic being built near the ocean, which Dr. Jonas is going to manage, and Dr. Chapman was furious. I don't blame him for the way he feels about Dr. Jonas, which is only human, because I read some of the reviews that Dr. Jonas wrote. Dr. Chapman asked me if I had seen Paul, and I told him I saw Paul go out early carrying a tennis racket and tin of balls. It occurs to me you can't play tennis by yourself. Who is Paul playing with? The young man across the pool is looking at me again. I think I'll take off my sun glasses and finish this later . . ."

♦   ♦   ♦

Always, before, when Mary McManus had played tennis with her father on Sunday mornings, he had seemed marvelously youthful to her. Even after a hard-fought set, in the most intense heat, his sparse hair lay neatly in place, and his strong face remained dry, and his breathing regular. His white tennis shirt and shorts were always spruce and creased and dapper.

But today, going to the net to retrieve the two balls—she had double-faulted on her first serve—and picking them up, she observed him through the mesh as he stood at the far base line, and she saw that he had changed. He's old, she told herself with incredulity. His hair was out of place, in wet knots; his face was beet red with sweat; his chest heaved beneath his damp, wrinkled shirt; and his belly was distended in a potty, unathletic way that she had not noticed before. He's an old man, she told herself again. But why shouldn't he be? He's my father, not my boy friend.

She walked slowly back across the baking asphalt court, her thick white tennis shoes making squashing and sucking sounds on the surface, toward her base line. Calculating backward, Mary tried to fix on the period when these weekly Sunday games at The Briars' Country Club had begun. Probably in her last year of junior high school, she decided, shortly after she had started taking lessons. Her father had always taken her along to the club, those Sunday mornings, and settled her on the terrace with a Coke, and gone below to play his doubles match, two out of three. One Sunday, Harry Ewing's partner had telephoned that he was held up, and Mary had been invited to play alongside her father. It had been a thrilling morning—she had acquitted herself stoutly and was highly praised —and soon after, her father had abandoned his weekly doubles to concentrate on singles with Mary. Except for those periods when he was out of the city on business, or one of them was ill, the weekly Sunday game had been continued all of these years.

Even after her marriage to Norman, when she had been so anxious for her father to know that she was not forsaking him, she had gone on with the Sunday match. At first, of course, Norman had been invited to join them, so that she and Norman alternated against her father. But Norman, able as he was at most sports, had neither the finesse nor the training for tennis. As a youngster, he had batted the ball about on various cracked public courts, and he still wielded the racket like a baseball bat. He was not a match for Harry Ewing, nor even for her, and though Mary encouraged him and complimented him, he eventually withdrew. Now it was his custom to sleep late Sunday mornings, while she enacted the traditional liturgy with her father. Most often, Norman was at breakfast when they returned home, and she was twice as attentive as usual in the afternoons.

"Are you all right, Mary?" Harry Ewing called out.

Mary realized that she had been standing at the base line for some seconds staring at the two balls in her hand. "I'm fine!"

"If you're tired, we can call it quits."

"Well, maybe after this set, Dad. What's the score?"

"Five-six. Love-fifteen."

She had lost the first set, three-six, and now she decided to lose this one, too, and have it over, legitimately or not. Some-

239

times, in the last half year, she had felt that with extra exertion she could soundly drub him. Her game was sharp, and recently he had been covering the court more slowly. But somehow she had never been able to bring herself to run him around and humiliate him. Especially on a day like today—when he was old.

"Okay," she said. She tossed a ball aloft and went high on her toes and into it, whacking down hard with her racket. The ball streaked an inch above the net, and then bounced. But Harry Ewing had it on the rise, off his forehand, and slammed it cross-court. Mary twisted to her right, watching the ball nick an inch into the alley and out, and then she ran after it.

"What was that?" he called. "Out?"

She snapped the ball off the asphalt with her racket, and caught it. "Right on the line," she said. "Love-thirty." She double-faulted on her next service, and her father advised her to let up a little on the second ball. Then, with the set at match point, they rallied briskly, until she charged the net, and he passed her for the win.

With relief, she congratulated her father and went into the subterranean women's locker room, welcoming the cement chill, and washed her face and neck and held her wrists under the faucet. After combing her hair and freshening her make-up, Mary locked her racket in its press and climbed the stairs to the terrace.

Harry Ewing, still red-faced and breathing heavily, was seated at a metal table, waiting. She sat dutifully beside him, observing by her watch that it was near eleven and wondering if Norman was awake yet.

"Well, you gave me quite a run for my money, young lady," Harry Ewing said. "I've worked up an appetite."

"When it's hot like this, don't you think doubles would be more sensible?"

"Nonsense. When they put me out to pasture, I'll take up doubles again." He snapped his fingers at the colored waiter clearing the next table. "Franklin—"

The colored waiter bobbed his head. "Yes, suh, be right there, Mistah Ewing."

"I *have* worked up an appetite," Harry Ewing said to his daughter. "Are you going to eat anything?"

"Mother'll be angry about lunch. I'll have lemonade."

The colored waiter came with his pad, and Harry Ewing

ordered lemonade for Mary and a plate of thin hot cakes with maple syrup and iced tea for himself.

As Mary watched the waiter leave, she saw Kathleen Ballard come up the stairs from the courts, followed by a tall, attractive man. They were carrying rackets, and Kathleen was wearing a short, pleated tennis skirt. Mary guessed that they had been playing on one of the rear courts, which were out of sight. Her escort said something, and Kathleen laughed.

"Kathleen—" Mary called out.

Kathleen Ballard stopped in her tracks, searched for a familiar face to go with the voice, and finally located Mary McManus. She lifted her hand in greeting, said something to her escort, and then they both approached.

"Hello, Mary."

Harry Ewing pushed himself to his feet.

"You know my father, Kathleen," said Mary.

"We've met. Hello, Mr. Ewing." She stood aside to expose Paul Radford fully. "This is Mr. Radford. He's visiting from the East. Mrs. Ewing—" She caught herself. "I'm sorry. Mrs. *McManus,* I should say, and Mr. Ewing."

The men shook hands. Kathleen insisted that Harry Ewing be seated, but he remained standing.

"Where's Norman?" Kathleen wanted to know.

"He's been working like ten dray horses," said Mary quickly. "He's so exhausted, we felt he should have one morning."

"Now there's a perfect wife," said Paul to Kathleen.

Kathleen beamed at Mary. "I won't disagree," she said to Paul.

After a few moments, they moved on to an empty table nearby, and Mary was alone with her father.

"Who is he?" asked Harry Ewing.

"I haven't the faintest idea," said Mary, "except he's attractive."

"I didn't think so."

"I don't mean like a movie star. I mean like a frontier scout —the tall in the saddle type—except—" she glanced off—"he looks like he also reads by the bonfire."

Presently, the lemonade appeared, and then the hot cakes and iced tea. While her father ate, Mary drank the lemonade and surreptitiously spied on Kathleen and Mr. Radford. They were sitting close to each other, he packing his pipe and speaking and she listening attentively. There was an air of intimacy suggested that gave Mary a wrench of loneliness. She and

241

Norman had not been together like that, not really, since their brief honeymoon. She missed Norman now, and didn't give a damn about tennis, and wished that Kathleen had seen her with Norman.

Harry Ewing had eaten as much of his hot cakes as he wanted, and now he shoved the plate aside and brought the iced tea before him, stirring it. "I suppose," he said, "Norman told you about the trial."

"Yes. Friday night."

"What did he tell you?"

"He said you had a poor case, and he did his best, but there wasn't a chance, and so you lost."

"You believed him?"

Mary was surprised. "Of course. Shouldn't I?"

"Well, I don't want to contradict your husband outright, or run him down. He's a fine young man, a promising attorney, a little wet behind the ears yet, and rash, but he'll develop. Right now, his problem is one of loyalty."

"What does that mean?"

"He lost our case not because it was poor—any one of our other men would have managed it properly—but because he didn't believe in it. He's still got a black-and-white mind—that's what I mean by professional immaturity—and he went into that court telling himself it was capital versus labor."

"Wasn't it?" Mary asked aggressively.

"Only to an obvious mind. No, it wasn't. Because an employee brings suit doesn't mean he's automatically right because he's an employee—the downtrodden—with a billion-dollar thug union behind him. Employers have their legal rights, too. Why does wealth automatically have to suggest piracy?"

"Because the history books are filled with the Commodore Vanderbilts, and Goulds, and Fisks—and a couple of guys named Krupp and Farben—and that's just the beginning."

"It seems to me there's a few words there about the Bill Haywoods, and McNamaras, and anarchists like Sacco and Vanzetti—"

"Oh, Dad—"

"But that's not the point. My son-in-law thinks my money good enough to accept every week. Therefore, he must earn that money. But to go into court, pretending to represent me, my firm, and knuckle under to those labor bullies—"

"Who says he knuckled under?"

"I have my means of hearing what goes on. I'm not blind."

"You mean your spies are not blind."

"Mary, what's got into you? A transcript of the case is available. Norman didn't use all his ammunition."

"He said most of it was unsubstantiated character assassination."

"I'll be the one who determines what's substantiated and what isn't. And that's not all. His final summation was filled with concessions, vacillating—"

"He was trying to be fair. He told me so. He's no gallus-snapping redneck, no rabble-rouser."

Harry Ewing was silent a moment. He wanted Mary to simmer down. She was like her mother, all unreasoning, when she was emotional. "When you go into court on a thing like this, Mary," he said, his intelligent voice at its softest, "you are going into an arena of combat, do or die and no quarter asked or given. It's not a debate society or bull session of egg-heads. It's for keeps. If Norman has too many left-wing prejudices to undertake such a case, he should withdraw before it starts, or tell me so. I'll confine him to paper work, where he's more useful. But to go in, on my behalf, with his secret sympathies on the other side—that's too much." He paused. "I gave him the case only because you said he was restless and wanted to flex his muscles in court. Well, he's had his chance. I'm appealing, and I've taken the case away from him. I think that's best all around."

Mary felt a sickness in the pit of her stomach. She could not look at her father. "Do what you think is best," she said at last. "Only try to be understanding and fair."

"When it comes to you, I always lean over backward, Mary—always will. As a matter of fact—well, I've told you I think he's capable—I've often told you that, haven't I?"

"Yes, you have."

"I'm sincere. I want to do what's good for both of you. I want to get the most out of the boy for all our sakes, make him live up to his potential, be proud of what he does. Yes, I've been giving Norman a good deal of thought. I think I've come up with something extremely interesting."

Mary looked up. Her father was smiling, and it softened him, and she felt a wave of relief and the old affection. "What is it, Dad? Is it something good for Norman?"

"Something wonderful, for a boy his age. You'll be pleased, too, I assure you. Give me a day or two. I'll have it worked out by the end of the week."

"Oh, Dad, I hope so." She reached across the table and

243

sought her father's hand, as she always had when she was a little girl. "Try to be tolerant of Norman. He's really so sweet."

Harry Ewing squeezed his daughter's hand. "I know he is, dear. Don't you worry. I want you both to be happy."

❖   ❖   ❖

Benita Selby's journal. Monday, June 1:". . . is Gerold Triplett, and he's an economist who works for a private company in San Francisco that has contracts with the Air Force. After I ate dinner with the others last night, I went out to the pool to cool off, and he was there again. We sat and talked until almost midnight. I didn't tell him exactly what I did, because when men find out you work for Dr. Chapman, they treat you like a nurse. I said I was visiting relatives in Pacific Palisades. He's here for three more days consulting with someone in Anaheim. He wanted to go to a concert tonight at the Philharmonic, but I haven't said yes, though I will. Gerold said he will be in Chicago for several weeks in August and wants to see me. Fate works in curious ways. We shall see. I had two letters from Mom this morning and only had time to read them hastily, since I overslept. She's slipped a disk, and Mrs. McKassen is helping her out. The Lord never made Job suffer more. Dr. Chapman is with Horace and Paul doing interviews today, because Cass had a relapse this morning. The virus, we think, and he's in bed. I called him a half hour ago to see if he's still alive, but the desk said he drove down to the drugstore to get something to keep from throwing up. . . ."

❖   ❖   ❖

Cass Miller sat behind the wheel of the Dodge sedan, parked alongside the curb of the side street, and brooded and waited.

He did not feel ill, really, except for the giddy and faint sensation when he tried to walk. The migraine usually came and went, throughout the day, although he did not suffer from it now. Perhaps he did have a touch of the flu, as he had told Chapman. More likely, it was fatigue. He could trace it back definitely to that Thursday-morning interview. When it had ended, he remembered, he had felt unhinged and irresponsible, and uncontrollably resentful, as he had that time in Ohio when the doctor called it a nervous breakdown, and he had been forced to take a month's leave of absence on some more acceptable pretext.

The street around, though merely two blocks from Wilshire Boulevard and the Beverly Hills shopping district, was incredibly empty and quiet. Far ahead, he could see the toy cars inching noiselessly forward, but no sound of their screeching and jamming and horns reached him. Momentarily, he was conscious of a stout mailman treading past, shuffling eternally through his envelopes. When the mailman was gone, he saw a tall, young, redheaded girl start out of the apartment beyond his door window. He twisted and watched her approach the sidewalk as she pulled on her white gloves. She glanced at him only briefly, then turned resolutely toward Wilshire. He continued to observe her as she meandered away, and then he deliberated on the fourteen months that had gone by.

The cumulative effect of those thousand interviews—there must have been a thousand or more that he had listened to personally—gave Cass Miller his own private mental image of the American married woman: a female beetle, turned on her back, legs in the air, legs waving in the air, wriggling and squirming but still on her back—until impaled.

In the streets of the cities at night, when he walked alone, and this he had done frequently and everywhere, Cass Miller had always watched closely the young women who promenaded ahead of him. He pictured them again: their full bottoms rotating provocatively beneath their tight skirts, their calves indecently encased in sheer nylon to thighs unseen, their high-heeled whorish pumps tilting them forward, steadily forward, to some vicious assignation. Sometimes they would halt to gaze into a window and thus give their profile to him, and he would have eyes only for the shameless protrusion of their unfettered busts. On such occasions, he would halt, too, and regard them with boiling hatred. They were harlots all of them, subtle and secret sluts. Not one of them was decent or trustworthy or faithful. They smelled of musk and body heat and the sick odor of sex, and you had only to touch them, and they would quickly lie on their backs, female beetles, wriggling bitch insects, wriggling. He hated women, and he lusted for them, and the emotions were one.

Absently rubbing the warm wheel of the Dodge, staring straight ahead, waiting for the sight of her, he recognized that the compulsion was not usual or widespread. Unconsciously, his mind gave it a vague rationale that was permissive. He was here because she was there, and she was misled and ill-used and wanted direction. He was here to meet her and give her his hand, and he would promise not to punish her too harshly. It was the least he owed his father, broken old bastard, racked by life and the beetle lust.

He waited with ruthless patience.

He had just consulted his wrist watch, and calculated the passage of nearly one hour and ten minutes, and allowed the unreasoning wrath to mount and possess him, when he looked up blindly—and there she was.

She had emerged from the apartment four doors ahead, patting the bun of dark hair behind her head, and hastened to the curb. For a moment, she glanced up the sidewalk, in each direction, and then began to cross over to her station wagon, parked on the same side as his car and faced in the same direction. She walked heavily, her legs full against the bright rayon dress, and then she went behind the car and opened the door and slid inside. She sat in the front seat a moment, occupied with something that he could not see, and he decided that she was lighting a cigarette.

He heard her engine sputter and catch, and then he watched, in a detached, dreamy way, as her vehicle floated forward. He waited until it had gone a block, slowing for the cross street, when he started the Dodge and unhurriedly followed her.

Sarah Goldsmith became fully aware of the Dodge at Westwood Boulevard. Its grill, reflecting the sun, and the dark, sullen face behind the windshield filled her rear-view mirror with a pounding remembrance and fear, and after that, for twenty minutes, it did not leave her mirror.

By the time she reached her street—with the safety of small children playing on someone's lawn, and a gardener guiding a power mower over another—she saw that her rear-view mirror was free of M. Javert (she had seen the movie on Sam's television, not read the book), and that only the placid, receding landscape was in sight. The choking fear was at once alleviated, and she began to feel that it was either a coincidence or a trick of hallucination.

She swung into the carport, parked, found her purse, and stepped out. She realized that there was no grocery bag, that she had forgotten to shop, but decided that the freezer would serve them adequately. She had started across the paved area toward the door when she was aware of a sedan wheeling into the street. She stopped short, staring off, and the white needles of dread and calamity punctured her forearms and legs. The

Dodge came to a halt three doors away, scraping the curb, and the engine idled. The face in the recess behind the glass was indistinct but pointed toward her. Even without seeing it plainly, she knew that it was dark and sullen.

Involuntarily, she gasped. Her legs were wooden, anchored. And then they moved. She stumbled, half running, to the door, shook frantically through her key ring, then opened the door, banged it behind her, and hysterically hooked the chain.

Her first illogical instinct was to call Sam, preserver of home and property, and then the police, and then the next-door neighbor, Mrs. Pederson, or Kathleen Ballard around the corner, and finally she saw the absurdity of all these impossible collaborations. Although her body was chilled rigid, her mind, so practical, reasoned out an explanation of M. Javert, and she knew that there was only one number she dared call.

In the kitchen, after hastily checking the service porch door, she snatched the receiver of the wall phone, making communication operative and rescue imminent, and she dialed Fred Tauber's number. After the first ring, she prayed that he was still on the bed. After the second ring, she was sure that he was in the bathroom. After the third ring, when her heart was sinking, he answered the phone.

"Hello," he said with incredible calmness.

"Fred!"

"Hello?"

"Fred—it's Sarah!"

"Yes—it's Fred—what's the matter?"

"I'm being followed," she gasped; "someone's following me—he's outside."

"What do you mean, Sarah? What are you talking about?"

"A man."

Fred's voice was steady, steadying her, but tense. "What man? Do get hold of yourself. Are you in danger?"

"No—I don't know, but—"

"Then calm down. Tell me as quickly as possible what is wrong."

She held the mouthpiece in one hand and drew closer to it. "When I left you, I noticed the car parked near, and then I started, and I guess it started. I was halfway home when I noticed it again, right behind, and then I kept watching, and it was still behind. And now it's two doors down—"

"Who's driving it? Did you see?"

"I couldn't tell very well. He's got black hair and a cruel face."

"Have you seen him before?"

"No—I mean, yes, I have. Saturday, I remember now. He was parked across from your apartment, the same car, and it came into the block here, but I didn't pay any attention then. Fred, who is he?"

"I don't know," he said slowly. "Is he still outside?"

"I suppose—"

"Go and look. I'll wait."

She let the receiver dangle and went into the living room. For a moment, alarm held her, but Fred was waiting, he was with her, and so she went out to the big window, the drapes partially drawn against the sun. She moved to the edge of the drapes and pulled one back slightly, and in this way hidden, she peered outside.

The street was before her. The Dodge was gone. She exposed herself more fully, the drape covering her like a broken tent, and searched the street, No car was in sight.

She freed herself of the drape and ran back into the kitchen.

"Fred—"

"Yes, I'm here."

"He's gone."

"You're sure?"

"I looked everywhere."

"Curious."

Threat was supplanted by mystery, and the anxiety in her voice was shaded by a subtle difference. "Fred, who can it be? Can it be about us?"

"It might be." He did not try to conceal his concern. "You're sure about the car shadowing you—Saturday and today?"

"Positively. I mean, if he got out and went someplace, or pretended to do something else, why, maybe I wouldn't be sure. But outside your apartment, and then right behind me, and parking here, just watching me, not pretending to be going anywhere else—"

"Be careful, Sarah. And don't use my name. The phone may be bugged." Fred's secret vice was television, after all.

Sarah was impatient. "If it's tapped, they've heard enough already. We *have* to talk. Maybe it's your wife—"

"My wife?"

"She suspects us. She saw me. I bet the man's a detective she hired."

"That could be. There's another possibility. He may have been assigned by your husband."

248

Sam? Ridiculous. "That's ridiculous," she said, and the moment she said it, she wasn't sure. Why not Sam? He wasn't the utter fool. Perhaps she had slipped up somewhere; perhaps she had been seen; perhaps there was gossip. An anonymous letter to the store. It took only a phone call and fifty dollars a day, she'd read somewhere, to hire a private eye. They existed. They even advertised in the yellow section of the phone book. "Investigations discreetly made. Call day or night." Sam. But no. If Sam even suspected, it would break out all over him like a rash, and there would be obvious innuendos or blunt accusations, and crying and turmoil. This wasn't Sam at all. It was Fred's wife. The juiceless one. Exactly what she would do. Yet it might be Sam. But if it was Mrs. Tauber—was that really her name?—was it so bad? Maybe she'd give him his divorce then. What was she thinking anyway?

". . . not so ridiculous," he was saying. "I'm sure your husband is as capable of doing this as my wife. In fact, Sarah, knowing my wife as I do—or did—I would say that she's less capable of this than your husband or anyone else."

"Why?"

He hesitated. "I don't think it would surprise her that I'd be interested in someone else. So I don't think she'd spend a dime to confirm that. No, I'm inclined toward your husband. That bothers me. I gather from you, he's not very sophisticated. Evidence about us might make him go haywire. He might behave badly. That's what bothers me."

"What should we do, Fred?"

"For one thing, keep a watchful eye for that same man and that car. See if he returns and hangs around. If he does, telephone me at once. Any hour. The other suggestion I'd make is that we stay away from each other for a little while."

"Fred, no—"

"Honey, just a couple of days, until we see if this is really trouble or simply nothing at all."

"How long, Fred?"

"A day or two. Let's play it cool, see what happens. If the coast is clear, call me Thursday morning."

"Thursday morning. Fred, I'll die."

"Honey, it's just as hard for me."

"Fred, do you love me?"

"You know I do. Now hang up, go about your work as if nothing's happened, and keep watch. I'll expect to hear from you Thursday morning. Goodbye, Sarah."

"Goodbye darling."

Benita Selby's journal, Tuesday, June 2: ". . . was lovely. After the concert, I told him it was so late I had better be taken right to the motel. But afterward we sat and talked until one in the morning, and then he took me to my door. He was such a gentleman. He asked if he could kiss me, and I agreed. I think I will see him once more before he leaves, and we leave. I look forward to Gerold's arrival in Chicago. It could be interesting. . . . There was a letter from Mom this morning, obviously written in pain. It's not a slipped disk but a dislocated hip. She'll have to remain in bed a while—not that she isn't anyway. I think we'll all be glad when this is over. Four more days of interviews, and Dr. Chapman's broadcast in 'The Hot Seat,' and then we leave Sunday night. Paul was as sleepy as I was this morning. He should be. I saw him come in late last night, while we were in the car talking. Cass is back at work. He came up behind me this morning and put his hands on my chest, the way he used to, and I was furious. He had such a nasty disposition. I amused Dr. Chapman when he came in an hour ago. I was reading the weekly newspaper they have in The Briars. It was called *The Alert,* and it is delivered door to door, free. Under 'Social Activities' I happened to see that a society woman named Teresa Harnish is giving a party Friday night for the elite of the community. It is a costume party, with buffet, and everyone is being told to dress as the person they would like to have been, or be, when Dr. Chapman interviewed them. Very clever. I clipped it and read it to Dr. Chapman. He laughed out loud. He has such a magnificent sense of humor, unlike most famous people. He also has a memorable memory, as I have already explained in this journal. After he laughed, he said that he remembered having personally interviewed Mrs. Harnish, and that she was a lovely lady and that he hoped her party would be a huge success. . . ."

◇　◇　◇

Teresa Harnish sat on the blanket at the perimeter of Constable's Cove, her shapely legs straight out before her, and for what seemed the hundreth time she adjusted the strap of her new bathing suit. She had been pleased when she purchased the white suit. The saleslady had said that it was ravishing (not that she listened to *them*), and had thought it might be exactly what she wanted, that is, if she didn't mind something

250

so daring (for it was a deeply cut maillot, drawn high against her thighs), but Teresa hadn't minded, and was satisfied that the suit showed off her trim figure in the best manner possible, and subtracted ten years from her thirty-six.

She had shopped for the bathing suit yesterday morning, after dropping Geoffrey off at the shop especially early, since he was making frantic last-minute preparations for the Boris Introsky show. She had kept the suit on, upon leaving the store, and driven directly to the beach. But the beach was devoid of life, and after a half hour of disappointment, she had driven home and puttered away the rest of the endless day in wretchedness.

Determined to continue her vigil until Ed Krasowski would appear again, she had hastened to the beach this morning. Again, it was desolate. She had been at her post ten minutes now, bookless and umbrellaless, for she did not intend to linger, once she had spoken to him. Since her brief encounter with him exactly one week ago, her mind had dwelled on almost nothing else.

Purposely, she had avoided the beach until yesterday, trying to sort out and examine each of her separate feelings. She was a reasonable, sensible girl—her family had always been prideful and boastful of this—and though now obsessed, she was not unreasonable, insensible. Byron had always disdainfully referred to his hapless wife, Annabella Milbanke, as the Princess of Parallelograms, meaning apparently that she was of a precise and mathematical turn, and implying some lack of emotion. Teresa had always regarded Byron with disgust, and, like Harriet Beecher Stowe, had sided with the admirable Princess Annabella. Over the long week end, Teresa had tried to review the situation coolly, as Byron's judicious wife might have done, but she perceived soon enough that this was impossible, for she was not a remote English lady, constricted and strait-laced, but a modern product, superior albeit, of a generation and time far advanced and considerably liberated. Still, constraint and sensibility and common sense were the proper words.

After hours of soul-searching, Teresa broke down her situation and problem satisfactorily. She had: (a) been married a decade to a gentleman, and had been the best of wives, and would continue to be so considered; (b) she was a female of special endowments, intelligence, wit, and a certain physical attractiveness, and the narrow boundaries of monogamy gave no room for further development and enjoyment of these gifts;

251

(c) she was thirty-six, and had much to offer, and much to share, and much capacity to enjoy, and it would be wasteful and an insult to the Divine Creator if she used her best years poorly because of bourgeois guilts that imprisoned so many; (d) she had no sentimental attachment for Ed Krasowski, who represented only a symbol of her goal of full attainment, but she felt that each of them, he and she, deserved more of the miracle of life; (e) she could accomplish true fulfillment of the life force by giving herself to a primitive, for there was an inexpressible Biblical beauty in this, the mating of the best product of civilization, the patrician wife of Hellas, with the barbarian of the north so recently removed from cave and club; (f) rather like Isadora and Essenine; and, finally, (g) her life would be richer, more meaningful, for it, and Geoffrey's, too.

Once the situation had been rationalized in an orderly fashion, Teresa was satisfied that she could proceed to the next step. The approach she had prepared absorbed and stimulated her more than any single activity since that occasion, several years back, when she had become engrossed in *bonsai*, and had spent an entire summer studying the Japanese art of dwarfing trees from its origin in the Ashikaga era to the present. Because she was emancipated beyond her sex— emancipated sufficiently to have been entirely truthful in her Chapman interview, which the other women had not been, she was sure—there was no need, she felt, to practice the degrading ceremonials of coquetry and seduction with Ed Krasowski. He would want to possess her, it was obvious, like the aboriginal that he was, and it would debase nature not to give herself in the same spirit.

The procedure was as simple as the object visited: go to the beach, wait for him, address him straightforwardly, and, finally, arrange the meeting that would enrich both their lives with added depth and breadth. Of spirit, she hastened to remind herself, breadth of spirit.

Her gaze picketed the beach, and, from time to time, she squinted out at the foaming whitecaps hurtling and breaking upon the wet sand. The ocean stretched endlessly to Cathay, and once, in their majesty, the lines from Keats climbed above the swelling breakers. "Then felt I like some watcher of the skies/ When a new planet swims into his ken;/ Or like stout Cortez when with eagle eyes/ He star'd at the Pacific—and all his men/ Look'd at each other with a wild surmise—/ Silent, upon a peak in Darien."

In a most casual way, they appeared far to her left, three of them, clad in bulky sweat suits, trudging down to the sand from the highway slope, and striding along the harder packed sand near the water. Closer, they came and closer, and Teresa's heart thumped. When they reached their game area, and spread apart until they had formed a triangle, and began tossing the football around, their faces became distinguishable to Teresa. Dismay pressed her heart. Ed Krasowski was not among them.

Her carefully arranged procedure was a shambles, but she did not panic. So single-minded was she about her necessary goal that she remained composed and imperturbable. She examined and evaluated possible actions. She might simply depart, and continue to return until she found Ed Krasowski present. She might seek out a telephone book and telephone him directly. She might write a note and leave it with his three companions. But none of these methods would immediately solve what was bothering her the most: what had happened to Ed Krasowski? Actually, two of her approaches would answer the question soon enough, but that would not be soon enough for her. She wanted no more daydreaming, no more fitful nights. She must know at once.

Emboldened by a desire that she had not known she possessed, she rose to her feet. By the direct approach, she was exposing herself to *them,* but her need surpassed human frailty and false modesty. No rationalization made the task easier. She felt her stiff, bare legs, one before the other, carrying her through the sand. She was within a few yards of the nearest of the three. He was squat and chunky, exerting himself with great exhalations, and his ridged back was to her.

In restaurants, she remembered, when she was still single and dining with women, she had always found it difficult to summon the waiter. Did you snap your fingers? Unladylike. Did you tap fork on glass? Autocratic and European. Did you call "Waiter!" as in "Fido!"? Or "Mister"? Or clear your throat loudly? The problem had been solved, at last, by marriage. Geoffrey snapped his fingers. But now this athlete, just ahead, unknown to her—here was another waiter.

"Oh, Mister," she called.

He had gone up into the air to catch the football on his chest. She waited until he had thrown it back.

"Mister!" she called loudly.

He looked over his shoulder, surprised. His hairline and

253

brow were low, and his countenance resembled a pumpkin that someone had sat upon. "You calling me, Ma'am?"

"Yes, please—"

He came toward her, puzzled.

"I had hoped to see your friend here today," she said quickly. "Mr. Krasowski."

"Ed? He's working."

"Regularly? Or will he be back?"

"He just got the job day before yesterday. Guess he'll be on it all summer, until we're back in uniform. Though he'll have some time off for workouts. But not here. He's through with the beach."

"Do you know where I can . . . reach him?"

"Paradise Park."

"Paradise Park?"

He looked at her as if she were a Martian. "The big amusement park—you know—between Santa Monica and Venice. He's got one of the booths."

"Will he be there tomorrow?"

"What's tomorrow—Wednesday? Yeah, sure. And Thursday, Friday and Saturday he's off, but he's got to work Sundays."

"I really appreciate this. Do you see him at all?"

"Every night, practically. We got an apartment together not far from here."

"I wonder—could you give him a message for me?"

"Sure thing."

"Tell him I'd like to see him about a . . . a private matter—at noon on Wed—no, better say Thursday. Thursday at twelve, at the amusement center. What's a good place to meet?"

This seemed to tax him a moment. He tried to concentrate. "It's awful big there," he murmured. "I know. After you go in, there's a pool for seals—everyone hangs around and feeds them fish."

"All right. Tell him I'll be there noon Thursday."

She was aware that for the first time he was impressed by her bathing suit. For a moment, she was unsure of the suit, and then she felt pleased. He would undoubtedly report her appearance to Ed. "Glad to oblige, Ma'am," he said finally. "Anything else?"

"No, nothing else. You won't forget?"

"Oh, no."

She flashed her best smile. "Thank you very much."

"Sure." He ducked his head, started to turn away, then halted. "Hey, I almost forgot—what's your name?"

She hesitated. "Just tell him, the girl—" she paused, remembering that to Ed she was not a girl but a lady, and she decided, exasperating as it might be, to keep her identity clearly defined—"tell him the lady he met on the beach, right here, last week, the one who was almost hit by his football. He'll remember."

He looked at her oddly, and she felt uncomfortable. "Okay, Ma'am," he said at last, and then he left to join the others.

Pleased with having accomplished what she had set out to accomplish, Teresa hastily gathered her few belongings, made her way to the car without once glancing at the other three, and drove swiftly to The Briars.

Once home, she efficiently made lunch and ate it. She discharged a half-dozen household phone calls. She wrote several thank-you notes, and one letter. She wrote checks for the bills. At three, she lay down for her daily nap—to which she attributed her continuing youth—but now, instead of dozing, she permitted herself the luxury of fantasying the divine union with her aboriginal. (In a way, she regretted that her meeting with Ed Krasowski had not occurred *before* the advent of Dr. Chapman. For now, she was permanently in his history as merely healthy; had Ed preceded the interview, she would have been immortalized as healthy *and* lusty.) At four, she was still wide awake, and rose to make up and dress meticulously for the Boris Introsky show. Minutes before five, she drove toward Westwood and the art shop.

Reaching the vicinity of the shop, she saw that parking places were difficult to find. Possibly it meant the show had drawn a large turnout, and she was pleased. She left her car in a nearby lot and walked to the shop. Approaching it, she saw several groups of people enter. Geoffrey was usually successful with these cocktail previews; his embossed announcements, mailed to a select list of opinion-makers (art critics, professional hostesses, wealthy divorcees, and film stars), were impressive and well received.

The small gallery was, indeed, crowded. Teresa swept in, her short cocktail dress rustling against her petticoat, nodding at some people she did not know, waving at some people she did know. Geoffrey, champagne glass in his left hand, stood center stage, like a captain in the pilot house—or was it fo'castle? No, rather like his idol, Ambrose Vollard at the old Galerie. Teresa pushed toward him, and took his hand, proffering a cool, wifely squeeze and her cheek, which his mustache brushed. He drew a small, emaciated, Rabbinical young man into their hub. The young man, perspiring profusely, was ridiculously immature for his shining bald head and short beard. Whenever she met a young man with a beard, Teresa always decided that either he had no chin or no talent. Geoffrey introduced him as Boris Introsky. Teresa did not mask her surprise. The name had evoked, when first she heard it, a grizzly, bearish Ukrainian, muscular, uncompromising, insulting. But this Boris, she guessed, had been born William, and raised in Coney Island, and been to Paris on the GI bill. His voice was thin, his eyes watery, and his opinion conventional. He will not sell, she decided.

Always, on these occasions, she had been valuable to Geoffrey. She mixed. She knew the patter. But now she had no stomach for it. She remained beside Geoffrey, until he whispered to her. Then she went to the punch bowl, and then she circulated through the overfilled, stifling room. The garish abstracts on the wall, no Duchamp or Kandinsky our Boris, gave her the impression of a nursery school, progressive, not of an art gallery, avant garde. She greeted Kathleen Ballard and a tall, serious young man named Radford, and she shook hands with three critics, and she shook hands with Grace Waterton and the Palmers. She circulated and circulated, dimly aware of the priestly Aramaic language of creativity ("but it's his sense of color harmonies . . . the texture, my dear . . . those rich blue areas . . . it draws you inside it . . . motion through multiple images, darling . . . new boundaries . . . sense of form . . . ultramarine . . . texture . . . inner eye . . . Montparnasse . . . vermilion . . . rebel . . . Hiroshige"), and wondered why Geoffrey had exiled the lovely ferrets of Pieter Brueghel for this, but knowing that this was a commodity available, to be bought cheaply and sold high, and had been made the fad.

Two hours had passed, and four champagne cocktails, and she decided that she should have a headache. Briefly, in the crowd, she had Geoffrey's ear. He was with buyers and nodded absently.

She pushed outside, where it was night and alive and not in the least abstract, no broken lines, and dabs, and dotted planes, and she thought of Ed Krasowski, who was closer to true Art, and wondered what he might make of all this. He would have seen it with her eye, she knew, and she felt closer to him.

How many of these beastly false shows had she ornamented? Where were those nights, those years?

Later, Geoffrey returned home an hour before she had expected him. She had intended to be fast asleep when he returned, since this was their night, and she was not in the mood for it. But here she was on the sofa, in the conversation group near the window, wide awake, and plainly well.

"It was a marvelous show," she said. "But you look so tired. How did it go?"

Geoffrey shook his head. "Disappointing. We only got rid of six."

She was pleased. "I'm sorry," she said sympathetically. "I was afraid of that. His work demands too much. People out here simply don't have that much to give. In Paris—"

"Ah, yes, Paris."

"Or even Rome."

"Mmm, yes."

"But you'll just have to concede something to mediocrity, my dear."

He nodded, staring at the beige carpet, then suddenly looked up. "How's your headache?"

"Better now." Then she added quickly, "I'm afraid it's that time of the month—"

She had never lied about *that* before, but, she told herself, this was an extraordinary transitional period in her growth. She would make it up to him tenfold, one day soon, and they would both be the happier.

"I'm sorry," he was saying. "Perhaps you should lie down."

She was on her feet, almost gay. "You're the one we're to worry about. Now, let's take your coat, and I'll get your slippers, and then we'll have a brandy."

She loved him so. And really, he *would* be happier.

❖   ❖   ❖

Benita Selby's journal. Wednesday, June 3: ". . . extraordinary thing that's ever happened to me, and I wouldn't write it down on paper except I think he's all right and will be my husband. After he became so drunk on those bourbons, I drove us back to the Villa Neapolis. We sat, and he started reciting his life—Mom's an angel next to his—and then he admitted being in analysis two years, and then he said he was a latent homosexual, which most men are anyway, but had never done anything wrong, and the analyst was curing him.

257

He put his head on my chest and cried and said he hoped to marry me. I was so sorry for him and wanted to take care of him always, and said we would talk about it. After a while, I agreed we would decide in Chicago, and when he left this morning, after we had breakfast, he was so nice. He needs me, there is no doubt, and since he is normal, as Dr. Chapman has proved, I think it may work out fine. We shall see. He makes $13,000 per annum. It is one-thirty, and my mood is good. In four days, we leave. There was a letter from Mom, and I don't blame her for quitting Dr. Rubinfeer. Who ever heard of a dislocated hip being psychosomatic? I'll write her tonight and give her moral support. I felt so good, I splurged at The Crystal Room. I was passing the table where Paul and Horace were eating with an attractive woman when he (Paul) stopped me and introduced me to her, Mrs. Ballard, and asked me to join them. I did. It was very friendly. When I was first passing the table, though, I heard Horace discussing his wife, which is why I slowed down, and they saw me, because since I have been with Dr. Chapman, I have never heard Horace discussing his wife. Of course, everyone at Reardon knows *why*. I mention it because a strange deductive fact comes to mind, which is, could Mrs. Ballard have been Horace's wife and now be married again? It could be, except she was so reserved, and the picture I have of Horace's wife . . ."

⟡   ⟡   ⟡

Naomi Shields sat woozily at the table beside the dance floor, where Wash Dillon had placed her after he had received her message, and with effort she brought the highball glass to her lips and downed the last of the gin.

She turned, scraping her chair, to call the waiter for a re-fill, and then the large dim room came into focus, and she saw that all of the tables in Jorrocks' Jollities were empty. A waiter was unbuttoning his white vest, and a Mexican in overalls had entered with a broom, and there was no one left, no one left, except herself and the orchestra.

She wrenched her face back to the dance floor and peered across it at the bandstand. The figures had a fuzzy quality, but she recognized Wash kneeling, laying away his saxophone, and there were the four others putting away their instruments and sheet music. She felt that they were her only friends, Wash especially, especially Wash.

Twice in the last eight days, three times counting tonight,

she had come to the bar of Jorrocks' Jollities, which was in the room next to the entrance, and had some drinks and wanted Wash to know and changed her mind and taken a taxi back to The Briars. Each successive morning, she had felt pride in her new chastity, the reformation, and each afternoon and night she had felt sick lonely and ache lonely and had realized that she could not go on unloved. Earlier this night, in her kitchen, food had revolted her, and she had begun to drink mildly (to work up an appetite), and more (to drown desire), and at last, at ten, she had phoned for a cab and come here the third time. This time, she had told the bartender, who was a trusted friend by now, to tell Wash, and after the medley, Wash had appeared and led her to the table.

She liked being one of the family. Twice, during breaks, they had trouped to the table behind Wash and pulled up chairs, acknowledging her, complimenting her, making amusing remarks to Wash (who always winked), and finally talking in a crazy way that she did not understand at all. About music, she thought. And musicians. Their names were . . . well, Wash . . . Perowitz . . . Lavine . . . Bardelli . . . Nims . . . no, Sims . . . Kims, whims, hymns.

She squeezed her eyes between forehead and cheeks and tried to match the names to the faces of the friends . . . the pasty face with the cigarette dangling . . . the Roman face with curled hair and jiggling knee . . . the black Negro face with scraggly goatee and all the rings on the fingers with long nails . . . the chewing gum face with thick beaked nose and twirling rabbit's foot . . . the long, long, long jaw face, sunken eyes, long, long body, arms, legs that matched Wash Dillon, arm around her, tickling her ear lobes with his lips.

She saw him coming across the slippery floor, ugly, desirable, in his tuxedo, and she tried to sit straight.

He was above her. "How's my baby?"

She lifted her head. His toothy, pock-marked visage doubled in her vision.

"You feeling all right, honey?" he asked.

"All right."

"Night's young. Like to have some more fun?"

Give the baby a toy, she thought, read her a bedtime story, put her in her trundle bundle, beddy-bed. Her mouth was cotton candy, pink. "Like to."

"You're mighty pretty, honey child, mighty delectable."

"If you like me."

Wash's smile was lipless. "Like you? Honey, ol' Wash isn't

one of your talkers. He likes to prove what he preaches. Honey, maybe you couldn't tell, but up there I was going crazy every minute wanting you."

She nodded. "I'm tired," she said.

She tried to rise, but it was impossible until he reached under her arms and easily hoisted her to her feet.

"On your feet," he said. He grinned. "Not for long, I'm hoping." He folded her arm inside his. "Come on, honey. We're going home." His arm around her was strong, and she felt better.

He started her through the empty tables, with their spotted cloths, half-filed ash trays, balled moist napkins, like all those mornings after.

"Hey, Wash!" someone was calling.

He stopped, and glanced over his shoulder.

"Havin' a game tonight?"

"More than that," he answered. "Little jam session, too." He looked down at Naomi. "Aren't we, honey?"

"Wash, I just want to lie down."

"You will, honey child. Ol' Wash'll take care of his baby good."

Outside, the cold air was a wet rag on her face, but although she partially revived, the universe remained invisible except for the towering, moving form beside her. Somewhere off far, the traffic hummed anonymously. High above, the twinkling dome of heaven tilted, and far, far below, the pavement was a concrete slide. On the leather of his car, it was easy to let herself be pulled toward him, until she smelled the satin and broadcloth of his suit, and the vague scent of some round flower in his lapel.

She was aware of being carried forward, of rocking on the turns, and bobbing gently, and his hand massaging the sweater over her breast.

"I knew you were it," he said, "the day I brought that post card over. Bet you felt it, too."

She laid her head back on the seat, eyes still shut.

"How long has it been, honey?"

"What?"

"Since you were loved?"

If she told him an eternity, since the cradle and since, he would think her mad. Besides, she was too tired. She said nothing.

The space ship went on and on, and then it was still, and she opened her eyes.

"Here we are," he said.

After a while, the door opened, and he helped her out. Arm around her, he helped her across the sidewalk, through the glass door, into the building. The rows of name plates and buzzers and brass-lidded mail boxes. The shadowed corridor past the staircase to the rear. The number five on the door.

The lights were on, and she stood unsteadily beside the green felt poker table in the center of his living room. He had returned from somewhere with two glasses, and one was in her hand.

"Come on, honey, drink up. We haven't got all night."

"I'm drinking gin."

"It's gin." He swallowed the contents of his glass in a single gulp. "Put it away, hon. It's for the road. We're going the mile."

She drank. The liquid was tasteless.

He set the glasses on the poker table, took her elbow, and firmly led her through the open door. He flipped the switch, and the overhead bulbs glared. She was beside the maple bureau, and beyond the chair was the double bed with the low maple headboard. An orange chenille spread neatly covered the bed.

"You're neat," she said thickly as he closed the door behind her.

"They throw in maid service. Mulatto broad. She puts out for a fiver."

He tore the chenille spread and maroon blanket off the bed, undoing part of the white linen sheeting that had been tucked in beneath, and dropped both to the floor. Then he threw the pillow aside.

"I like plenty of room," he said. He favored her with the lipless smile. "What about you, honey?"

"What about me?"

He went to her, half lifting her from her feet, and pressing his mouth hungrily to her own. Arousal surfaced slowly through the vapor layers of intoxication. It wasn't the kiss, but the pressure against her sore breasts and his hand on her hip. He released her, and they both labored for breath.

"Let's go, honey," he said.

He began unbuttoning his shirt. She moved slowly toward the bed, intending to undress, but finally just standing there. The momentary urge to copulate had diminished, and what was left was the apathetic void. Behind the dizziness in her temples, there was a sobering, and the unadorned bed was less

261

inviting. No desire stirred her—no desire to see him naked and taut, for there had been so many; no desire to be joined with him, for there had been too many. Why was she here? If she told him, explained, maybe there was hope.

"Hey, honey—" he said.

She turned wearily, intent upon logic and reason, and then she saw his endless, hairless, bony frame, and knew it was futile. She had wound up the machine; it must run down.

". . . what's holding you. Come on."

With sad regret, she took the bottom of her sweater and slowly, slowly, began to draw it up across her brassière.

"Hurry it up, dammit!"

He was over her, grabbing the sweater, yanking it over her head. His hands were behind her, trying to unfasten the brassière, and finally, powerfully, ripping it apart. As it fell to the floor, and her enormous breasts burst free, she tried to protest. But his hands were on her, painfully, and she was off her feet and harshly on the bed.

"Wash, don't—"

"Goddammit—"

Her nylon pants were being torn roughly down her thighs.

He was beside her, and over her.

"My stockings—" she gasped.

"To hell with that."

"No, please—"

She tried to rise. She mounted an elbow. She only wanted to explain. There was a certain code to love, and a lady didn't lie unclad except for stockings. The stockings were indecent, absolutely indecent.

His arm fell like a crowbar on her throat, and her head slammed into the mattress. His hands were gritty on her breasts, and she moaned for the indignity of the stockings.

Once, opening her eyes, she saw him and was frightened. "Don't hurt me," she cried.

His voice was anger, impatience, passion. An animal chant dinned against her ears, and she closed her eyes, sinking in the darkness, offering her flesh so that the death would come sooner, and the pain be ended.

At last, the expected sensation—skin peeling before the scalpel, she thought, lacerating, lacerating, but soon healing, soon healing—and she was grateful because the sensation was now bounded, now limited, now familiar, now known. Her body recoiled and recoiled from the rhythmical beat, but it continued interminably, unceasingly, until the searing agony was joined by pleasure, so that agony and pleasure were one and the same, and at last her hands grasped his back. "I love you, Horace," she murmured.

But later, it was done, and she felt limp and victorious, even in this defeat. For she had always given, as she told the man behind that foolish screen, and tonight he had given, but she had not. The pleasure of this dominated any other pleasure she had known.

She turned her head on the mattress and looked off. Wash was buckling his belt.

He saw her and grinned. "You'll do, kid. Want a drink?"

She shook her head. "Take me home." She started to rise, but he came to her and pushed her down gently. "Not so fast," he said. "It's not polite to eat and run." She lay back, weak and groggy, and watched as he went to the door and opened it. Through the doorway, the mingled sounds of clattering chips and indistinct voices came to her.

Wash called off. "Okay, Ace—you're on."

Suddenly, a stranger came through the doorway—not a stranger but the Roman face with curled hair. Shocked, she reached for something to cover herself, but there was nothing but her hand.

"Sa-ay now," said the Roman face.

Wash formed the lipless smile. "Bardelli, tonight you are a man."

Bardelli began to remove his shirt. Naomi sat up. "What do you think I am?" she shrieked at Wash.

She tried to swing off the bed, but Wash caught her by the shoulders and pressed her backward. She flayed at him with her fists, until he grabbed her forearms and pushed her flat.

"Guess you didn't make her happy," said Bardelli. "Too much fight left."

Naomi tried to scream, but Wash stifled it with his arm. "Come on, you old bastard," he called behind him. "This is a tiger."

Unable to move her arms or cry out, Naomi thrashed her legs wildly. But someone pinned them down, and above Wash's arm she saw the Roman face with curled hair, and in a moment the curls were on her face and the garlic mouth on her mouth. She twisted and squirmed, and once she saw Wash grinning from the door, and after that she saw only the Roman face. She kicked him, and he grunted, and smashed his palm across her face. She sobbed, and tried to bite, and again felt the sting of his big hand, and after a while, she stopped fighting, and he stopped slapping, and she let him handle her as he would a rag doll.

Again, it was interminable, the stitching pain, the cramped pain, the savage violence of it accompanied by a door somewhere opening, closing, opening, closing, and far away voices entreating Bardelli to get on with it, get on with it, and the Roman face hung from above like a contorted lantern, curls greasy and wet.

And when it was done, she could not rise. No will on earth could make her lift her racked flesh. And now the victory of not giving was no victory at all. She lay panting, her huge pointed breasts heaving, her eyes staring and waiting. Her innards had been scooped hollow of resistance, and she lay prostrated, staring and waiting.

The door opened and closed, and there was laughter, and there was the thick nose and the chewing jaws and hands on her breasts and thighs on her thighs . . . Lavine, Lavine . . . and now the black one, Sims not Nims, Sims she had learned at last, and shutting her eyes, she remembered there had been one like this one before—when?—the bartender, the intellectual who read so many books and told her that the race problem in the South stemmed from the psychotic fear white men had that black men were better endowed. . . . Sims, don't, Sims, until she screeched hoarsely . . . and when she opened her eyes, it was no longer Sims but a pimpled flour face twitching . . . and during this, she sank into unconsciousness. . . .

When she opened her eyes, she was upright, propped upright between Wash and Sims, who was driving. Both windows were open, and the wind was cool as a brook.

"You all right?" Wash was asking. "We're taking you home."

She looked down and saw that someone had dressed her. Real gentlemen, real gentlemen—for a lady fair.

"Now don't go flipping on us," Wash was saying. "Any ol' sawbones will tell you five's no worse than one. What little girls got don't wear out. Only listen, honey—you're—well, you got to be careful—one of the boys, he—you've been hurt a little—but nothing serious, nothing at all. Hey, Sims, over there, pull up there."

She felt the car swerve, and jarringly halt, engine idling. Wash opened the door. "We're letting you off a few doors away, honey, in case somebody's waiting up."

He offered to help her out, but she didn't move.

"Lend a hand, Sims."

Together, pulling and pushing, they maneuvered her out of the car. Wash propped her against a tree. He pointed off. "That way, honey." He offered his mock smile and inclined his head. "Thank you for the evening."

After the car had gone, she remained against the tree. At last, she stretched a leg, to see if it would move, and she saw that her stocking was below her knee, torn and stained.

She began to run, stumbling forward, sobbing and running.

When she reached her lawn, she collapsed, dropping in a heap on the cool, moist grass, wailing uncontrollably.

But then she heard footsteps on the pavement, muffled on the grass, approaching swiftly. She tried to stop crying, and lifted her head, expecting a policeman and finding herself not at all surprised that it was Horace who was beside her, saying something she could not understand, before she shut her eyes and brain to all sensibility.

10

AT TEN MINUTES after eight on Thursday morning, Kathleen Ballard, in answer to Paul Radford's urgent summons of almost an hour earlier, arrived at Naomi Shields' house and was admitted by Paul.

The reason for the emergency was still not clear to Kathleen, except that Paul had said on the telephone that Naomi had been on a date with some hoodlum, had been mistreated, had been put to bed by her doctor, and that a friend or neighbor was needed to stay with her until the registry found an available nurse.

Although Kathleen was not a close friend of Naomi's, and saw her infrequently (the last time had been the occasion of Dr. Chapman's lecture at the Association), she had responded immediately. Her private feelings about Naomi had always been ambivalent: at once a secret kinship for another who had been married and was now husbandless, and a secret discomfort in the presence of one whose unrestrained sexuality (if all those terrible stories were true) had become standard parlor gossip in The Briars. Now, for Kathleen, another element had been added. She had met Horace at lunch yesterday and learned that he was formerly Naomi's husband, and because she liked Horace (and, in fact, everyone and everything associated with Paul), she was compelled to look upon Naomi as on official member of the new circle into which she had been drawn.

"How is she?" Kathleen asked as she entered Naomi's attractive but obviously decorated Chinese-modern living room, and realized with surprise that it was unfamiliar to her.

"Dozing," said Paul. "She was heavily sedated last night. She'll be all right." For a moment, he enjoyed Kathleen's morning face.

Conscious of his eyes fixed upon her, Kathleen lifted her

fingers to her cheek. "I must be a sight. I hardly had time to make up." She glanced off worriedly. "Is there anything I can do for Naomi?"

"Nothing, for the moment, except standing sentry," said Paul. "I can't tell you how grateful we are, Kathleen. Horace and I don't know Naomi's friends. We didn't know where to turn."

"You did the right thing."

"What about Deirdre?"

"I dropped her at school on the way and left a note for Albertine to watch for the car-pool auto at noon and stay on until I returned. Have you had breakfast?"

"I don't remember."

"You've got to have something. Let's find the kitchen."

There were neither eggs nor bacon in the refrigerator, and the bread in the white metal box was several days old. Dirty dishes filled the sink. Kathleen dropped two slices of bread in the toaster, prepared coffee, and then washed and dried several dishes. As she worked, Paul settled himself on a dinette chair with a grunt and explained what had been happening.

Several times, since Horace had learned Naomi lived in The Briars, he had called upon her, but not once had he found her home. Last night he had tried again, and when again she was not present, he had parked before her porch, determined to await her return. After midnight, she had appeared on her lawn, drunk and mauled. Horace had carried her inside, revived her, learned the name of her physician, and called him. The doctor had come at once, and had reported that, except for requiring three stitches, her injury was mainly psychic. He had recommended that she be placed in a sanitarium and be given intensive psychiatric treatment. He had left the names of several analysts, and by daybreak, Horace, exhausted and confused, had telephoned Paul for his advice.

"What could I tell him?" Paul said to Kathleen as she served the buttered toast and coffee. "We're strangers out here. And, knowing what I know of Naomi, it was something you just don't play by ear. Of course, Dr. Chapman has the best medical connections, but Horace and I agreed that this was something we had best leave him out of. He'd have immediately worried about the newspapers. This was strictly Horace's personal matter, to be handled as quietly as possible. Then I remembered Dr. Victor Jonas."

Kathleen, seating herself across from Paul, remembered Dr.

267

Jonas, too. Paul had spoken of him with affection on one of their first dates.

"And even though, technically, he was Dr. Chapman's adversary, I knew Naomi's problem was in his area and that he could be trusted. So I called him from the motel and explained the situation, and I met him here. And then I called you."

"Is Dr. Jonas here now?"

"In the back, talking to Horace. I told Horace to accept whatever he has to say."

There was little to add. They drank their coffee in silence. Kathleen remembered the time when her sister had been in the hospital to have her adenoids and tonsils removed, and after the surgery, while her sister was in the recovery room, she and her parents had gone down to a cafeteria and had sat in the early morning drinking coffee, and it had smelled like this. But then, placing it in time, she realized that it must have been her parents' coffee that smelled like this. She would have had milk.

They heard footsteps, and Dr. Victor Jonas came into the kitchen. Paul tried to stand, but Dr. Jonas kept him down with a hand on his shoulder, acknowledged the introduction to Kathleen with a warm smile, and decided that he would pour himself some coffee. Consciously, Kathleen had to cease staring at him: his rumpled hair and suit, and the prow of a nose, made him seem so unprofessional and eccentric.

"Horace just went to look in on her," said Dr. Jonas as he brought his coffee to the table and sat. "I think he understands what must be done."

"Is there hope for her?" Paul wanted to know.

"Maybe," said Dr. Jonas.

Paul and Kathleen exchanged a glance, he perturbed, she perplexed, for they had expected the usual confident social platitude which ranged from "of course" to "where there's life, there's hope." Paul had momentarily forgotten, and Kathleen did not yet know, Dr. Jonas' habit of candor.

"What does that mean?" asked Paul.

"Psychiatrically, there's every likelihood that this thing can be cured. It's really in their own hands, more in Horace's, I'd say. If she's to be helped, she's got to understand that she can be helped, that this is an illness, the symptom of a deeper illness. But since she is the one afflicted with a wish to self-destruction, she'll need a hand. So that puts it squarely up to Horace. He's got to know that she's not depraved but sick. Not so easy for him. He's educated, oriented, but there's an enemy, and that's his old religious upbringing. If he decides that he wants her, that she's worth saving for himself, then he'll come around. And he can bring her around. Then I have the place for them and the man. In Michigan. It wouldn't be too far for him."

"Have you actually seen cures in cases like this?" Paul asked.

"Of course. I told you, nymphomania's a symptom of something that can be healed. Reach down, touch it, treat it, and there's no more reason for nymphomania."

Kathleen felt the inner tremor of shock and hoped she did not show it. That word, always the word in a joke or rental novel, had now a frightening quality, for it was real, and Naomi, sedated, was real. Suddenly, Kathleen recalled the gossip and shuddered. The stories were true. But how could any woman behave that way? But then, he had said, she could not help it, she was helpless, she was ill.

"What are the causes?" Kathleen found herself asking.

Dr. Jonas finished his coffee. "They vary. In this case, from the little I've heard, I'd guess she wasn't much loved as a child." He felt his pockets for the corncob pipe and found it. "I'm oversimplifying, of course. But this hypersexuality could be one means of trying to get that love now, as an adult. But it doesn't work, you see—no man, no hundred men, can give her what her parents failed to give her twenty-odd years ago." He filled the pipe and lighted it. "I tried to explain this to Horace. I told him she'd grown up without tenderness, security, authority, without the feeling of having been a person of value, and so the problem grew as she grew, and then she tried to run away from it by this endless series of unsatisfying episodes with other men. When I was through, Horace said, 'You mean, it's not just sex she's looking for; you mean, she doesn't want all those men?' and I told him no, she doesn't. In fact, underneath, she's deeply hostile toward men. That may have opened his eyes a little. And it's true." He looked at Kathleen and welcomed her again with a shy but reassuring smile. "Analytic treatment can help fill in what has been missing. It can make her learn who she is, and why, and that she is a person of value. It will restore her identity. These suicidal sexual episodes will cease." He shrugged. "It's up to the two of them."

After a few minutes, Horace, wearily rubbing the bridge of his nose with the hand that held his glasses, appeared. He glanced at the three around the dinette table with a blank expression. Kathleen tried to smile, and at last Horace recognized her and greeted her.

"She's still sleeping," said Horace, "but she seems restless."

"Naturally," said Dr. Jonas. "That wasn't exactly a picnic last night."

Horace looked at Kathleen. "It's good of you to come, but maybe I'd better be here until the nurse arrives. In case Naomi wakes up. I think I'll call Dr. Chapman and have him take over for me."

Horace found the Association number in his billfold, and then telephoned. He got Benita Selby on the other end and explained that he might be detained and wondered if Dr. Chapman could manage for him until noon. He listened then, nodding at the phone, seeming sadder than before, and finally said that he and Paul would be on hand for the first interviews.

Returning the receiver to the cradle, Horace faced Kathleen. "Well, they can't spare me," he said. And then, to Paul. "Apparently Cass is down with the flu again, so Dr. Chapman's taking his list."

"Don't worry," said Kathleen. "I'll look after her."

"If she wakes up," said Horace, "explain that I'll be here right after work, by six-thirty, if possible."

Kathleen nodded. Paul and Dr. Jonas stood up. "I think she'll sleep most of the day," Dr. Jonas said to Kathleen. "You might look in every once in a while, to see if she's comfortable."

There was a mournful canine wail from the maid's room. "Christ, the dog," said Horace. "I forgot." He looked helplessly about. "Who's going to take care of it?"

"I will," said Dr. Jonas promptly. "My boys can care for the dog until Mrs. Shields is on her feet." He disappeared briefly through the service porch and then returned with the grateful cocker spaniel in his arms.

Kathleen followed the men to the front door. After Horace and Dr. Jonas had gone out, Paul lingered a moment.

"Special thanks," he said to Kathleen. "I'll call you at noon to see if everything's okay. May I see you tonight?"

"That would be nice."

"Dinner?"

"I won't have you leaving California flat broke. A hamburger at a drive-in would suit me fine."

Paul smiled. "You're not the type, but whatever you say."

"Are you sure you know what type I am?"

270

"Pheasant under glass and caviar with a sprig of Edelweiss."

"Sometimes, yes. But also hamburger with a sprig of grass roots." She wrinkled her nose. "Have a good day."

After she had closed the door, she went into the hall, tiptoeing as she sought Naomi's room. Finding the bedroom, she peered inside. The shades were drawn, and the room was in semi-darkness. Naomi lay with her head resting on her curled arm.

Turning away, Kathleen had an image: a creature from her private mythology, from the neck up an angel, from the neck down, a strumpet. Quickly, she was ashamed of the image and banished it.

In the overdecorated living room, surveying the pieces, she realized that what had at first seemed studied chic, now appeared garish. The fine old Chinese porcelain lamps were not genuine but cheap San Fernando Valley copies, and the vases were not cut crystal but pressed glass. Suddenly, she felt ashamed for these discoveries, as if caught peeking into private drawers when the owner was away. Because she didn't care about other people's furnishings anyway, because she had no such snobberies, only the knowledge of what was tasteful and what was not, she turned from the pieces and sought a book.

In a few minutes, she had found a rental-library mystery and decided that it would help consume the morning. Arming herself with cigarettes, matches, ash tray, she made herself comfortable on the thick sofa, crossed her legs, carefully put her heels on the coffee table, and attempted to read. But it was difficult. Her mind had fastened on Paul Radford.

During the past week, she had seen him every day but one. She had never before felt so contented, so quickly, with a man. Yet the old worry hung over her like a naked sword. She would not dare to let herself think of it or of what might happen between them, before he left on Sunday. Now, as she invited him to wander through her head, she felt suddenly cheating and unworthy. She tried to think about the other women that she knew in relation to Paul. How would they manage him? Who did she mean? Naomi? Oh, God, no. But someone as . . . as cool and controlled, outwardly, as herself. Who was like herself? No one, really. Yet, there was Ursula Palmer. She was a writer. Paul was a writer. Things in common. More than that, Ursula was so in-control-of and self-assured. Those were characteristics required in a situation like this. None of the black uncertainty. She envied Ursula. . . .

"Well," said Bertram Foster at last, after having placed the glass of champagne on the coffee table before her, "I bet this is the first time you ever had bubbles in your nose at breakfast."

"Yes," said Ursula Palmer dutifully.

The day before, Foster had telephoned her to change the time of their meeting. He had complained that Alma simply would not give him a night off, even to work, and so he had arranged the next best thing. He had conspired with a studio to have her taken on a visit to a location shooting at Lake Arrowhead. She would be back by dinner. But, at any rate, this would give Ursula and himself all of Thursday morning and afternoon together. He had suggested that they begin by breakfasting early in his suite.

Ursula had felt better about the breakfast. Increasingly, the dinner date had troubled her. Breakfast had an uninvolved, unromantic, anti-sexual atmosphere. After all, who could be inspired to fornicate after Wheaties? But when she had arrived, morning attired, in her open-throat blouse and pleated light wool skirt, she had been dismayed to find Foster wearing a thin, polka-dot silk robe over his gray silk pajamas. His round face was freshly shaved and smelled of pine and talcum. And behind him, on the breakfast cart, was the open bottle in the iced bucket.

He held his glass aloft. "Piper Heidsick," he said. "The best money can buy. Go ahead, go ahead—try it."

He drank and watched over his glass as she brought her glass to her lips. Ursula tried to keep from grimacing. It tasted like something squeezed out of wet wood. "Delicious," she said, and felt the heat of it rise to her temples.

"Umm," said Foster, drinking. "Breakfast can wait." He came around the table to her, set the glass down, and dropped heavily on the couch beside her. He peered owlishly at the cleft made visible by her open-throat blouse. "Well, Miss Editor," he said, "where is it?"

For Ursula, the long-deferred, dread moment had finally arrived. "Here," she said, patting the large manila envelope beneath her purse. The completion of the notes on her sex history had been a miracle of ambition. Constantly during her typing of it, she had been delayed and held up by involuntary mental odysseys into her childhood, her years with Harold, her inadequacies as a sexual partner. In a busy, eventful life, where love had been sublimated to a lesser part of it, her short-comings had never been fully faced or even partially apparent to her. But once concentrated in one place, as a separate biography of her behavior, this portion of her life loomed larger than heretofore, and its failures were evident and haunting. The distasteful task of reliving this segment of her biography, of knowing it would be soon seen by another, these facts as well as the knowledge that her husband was being serviced in his office by a German chippy, had made the last days unbearable. Several times the thought, unthinkable weeks ago, that the cover line and the job in New York were not worth the price, had crossed her mind, but in the end she had gone on and finished the loathsome assignment.

Now, unclasping the manila envelope, opening it, extracting the clipped pages of typed notes, she wondered if it would be less galling simply to sleep with Foster rather than let him peek into the bedroom and watch her perform through the years.

"It's twenty-seven pages," she said, and she handed it to him.

He held the notes in his hands, and held also a serious, businesslike face. "A real contribution," he said.

"It'll take a while to read, Mr. Foster. Maybe I could go for a walk and come back."

"No. I want you here to discuss. Have champagne."

Already he was eagerly reading. Ursula tried to avoid his face, but several times glanced sidelong at it and saw that this was the face that stared at stag films in darkened living rooms and avidly read the classic eroticism of John Cleland. Ursula swallowed her champagne, feeling sick at heart, feeling Belle Boyd delivering Harold's secrets to the enemy, feeling betrayer of the only God-chosen private part of her life. (When you sold this, what else was left?)

She was aware that he was beginning to skip pages, hur-riedly.

"What's the matter, Mr. Foster?"

"The kid stuff—who cares? Where's the grown-up part?"

"You mean premarital?"

"Whatever you call it," he said impatiently.

"Page eighteen."

He found the page and began to read again. His eyes did not blink. He kept wetting his lips.

After a while, he looked at her. "So you put out before?"

"I was very young, Mr. Foster," she said hastily, resenting her defensiveness but not wishing to give him license.

He read on and looked at her again, and she had the strange sensation that his eyes reflected not Ursula Palmer but a side of stripped beef. "You live and learn," he said.

"What?"

"Position is everything," he said, and he showed his teeth and winked. Her skin went cold.

He read on. She saw, from the corner of her eye, the pages steadily flipping. She judged that he was reading about her life with Harold. She despised herself and wanted to snatch the manuscript from his fat hand.

He held his finger on the page and shifted toward her. "He's not so much," said Foster.

She met his eyes. "Who?"

"Your husband."

She was blinded by indignation. "He's as good as anybody— as you or anybody."

"Not by my book."

Losing restraint, she fought back. "Why are men so conceited? They always think they can do better for a woman than her husband."

"Loyalty, I don't knock—but facts are facts." His lardy lips spread. "Excuse me; maybe he improves with age."

He resumed reading. She trembled with the outrage of it. This misshapen old lecher, with his soiled brain, derogating and mocking Harold, dismissing her whole married life with his filthy tongue.

He had turned a page, and now he brought it back again and reread it slowly. His lips silently formed the words. He held the page stiffly, not turning it. He began to speak without looking at her. "It says here, 'Question: Do you—'" His bloated face was turned toward her. "Come here," he ordered. His finger was on the page. "Read this and tell me if I understand."

Tensely, she edged beside him, inclining her head to follow his finger on the page. She felt his asthmatic breath on her cheek.

"What does that mean?" he demanded.

She pulled back, sitting upright. He stared at her. She wanted to burst into tears. His expression was queer. He was breathing through his mouth only.

"What does that mean?" he repeated.

274

Her voice was almost gone. "What it says."

"What I think?"

"Yes, but . . . it's different—"

"Ah—" he wheezed.

His face was before her, and his command came in a harsh undertone.

Her temples were ablaze. "Mr. Foster—"

"Yes!" he shouted, reiterating his command.

He reached for her, but she tore free of his grasp and slapped him with all her strength. "You pig—you filthy pig!"

"You're the pig."

She leaped to her feet, to evade him, grabbing for her purse and then the manuscript.

He sat, wheezing, and his voice was now a pleading whine. "Ursula—listen, sweetheart—I can help you—anything—"

She started for the door.

"You did it before!" he shouted. "You like it!"

She had the doorknob.

"You leave, and you leave the job—everything!"

From the open door, she wheeled. "You know what you can do with your job?" she shouted back. And then, like a long-shoreman (she would remember later), she told him. And then she fled, past the elevators, down the three flights of stairs, through the lobby, and she did not stop running until she had reached the car. Then, and only then, did the full impact of her break with the past, not the future but the past, strike her forcefully.

Curiously, she felt no need to weep. Through the windshield, between the two tall, gray office buildings ahead, she could see the towering blue-green mountains to the north, every furry crag and crevice defined. It was a wonderfully clear day for California, she was pleased to note.

❖   ❖   ❖

Still comfortable on Naomi's sofa, Kathleen Ballard had hardly moved in a half hour. A dozen playlets, produced by daydreams, had intervened between herself and the mystery novel on her lap. In each playlet, the hero was always Paul, but the heroine bore a different countenance imposed upon her own person. Ursula Palmer had come and gone, and Ruth Joyce, and Felicia Scoville, and now she had introduced Sarah Goldsmith into her corporeal being, on her private stage, and had presented her to Paul.

Considering Sarah, Kathleen could see how her natural warmth, her down-to-earth housewifeliness, her air of fecundity, would appeal to a man like Paul. Surely, in Kathleen's situation, she would react affectionately and generously. It was a matter of the forty-eight chromosomes, in the end. How did the Creator distribute them? How Sarah hers, and how me, mine, my mashed, dried gelatinous genes that gave me my meness? Genetically, Sarah has it by a unanimous decision.

✧   ✧   ✧

Never, since that Halloween night when she was six or seven and the headless skeleton had risen shrieking from behind the fence, and she and the others had bruised and bloodied themselves in their heart-stopping scramble to the illuminated shelter of the main street, had Sarah Goldsmith known such icy fear.

Flattened against the living-room wall, behind the drape, beside the large window, she peered outside. The Dodge had not moved, nor the dark avenging spirit of haunting guilt that was inside it. Withdrawing from the glass pane with a breathless gasp, Sarah pushed herself from the wall, and, steadying herself on the furniture she passed, made her way on collapsible legs to the kitchen.

For the third time this morning, since she had first sighted the car and the driver after Sam's departure, she was dialing Fred's number. Since the terror of Monday, she had awaited the return of the avenging spirit, the adhesive conscience, the all-knowing eye. But on Tuesday, and again Wednesday, the street had remained empty, and, following Fred's advice, she had remained away from his bed and stayed anchored to Sam's house.

This morning she had mystically, neurotically, compulsively, latched her peace of mind to the number three. If three days would pass with the street empty, then she and Fred were safe, and it had all been a coincidence. But on this, the third watch, the Dodge had been inexorably waiting, and her magical incantation had melted before a demoralizing reality. Even as she had telephoned Fred to report the terror, her dependence had been on the number three, the third call that would find him in his apartment. But her wizardry had vanished. The devil rode a Dodge, and bewitchery had fled from her hands to his.

The telephone buzz hummed persistently, mechanically subdued, controlled, unable to exclaim the urgency of her panic.

At last, she returned the receiver to the hook. Fred was out, and she was alone with their evil. The slant walls of the house were the rising tide, engulfing her, and the only refuge lay in the sun, where also waited the danger. But outdoors was the sanity of her living street, and friends, and the path to Fred's apartment, and ultimate safety.

Who was the shadowing, four-wheeled figure anyway? A man. A car. A detective on duty. A commercial shadow, fifty dollars a day, hire, fired. By whom? Mrs. Tauber? Sam? But look, she was invincible, Sarah told herself, free, white, a mother, a shopper, with daylight her armor. How could the four-wheeled figure harm her more? Follow again? Make another note? For Sam? Mrs. Tauber? There were notes enough, surely, already. More did not matter. What mattered was seeing Fred, measuring, evaluating, deciding, knowing someone stood beside her, flintlock in hand, defying the world to jeer her scarlet letter.

She found her leather jacket in the closet and reached the front door and opened it. For a moment, she hesitated, saw the gardener across the way, then the Dodge, and then she hurried into the sun and daylight. Once in the cool station wagon, she swiftly started it, backed out, attained the street, made the turn away from the parked conscience, and then turned again, and when she was in the traffic on Wilshire Boulevard, she was relieved to find no reflection of the Dodge in her rear-view mirror.

There was no memory of the ride to Beverly Hills, and no sight of the terrifying shadow. But crossing Santa Monica Boulevard, past the great hotel, she thought she saw in her mirror, two cars back, the familiar grill. She made the right turn south, then two blocks, and, across from Fred's apartment, she parked. She tore herself from the front seat, searched behind, and felt limp pleasure in the view of the street barren of traffic and enemy.

She hastened into the apartment building, up the flight of stairs more familiar than Sam's front door, and it was when she turned to touch the doorbell that she saw the sheet of paper pasted with Scotch tape above the knocker.

There was a message, classically slanted, printed, in Fred's hand. "Reggie," it began—a name unknown to her, but male —"Had to skip out early to the barrister—" jocular, although maybe not, but indicating no crisis—"and will be closeted with him through lunch. Will settle the matter and call you late afternoon. Forgive me. Sit on the phone and wait. Fred."

Sarah's disappointment at Fred's absence was now tempered by a new bright hope. It would require no Champollion to decipher this discovery. Fred had spoken often about seeing an attorney to divest himself from the juiceless Mrs. Tauber. But always Sarah's questions had hung unanswered, deferring to the immediacy of their clinging bodies, and afterward the questions had evaporated into thin air; nor did she mind, for the more demanded answer had been given.

She had removed her spectacles, before ascending the staircase, and now she returned them to her face. She studied the note for a word wrongly read, a phrase misunderstood. But the message was all clarity. Fred was closeted with his attorney. This could mean, at last, at long last, he was arranging the divorce, a proceeding, a word, not yet part of their vocabulary of love. Her body was permeated by the marvel of it, the glittering utopia of it. A divorce. But who was Reggie? Here was needed Champollion. Or merely Fred.

She opened her purse, dug through a miniature cosmetic warehouse, and found the gold pencil. She reflected a moment, and then, at the bottom of the sheet pasted to the door, she wrote: "Fred—came calling to discuss business—will call later today—S." She considered her handiwork, crossed out *business*, and replaced it with *Dodge*. This was unmistakable.

As she descended the staircase, a momentary trepidation held her elbow, escorted her to the heavy door. Outside, she met her car. She examined the street, right and left. There was no other car.

As she crossed the street, a deduction entered her mind. It was so obvious that it had almost eluded her farsightedness. Why was Fred conversing with an attorney today, why now, after these many weeks? Because of her urgent call Monday, because of M. Javert. Fred was anticipating Mrs. Tauber. Or Sam. The inevitable detective had produced the inevitable crossroad of decision. Why await confrontation? Scandal? A grand slam? Anticipate. Disarm. Poor Mrs. Tauber. Or Sam.

She had reached the car. She was proud of Fred, her Fred, her Fred. The Dodge was ineffectual now. Pitiful Dodge. Stupid, foolish Dodge. Those wasted notes ("Subject left home 10:32. Entered Tauber ap't. 10:57. Emerged 12:01. Halted to comb hair, adjust make-up"), so promisingly erotic, so suddenly respectable. She wondered if it would be in the news-papers. She remembered that she had promised Jerry and Debbie that she would not disgrace them again by forgetting the PTA paper drive. Nevertheless, she felt almost gay.

♦   ♦   ♦

Kathleen Ballard had finally got past the first chapter of the mystery novel, aware early that it was of English origin because *honor* was spelled *honour* and aware also that the nephew Peter was too detestable to have done it (yet the au-thor—at his twenty-fourth novel—would surmise that Peter, being detestable, would be dismissed, and therefore it might be wise to make it Peter, after all). She turned the page, hav-ing just met Lady Cynthia returned from Nepal, when the telephone shattered the stillness.

Kathleen swung to her feet, limped on the leg that had almost gone to sleep, and snatched up the receiver in the kitchen after the third peal. A remote telephone operator's voice announced the nurse's registry. Miss Wheatley, who had been assigned at noon, would be detained until six. But she would definitely appear. Kathleen protested. There was a patient re-quiring expert care. Wasn't anyone else available? The remote voice avoided involvement. No one available before evening, but then Miss Wheatley would be on hand. Kathleen fought the detached system. What if there was an immediate emer-gency? Would they have a nurse then? The remote voice would not be baited, no more than would a phonograph rec-ord. The voice was in no position to reply to the questions. The voice accepted messages and delivered them. Good day.

Kathleen was used to these lesser disappointments, and once having adjusted herself to the six hours ahead, she took inven-tory of the kitchen for sustenance. Naomi, it was evident, always ate out. Or, more likely, based on the single stocked cupboard, did not eat at all, but drank her meals on the rocks. A determined search disclosed, at last, a bent can of pea soup, a mammoth can of beef stew, a dusty, unopened box of cheese crackers, and several bottles of Seven Up (seasoned survivors of an old lost battle against gin). Kathleen decided that the beef stew would suffice, and this was a good day to start a diet, anyway.

She had succeeded in decapitating the mammoth can when the telephone rang a second time. The caller was Paul, and, hearing his voice, she was grateful for the companionship, and then certain that he would not have been happy with Sarah Goldsmith at all.

She told him about the nurse, wanting only the affection of his concern, and was then able to tell him that she would manage very nicely until six. Was she sure? Absolutely. Damn sorry to have gotten her into this mess. Of course not; it was the least that she could do. What about Naomi? Sleeping. Good, good. Horace would be relieved. She hadn't forgotten dinner, had she? Oh, no. Well, until later then. Yes, later.

The stew was in a pot and heating over a burner when she heard Naomi's outcry. "Horace!"

Kathleen turned the burner low and hurried toward the bedroom. When she entered, she found Naomi on her back, beneath the blanket, eyes pointed to the ceiling.

Kathleen went to the bed. "Are you all right?"

The eyes shifted. "What are you doing here?"

"Horace had to go to work. The nurse hasn't come on yet. So I'm filling in."

"Why you?"

"I . . . I've been seeing a friend of Horace's, and they called me."

"I don't need anyone. I don't need a nurse."

"Well, the doctor—"

"That horse's ass."

Naomi did not move. She closed her eyes, then opened them. Kathleen, worried, walked closer to the bed.

"Naomi, can I get you anything?"

"No. I'll be up soon as this junk wears off."

"How do you feel?"

"Like someone's pinching my crotch."

"Stitches."

Naomi averted her head on the pillow. "Bastards," she said from profile and with no anger. She was still again, and Kathleen stood waiting uncomfortably.

"Do you know what happened last night?"

Kathleen quickly shook her head. "No."

"I was gang laid."

"Oh, Naomi—"

"It might have been instructive, if I'd been sober. I'm submitting a supplementary report to Doc Chapman."

"You mean they forced—"

Naomi met her eyes. "I'm not so sure." She created the brief facsimile of a smile. "Go away. I contaminate. I'm a slut."

"Don't talk like that."

280

"Men's language. I like it. The only true language. They don't know women. But they know sluts."

"Naomi, try to rest."

"Who was here? This morning?"

"Your doctor. Then Horace brought a psychologist."

"Head-shrinker?"

"No. He was just trying to help out, give advice."

"What did he advise?"

"I think we should wait until Horace—"

"No, you."

"I'm not sure."

"Get off it, Katie. I've been banged by a battalion. I've got to know what the high command says."

"They spoke of treatment, analysis."

"You think lying on a couch for a year telling dirty stories will help?"

"I can't say. I suppose they know."

"Screw that." She turned on her side. "Let me sleep." Her voice was fading.

Kathleen looked on helplessly a moment, distressed by Naomi's sickness, sickness and sickly vulgarity, and then turned to leave. At the door, Naomi called out to her.

"What's Horace doing here?"

Kathleen was surprised. "I thought—why, he's with Dr. Chapman."

"I didn't know." Her voice drifted off. "No kidding?" In a moment, her labored nasal breathing told Kathleen that she was asleep. Softly, Kathleen drew the door shut and went into the kitchen.

Later, having eaten only a small portion of the stringy beef stew and finished the soft drink, she returned to the sofa and the mystery novel. All through the meal she had thought of Naomi, trying to reconcile her beauty with her coarseness, trying to separate her sensuality from illness. She wondered if men, taking that voluptuous body, were ultimately conscious of the decay beneath. Would Paul, given the opportunity, take her? Enjoy her? Or be repelled? Of course, Naomi's aptitude was sex. Her physical loveliness and dexterity might offset all else. Committed to lust, no man was a sensitive, perceptive, thinking animal. When he was that way, Boynton would have ravished a corpse. There was a medical name for that. Boynton, yes, but not Paul. No, Paul would not enjoy Naomi, ever. He would prefer someone tidy, composed, restrained. Like herself, of course. Not herself, no, for she was merely the

281

polar opposite of Naomi, which also was a kind of sickness, although less obvious and appalling. Who, then, tidy, composed, restrained? Who, normal? Teresa?

Sitting on the sofa, the unlighted cigarette between her fingers, she considered Teresa Harnish and Paul. Teresa's practicing intellectuality and artiness might become a bore. But she *was* attractive, she *was* a lady. . . .

◇   ◇   ◇

Teresa Harnish had arrived ten minutes early, and now he was ten minutes late. She began to worry for the first time whether or not he had received the message. Even if he had received it, would he take it seriously, would he be free, would he remember her?

Impatiently, she circled the pool of seals just inside the entrance of Paradise Park, and disinterestedly she scrutinized her fellow pleasure-seekers. A dumpy, shapeless young mother with a sticky boy in knee pants. Several teen-age girls, in some kind of middy uniforms, giggling behind their hands as if it were sinful and not allowed at the seminary. An elderly, gray gentleman in a blue serge suit that had the shine his shoes needed, elbows on the rail, mournfully throwing dead fish from a bag to the slimy black seals below. She listened to the barking of the seals and abhorred their hoarse, guttural gruntings.

She wondered if the breeze from the ocean beyond the pier had disturbed her hair. She fished in her purse for the French silver compact, sprang it open with her thumb, and regarded her hair and make-up. Everything was in place, unmussed, unsmeared. Returning compact to her purse, she examined her attire and was pleased. It had taken her half the morning to select the proper outfit. Over her shoulders, the tawny cashmere sweater. Pressed by the wind to her body, the transparent white silk blouse, almost revealing the lace brassière beneath. Flaring below, the short, full, tan piqué skirt. Legs stockingless; Rembrandt-brown leather moccasins simulating ballet slippers. The effect: youth.

The morning's choice had been between provocation and juvenescence. After leaving Geoffrey at the shop, she had returned to the study, located Dr. Chapman's previous book and learned that the male achieves greatest potency between the ages of eighteen and twenty-eight. (Also, the happy footnote quoting the Terman and Miles M-F tests: athletes scored highest in masculinity; artists scored lowest.) She calculated, based on education, graduation, football service, that he could be no more than twenty-five. It was all-important that the eleven-year chasm be narrowed. Her wardrobe reflected her final decision. Now his youth vigor, he would see, would be matched by her own.

She peered down at her platinum wrist watch and saw that he was sixteen minutes late. Unless her watch was fast. She swung about girlishly, scanning the whip, the ferris wheel, the roller coaster, the hall of mirrors, the visit to the moon, and then, from somewhere, he strode into her vision.

He wore a jaunty white sailor cap, a t-shirt bearing the fresh imprint that read "Paradise Park," khakis and open brown sandals. His face was Apollo, and the bulging biceps and chest, Milo of Greece.

She watched Ed Krasowski come to a halt across the pool, searching for her, looking directly at her, and still searching. She hurried around the pool toward him, and then he recognized her.

"Hiya," he said. "Didn't see you at first."

"Because I have a dress on," she said. "You always see me in shorts. Besides, if you're used to seeing a person in one place, and suddenly you see them against a different background, they look different."

"Yeah," he said.

There was an uneasy pause.

"I'm glad you could make it," she said quickly.

"Sure. Jackie told me."

The teen-agers were giggling again. Ed glanced at them, and Teresa followed his glance.

"Can't we find somewhere to talk?" she asked quickly.

"You mean to sit down?"

"Anywhere."

He held up his large steel wrist watch. "Well, lady, I got only half an hour for lunch—old Simon Legree don't like me late—so maybe I better eat while you talk."

"I'll have something, too. Is there a restaurant—"

"Couple fancy ones. But I'm not blowing my bankroll there."

"I'd love to treat."

He bridled. "What do you take me for? No. Dutch."

She felt a wave of pleasure at his manliness and his gallantry. "I'm sure any place you say—may I call you Ed?"

"Everybody does." He nodded toward the main promenade. "Tuffy makes the best dogs in the Park. Come on."

She walked hurriedly beside his hugeness, skipping several times to keep up, and feeling proud and possessive of his size. He uttered not a word as they progressed, until they reached the whitewashed wooden stand with the monstrous metal frankfurter on top and the four empty stools below, and then he said, "Right here."

She ascended a stool, elegantly, and he squatted on the one beside her. He wheeled toward the counter. "Hey, Tuffy—"

A wrinkled, toothless old man, wearing a ridiculous starched chef's hat and a spotted apron, appeared from a rear room, hoisting in greeting the arm tattooed with an anchor. "Hiya, Rams."

"What you doing back there, Tuffy, burying money?"

"Got better to do with money."

Ed Krasowski wheeled toward Teresa. "What you having?"

"Whatever you have."

Ed winked, pleased. "Specialty of the house. Two dogs, Tuffy. The supers. Everything."

Teresa observed Ed's arms, the subtle play of muscles beneath the tanned surface as he cracked his knuckles and then proceeded to arrange toothpicks on the counter in some curious formation.

"Are you going to be working here long?" she asked.

"Couple months maybe. Until we go back to practice."

"Do you like it?"

He shrugged the big shoulders. "Makes no difference."

"Your friend said you had one of the booths. Which?"

"Knocking over the wooden milk bottles."

"What do you have to do?"

"Nothing much. Make change. Pick up the balls. Set the bottles. Jolly the dames and kids along. It's like finding money."

"I'll bet you meet interesting people."

"Never noticed."

She pushed on like this, leading him, understanding his halting, monosyllabic answers, appreciating the inarticulate strength of the man of action. The change was stimulating, exhilarating. How many years had she wasted listening to cultivated, hollow words? Listening all those dull years, listening to all those chattering effeminate men? She stroked Ed with a glance. What had Napoleon said? *Voilà un homme!*

The burned frankfurters were served. They were mammoth, twelve inches in length, protruding from either side of the roll, heavy with chopped onion and relish. She held the elongated frankfurter awkwardly, gazing at it, and then at Ed.

284

She nibbled. He chewed. He swallowed a mouthful, spun partially on the stool toward her. "Jackie said you had some private business to talk to me about."

She nodded, as he made inroads into his frankfurter. Until now it had seemed vaguely possible, less and less so, but possible, that her planned and rehearsed proposal of mating could be openly broached. But the frankfurters made it impossible. Amid such wine as this—root beer on tap—could Isadora and Essinine flourish?

His nearness was maddening. The magnificent thing must be kept alive. Another way? "I . . . I've watched you—on the beach—"

"I thought you was always reading."

"I read, too. Don't you?"

"Sure. Not books, though. Takes too long. Hated them in school. Coach got the grinds to cram me. Mostly I got time only for magazines nowadays. Anyway, about the beach—"

"I observed you playing ball. You're extremely agile. You have a good body for it."

"I keep in shape," he admitted with undisguised pride.

"Well, that brings me to why I wanted to see you." She put down the ridiculous frankfurter and faced him earnestly. "I'm an artist, quite a good one," she said, almost believing it, "and from the moment I saw you, I said to myself, I must capture him on canvas."

His forehead was puzzled. "Paint me? You mean a regular picture?"

"Dozens of pictures," she said enthusiastically. "I've watched you, as I said, closely, and you're a human being of many facets. I want to know all of them. I want the world to know you as Greek God, Olympian, Roman Emperor, Gladiator." She had heard Geoffrey's artists sometimes speak like this, not precisely so, but similarly, and she was sure it sounded correct. "I hope you'll consent."

"I never thought about it. Who are the pictures for?"

"Myself. Exhibits. Perhaps some will be reproduced in magazines or books."

"Does it take a lot of time?"

"An hour or two a day, no more."

He finished the frankfurter and wiped his mouth with a paper napkin. "I don't know. I ain't got much time what with this, and practice, and a man's got to relax a little."

"You'll find it relaxing."

"Not what I mean."

"What do you call relaxing?"

"Few beers with the boys, maybe a movie, and—well, some fun."

"You mean, girls?"

"Yeah, that's right."

Her lips were compressed. She wanted to shake him, scream at him: I'm girls, look at me, all girls, all women, the best, the best you ever met, I'm attractive, well dressed, witty, cultured, I have a large home in The Briars, I'm desirable. *I am fun.*

She swallowed. "Well, I understand that. But, Ed, you'd be surprised at what good sport this can be."

"I don't know," he said.

Desperate measures were indicated. Finger on the emergency button. Press. "Of course, I don't expect you to model for nothing."

He looked up sharply.

"I told your friend I wanted to see you about business," she added. "What do you make here?"

"Eighty bucks a week."

"I'll pay you twenty dollars for each . . . each session you pose."

"You mean for a couple of hours?"

"That's right."

He grinned broadly. "Lady, you got a deal."

Inside her, something eased. She had not wanted it to go this way, nor would he want it this way, once he understood her better offer, but for the moment this was enough. There would be the private meeting. It was all that she desired. And now she ached to have it at once.

"Wonderful," she said. "When can we have our first . . . meeting?"

"You name it."

"Tomorrow—eleven in the morning."

"I'm not free tomorrow until five."

It was so long a time to wait. But, all right, anything. "I can meet you at your place at five-thirty." She opened her purse and took out pencil and the white leather pad on which she jotted her aphorisms. "Here, write your address."

He wrote it, returned pad and pencil, and looked down at his metal watch. He rose from the stool. "Back to the salt mines," he said.

She slipped off the stool. He hesitated, staring down at her.

"Funny," he said.

"What?"

286

"You don't look like a painter."

"No? What do I look like?"

"Well, I don't know—"

"You mean—I look like . . . like just a woman."

"Something like that."

Her heart leaped. "You're very nice," she said. "I'll be looking forward to tomorrow."

"Okay. Be seeing you."

She watched him lumbering off, swaying, Brobdingnagian, magnificent. She wondered exactly how it would happen finally, and what it would be like, and she shivered. She watched the ferris wheel revolving and somewhere heard a calliope. She didn't feel like de Pompadour or de Poitiers, that was for sure. But she felt like more, far more, than she had been before, and that was good enough.

✧   ✧   ✧

By five-fifteen, the sun no longer high through the kitchen window but the afternoon still bright, Kathleen had abandoned the mystery novel and busied herself heating water for tea.

When the telephone rang out, startling her, she hastened to pick up the receiver, to prevent it from awakening Naomi.

"Hello?"

"Naomi?" The voice was a girl's voice.

"I'm a friend of Naomi's—Mrs. Ballard."

"Kathleen?"

"Yes?"

"Mary McManus. What are you doing there?"

"Oh, hello, Mary. I . . . well . . . Naomi wasn't—she came down with a bad cold, and I'm baby-sitting until a nurse comes in."

"Nothing serious, I hope?"

"No, no."

"I'm sorry about Naomi. I've been promising to get together with her, and tonight Dad's having some people in for a barbecue—and, well, Norman couldn't make it, and we have extra food, so I took a chance that maybe Naomi was free, but, this way—"

"I know she'll be glad you called."

"Tell her I'll talk to her tomorrow. How have you been?"

"Domesticating."

"What?"

"Synonym for vegetating. No, I've been fine, Mary. Do cal me some afternoon and come over for tea."

"I'd love to. I really would. Tell Naomi I'm sorry. She's going to miss a good steak. Well, good to talk to you, Kathleen. 'Bye."

"Goodbye, Mary."

After she had poured the hot water and then removed the tea bag, Kathleen drank, admired the built-in stainless-steel gas range, and thought about Mary McManus. She decided that Mary was an argument for zest over beauty. Mary's bronzed outdoor vigor, her bouncing enthusiasm, made Kathleen feel old. She supposed that she was really no more than six or seven years Mary's senior, yet she felt used and worn, deep inside. Only technically could she offer Paul a chassis less than thirty years old. Mary, on the other hand, could give a bachelor the miracle of resurrection. Wasn't it curious, though, that last Sunday she had been at the tennis club with her father and not her husband? Well, young girls and their fathers. . . .

◇   ◇   ◇

Mary McManus went out on the cement patio where her father was still poking at the heating charcoal in the brick barbecue grill. Nearby stood the portable table, the layers of thick red steak, separated by wax paper, piled majestically high. Mary watched a moment and then sat on the edge of a checkered lounge.

"Put one steak back in the freezer," she said. "Naomi can't make it."

"You're sure Norman won't come down?" Harry asked without turning.

Mary was faintly irritated with the way the question had been posed. Unaccountably, she felt like bickering. "It's not a matter of 'won't come down'; he can't, he doesn't feel well—don't you ever feel that way?"

Her father spun about and blinked at her. "Aren't we a little touchy about semantics tonight?"

"I just thought you wanted to say it that way." She hesitated. "I'm sorry. But he did come home with an awful headache, Dad. You should know; you drove with him. He was sure a nap would get rid of it, but just now he said he felt no better. He doesn't want to throw a wet blanket on the party."

"It seems to me he's getting more than his share of head-

288

aches lately—for a healthy, strapping young man. Why don't you get him to see a doctor?"

"He insists he's all right. They go away."

Harry Ewing grunted, seemed lost in thought a moment, pursed his lips, absently wiped his hands on the comical chef's apron, and walked slowly to the lounge across from Mary.

"Did he tell you we had a talk today?"

Mary raised her eyebrows. "No."

"We did. About his new assignment."

"New assignment?"

"Remember—Sunday—I told you I was cooking up something extremely interesting?"

Mary nodded eagerly.

"Well, we've decided to tackle those Essen people on the pre-fab patent case. We're going into the German courts. I'm shipping Norman and Hawkins off next month."

"To Germany?" Mary clapped her hands with delight. "It's one place I've always wanted to—"

"No, Mary," Harry Ewing said quickly, "not you. He'll be up to his neck there. No place for wives. I told Hawkins he couldn't take his missus, and I can't show partiality to Norm because he's my son-in-law. It would be demoralizing, bad precedent."

Mary's delight had given way to somber concern. "How long?" she asked.

"Who knows? Those court things drag on. And there's a good deal of preparation to be done on the scene with our German—"

"How long?" she persisted.

"Oh, four months—at the most six."

"Without me?" Her tone was ominous.

"Look, Mary—"

"What did Norman say?"

"Well, I will admit he didn't take too kindly to it. I wanted to keep this from you. But he was most disappointing. I reminded him that, family or no, he was still an employee. No preferential treatment. It was an important job, and I expected him to do it."

"But will he do it?"

"He'd better. He said he'd talk it over with you. 'It's up to Mary,' he said. I'm depending on you to pound some sense into that boy. I'm through coddling him."

Mary sat rocking her body on the lounge, staring at her father in an odd, new way.

Harry Ewing met her gaze, then exhaled. "Well, the steaks—" He began to leave.

"You want us apart, don't you, Dad?" Her voice held no harshness, merely understanding.

"Are you crazy?"

"I think you even want him to fail—"

"Mary!"

"Yes." She stood up. She started inside.

"Where are you going?" Harry Ewing called after her.

"To give Norman my answer."

She climbed the stairs gradually, giving herself time to adjust to the new decision, like an ascending deep-sea diver surfacing slowly against the changing pressure.

Upstairs, she moved to the bedroom, opened the door, closed it behind her, and turned the key.

Norman, lying on the bed, on his back, arms behind his head, staring at the ceiling, now watched her. She went to the foot of the bed.

"How's your headache?"

"I never had a headache."

She nodded. "That's what I thought. Norman, he told me."

"Deutschland über alles?"

"Not *über alles*—I told him."

"Oh?"

"Not *über* us."

She kicked off her shoes, and crawled on the bed, and lowered herself beside him.

"Norman, I love you."

"Ditto."

"Just you."

He examined her face warily.

"Norman—"

"Uh-huh?"

"I want us to have a baby."

He lifted himself to an elbow. "When did this happen?"

"It happened." She tried to smile. "We can travel when the baby's grown up."

"You mean it, don't you?"

"With all my heart."

He reached out for her, and she went into his arms, cuddled close to his chest.

"When?" he asked softly.

"Now, Norman—now."

❖   ❖   ❖

Miss Wheatley, the special, a large masculine woman with down on her upper lip and a severely starched nurse's uniform, had appeared at six-twenty, and Kathleen had rushed home to assist Albertine in feeding Deirdre and to change for dinner.

Paul had picked her up at eight, and instead of hamburgers, they had driven east to an Italian restaurant on the fringe of metropolitan Los Angeles. Although no Angeleno, and especially no native of The Briars, would have been caught dead in that unlovely business part of the vast city after work hours (except for the Philharmonic season and the New York plays), Kathleen had remembered the restaurant as charming, from a visit once paid to it with Ted Dyson.

The intimate, candlelit room, decorated with hanging Chianti bottles, made them feel near and private. They had ordered minestrone and lasagne, and consumed great numbers of breadsticks and a greater quantity of red wine. They had talked a long time of Paris—she had visited it with her family in the summer between high school and college, and he during weekends from the job in Berne—and she had remembered "Just Tell the Driver 'Sank Roo Doe Noo' " and he had remembered the chansonniers in Le Lapin Agile, and both had recalled the view from the Sacre-Coeur.

They had returned to The Briars slowly, reluctantly, through the balmy night, conversing less, and self-conscious for being so close and yet so far apart.

Now they were parked in the darkness of Kathleen's driveway.

He looked at her: the achingly delicate profile, the full scarlet lips, the blouse draped from her breasts, the silk skirt outlining her thighs.

She turned her head and looked at him: the wonderfully creased and lived-in face.

"Kathleen," he said.

"Yes," she said, almost inaudibly.

The moment was understood by both. Without thinking further, he did what he had not yet done. He drew her to him, and as she shut her eyes and parted her lips, his mouth found her lips. The kiss was long and electric. For a moment, he released her, both breathless, and when he sought to bring her to him again, closer, his arm went fully around her back and

291

his hand came to rest on her breast, cupping it fully. Before he could withdraw it, for it had been accidental, she stiffened in his arm and wrenched free. The moment was ended.

"Kathleen, I didn't mean it."

"It's all right."

"I didn't know—I was—I wanted you as close to me as possible."

How dreadful, she thought, to force such an apology. Her swift anger had turned away from him and inward. Here she was, an adult female of twenty-eight, married once, inviting tenderness, love, desiring it from a man she had imagined in every high-school dream, and yet reacting, behaving, as no juvenile teen-ager, no gauche or frightened adolescent, would behave. But then, as a female, she was a fraud, and now he would know it, at last. There could be no recovery. She, not Naomi, she more, needed the analyst. What had Ted Dyson called her?

His troubled face. She was so ashamed. "Paul," she said with difficulty, "I didn't mean—"

The vestibule lights went on, and in the glare, they both started. She swerved in the seat. The front door was open, and Albertine stood behind the screen, craning her neck, peering toward them.

"Mrs. Ballard?" she called.

Kathleen hastily rolled down the window. "Is anything wrong?"

"There's been two urgent calls for your gentleman friend. One not five minutes ago."

Paul leaned across Kathleen toward the open window. "Who was it?"

Albertine consulted the pad in her hand. "Mr. Van Dooten."

"Horace," said Paul.

"He said to watch for you and have you call the motel."

Paul frowned. "Must be something wrong."

He jerked the handle of Kathleen's car door and shoved it open. She stepped out, and he followed her. They hurried into the house.

In the study, Paul dialed the motel and asked for Mr. Van Duesen. He waited, and at last Horace came on. "Hello?"

"It's Paul."

"Thank God! Listen—Naomi's gone off; we don't know what the hell's happened to her."

"I don't understand."

"Naomi—she ran away. The nurse went to the bathroom—

around nine, she says—and when she got out, Naomi was gone. Her car, too. The nurse didn't know where to turn."

"Were you there?"

"That's just it, I wasn't. I was stuck with Chapman until about nine-thirty. When we broke up, I phoned to ask Naomi if she wanted anything before I came over. That's when I found out. The most I could get straight was that she blew her cork, because I wasn't there with her when she woke up. I guess she figured I was letting her down."

"Forget it. You know she's not very rational right now."

"That's what worries me. I'm worried sick. I don't even know where to start looking. Maybe she went to some friend's place. That's what I'm hoping. Ask Kathleen about her friends."

"All right." But something else had occurred to Paul. "There's another possibility—"

"What?"

"I'm not sure. I'll tell you when I see you. Look, Horace, sit tight. I'll be right over. We'll hunt for her together."

After hanging up, Paul explained to Kathleen exactly what had taken place. Kathleen knew none of Naomi's close friends, except Mary McManus, if Mary was a close friend. Immediately, Kathleen telephoned the Ewing residence. Harry Ewing answered the call. He sounded distant and cotton-mouthed. He said Mary couldn't come to the phone because she was asleep, and he had seen nothing of Naomi Shields. Undiscouraged, after she had finished with Ewing, Kathleen remembered that Naomi had once mentioned her father in Burbank. She tried information, learned there were several Shieldses in Burbank, and took all their numbers. The second proved to be Naomi's parent. He was gruff, unpleasant, and said he had not seen his daughter in months.

After this rebuff, Kathleen had one more idea. She telephoned the agitated, defensive Miss Wheatley and ordered her to search Naomi's kitchen and bedroom for an address book or list of personal phone numbers. After five silent minutes, Miss Wheatley returned to the mouthpiece empty-handed. She had been unable to produce an address book of any kind. Firmly, Kathleen told her to remain where she was, in case Naomi returned, and, if Naomi did return, to contact Horace Van Duesen at the Villa Neapolis at once.

During all of this, Paul had hovered restlessly nearby. Now Kathleen set down the telephone and confronted him. "Well," she said, "I guess I have struck out."

Paul nodded grimly. "There's one more longshot."

"What's that?"

"The nightclub where she got herself picked up last night. It's out on Sunset Boulevard. Horace knows the name."

"Why on earth would she go back there?"

"If she wanted to kill those men, that would be logical. But maybe she wants to have them again, and kill herself. That would be abnormal, but for her, in her present state, perfectly logical. Don't you see? Perverse logic. Indulging the self-destroying death wish."

"I can't believe it."

"She despises herself, Kathleen," he insisted. "This would be the ultimate flagellation. Anyway, we'll know soon enough."

Kathleen trailed him to the living-room door.

"Paul—"

Hand on the knob, he waited.

She hoped to explain about that moment in the car, that she hadn't meant it, that she cared for him, but now it seemed too callous and trivial in the light of Naomi's disappearance. Still, she supposed, it must always be like this with everyone: you set the human brain on a track marked sorrow, but it does not always stay there. What did people *really* think during a funeral? She recalled the rites around Boynton's grave, before the coffin was lowered.

"Paul . . . I . . . I hope you find her. And look out for yourself."

He nodded solemnly.

Suddenly, blindly, she ran to him, finding his cheeks with her hands, then standing on tiptoe to kiss him. This was wrong, too, she supposed, staying the Minute Man from his emergency, but, dammit, dammit, she was as lost as Naomi. For a moment, as their lips met, her instinct was to lift his hands from her hips and place them on her breasts. She wanted to do it, boldly, to show him that she had not meant her earlier prudery, to assure him that she was as warm as any woman alive. But what surprised her most was her dominating emotion: she wanted to do it because the flesh of her breasts strained for his touch. She held the desire and held it, but a cold paralysis gripped her, and then the kiss was ended and it was too late.

At last, she was sorry to have delayed him. "You'd better hurry. Let me know if you have any luck."

"I'll call you in the morning." For another moment, he

stared down at her. "You know what? You're the most beautiful girl I've ever known."

And he was gone.

She leaned against the closed door and thought the cliché: But beauty's only skin deep, and my hidden ugliness is deeper, much, much deeper, the greater part you cannot see, below the surface like an iceberg, like a lump of dough in a buried coffin.

⋄　⋄　⋄

Sitting at the ringside table in the noisy, smoky nightclub, only half aware of the gliding shadows of dancers before her eyes, Naomi Shields wondered why she was not drunk.

She had consumed six, seven, eight gin somethings, and her head was clear; she was sure it was clear. True, the knifing pain of the stitches had dulled, and the hurt of Horace's absence had numbed. But the clarity of her original desire had not blurred: to be impaled on a cross, on a bed, until she bled to death and found peace, at last.

The music had ceased, and now there remained overhead the shrill cacophony of human voices. A tall presence loomed, then lowered itself to eye-level in the chair across. The beloved, pocked death head. The lipless smile. Here, the Reaper, beloved Reaper, to wrap her in a shroud.

"How's my honey child?" Wash was asking.

"I'm tired of waiting," Naomi said.

"You don't want to wait?"

"No. Now."

He shook his head with admiration. "You're something, honey."

"Now," she repeated.

"You know, you're getting me excited. Maybe it can be arranged. You really want ol' Wash, don't you?"

She wanted calvary, the purge of pain, and the final nothingness. She nodded.

"Okay, honey, you got me." He rose to his feet.

"Not jus' you," she said. "All."

Wash whistled under his breath. "Christ."

"All—" she insisted.

"Okay, honey, okay. Come on. Let's get the show on the road." He helped her from the chair and led her across the slippery dance floor. As they passed the bandstand where several of the boys were relaxing, smoking, he held up his hand, joining forefinger and thumb in a circle. He opened the side exit and started her along the edge of the parking lot beside the kitchen.

"My car's behind there," he said, "all by itself."

"Where you taking me?"

"Nowhere, honey. I got a nice private backseat."

She heard a motor behind, and stopped, and looked off toward the bright area nearer the street. The car was an MG. An attendant was holding a door open, and a girl stepped out. Her face was indistinct at the distance, but she was young, patting down her taffeta and petticoats, and holding her corsage of camellias, and her escort was young and straight. Later, at her door, they would kiss, and tomorrow she would build a dream house, a dream life, a dream universe of happiness.

"Come on, honey. I got it bad now."

Naomi stared at the hideous death head, and suddenly the revulsion filled her throat. She was alive, a living entity, and all around, all around, were the living, the fresh, clean, alive living, and they were the race to whom she belonged, they and not this gruesome skeleton.

"No," she said.

"Come on."

"No, not in the car. What do you think I am?"

She pivoted uncertainly and tried to move away. Wash's hand was on her arm and she winced. The lipless smile was gone. "You're my girl, an' you're coming with me—so let's not have any trouble."

Dignity, dignity. "Let go of me," she said archly.

"Look, honey, no little bitch is getting me hepped up, and taking a powder. This is the big leagues, honey. We deliver. You're going with ol' Wash—and the boys, the boys, too. I'm not letting them down for nothing."

"I'm sick," she said suddenly. "You can't hurt somebody who's sick."

"You'll be sicker if you give me any more trouble."

He wrenched her violently after him and hastily dragged her toward the corner of the kitchen and the shape of the vehicle in the blackness beyond. Off balance, she stumbled after him, choking, trying to find her voice. She fell to her knees on the gravel. As he pulled her upright, she tore free. She tried to scream but felt his hand smashing across her face.

She sobbed. "No, Wash, no—"

He had her about the waist, off her feet. She tried to tear at him, tried to kick, but he continued with her toward the blackness. There was no sound but their breathing and his feet biting the gravel, and then there was a shaft of light behind, a door slamming, other feet.

Wash dropped her and whirled about, too late to lift his hands, as Horace's fist exploded in his vision. The blow sent Wash reeling backward, crashing into the side of the car. Grotesquely, he hung there, then slipped down to the ground. Horace was over him again. Groggily, Wash pawed for his legs, missed, and received the full impact of Horace's shoe on his jaw.

By the time Wash had brought himself to a sitting position, the pair of them were beyond the bright area and out of sight. Wash touched his mouth, a meaty mass, then considered the palm of his hand that now held his blood and a broken tooth. He blinked incredulously. All this, and she wasn't even a *good* lay.

When Horace reached the car, Naomi's hysteria had subsided. Until then, she had clutched him desperately, and wept, to the bewilderment of the parking attendant and a passing couple, and not once had she spoken a coherent word.

Paul was waiting with the car door open.

"Is she all right, Horace?"

"I think so. I caught up with them in the parking lot. I really slugged him."

Horace worked her into the front seat, then pushed in beside her.

"We'd better move," said Paul. "We'll have the whole gang on our necks."

"I don't think so," said Horace. "One of the men in the orchestra told me where she was. For twenty bucks."

Later, as they were driving alongside the bridle path through Beverly Hills, after she had wiped her eyes with Horace's handkerchief, and blown her nose, Naomi spoke at last.

She pointed to the torn knees of her stockings. "Look at me," she said.

"You're all right. That's all that counts," said Horace.

"Never leave me, Horace—never, never leave me."

"Never, I promise."

"I'll do what you say—whatever you say. Get me an analyst, put me in a place, a sanitarium—have them help me, Horace. I want to be well, that's all I want."

297

He brought her close to him. "Everything's going to be all right, darling. From now on. Just leave it to me."

Her voice was muffled. "You won't think of the other?"

Horace's eyes were full. But he tried to smile. "What other?" he asked.

❖   ❖   ❖

After leaving Horace and Naomi at her house, Paul returned to the Villa Neapolis.

Now, trudging between the stately royal palms to the motel entrance, Paul thought once more of Kathleen. The incident in the car had been curious. As curious as her temper the first night he had met her. As curious, in fact, as the spontaneous kiss she had favored him with as he left her several hours before. And then, so long ago it seemed, the sex history she had recited at him through the screen. No truer woman on all the earth existed, of that he was certain, yet her history had been incredibly false. Or credibly false? It depended on the point of view. She seemed to care for him, that was evident, and he knew the churning excitement he felt this moment, thinking of her. Yet, between them, stood an unidentifiable barrier, as real as the cane and walnut folding screen that had separated them the day of the interview. Perhaps between every woman and man, there rose this screen, defying total intimacy. Perhaps between every woman and the entire world, there was a screen, always. . . .

At the reception desk, the night clerk, who resembled a retired jockey, gave him his key and a sealed envelope. Puzzled, Paul opened the envelope and extracted a penciled note.

"Paul," it read, "Ackerman just called and is coming over. I'm anxious that you be present during this meeting. Whenever you return, come to my room. Urgent. G.G.C."

The wall clock above the desk showed the small hand between the twelve and the one, nearer the one, and the big hand on the ten. Twelve-fifty. Could Dr. Chapman possibly want to see him at this hour?

Paul went outside, past the placid pool, then mounted the wooden staircase. At the door to Dr. Chapman's suite, he paused and listened. There were voices behind the door. He knocked.

The door was opened by Dr. Chapman, whose casual blue smoking jacket did nothing to offset the tension at the corners of his mouth.

298

"Ah, Paul," said Dr. Chapman. "I'm glad you made it before we broke up. You know Emil Ackerman—" he indicated the portly Ackerman, and then waved his hand at a small, slender young man, of college age, with a high head of hair combed back, bulging eyes, and a sallow face, slumped in the chair across the living room—"and his nephew, Mr. Sidney Ackerman."

Paul crossed to shake Ackerman's genial hand, and then went to the nephew, who tentatively made an effort to rise, and Paul shook his hand, too.

"Have a seat, Paul," said Dr. Chapman. "We're almost finished."

Paul took a straight chair from the wall, carried it closer to the group, and sat down.

"I like to have Paul in on everything I do," Dr. Chapman was telling Ackerman. "He has good judgment."

"Maybe you better bring him up to date, George," said Emil Ackerman.

Dr. Chapman bobbed his head. "Yes, I intend to." He shifted on the big chair toward Paul. "You know, of course, how deeply interested Emil is in our work."

"Yes," said Paul, "I do."

Ackerman beamed. The nephew, Sidney, scratched his scalp and worked his upper lip over his yellow buck teeth.

"I think, in a way, he's appointed himself my West Coast representative," said Dr. Chapman.

Ackerman chuckled, pleased.

"At any rate, Paul, to make a long story short, Emil has been looking out for our interests and keeping an eye on the activities of his nephew Sidney."

"I've guided him every step of the way," said Ackerman.

"I'm sure you have, Emil," Dr. Chapman agreed, projecting admiration. He sought Paul's attention once more. "Sidney's a sociology major at the university here. He graduates in two weeks. The young man's ambition is to be associated with our project. Emil feels he can be most useful to us."

"I'm positive of it," said Ackerman.

"I've tried to explain," Dr. Chapman continued to Paul, "that our roster is temporarily filled, but, of course, we'll be expanding very soon. He knows we have an impressive waiting list, many eminent scientists with excellent records—still, as Emil has pointed out, we dare not shut our eyes to fresh young minds, eager young newcomers."

"Plenty of rookies have helped make pennant winners," said Ackerman.

"Indeed they have," agreed Dr. Chapman. Then to Paul: "I've been briefing Sidney on our operation, and I've been inquiring into his background. And that's where we stand now." He looked across the room at Sidney. "Perhaps you'd like to ask some questions of us?"

Sidney hoisted himself erect, crossed his legs, and then uncrossed them. He picked at his scalp nervously. "I read your books," he said.

Dr. Chapman nodded paternally. "Good."

"I've been wondering—what's your next project?"

"We haven't determined that yet, Sidney," said Dr. Chapman. "We have several under consideration. We may undertake the whole subject of motherhood—a survey of mothers."

"You mean, a lot of old women?"

"Not exactly. There are millions of young mothers, too—in fact, some very young ones. After that, we may tackle married men."

"I'd like to be on the women survey," Sidney said flatly. He grinned, revealing the protruding yellow teeth. "That's normal, isn't it, Doctor?"

The good-natured social expression on Dr. Chapman's face hardened. He moved his bulk uneasily in his chair. "Yes," he said, "yes, I suppose it is."

Paul tried to watch Sidney's face without too obviously staring. Perhaps he was being unfair, but he felt that he had detected a bright, leering quality in the young man's bulging eyes. There was about his manner, his voice, the rancid air of unhealthy sex. His questions reflected the voyeur, not the scientist. Paul had seen him before, in many places, lounging before small-town drugstores to comment on girls' bosoms and legs, telling a dirty story as he cued the tip of his pool stick in some shadowed billiard parlor, standing at a magazine rack devouring the semi-nude reproductions of models and starlets. Paul decided: He thinks our project is like attending a daily stag film.

"Uncle Emil will tell you," Sidney was saying, "I've always made a study of women. I've read everything that exists—history, biology, sociology."

"That's right, George," Ackerman said to Dr. Chapman.

"I want to be part of your great movement," Sidney went on. "I think when you can get women to talk about sexual intercourse, that's an important advance. Like the survey you're

300

just finishing—it's like the bachelor one you wrote about, isn't it?"

"Yes," said Dr. Chapman quietly.

"Well, I think that's something," said Sidney. He scratched his scalp with his nails. "Imagine getting women to talk about . . . about how they feel. They do, don't they?"

"Most of them," said Dr. Chapman grimly.

After ten more minutes, the meeting was concluded. Dr. Chapman and Paul walked Ackerman and Sidney down to the guest parking area, beside the top of the road, where Ackerman's shining Cadillac stood alone.

Before getting into the car, Ackerman looked at Dr. Chapman. "Well, George," he said, "what do you think?"

"You're sure you want him in this kind of work?" asked Dr. Chapman. "It's drudgery and exacting, you know."

"It's what he wants. That's the important thing, I think. Enthusiasm."

"Mmm. All right, Emil. Let me see what I can work out. I'll do what I can."

After the Cadillac had gone down the hill, Paul and Dr. Chapman remained standing by the roadside, in the cool night.

Paul hated to look at Dr. Chapman, but then he did. He knew what his eyes sought: the crack in the armor. As he had waited to find it in Dr. Jonas, and had not, he waited now for sight of it in the giant figure who, heretofore, had been invincible. He waited, his chest constricted by the suspense. He waited.

"Imagine the nerve of him," Dr. Chapman said angrily, "trying to foist that snot-nosed pervert on us. Did you hear the little fiend? He thinks we're staging sex circuses and films." He took Paul's arm and guided him toward the motel. "Remember, I once told you Ackerman's in the business of making people beholden to him. Well, this time, I assure you, he's not getting paid off. I'd sooner junk the whole project than take that little brute on. I'll placate Uncle Emil with a letter that will be a masterpiece of generalities. I'll tell him we're keeping Sidney on file. He's got as much chance of getting out of that file as out of a time capsule buried in concrete. Right, Paul?"

"Right," said Paul, and even on this moonless night, he could see that Dr. Chapman's armor shone brighter than ever.

11

TERESA HARNISH had just swung the convertible to the
curbing, preparatory to delivering Geoffrey to the art shop,
when the announcer on the car radio began the weather
forecast.

Geoffrey had opened the door to leave, but now, one foot
still on the convertible floor board, he listened to the forecast. ". . . although today, Friday, June fifth, promises to be
the hottest June fifth in twenty years, with the temperature
reaching a high of ninety-five or thereabouts, there is every
likelihood that by nightfall the temperature will drop to the
low seventies."

Teresa turned off the radio, impatient for Geoffrey to leave.
The forecast had made her aware of her discomfort. The boiling air had the consistency of an updraft from a blast furnace,
dry and scorching. Geoffrey stepped out of the car and
squinted toward the sun.

"A real sizzler," he said. "Thank God, it'll cool down tonight. Maybe we should serve drinks and the buffet in the
patio?" Teresa's head jerked toward him, revealing an expression of surprise.

The expression on his wife's face puzzled Geoffrey. "Anything the matter, Teresa?" he asked.

What had astounded Teresa was Geoffrey's sudden reminder
that they were giving a large party this evening. Since the day
before yesterday, the event had left her mind completely.
Even since breakfast, an hour ago, she had been preoccupied
with the greater event eight hours off. Yet, suddenly, at almost
the same time, she was expected to perform as wife and
hostess.

Geoffrey was still gazing at her curiously. Quickly, danger
signals blinked red warnings across her mind. In the recent
past, the Dark Ages, parties and dinners had been her most

devoted activity and favorite social pleasure. To have forgotten this would invite grave suspicion.

Don't just sit, she told herself; say something, anything. She said something, anything. "There's nothing the matter," she said, "except I've been so busy arranging the dinner, I completely forgot to rent a costume."

"Didn't you decide to cancel the costume part of it?"

She remembered that she had, indeed, decided just that, but had neglected to inform her guests of it. "No, I changed my mind again. I decided it would be more fun to keep the status quo—women in costume, men optional."

"Well, fine. You've got the whole day to find something. What do you intend to wear?"

"I haven't had a moment till now to think about it."

"What about the get-up you wore at that Waterton supper party—you know, New Year's Eve—three years ago?"

"George Sand?"

"Absolutely. It was most becoming. Isn't she the person you wish you had been when Dr. Chapman interviewed you?"

"Of course not. She's too *masculine*. Still, it's an idea. The only thing that bothers me is that I'll be repeating myself; it won't seem very imaginative."

"Oh, hell, half the crowd hasn't seen it before." He dug the shop keys out of his linen jacket. "Do as you wish. I suppose you'll want me home early?"

"No," Teresa answered quickly, "that won't be necessary."

"Well, scoop me up no later than six, anyway. I'll want time to shower and dress."

As he turned toward the shop, she called out after him. "Dearest, is it dreadful of me to ask you to take a taxi home tonight? I'm so afraid I'll be up to my ears in Mrs. Symonds and Mr. Jefferson." Mrs. Symonds was the German cateress who prepared the hors d'oeuvres and dinner for a fee of twenty-five dollars, and Mr. Jefferson was the elderly, solemn, colored bartender.

"Very well," said Geoffrey. "Don't forget the cigar."

"Cigar?"

"George Sand."

"Oh, yes."

After Geoffrey had unlocked the front door of the shop and disappeared inside, Teresa remained a minute longer before the yellow curb, trying to gather her wits about her. She had promised to meet Ed Krasowski, in his beach apartment, at five-thirty. She had invited ten couples to come to drinks and

303

dinner at seven. That meant the first arrivals would appear at seven-fifteen. The Goldsmiths were always early.

Teresa calculated the time. Between five-thirty and seven-fifteen lay—lay, now wasn't that clever of her?—one hour and forty-five minutes. Subtracting the thirty minutes it would take her to drive back to The Briars from the beach, there was left one hour and fifteen minutes. This was insufficient for what she had to offer, and for what Ed would give her. Grand romance could not be constricted by the clock. What to do? Common sense dictated that she should call him at once and postpone the assignation for another day—tomorrow or—no, that would be Sunday, and Geoffrey would be home—tomorrow or the beginning of next week. But now the ardor that burned within, across her chest, across her loins, was too demanding, too insistent, too immediate. Common sense was decimated and routed. And at once she was happy again.

It would be today, this afternoon, exactly as planned, she decided. She would simply be late to her own party. It was even amusing. George Sand had not been without similar audacity. But a foolproof excuse must be invented. What, possibly? She recalled that at the time she had conceived the party, she had considered as the *pièce de résistance* of her dinner buffet a Danish ham baked inside a bread. She had featured this gourmet's delight once before, and it had been a gastronomic sensation and earned her gratifying compliments, but this time she had rejected it finally because the bakery was a forty-minute drive out Ventura Boulevard in the horrible valley. The valley would be an oven today, but the exotic Danish ham seemed to make Ed Krasowski possible.

Now, then, the *modus operandi*. She would telephone the bakery, place a rush order, and pick the ham up before noon. She would smuggle it into the house, to preserve it from the heat, and then return it to the luggage compartment of her car before going to Ed's. At five o'clock, departing for the beach, she would leave a note for Geoffrey: Have decided on Danish ham in bread and gone to valley to pick it up. Will be back shortly. Everything under control. In haste, Teresa.

Then, thinking, more *modus*, more *operandi*. She and Ed would have consummated their love—it was now "their" love —by seven-thirty. It would probably be difficult parting from Ed, she recognized that; he would want her to stay the night, the evening, anyway, and she would want it, too, but she would be firm. Poor dear boy. Well, there was a life of nights ahead. She would assure him. Anyway, anyway, seven-thirty, yes. She would drive to the first public phone. By then there would be guests, and Geoffrey would be worried ill. She would inform him that, returning with the ham in bread, the car had stalled in the middle of nowhere and was this moment being repaired by the nearest gas station. Carburetor trouble sounded the right note. She knew nothing about what made vehicles go, but Geoffrey knew less. She would reassure Geoffrey of her return within a half hour and promise to be on the receiving line, in costume (with cigar), within fifteen minutes of her return. There, now. Easy?

Teresa shifted the gear, and the idling convertible was propelled forward into the day, as was Teresa herself. As the day grew older, Teresa was never unmindful of the oppressive sun. Everywhere she went, an afternoon newspaper met her with the boldfaced streamer: ANGELENOS SWELTER IN RECORD HEAT WAVE. There was a large photograph, beneath, of a leggy model, generally unsheathed, dancing gratefully beneath a hose of water applied by two briefly clad starlets, their latest motion-picture credits advertised in the caption. Teresa disliked heat because it undid neatness of person. But this day, she resented it less. Somehow, tropical weather seemed appropriate for her passion, although, most likely, Ed's lovely beach place would be cooled by the nearness of the lapping waves.

Teresa moved steadily, efficiently, toward five o'clock. From a stifling glass booth beside the filling station, she telephoned the valley bakery and ordered the ham in bread for one o'clock. Then she telephoned Mrs. Symonds to advise her to include the ham in bread on her menu and ignore the cold cuts. Leaving the booth, she remembered the original purpose of her meeting with Ed. She located an art-supply store, intending to purchase easel, canvas, and paints, and then thought this camouflage too elaborate and foolish, and settled for charcoal and pad.

Going back to The Briars, she tried to remember where she had stored the George Sand costume, and then remembered. She found it in the large bottom drawer built into the bedroom wall. The outfit, inspired by Delacroix's portrait of Sand done in 1830, consisted of a top hat, now somewhat bent, a dark stock, loose coat, and men's slacks, all badly creased. She telephoned Mr. Jefferson, who was out on his day job, and left word with his landlady that he remember to bring ice cubes and one cigar; yes, one, no particular brand.

She braved the suffocating heat again to drive to a cleaning shop in The Village Green, and there deposit her Sand costume to be brushed and pressed. She then steered her car eastward, past the atrocious Villa Neapolis, past the university, through Beverly Hills, into Hollywood, where she turned north on Cahuenga.

She fought the freeway traffic, feeling the wheel flaming under her tight grip, until she reached Studio City, where she made the turn-off to the bakery. The eighteen-inch ham in bread, still warm, was ready. She wrote a check for twenty dollars, carefully placed the box in her luggage compartment, and then completed the circle by driving on Ventura to Sepulveda Boulevard, and thence to Sunset and The Briars. She double-parked at the cleaners, where the Sand costume waited, neatly pressed, and then hastened back to the house, where Mrs. Symonds, mopping her chins with a white handkerchief, impatiently waited in her vintage coupé.

In the kitchen, Teresa briskly reviewed the hors d'oeuvre list and dinner menu with Mrs. Symonds, then got out the good silver, dishes, and platters, finished the floral arrangement for the buffet (green Bells of Ireland and white Agapanthus resting on a glass-covered Miro collage), rearranged the seating in the studio modern living room, and then retired to the master bedroom.

She removed five outfits from her closet, hung them in a row, and stepped back to study them for utility as well as beauty. At last, she selected the Parma-blue silk dress, because it did wonders for her bosom and hips, and because the long zipper in back made it easy to put on and remove. She examined her underwear with care, settling finally on the sheer black brassière and nylon crepe panties; then returned the brassière to the drawer, settling for the black panties and a half-slip. She considered stockings, but the necessity of a garter belt was a nuisance, and she decided that she would remain provocatively bare-legged, and wear the high-heeled blue leather pumps that complemented the dress. She opened the jewel box, removed her wedding band and deposited it, leaving only the diamond engagement ring on her finger. She poked through her accessories, held up the fragile necklace with the small gold cross, and liked it.

She filled the tub, added several drops of a French bath oil, and then immersed herself in the fragrant water and soaked. She thought about the last year in Vassar, and the Greenwich Village period with the poet who never bathed (what had happened to him?), and she tried to picture Ed's apartment overlooking the ocean. She thought about the interview with Dr.

Chapman, and all she could remember of it were those questions about the exhibits. She had, she remembered, given her reactions to a half-dozen photographs, and to a passage from Casanova, and then she had been offered the option to read or refuse to read a passage from *Fanny Hill*. She had read the passage, of course. "My bosom was now bare, and rising in the warmest throbs, presented to his sight and feeling the firm hard swell of a pair of young breasts. . . ." What had she answered? Yes, somewhat aroused. Perhaps she should have answered strongly aroused. No, somewhat was more accurate. She tried to picture Ed's apartment again. At last, an eye on the clock, she stepped out of the tub, dried herself, touched up her well-formed figure with cologne, inserted the diaphragm, and then slowly garmented herself with the attire selected.

At ten minutes to five, she wrote the note to Geoffrey about going to pick up the ham in bread, and reminded Mrs. Symonds to be sure to see that Mr. Harnish received the note so that he would not be concerned with her absence. At five o'clock, precisely, she settled behind the wheel of the convertible and prepared to leave for the beach.

The address that Ed Krasowski had given her, she was surprised to learn, was not in Malibu as she had expected, but much before Malibu and closer to the widely patronized Santa Monica pier. There was a large dirt parking area, and the soiled gray wood building, a dozen units perhaps, was of indifferent clapboard construction, and rose in humpty-dumpty fashion above a cliff that hung over the beach. It was flanked by a cheap hotel and a hamburger shanty. Teresa told herself that this was Bohemia, such as she had left behind in Greenwich Village, but this was better, and it was good to be back among teeming and vital life.

Ed's apartment proved to be on the second floor. Carrying pad and charcoal and her white summer purse, Teresa climbed the slippery, creaking steps to the outer veranda above. Two dirty, tanned, sopping children, possibly female, brushed past her, one chasing the other down the stairs, and Teresa saw that her dress was only slightly spotted. She continued along the veranda, side-stepping several pools of water and a hole where the planks had broken or rotted apart, and at last she reached the sanctuary of Ed's apartment.

She rapped.

"Come in!"

She opened the door, a chipped green, and entered. For a moment, she stood inside the door, closing it behind her and

307

trying to accustom her eyes to the shade. Ed sat in a big over-stuffed chair, one leg thrown over the side, sucking beer from a can and listening to a blaring baseball broadcast on the portable radio. He was wearing a T-shirt again emblazoned with the legend *Paradise Park*, and white shorts, wrinkled, the stripes faded along the sides. Although his face seemed puffier than she had remembered, the shirt and shorts wonderfully pointed up his bursting strength and manliness. His biceps were incredible, still, and the thighs grew out of his shorts like barkless tree trunks.

"Hiya," he said, waving. He indicated the radio with a nod. "They're in Philly, all tied up in the third."

Teresa bobbed her head as if she understood. Ed finished his beer and then, remembering manners, lifted his enormous bulk to his feet. "Well, make yourself at home," he said.

"Yes, thank you, Ed."

She placed her sketch equipment on a table.

"See you came prepared," he said.

"That's right."

"What about a beer? Set you up."

"If you'll have one with me." She had never had domestic beer in her life. It was a day of adventures.

"I've had three already, but I'm not the one to say no. Excuse me."

He went into what appeared to be a kitchenette. For the first time, she surveyed their Charterhouse of Valdemosa, their Palma, their Majorca. A large oval, braided, early-American rug, its ancestry traceable to Sears, Roebuck, covered a worn floor speckled with sand. Besides the overstuffed chair and raucous radio, the remaining furniture consisted of a green divan with broken springs and several fraying rattan chairs. There were two intensely modern reflector lamps. On the walls hung a reproduction of Millet's *The Angelus*, probably the landlord's, and a reproduction of Bellows' *A night at Sharkey's*, probably inherited from a previous and more pugilistic tenant. There were three magazine pages of nude females with abnormal bosoms and buttocks, taken from a publication unknown to her—*Playboy*—tacked to the wall. There was an autographed photograph of someone who signed himself Harold "Red" Grange. There were two photographs, happily framed, one of Ed in football togs, crouched and ferocious, and the other of the person she remembered as Jackie.

Teresa moved to the windows—the soiled mesh drapes were parted—and regarded the rocky beach below. There was a fat woman seated cross-legged on an army blanket slicing a sausage. There was a skin diver adjusting his Martian headgear, with a thin rail of a peroxide blonde assisting him. There were armies of screaming wet children.

Discreetly, Teresa shut the open window, but still the noise came through the glass and thin walls. She moved on to the black hole of a bedroom, crowded with two twin beds without headboards and both halfheartedly made up, and two more rattan chairs and a secondhand peeling brown bureau.

"Not bad, eh?" she heard Ed call out.

She pirouetted in time to accept her beer, which was in a glass, and to notice that he preferred his own directly from the can. If he was devoted to beer, she decided, she would surprise him with a case of imported German lager. It would make a splendid little gift.

"Well," he said, holding up his can, "here's to lots of famous pictures."

"I hope so," she said.

She swallowed a great gulp of beer, and although it was malty, she drank again, and smiled at him.

"Why don't you sit down?" he said.

She nodded, then frowned at the frenzied radio. He saw her disapproval. "Bother you? Here, let me lower it." He turned it down, and now the children's voices, from below, were louder.

He sat heavily on the divan and indicated that she could have the favored overstuffed chair. But, impetuously, she sat on the divan several feet from him.

"It's not so comfortable," he said. "The springs—"

"It's all right."

"That's the way it was when Jackie and I moved in. The landlord's strictly do-nothing."

"Where's your roommate?"

"I kicked him out for now."

Her heart hammered. Had there ever been a greater show of love? He was trying to demonstrate that he had need to be alone with her.

"I ain't letting that bench jockey heckle me," he went on, "while I'm being painted."

Somewhat taken aback, she finished the horrid beer. "You like the beach, don't you, Ed?"

"Sure do. Nothing like doing a workout in the sand every morning to build those leg muscles. And I like the surfing.

Besides, it's the only place where a man can live like a millionaire at these prices."

"I can understand that. I suppose, in your profession, you must take care of your body."

"Like a baby," said Ed solemnly. Then he shook the can, and his Slavic face broke into a grin. " 'Course, man's got to have one vice." He brought the can to his mouth and drank.

"You mean to tell me that's your only vice?"

"Depends what you call vice."

"Well, female companionship—"

"That's more necessity. If you'll pardon the expression—a man's got to have an outlet."

"Oh, I agree with you," she said quickly. "It's a part of normal good health."

He grinned at some remembrance. " 'Course, you wouldn't think that if you met some of the flipperoos that come around."

"Women, you mean?"

"It takes all kinds to make a world, and all kinds sort of wash up on the beach."

The thought struck her: Could Isadora's Essinine be a puritan at heart? She dismissed it: Aren't all men?

"I suppose you're popular," she said.

"Well, I don't know," he said modestly.

"I don't mind confessing that it was seeing you on the beach, in your natural element, observing your bodily grace, the freedom of your limbs, that first attracted me to you." She watched him. "You have a perfectly symmetrical body," she added.

He did not disagree. "Yeah, I guess so," he said. "Like I said before, I baby it. I got good development—smooth, no knots. I don't go for that weight-lifter bit—you know, overdevelopment. It's no good, ties you up. I like to keep it well proportioned." He spoke of his body as if it were an entity apart from himself.

She was intrigued. She had discovered a subject that interested both of them.

"I think you're far better looking than most of the motion-picture stars. You look more manly."

"That doesn't take much doing," he said. "Those queers—if you'll pardon me."

"I think that's why I wanted to sketch you first as a Grecian Olympic hero—to contrast your basic virility with the pallid men who surround us today." The points of her breasts, her legs, ached with desire. "Have you ever seen the classical statue of the discus thrower?"

"No."

"Inspired by your body, I feel I can surpass Myron the Greek. He did the discus thrower. He also did Lais, the courtesan. I'd like to do you in exactly the same way. In fact, I'd like to start right now."

"Sure. What do I do?"

"Well, the discus thrower was nude, of course, like all Greek Olympians. I would want you to pose that way."

He straightened his bulk on the sofa. "With nothing on?" She tried to assume an unemotional, businesslike tone.

"Yes, in the classical tradition. If you'll just disrobe while I get ready—"

"Hey, wait a minute, lady. You don't expect me to take off all my clothes in front of a woman?"

"Why not? Do you suffer false modesty? I'm sure you've done it a hundred times before—in front of women."

"But not to be looked at. When I strip down, it's for different reasons. And then, the dame's always naked, too."

"Is that what's bothering you, Ed? That I'll be dressed, and you won't? Very well. I'll gladly take off my clothes, too."

He was certain that he had not heard her right. "What did you say?"

"You heard me correctly, Ed. If it'll make you happier, I'll undress right now."

His face was all confusion. "Just to paint me?"

She heard her heart, and wanted to be buried in his arms forever. Her voice, when she found it, was foreign to her ears. "Of course not, silly boy. I can paint the next time. I want you to do to me what you do to those other girls."

He sat gaping. She jumped to her feet and stood before him, legs apart, her knees touching his, her hands clasped behind her back so that her breasts were distended.

"Ed, don't you even want to touch me?"

The turn of events anchored him in bewilderment. "Sure, but—"

"But what, Ed? You think I'm too much of a lady to behave like this? Well, I am a lady, but I'm also a woman. From the moment I first saw you on the beach, I fought the feeling inside me. I knew I was becoming enamored of you—foolishly so—but women in love are foolish, and now, all I want is your love." She stared down at him, too aroused to smile or make light of it. "Touch me, Ed. You might enjoy it."

311

He grabbed out at her and roughly yanked her down to his lap. Her hands were in his hair, and her mouth met his, pressing so hard that her teeth hurt. Gasping, they were apart.

"Holy geez," he said.

"Those others—what do you do with them?"

"Those broads are different—run-of-the-mill snatch—but you—"

"What about me?"

"I should've known. I just didn't figure you—like Jackie, when he brought me your message—ol' Jackie said, 'Ed, you should've seen her in that swim suit—built like a—' And then, he said, 'I gotta hunch you can maybe make time there—there's a lotta pepper in that tomato.' But I told him he was nuts."

"You see, Ed? Even he could tell how I wanted you." She placed her face against his. "Aren't you going to undress me?"

"You bet your life!"

Awkwardly, he fumbled at her dress.

"The zipper's in back," she whispered.

He found it, and suddenly he remembered something. "In the bedroom," he said. "Get in there."

He pushed her to her feet and stood up. She started for the bedroom, watching him as he strode to the door, locked it, then hurried to the windows and drew the drapes closed.

In the darkened bedroom, she kicked off her pumps and felt the chill of the carpetless floor on her soles. She had released the dress to her waist when he returned, breathing audibly. She wriggled, letting it drop, then stepped out of it. She stood barefooted, very small in her half-slip, naked from the waist up, shoulders drawn back.

"Holy geez," he said admiringly.

"Should I undress you?"

"No, I'll do it. You lie down and wait."

He hastened into the bathroom. She removed slip and pants, threw back the blanket, and stretched herself on the bed. She gazed into the living room, listening to the screams on the beach, the wet feet on the veranda, the humming voice on the radio. The room was close and tepid. And there was some gritty discomfort beneath her. She ran her fingers across the bed sheet: sand.

"You ready?" he called from the bathroom.

"Yes, darling."

He appeared wearing only an elastic athletic supporter. It accentuated the muscular layers of his stomach and torso. He pulled down the supporter and kicked it away, and faced her fully. The discus thrower, she thought, and then she observed his total nudity for the first time, and for a moment she was nudged by surprise. The surprise was that he was, in one way, no more extraordinary than Geoffrey—in fact, far less so. He advanced toward her, and the surprise was forgotten. The appeal of his towering frame was Godlike. He had come to her, from Olympus, at last.

She held out her arms. "Come to me."

She tingled in anticipation of the long, excruciating feast of love that would now begin. Every inch of her being waited to be brought to the peak of desire. The bed trembled as he knelt on it, and, as she waited to accept his kisses and caresses, she was suddenly shocked to find him directly atop her, pinning her shoulders, crushing her beneath his terrible weight. And then she cried out, not with pain but with outrage, when she realized that he was making love to her.

She twisted her head aside, protesting this madness. "Ed, not yet, not yet—you haven't—I'm not—"

Ignoring all but her body, he went on, frenzied. She reached to push him away, but she might as well have tried to move the Empire State building. She closed her eyes and made an effort to understand: He's treating me like one of those Japanese rubber torsos sailors buy in Kobe—he hasn't kissed me but once, not even touched my breasts, not my body, not whispered a single endearment.

She opened her eyes. He was performing quite apart from her, like a senseless animal. She felt nothing, no connection with him, beyond the ridiculous pressure, that and the irritating sand on her bottom, that and the stale beery breath above, the panting harmonizing with the yelling children beneath the room. She smelled his sweat, and the smell of kelp and seaweed, and the horrible fish market smell of the public beach. And she hated the lumpy mattress that hurt, and the uncoiled springs, and his monstrous weight.

"Ed, listen—will you—listen—"

She tried to free herself of the tiresome burden, but when she did so, he frightened her by squealing like a pig and exhaling an explosion of breath. And then, after a moment, he disengaged himself and fell on his side.

She sat up the instant that she was free and regarded the fleshy mountain incredulously. He lay biting the air for oxygen, and finally he opened his eyes and met her gaze. He smiled and winked at her. "Holy geez, honey, that was great.

313

You can put your shoes under my bed any day of the week."

She continued to stare at him, too stunned to articulate a word. This . . . this orangutan. He had treated love like football practice. Several lunges, and a day's work done. This was primitive man? My God, she thought, my God, maybe it was like this, really like this, when you clubbed a woman and dragged her to the hole in the hill and employed her as a handy receptacle. God, oh, God, Isadora, Isadora, this is funny.

She remained sitting, immobilized by the wonder of it. Great expectations. Says who? Dickens. She felt as unmoved, as uninvaded, as untouched, in fact, as the moment before she entered this cheap little hovel. Yet, this had been love, too. Who on earth would know this besides herself? Dr. Chapman, of course. No, not Dr. Chapman. He had no chart of statistics to measure great expectations. Who then would understand? Stendhal, yes, he alone. Inevitably, the line, following his first sex act, came to mind: *Quoi, n'est-ce que ça?* She stared at the filthy, unkempt cell that was a bedroom, saw the nails in the wall that held no art, and the plasterless portions of the ceiling, and a football in the corner.

She worked her way to the edge of the bed.

"How was it, honey?" he asked.

My God, she thought, he wanted her gratefulness. "Great," she said.

"Well—any time."

She dressed quickly, not looking at him.

"Hey, you're not going already?" he asked.

"I'm afraid I have to."

"When's our next date? Remember, you're painting me." He laughed with child's delight.

"I'll let you know."

She zippered her dress and stepped into her pumps. She picked up her purse and started into the living room.

"Wait a minute," he called out. "I don't even know your name."

She kept going, as fast as she could, through the living room, abandoning the sketch materials, fairly fleeing through the door. On the veranda, a wet child stamped past. She drew aside, then made her way over the slippery surface to the stairs. Descending, she glanced at her watch. She had come to this place, she recalled, at five thirty-five. Now her watch told her it was five fifty-two.

She would be home in plenty of time to greet the first guests.

Although dinner was still a half hour from being served—
Mr. Jefferson was on his third round through the living room
and patio, delivering highballs from his tray, taking new orders
—the Danish ham baked in the bread, sliced in two, centered
on the buffet before the floral arrangement, was the major success of the evening.

Already Teresa, on her husband's arm, had received four
compliments.

"Clever of you, dearest," Geoffrey whispered with pride.

Teresa snuggled closer to him. "I love you." Her top hat was
askew. She corrected it and waved her cigar at the clusters of
friends. "Isn't this fun?" she exclaimed gaily. Not in months
had she so savored the pleasures of her richly appointed home,
the riot of lovely paintings on every burlap wall, her distinguished husband, her intelligent friends, as she did this night.

"Oh, look," she cried, pointing to the front door that Mr.
Jefferson had just opened. "There's Kathleen! Isn't she lovely?"

Kathleen Ballard had slipped the mink stole from her shoulders, and Paul took it and handed it to Mr. Jefferson. Kathleen
was swathed in clouds of filmy white, full and Grecian and of
daring *décolletage*. After making the garment, she had been
embarrassed by it but, in the end, had determined to wear it
unafraid. After all, this *was* the woman she would have wished
to have been the day Paul interviewed her, and perhaps it
would help him appreciate her subconscious self.

Teresa, followed by Geoffrey, was upon her. "Kathleen,
you are divine. Whatever are you—a Vestal Virgin?"

"Lady Emma Hamilton, I hope," said Kathleen. "This was
the way she dressed."

"Of course!" said Teresa, standing back, framing Kathleen
with her hands. She turned to Geoffrey. "Romney's *Lady
Hamilton*."

Geoffrey nodded sagely. "National Gallery. London."

"I suppose that was the picture I saw in the book," said
Kathleen.

"The most innocent, fawnlike, beautiful portrait of a
woman ever put to canvas," said Geoffrey. "Romney surpassed
himself."

"God was the artist," Teresa said to Geoffrey.

"*Olé*," said Geoffrey, pleased.

Kathleen had Paul's hand. "This is Mr. Paul Radford; our host and hostess, Teresa and Geoffrey Harnish." As the introduction was acknowledged, Kathleen remembered that she and Paul had agreed not to mention his connection with Dr. Chapman. "Paul's a writer," Kathleen added vaguely.

✦   ✦   ✦

Kathleen and Paul, fortified by a second serving of Scotch and soda, were conversing with Mary and Norman McManus. Originally, Mary had intended to appear as Florence Nightingale, doer of good works, her father's suggestion. But this morning, after breakfast, she had decided that the lady with the lamp was too saccharine. She had felt as reckless and independent as any pioneer woman who had ever trod the uncouth West. After careful consideration, she had rejected Jessie Fremont for Belle Starr, and now wore cowboy hat, black shirt, holster and pearl six-shooter, and a leather skirt, all rented from a costume house on Melrose.

"I'm truly sorry Naomi couldn't make it," she was saying to Kathleen. "But she is better?"

"Much better," said Kathleen. "You know how these colds hang on. I believe she's planning a trip East, the moment she's strong enough."

"How wonderful. She was raised there, wasn't she?"

"Yes, I believe so."

"Well," said Mary, taking Norman's hand and beaming up at him, "Norman and I are taking a trip, too—in a way."

"Really?" said Kathleen conversationally.

"Not really," said Norman. "But we're looking for a house of our own."

"That's the smart thing to do," said Kathleen. "If you run into any trouble, you should speak to Grace Waterton. She knows every realtor in The Briars."

"Thank you, Mrs. Ballard," said Norman, "but I'm afraid it won't be The Briars. You see, I'm going on my own—that is, I'm forming a partnership with a friend of mine who has offices downtown."

"What profession are you in?" asked Paul.

"Law," said Norman. "It'll take time to get a foothold." He turned to Kathleen. "Anyway, if you hear of anything reasonable in the valley, let us know." He examined his highball glass. "Excuse me. I think I want a refill."

He went off toward the bar. Mary lingered a moment. She

moved her face close to Kathleen's ear. "We're going to have a baby," she whispered.

"Oh, Mary—when?"

Mary winked. "Soon. It's in the works." She hurried off after Norman.

◇　◇　◇

Mary and Norman McManus had accepted their refills from Mr. Jefferson in the dining room, and now they were chatting with Ursula and Harold Palmer. Ursula, after considerable soul-searching, had attired herself as a modernized version of Lucrezia Borgia. She wore a jeweled cap on her freshly coiffured hair, which was circled by a dramatic braid, a gauzy veil about her throat, a full-length gown of emerald-green satin, a silver girdle, and sandals studded with costumed stones.

"I couldn't stand that damn magazine another day," Ursula was telling Mary and Norman. "That nauseating motto, 'The magazine of companionship—serving your heart and hearth.' Enough to make you upchuck."

Mary did not know what to say in reply. She had subscribed to *Houseday* since her marriage and had assigned it a place of authority beside Harry Ewing, Hannah and Abraham Stone, the New Testament, and Dr. Norman Vincent Peale. Now she would not admit to being Constant Reader, and secretly decided to relegate the publication to a lesser position, like the recently demoted Harry Ewing.

"I don't blame you, Ursula," she said lamely. And then she added with more reassurance, "People grow."

"Exactly," said Ursula, who was beginning to feel the liquor. "The publisher had grand plans for me, an executive position in New York, the works, but I couldn't see Harold and me becoming ensnared by the Madison Avenue bit, the commuter bit—" this had been the expurgated official version released to Harold after the shameful session with Foster— "especially since Harold is doing so marvelously in his new business."

"I got the Berrey account," Harold explained to Norman. "He's drugstores."

"Oh, yes," said Norman. "I'm very interested in knowing what it's like to be on your own. You see, a friend of mine, Chris Shearer—we were in law school together—we're opening offices—"

"It's not all caviar," said Harold expansively. "You've got to expect to struggle a little."

"Oh, I do," said Norman.

"But before long you'll be right up there," continued Harold. " 'Specially if you have the little woman behind you." Ursula turned the full glow of her drunken smile on her husband. "Might as well tell you," said Harold, "Ursula's moved into the office to lend a hand. I had a girl, but Ursula's ten girls in one, and that's what a man needs." He wagged his finger at Mary. "You just stay behind him, Mary. Look behind every great man, and you find a greater woman. Richelieu." He understood that this made no sense, and that he should have allowed the bartender to put *some* vermouth in the martinis. "Mrs. Roosevelt," he amended. "After a while it's peaches and cream."

Mary's hand moved inside Norman's hand. Her forefinger tickled his palm. Harold was still speaking. "A little nerve is all you need. Take the time I went after Berrey—"

❖   ❖   ❖

Mrs. Symonds, in her white kitchen uniform, offered the tray of crab meat in canapé shells and hot curried meat balls to Ursula and Harold Palmer, who were in the patio holding a discussion with Sarah and Sam Goldsmith.

Harold absently accepted the canapé his wife had passed him and continued to stare woozily at the exposed expanse of Sarah's belly. Sarah had defied Sam's conventionality, to convert halter and tights, once used in a class of the modern dance, into the costume of Mata Hari. Four beaded scarves now modified the tights, and a larger scarf was wound around the halter, but her belly was still bare, to Sam's acute discomfort.

Earlier, to gain Sam's affection and perhaps acquire his clothing-store account, Harold had questioned Sam about his business. Sam, his worried eyes shifting constantly from his wife's indecent costume (what gets into these women—a mother of two, yet?) to the glances of other males in the patio, and back to Harold, discoursed in a steady, complaining drone on the rising cost of merchandise, the perfidy of hired help, the sales tax, the property tax, the income tax, and the trickery of monopolistic chain establishments.

Ursula, tranquilized by alcohol and half listening, murmured agreement and assent from time to time, instinctively

318

understanding that the speaker's business could enrich their business.

Sarah, not listening at all, fiddled with the bun of her hair and then rearranged her scarves, finding little enjoyment in the brevity of her costume, yet not regretting any gesture that might distress Sam. Observing Sam's profile, the heavy jowls shimmying like a mastiff's jaw, she thought of those Semitic caricatures once fostered by Streicher in *Der Stürmer*. But the comparison was not fair, she acknowledged, and the jowls weren't what actually aggravated her. It was the oppressiveness of his private, and now social, banality that embarrassed the most. The frustration of being among people like these, who mattered, with a mate who was a dolt, who in no way represented her mature taste in men, instead of with the mate whom she truly loved, who would have reflected her fine judgment and her own desirability, was what she could not bear.

She saw Grace Waterton enter the patio, and she signaled to capture Grace's attention. Anything, she felt, to interrupt Sam's boring monologue on small business. Grace responded with her handkerchief and hastened forward, rustling loudly in her unbecoming Tudor dress that was meant to be a representation of Anne Boleyn.

"Sarah, I've been looking everywhere for you," Grace said rapidly. "Actually, I was just looking for Mr. Waterton—" she always referred to him thus, and she scanned the patio quickly—"but I did want to have a talk with you."

Sarah saw that neither sleet nor storm nor Waterton would halt the forensic Sam, and so she turned her back on Sam and the Palmers and confronted Grace.

"Aren't you divine?" said Grace, surveying the tights and scarves. "How do you manage that schoolgirl figure?"

Sarah was pleased. "No lunches and no desserts," she said simply.

"Sarah, we've been talking seriously about doing another fund-raising play this summer. The other was such a success." Sarah's heart stood still. She said nothing. Grace was going on. "You were such a hit in it. We're trying to get the same cast back. Perhaps do *Lady Windermere's Fan*. You'd be the perfect Lady Windermere—you have just the bearing—though, of course, you could do Mrs. Erlynne, if you preferred. We've just begun to make inquiries."

"I . . . I'm afraid I couldn't manage it, Grace. It's been so hectic. The children—"

319

"But we wouldn't do it before August. You'd have the kids in camp."

"I don't think so, Grace. Anyway, Sam and I might be away."

Grace sighed. "Oh dear, everyone traveling. That makes my second turn-down in a row, and for the same reason."

Some intuition restrained the question on the tip of Sarah's tongue, but she forced it out anyway. "Who was the other to turn you down?"

Grace's gaze had wandered in search of her husband. She returned it now to Sarah. "Fred Tauber," she said. "Remember him?"

"Yes, I do."

"I figured, let's start with the director. After all, the big job is his. I phoned him this morning."

Sarah's cheeks were warm. It was odd listening to someone else bandying Fred's name, invading the secret preserve of her life, where she was hidden with Fred. She remembered— at no time this evening had she forgotten—that she had telephoned Fred from a booth in The Village Green late yesterday afternoon. She had found him in, at last, but disturbingly remote. She had telephoned him innumerable times, with no answer, she had said. He had been out on a series of business meetings, he had said. She had come to see him in desperation, because of the man in the Dodge, she had said. He had been to his attorney, he had said. Then, hopefully, she had wondered about the attorney—was anything wrong? No, he had replied impatiently, it was a contract matter—in fact, he was in the midst of a conference that moment—and she had been relieved to have this explain his remoteness and impatience. She had wanted to know when they could meet, reminding him they had not seen each other for four days, and he had explained that he would be out tomorrow morning but that he might be in Saturday morning. He had advised her to contact him then.

". . . and we had a brief talk," Grace was saying.

"You phoned him *this morning?*"

"Why, of course. Why not?"

"I . . . I should suppose he's working."

"Oh. Well. I'll tell you all about *that,* my dear. But the point is, I told him how everyone adored his work on the last show, how charitable and gracious it had been of him, and how we needed him again. Of course, I thought I had him in the bag, because of what I'd heard."

"What did you hear, Grace?"

"He's a has-been. No one would touch him with a ten-foot pole. He makes a big show of disdaining television, of turning down everything but the best—hell, he hasn't been offered even a puppet show in two years."

Sarah felt her nails in the palms of her hands. She wanted to scratch Grace's eyes out. With difficulty, she restrained her voice. "I don't believe that cheap gossip. He's a genius. All of us thought so who worked with him."

"Don't take it to heart. What did you do, transfer to your director or something? So he's a genius—a genius who can't buy a job. Anyway, I'm only repeating. At any rate, back to that phone call. I thought we had him, but, by God, our luck, he just *did* get a job a couple of days ago."

"Really? What?"

"A television series they're going to shoot down in Mexico and Central America. 'The Filibusters,' I think he said it was called—you know, William Walker, soldiers of fortune, adventurers. Not a bad idea. Maybe some banana company will sponsor it. Anyway, he's leaving for Mexico City tomorrow to shoot the pilot film. Isn't that the damnedest luck?"

"Tomorrow?" said Sarah dully. Every organ inside her body had given way.

Grace seemed not to have heard her. "But that's not the juicy part. Even that job's a fluke. I had to call Helen Fleming this morning—she's on the play committee—with the bad news. Well, her husband's in the studios, and a friend of his, someone named Reggie Hooper, created the series. Well, it seems that Fred Tauber's wife—did you know he had a wife?"

Sarah shook her head.

"His wife is the daughter of one of those Hollywood big shots. She's society and loaded with gilt-edged and quite a bit older. I suppose Tauber married her because he expected it would help. Well, it helped a little, I'm sure, but not enough, and he got bored and began pinching starlets, and she found out. There was some kind of noisy showdown in Romanoff's, and he left her. So she went to big-shot Daddy, and Daddy got Tauber blacklisted until he came around. But Tauber wouldn't come around, jobs or no jobs—he didn't have enough talent to get anyone to defy his father-in-law—so he just sat in limbo, reading Hedda Hopper and pinching starlets. But here's the pay-off. Apparently, his wife really loved him—either that or she didn't want her name dragged into the divorce courts— there's a kid somewhere around—so at last she was the one

321

to come around. I think she helped him a little with money for a couple of independent projects that fell through. Anyway, lately, she got wind that was he going hot and heavy for someone, an actress, I think, and she decided to put a stop to that. She bought this television property and offered Tauber a partnership if he would take it down to Mexico and produce and direct it. I don't think she gives a damn about anything, except getting him away from here. So who suffers in the end? *We* suffer. If anyone knew what the Association goes through . . ."

❖ ❖ ❖

An unfamiliar voice, male, answered the phone, and Sarah asked for Mr. Tauber.

"Just a moment, please," said the voice.

She sat on the edge of the hassock, in the study, telephone in her lap, rocking to and fro and wanting to wail. Her temples throbbed, and the back of her neck was agonizing.

Minutes before, she had pleaded the powder room and escaped Grace, who had moved on to Sam and the Palmers, and stumbled into the dining room where Geoffrey was showing off the ham baked in bread to a professorial guest. She had whispered to Geoffrey that she must make a phone call in privacy, and he had cheerfully placed an arm around her bare back and led her to the study. Inside, he had nuzzled her neck with his mustache and told her that no one would disturb her if she pressed the lock from the inside. He had left, reluctantly, and she had shut the door and pressed the lock.

"Yes?" It was Fred's busy voice.

"This is Sarah."

"Look, I'm tied up right now."

"They can wait. You listen to me."

Her tone of voice had given him pause. "All right," he said slowly. "What is it?"

"I know all about your damn television series, and Mexico, and going tomorrow. I'm at a party, and I overheard it. I just want you to tell me if it's true. I just want to know it's true. I want to hear it from you."

"Look, let me explain—one second—" He had apparently partially covered the mouthpiece with his hand. She tried to visualize what he was doing. He was explaining to the others that it was something private. They could stay put, and he

322

would let out the extension cord and carry the phone into the bathroom behind the living room.

He came on again. "All right, now I can talk. Look, Sarah, I didn't dare call you—I was going to write you a note after tonight's meeting—"

"A *note?*" She knew that her voice was shrill and didn't give a damn.

"A letter, explaining—"

"You knew this yesterday when I called. Why didn't you tell me then?"

"There were people in the room."

"Your wife, you mean."

"All right. Yes."

"You should hear what I heard. It's all over the place. She knows about us. She got you this series to get you out of town."

"Who told you that crap?" His voice was furious. "Nobody's spending fifty thou on a pilot to get me out of town, not even my wife."

"Are you going to tell me she isn't putting up a dime?"

"I'm saying nothing of the sort. She's one of the backers, of course. She's a businesswoman. She knows what I can do. But there are others, too."

"She wants to break us up, and you're letting her—for a lousy job."

"It's got nothing to do with her. Sarah, be reasonable. I'm a man. I'm a director. I've got work to do. This is something that's come up that I like, and I want to do it."

She rocked on the hassock, blind with hurt, wanting only to lash out, to hurt him. "All the time, your arty talk, looking down your nose at television, and the first piece of junk that comes along—"

"Sarah, what's got into you? I can't believe this is you. Knowing me as you do, do you think I'd do anything I didn't believe in? You're just upset because you heard about it this way."

"I am, I want to cry."

"I told you I was going to explain. I was planning to leave time for it tonight. You mean a good deal to me. You're the most important thing in my life—except for my work, I'm a man—I've got to work—but you're everything else—"

She loved him so, that broken face, that tender touch and voice, her life, her entire life.

". . . and I'll be back in six weeks," he went on. "We'll be together as before."

"I can't live six weeks without you. I'll die."

"I'll be back, Sarah."

"And after that? More trips? No—no, Fred, listen—we can't go on like this. I've made up my mind. Nothing will change it." Overlapping her words was the memory: she had made up her mind during the interview, or right after, discussing her life with Sam, then Fred, and bringing everything into clear focus. What had deterred her from acting at once had been the children, the children and the wave of scandal that would wash her away from relatives and friends. But then she had determined to live her life as it must be lived. Eventually, she would have the children again. Eventually, she would regain the regard of relatives and friends. People remarried every day, and it was acceptable. Sam had the store and the twenty-one-inch screen. To hell with Sam. Because he was dead, must she also be entombed? "I'm going with you," she heard herself say. "I'll meet you at the airport in the morning."

"Sarah, you can't mean that? You're not making sense."

"I'm making sense——for the first time, yes—I'll meet you."

"Your family—"

"I don't care. You're my family."

"Sarah, I'm going down with a crew. There'll be no women. I couldn't—"

"I'll take the next flight, then. Where will you be?"

"All over the place. I'll be busy every minute."

"Where will you be? There's got to be one place."

"The Reforma Hotel," he said unhappily. "I wish you wouldn't, Sarah. I wish you'd sleep on it, think about it."

"No."

"I can't keep you from coming to Mexico, of course not—"

"You can keep me from coming. Tell me you don't love me. Tell me you don't want me, ever again. Tell me that."

There was a momentary silence. "I can't tell you that, but—"

Someone was knocking at the study door.

"I have to hang up now," she whispered. "I'll see you."

She returned the receiver to the cradle, set down the telephone, straightened the scarves so that they covered her tights, and opened the study door. It was Geoffrey holding up two drinks.

"Scotch or bourbon? Your choice of weapons."

"Bourbon."

He extended the glass in his left hand, and she accepted the drink.

"I thought you needed it," he said.

She smiled wanly. "Mata Hari doesn't," she said. "But I do."

❖   ❖   ❖

The first guests had begun to depart at twelve-thirty, and by twelve forty-five Kathleen and Paul had taken their leave of the Harnishes and were headed toward Kathleen's house a dozen blocks away.

Kathleen had enjoyed the dinner, and so had Paul, both fully aware that this had been their formal social debut as partners. Now, remembering incidents at the party, they laughed, and Paul hardest at the memory of the Palmers so drunk, enacting an impromptu playlet of Dr. Chapman interviewing Lucrezia Borgia on her sexual behavior.

Kathleen shook her head. "Imagine, if they had known you were one of the interviewers."

"She would have gone ahead anyway. She was tanked."

Kathleen looked at him out of the corner of her eye. "You weren't offended?"

Paul chuckled. "I wish I'd written that skit. . . . Hell, no. We're fair game."

Turning into Kathleen's street, they both fell silent as if by mutual consent. The thinnest slice of moon hung high above the street lights, circled by dots that were stars sparkling on and off. On either side of the thoroughfare, casting weird silhouettes on the street, the rows of eucalyptus bowed respectfully, like ancient retainers. In the unstirred air remained the faint exotic odor of gardenia bushes.

Paul bent the car into Kathleen's driveway, and in a moment they were before her entrance. He turned the ignition key, and the motor lost its voice to the cadence of the crickets in the grass.

Kathleen pulled her mink stole about her, then folded her hands in her lap, and turned to face Paul. "I'd ask you in, but it's so late."

Paul's eyes watched her face. "What did our host say? Romney's portrait—the most beautiful face ever put to canvas? Someday, we'll see, and then I'll show you—not half as beautiful as you, Kathleen."

"Don't say things like that, Paul, unless you mean them."

325

"I love you, Kathleen."

"Paul . . . I—"

She closed her eyes, red lips trembling, and he embraced her and kissed her. After a while, as he kissed her cheeks, and eyes and forehead, and hair, and found her mouth again, she took his hand in her own and brought it to her chest, and then pressed it down beneath the veiled bodice and inside her brassière. Gently, he caressed the soft breast, then withdrew his hand and touched her hot cheek with his fingertips.

"Kathleen, I love you. I want to marry you."

Her eyes were open, and, suddenly, she sat up, staring wordlessly at him. Her eyes were odd, almost frightened.

"I'm supposed to leave Sunday," he said, "but Dr. Chapman owes us vacations. I could ask to stay. We could fly to Las Vegas—or a church, if you like—"

"No," she said.

Paul did not conceal his astonishment. "I thought—I'm trying to say I love you, all the way—and I thought—it seemed to me that you felt—"

"I do, I do—but not now."

"I don't understand you, Kathleen."

Her head was bowed. She did not speak.

"Kathleen, I've been a bachelor a long time. I knew that when it finally happened, it would be right. I knew it—and I know it now, this moment here. You're right, and I'm right, and I think we should be together for the rest of our lives."

She looked up. There was a secret misery in her face that he had not seen before. "I can't now—I want you, but not now —and don't ask me to explain."

"But this makes no sense. Is it your first husband?"

"No."

"Then what is it, Kathleen? This is the most important moment in our lives. There can be no secrets. Tell me what's bothering you, just tell me—get it over with—and then we can have each other."

"I'm too tired, Paul." She opened the car door, and before he could speak again, she was standing in the driveway. "I can't answer you, because I can't. Don't ask for logic. I'm too tired now to talk—just too tired."

She turned and went swiftly to the door. She inserted the key, and hurried inside, and closed it against him, not once looking back.

Paul sat behind the wheel, unmoving, for many minutes. He tried to understand, but without information, without logic, without communication, there was no understanding. The incredibility of the situation overwhelmed him. For most of thirty-five years, he had sought this woman, this delicate, ethereal Romney portrait, and after the endless odyssey, the trial by loneliness, he had found her. Yet, he had found no one, no person, but an image that had neither substance nor reality. He could not possess, he realized, what did not exist. The weight of the disappointment crushed him.

He turned the ignition key and started the car. Sick at heart, sick beyond breathing, he drove through The Briars toward the refuge of the only reality that held back no secrets, offered no disappointments—the refuge of numbers, cold and clear, even welcoming warm in their calm and orderly array.

12

HAVING COMPLETED A short letter to Gerold Triplett in San Francisco, and a long letter to her mother in Beloit, Wisconsin, Benita Selby sat at her desk in the corridor on the second story of The Briars' Women's Association and tried to determine what she should undertake next. Since it was too early to clean out the desk, she decided that she would make the final California entry in her journal.

With some difficulty, Benita worked the journal out of her handbag, cracked the booklet open on the desk, peeled the pages slowly, fleetingly admiring some gem of perception, until she reached the first of the few remaining blank pages.

Taking pen in hand, she began to write under Saturday, June 6: "Well, toot the trumpets, the Last Day of Judgment is here. Because of several cancellations this past week, as expected, today will be an abbreviated day of interviewing. Dr. Chapman, Horace, and Paul are scheduled for four interviews apiece, from ten-thirty this morning until five-thirty this afternoon. That will conclude 187 interviews of married women in The Briars and 3,294 nation-wide in fourteen months. That will end the married female survey, as far as field work is concerned. Cass is still ill. He was miserable all yesterday, and this morning early he drove off to see his doctor again. Dr. Chapman is working in the conference room, preparing his notes for tomorrow morning's network television program, Borden Bush's 'The Hot Seat,' in which he is the guest of honor who discusses his work with three experts in his line. The network says Trendex expects the largest morning audience this year. Dr. Chapman said to me, 'It is very important, Benita,' and he is giving it his all. The rest of us are free tomorrow to pack and do as we please, until the streamliner leaves Union Station at seven-fifteen in the evening. I will buy presents for Mom, Mrs. McKassen, who's been so helpful, and the girls at school . . ."

The sound of leather heels on the corridor floor stayed Benita's penmanship, and she looked up to see Paul Radford approaching. He appeared overheated, carrying his suit coat on his arm, and unusually absorbed. Hastily, Benita closed her journal and pushed it into the handbag.

"Good morning, Paul. Hot, isn't it?"

"Murder."

"But at least not humid and sticky, like the East. I'd love to live here, someday—or maybe north, like San Francisco—wouldn't you?"

"I haven't thought about it. Am I the first here?"

"Dr. Chapman's in the conference room. Cass went to his doctor, and—oh, Paul, someone's waiting for you."

He had started for the conference room, but now he came back to the desk, surprised.

"For me? Who?"

"Mrs. Ballard."

He threw his coat over the other arm. "Where is she?"

"I put her in your office. You won't be using it for another half hour."

Paul moved toward his office. "Has she been here very long?"

"Ten, fifteen minutes."

"See that we're not disturbed."

He continued into the office. He expected to find her in the chair, but she was leaning against the wall, legs crossed and arms folded over her bosom, smoke curling from the cigarette between the fingers of one slender hand. She was staring at the side of the brown folding screen when he entered, and she greeted his entrance without a smile.

"Kathleen—"

"Good morning, Paul."

She wore a sleeveless magenta silk dress, and for that moment of elegant loveliness, he forgave her for upending a life of tidiness and making it one of chaos and turmoil. Yet, though she was present before him of her own initiative, he could not forget her enigmatic elusiveness of the night before. He tried to arrest the curve of rising hope. Through the restless night and bleak dawn, he had almost made the adjustment to a future that must perforce continue lonely. He would not permit himself another cycle of optimism because he would not suffer another fall into solitude.

"If I'd known you were coming here—" he said.

"I called the motel. You were out."

"I was walking."

"Then I phoned Miss Selby and came over."

He indicated the chair, noticing that there were already two cigarette butts in the ceramic tray. "Why don't you sit down Kathleen?"

She passed before him, eyes on the brown screen, and finally sat. "Why do you use a screen?"

"Dr. Chapman worked without one in the beginning, during the adolescent study, but finally decided that face-to-face interviews were too inhibiting for the subject. He thinks it's better this way."

"I don't think so. Perhaps, if there had been no screen between us—" she hesitated—"it might have been easier."

"Wouldn't you have been embarrassed?"

"At first, yes. But when a person is looking at you, it's—" She halted and drew twice on her cigarette.

"It's what, Kathleen?" he asked.

She raised her head toward him. "I'm trying to explain something to you, Paul—something terribly important—and I'm trying to lead into it gracefully." She shrugged. "I think that's impossible."

"Does it have to do with the way you reacted last night?"

"Yes, entirely."

"By the time the sun came up this morning, I'd decided that you wanted me a little, but not enough, not enough to be forever. I'm extremely possessive, Kathleen. I think you may have guessed that. It would have to be forever."

"How does one ever know before? How can one be sure?"

"When you've waited as long as I have, you're sure."

"You're being unrealistic, Paul. I've been married. Once, I wasn't, and then I was. There's a tremendous difference. Momentarily, you think someone is right, and you say forever, but afterward, forever becomes—what?—it becomes snoring and bad breath in the morning, and diarrhea, and menstrual cramps, and fights over money, and sucking your teeth, and hair curlers, and the same tired one in bed, imperfect, saying the same words, reacting the same way—forever. That's forever, too."

"I'm no child, Kathleen. I've known many women—"

"Not like that—not forever."

"I've just finished listening to a good portion of three thousand of them."

330

"The questions you ask don't always bring the . . . the full answers."

"I'm surprisingly bright, Kathleen. I can project a laconic answer to the ultimate fact—"

"To the ultimate disillusion?"

"That would never happen to us. Even if passion becomes habit, and high regard or affection, let's say, it may be what should evolve with the passing years. Isn't a long intimacy, a total intimacy, enough foundation?"

"Is it? I don't know."

"Why are you here, Kathleen?"

"You proposed to me last night. I didn't say no. If I had said no, I wouldn't be here."

"You didn't say yes, either. Matrimony requires full affirmation on both sides."

"I don't know if that's possible on my part. I suspect it isn't. I think this is one of those . . . those encounters where you meet, and dream a little, and go on your separate ways. Because you never knew you'd meet, and, besides, nature didn't equip you, prepare you, for the encounter. It wasn't fated to be. Like the sperm missing the egg."

"Is that how you feel?"

"About myself. Not you. I feel you came prepared. I'm the one who's not equal to it."

He was silent.

Angrily, Kathleen ground her cigarette stub into the tray. "Hell—circles—around and around I go. I'm here because, dammit, you've got to know."

There was a tentative rapping on the glazed door pane. Paul muttered a curse under his breath, strode to the door, and yanked it open.

Benita Selby recoiled. "I . . . I'm sorry, Paul, but Dr. Chapman wants to see you right away. I told him, but he insists. He's all steamed up about something. He said to break in on you."

"Can't you tell him to wait a minute?"

"You tell him. Not me."

Exasperated, Paul said, "All right. I'll be right in." He left the door open as he turned into the room. "Kathleen—"

"I heard. You go ahead, please."

"Will you wait? I want to know."

"I'll wait. I'll be right here."

He nodded gratefully and hurried into the corridor.

In the conference room, Dr. Chapman was pacing near the

far end of the table in a state of uncontrolled agitation. Paul shut the door and went to him.

"Where's Cass?" asked Dr. Chapman. "Have you seen Cass?"

"He was going to the doctor."

"He says. Three days ago I sent him to an internist, Perowitz, a friend of mine. Out on Wilshire. Cass said he went and this morning he left to see the doctor again."

Paul waited. Dr. Chapman resumed angrily.

"I worried about him all morning—we *are* leaving tomorrow—so I called the motel. They said he's still out. So I telephoned Perowitz to find out if it's serious. You know what Perowitz told me?"

Paul had not the faintest idea.

"He's never seen or heard of Cass Miller. Do you understand, Paul? Cass has been bluffing us. He's never been to a doctor. I'm beginning to suspect he wasn't even ill."

"There must be some logical explanation."

"You're damn right. There'd better be. And that's what we're going to find out right now. You and I—we're going out on a Cass hunt, and when I find him, well, he'd better have his reasons, and they'd better make sense, or he's through, right now, today, through."

Paul glanced at the wall clock. "We have interviews in eighteen minutes."

"Benita can have them wait. I want to settle Cass right now."

"Where do we begin?"

"Never mind. I want to question the clerk at the motel and the gas station attendant where he takes the Dodge."

He went to the door. Paul followed him into the corridor. "Are you sure you need me, Doctor?"

Dr. Chapman did not hide his vexation. "Look, Paul, I think this is important enough to investigate personally. Certainly, it's not what the head of a project is expected to do. But I've never looked upon Cass, or you or Horace, for that matter, as subordinates or employees. We're partners, and when one of us founders, is derelict in duty, it affects and involves all of us." He caught his breath. "Certainly I need you. How do I know what's happened to him? Maybe he's drunk. Maybe it'll take two of us."

It was Paul's turn to be irked by what he considered an unnecessary chastisement. "Okay," he said curtly. "Let me get my coat."

Paul entered his office. Kathleen had not moved from the chair. She sat staring at the screen, smoking. She looked at him as he picked up his coat.

"Kathleen, I'm sorry. A minor crisis. Dr. Chapman needs me with him on a mission. Then, the interviews—"

"That's all right. But I do want to talk to you today." She hesitated, and seemed suddenly tired and uncertain. "If you want to."

"I want to. I'm finishing here around five-thirty. No, it'll be later now. Probably closer to six. Can I just come right over?"

"Yes." She held up the cigarette. "May I finish this before leaving?"

"Take your time. The office will be empty another half hour or more."

He bent, brush-kissed her forehead, and hastened out to join Dr. Chapman.

❦ ❦ ❦

It was after ten o'clock, and Sarah Goldsmith still sat at the antique slant-top desk writing the final draft of the note.

Her matching gray airline luggage, packed after the children had gone off to school and Sam had clumped off to a meeting in Pomona, had been hastily packed and now rested inside the front door. The telephone call to the sitter service had been made, and there would be someone to use the key under the rubber mat and be on hand to greet the children. All that was left was the note. Sarah had written it three times and discarded three versions, and this was the last, for the passenger plane to Mexico City took off in two hours, and the airport was a long drive.

The note was done, and now she read it.

"Sam. After twelve years, it's hard to write a letter like this. But you know, for the last years, we have not been happy and there's no use lying to ourselves. I have been miserable. It could have less to do with you and more to do with me. I have stayed with you until now, and tried to make a home and family life because of the children, mainly. But it's no use now, and, anyway, I don't think everyone was meant to live together because they married. So I have decided to call it quits while we are still young and can do something separately with our lives ahead. Believe me, I'm sorry about this, but circumstances are such that I have to think of myself for a change. Therefore, I am making a clean break, to get it over with all at once. Much as I hate to hurt you, but to help you

333

understand, I have been in love with another man, a fine gentleman, for some time, and still am. I am leaving this morning to go to a foreign country to join him. Eventually we hope to be married. I know this will shock you and the family, but this is life. You can tell the family and people here anything you want—that you kicked me out or that I wasn't well, and we both thought a separation better, or anything like that. Don't be cruel about me to Jerry and Debbie, because I am still their mother and had them with my body. Look after them, and spend more time, and tell them I will see them soon. When I arrive, I will write you and let you know where to write me, and I will get an attorney for an arrangement. I have drawn my money out of savings and closed the account. Please take this like a man, Sam, and don't hate me too much. I can't help it, and maybe you'll be better off. Regretfully, Sarah . . . P.S. Get a nurse for the children right away or, better, send for your cousin, Bertha, who is single and would look after you, with Jerry and Debbie. Goodbye."

Satisfied that no more could be written in a note, Sarah blotted it, searched the upper drawer for a long, plain envelope. Then she printed "For Sam. Confidential. Important. From Sarah" across the envelope, folded and inserted the page, licked the back of the envelope, sealed it, and cast about in the room for a conspicuous place where Sam would find it at once and Jerry not reach it. At last, she went into the kitchen, tore off a piece of Scotch tape, then carried the envelope into the large bathroom and secured the envelope to the medicine cabinet mirror with the tape.

She remained a moment before the mirror, studying her image, partially obscured by the envelope, and trying to see it as Fred would soon see it in Mexico. She lifted her wrist to the window light, scrutinizing the tiny dial for the time. There was little time left, but dressing would take no more than five minutes. Her hair was done, and her face, and beneath the housecoat she had on her garter belt and sheerest nylon stockings. Undoing her short cotton housecoat, she started for the bedroom to change into brassière, slip, and gabardine suit.

On the way to the bedroom, she heard the front door bell chime. This would be the postman, she thought as she changed her route to the living room, knotting her belt as she walked. Sam's relatives were always writing postage due. Without bothering to peer through the circular peephole in the door with its one-way glass, for she rarely used it in the daytime, she turned the knob and pulled the door fully open.

Startled at first because he was not the postman in uniform with laden pouch, she did not recognize the dark, intense young man in the doorway.

"Mrs. Goldsmith," he said politely, not really asking if it were she but flatly stating the fact as if something had just been accomplished.

And then, with a clutch of terror, she saw the familiar Dodge over his shoulder, parked across the street, and she associated him with the persistent fear of the week gone by. She meant to slam the door, but the recognition had been slow, and then the audacity of his materializing had petrified her, and now he was inside the living room, and if she shut the door she would be shutting it to keep safety out and terror in.

"What do you want?" she gasped.

"I'm Cass Miller," he said tightly. "I'm with Dr. Chapman."

For a split second, she could not place Dr. Chapman, and then she recollected the interview, and fear gave way to relief. So clearly had he been fashioned in her brain as a detective, an enemy to Fred and herself, that the revelation of his true identity was almost exhilarating.

"Yes," she said. "What can I do for you? I'm in a terrible hurry—"

"This won't take long." She found it difficult to hear his voice, which seemed strangled, and she felt uncomfortable before the eyes that would not meet her eyes. "I've been watching you," he said.

Goose pimples raised on her arms. "I know. You've had me frightened. Is it part of the survey, or what?"

"I know about you and Mr. Tauber," he said. An ominous and relentless dullness pushed his words forth. "Why are you cheating on your husband?"

"Why, I like your nerve—"

"Don't lie to me. I know everything." He intoned the litany: "Three months, four times a week average, husband doesn't suspect, coitus half hour, orgasm, yes, forty minutes, fifty minutes, on your back, married, two children." Suddenly, his eyes widened, the pupils pin points, and his face contorted. "Whore!"

She stumbled backward, arm to her mouth, fear throttling her throat.

He pushed the door shut behind him and advanced toward her. "Whore," he repeated, "whore. I read your questionnaire. I saw you go there. Cheating, every day cheating."

"Go away!" she shrieked hysterically.

"Scream and I'll kill you."

She breathed convulsively at the nearness of his maniacal eyes and stood her ground, panting, afraid to raise her voice.

"You," she said chokingly, "why . . . why are you here?"

"I like whores. I like them much. I want what you're passing out."

"You're insane."

"Give it to me, like you give him—forty minutes—the same, and I'll go away. If you don't, I'll tell your husband—now—I'll tell him now."

"I already told him—he knows!" Reason with him, reason. "It's no secret any more. There's nothing wrong any more."

He wasn't listening to her. He wasn't hearing. "Let your hair down—down—"

He reached for her hair, and she swung at his arm with an outcry, and spun around, bumping into a chair, staggering against the wall, then running for the kitchen and the back door.

Bursting into the kitchen, almost falling, she flung herself at the door and wrenched wildly at the knob. It was long seconds before she realized that she had locked it from the inside. She fumbled for the upper bolt, twisting, when she heard him and turned.

Cass grabbed for her shoulders, wanting to smother the terrified face, but she ducked under his clawing fingers. His fingers tore at the shoulder of her housecoat as she grasped the edge of the sink to maintain her balance. Cornered, she straightened to meet him.

For an instant, he hesitated, staring at the housecoat ripped open, at the mother's breasts rising and falling, at the overflowing mother's flesh above and beneath and below the nylon pants, breathing now like some forest thing mortally wounded and shuffling closer and closer to her.

She watched him, mesmerized, helpless, and the picture froze in its incredibility: the maddened rapist, twitching face and sick to his bowels, and the housewife alone, you always read it in the morning paper, you always read it, and it had happened on some obscure street, unpronounceable, in some depressed outlying district, among the poor, the wretches, the slatterns, who had no expensive houses in The Briars, no expensive locks on their doors, no expensive kitchenware, neither clothes, nor friends, neither police, nor importance. It happened always to the anonymous dregs, but she was Sarah Goldsmith, of New York, with horn-rimmed glasses (where were

336

they? you can't hurt someone with glasses!), and a clothing store, and a seat in the synagogue, and membership in the Association, and shares in American Tel and Tel.

No!

With all of her strength, she threw herself past his out-stretched, groping arms. She felt the clubbing weight of an arm against her breastbone, and then the exulting freedom of open space, and then her feet sliding upward from under her, and the floor and stove rising, spinning crazily into vision.

As the side of her head smashed against the corner of the stove and her body hit the floor, she seemed grotesque and misshapen, and then she rolled limply on her back. Cass tottered toward her, quickly dropping to his knees.

"Don't run," he said. "No more," he said. "No more."

She lay soft and doughy beneath, spread-eagled and compliant at last, and he lifted the long-known fleshy thighs with each hand, and he violated her, punishing, punishing.

All through it, on the hammered anvil of hate, he was the mover, and she moved not at all except to his movement, and even after, she lay still, inert, quiescent, not angry, not pleased, and then it was, touching fingers to her icy cheek and lids and pulse, it was only then that he realized she had been dead all the while, killed dead, neck broken, by the fall against the stove.

"Oh, Mother," he sobbed, "Mother," wanting the comfort of the swollen mother breasts and knowing that they were life-less to him for all eternity. . . .

◇　◇　◇

After Cass Miller had returned to the Villa Neapolis, leaving the Dodge in the guest parking area, he took a sheet of the stationery bearing an aerial photograph of the motel ("Your Luxurious Home away from Home") and, standing at the corner of the reception desk, wrote in stilted hand his memorandum to history.

Later, in the car again, turning westward from the motel, he stopped beside the pumps of the first filling station, and, keeping the engine idling, he called out to the nearest attendant for the best neighborhood mountain drive. He printed the directions inside his skull, the last of them being for Topanga Canyon.

Later still, riding the outer rim of a rising paved road, he climbed steadily into the blue hills of the range. Once, through the outer window, he saw the whitewashed toy homes in the clusters of make-believe miniature trees far, far below and was reminded of an electrical train set under a gaudy Christmas pine. Once, he thought of Benita Selby in the lavender bathing suit and her unattractive slat ass, and then of the blonde who wasn't blonde at all on the train from East St. Louis, and then unaccountably of the sweet Polish girl in the white organdy formal whom he had taken to the high-school prom. Once, he thought about great men dying, all surely feeling duped at having to leave, after so much complexity, all with their grand last words, Nero saying, "What an artist is now about to perish!" O. Henry saying, "Pull up the shades, I don't want to go home in the dark," Henry Ward Beecher saying, "Now comes the mystery," someone saying, "God will forgive me, it is His business." All the bravura, all the pack of lies.

He saw that the road had narrowed and that only a flimsy metal guard rail protected the lane from the sheer drop thousands of feet below.

Yet, he thought, he wished he had added something with style to that note, perhaps the lines by Edgar Allan Poe: "The fever called 'living' / Is conquered at last."

Then he saw, off along the mountain's side, two vehicles, a sedan, a truck, approaching in the inner lane. Then he saw, again, coming fast, the metal guard rail. There will be witnesses, he thought, and plunged his shoe into the gas pedal. The rail loomed big, more quickly than he had planned, and then without thought, before he could change his mind, he swung the wheel hard right, swerving at full speed, catapulting toward the metal rail.

The massive machine heaved high beneath him as the metal and wood exploded with his grill and hood and radiator, throwing him from the cushioned seat into the bending wheel. Conscious he was, of the strange suspension between the blue above and the green below, conscious, too, of infinite space and roaring winds, wondering what he should think this moment here. A last word, words, dignity of man, yes, bravura, yes. The seat beneath him was leaving the floor, which was ridiculous, and he was sorry it was a rented car, and then, the hurtling sarcophagus shuddered, the atoms dissolving before him, and something flat and black swung toward his face, his neck nailed in too tight to move, and he thought a last, last word, words, phrase to remember me, immortal me, take it, Benita, valediction, epitaph: Fuck you, one and all.

At five to six, the day still light and muggy, Paul directed the cabbie to Kathleen's driveway, then paid him the fare, and stepped out of the taxi.

The morning, the search for Cass, had been utterly futile. All that he and Dr. Chapman had been able to learn was that Cass had gone off somewhere, early, in the Dodge. Dr. Chapman had taken the wheel of the Ford back to the Association building, fuming all the way. Once inside, because they were behind schedule, Dr. Chapman and he had conducted their interviews right through lunch, taking only two coffee breaks. When Paul had concluded his final interview at five-thirty, and met Horace in the corridor after the women had departed, both were surprised to find that Benita had gone, in some haste apparently, for her desk was still in disarray, and Dr. Chapman was nowhere to be found. To add to the mystery, the Ford was missing from its accustomed parking place. Briefly, Paul and Horace had discussed phoning Villa Neapolis to check with Dr. Chapman, but there seemed no point to it, especially since each was eager to keep an appointment. They had walked to The Village Green together, found taxis, and Horace had gone off to relieve the nurse at Naomi's, and Paul had given the cabbie Kathleen's address.

Now, entering the driveway on foot, Paul could see Kathleen's Mercedes parked past the curve of the half circle. Reaching the front door, Paul touched the doorbell. Albertine appeared at once, carrying Deirdre.

"Hello, Albertine." He placed his hands under the curly-haired Deirdre's arms and took her to him. "How's my favorite octopus today?" The last time, when he had greeted the child by name, she had corrected him, informing him that she was "a little octopus." Now she settled in his arms. "I'm not an octopus," she said with the gravity of a diminutive adult. "I'm me. Do you want to eat with us?"

"Well, I'd like to," Paul said, "but—"

Deirdre twisted toward the housekeeper. "Can he, 'Bertine?" Albertine shrugged. "Jus' means opening another can."

But already Deirdre's mind had shifted to more immediate pleasures. "Give me a rocket ride like always," she said to Paul.

He hoisted her high above his head, whirling her round and

339

round as Albertine backed off, and then he lowered her to the carpet. "There," he said. "We're on the moon." Straightening, he faced Albertine. "Is Mrs. Ballard in?"

"She went scootin' off to Mrs. Goldsmith' couple hours ago and said for you to come there. Seemed awful fussed, like she was workin' up to a good cry."

"How do I get there?"

"Goldsmith's? Go left two blocks, left again, Hayes Drive, then the third from the corner, left. Name's on the box."

"Thanks, Albertine. . . . See you in a little while, Moon-maid."

Walking south on the wide thoroughfare, close to the curbing to avoid the occasional oncoming car, he wondered why Kathleen had been fussed, as Albertine had described it, and what she had come to the office to tell him this morning.

The mingled fragrance of a thousand flowers engulfed him, and he peered past the rows of eucalyptus, the hedges and bushes and ferns, the grilled gates, and once saw a fabulous bed of geraniums, and then orange and pink hibiscus, and, beside a banana tree, a profusion of purple asters bordered by white petunias.

How difficult, he thought, to reconcile this outer front of utopia with the people who inhabited it, especially the women he had interviewed these two weeks past, the specific mistresses of these specific mansions. Look at them, he thought, staring at the front lawns and gardens and magnificent mansions, here everything is regulated and aesthetically enticing. The thick foliage the greenest, the homes the largest, the garages crowded with gleaming chariots, the sun-touched children, the maids. Here is an earthly heaven, you would say, placid, solved, happy; and the mammals within, placid, solved, happy—this you would say, until you had been inside. For he had been inside, he and Horace and Cass and Dr. Chapman had been inside, and what had they found behind the gracious façade?—crouching creatures fighting the human plagues that infest, not only here but everywhere, stagnation and dry rot of the mind, famine of the heart, and the airless dying of the soul. Everywhere? He tried to recapture fragments of interviews, the ones reinforced by warm strong love, true intimacy, the fully integrated ones. There had been some. A few. Very few. But for the rest . . . and which was Kathleen?

He was approaching Hayes Drive when he saw her come around the corner toward him, rust cardigan over her shoulders, blouse and skirt and low-heeled shoes. He waved and waited. She made no acknowledgment in return.

When she was beside him, he observed the strain on her features. "I was just going to find you, Kathleen."

"Do you have a cigarette? I'm all out."

"No," he apologized, lifting his pipe stem from the coat pocket.

"It doesn't matter." Her hands were nervous. "It's just been terrible. Have you heard?"

"What?"

She resumed walking toward her house, and he fell in step beside her.

"Sarah Goldsmith," she said. "She's dead."

"Who?"

"Sarah—you met her, Paul, last night, just last night. She was the one with the black hair pulled back in a chignon, like a Spanish dancer. Mata Hari."

At once, he recalled her. He remembered a Latin face to which the Semitic name had not seemed to belong. And the tights and beaded scarves. And the rounded thighs.

"Yes," he said, "I remember. "What happened to her?"

"No one knows. The police say her husband murdered her."

It was easier to recall the husband of Mata Hari. A nice rumpled blob, with apologetic eyes and a hand like gelatin. Aaron? Abe? Sam? Yes, Sam.

"Sam Goldsmith," he said. "Why did he do it?"

"It's all garbled, I'm sure. I got it secondhand. Her neighbor, Mrs. Pedersen, phoned me after the police and ambulance left. She found my name in Sarah's personal phone book. I was the nearest neighbor friend, so she called. She has her own children, and the sitter was too upset to stay. So I went over to help out, after the children came from school."

"They arrested Sam?"

"Yes, I think so. No, they took him in for questioning. That's it. They found a note in the bathroom and her luggage packed. Apparently, she was leaving Sam this morning—going off to meet another man—she'd been having an affair—of all people, Sarah. I swear, I can't believe it."

"It happens," he said gently.

She looked at him with troubled eyes. "Yes. I'm sure you hear it all the time. But Sarah—"

"The police, I suppose they figured Sam heard about it and tried to stop her?"

341

"That's right. They said he came home—he wasn't in the store this morning, it turns out—and found her leaving, and maybe the note, and he tried to stop her. They fought. He killed her. I can't believe it, though, even under the circumstances. He's the sweetest man."

"Someone did it, Kathleen."

"Maybe it was an accident?"

"How did it happen?" Paul asked.

"The sitter got a message to be there at noon, the key was to be under the mat, and wait for the children. She arrived a little late, and no one seemed home, and she went into the kitchen—and there was Sarah on the floor. The police said her neck had been broken."

They had arrived at the front door.

"I suppose you're not in the mood to have me in," said Paul.

"That's not it. I promised to go back. Mrs. Pedersen and I are going to sit with the children until one of Sam's family comes. His lawyer called a relative in Chicago, and she's flying out. I think she'll get in about one in the morning." Kathleen unlocked the door. "I just came back a few minutes to see that Deirdre is properly fed and to get my coat. Would you like a sandwich, Paul?"

"No, I'll just call for a cab."

"Take my car. I won't need it tonight or tomorrow." She gave him the keys. "Please."

"All right. I'll have a snack at the motel, and then I'll have to pack." He waved the keys. "Does this mean I can see you tomorrow?"

She stared at him. "I was hoping to see you, if you want to."

"I'm leaving with them tomorrow night. Only one thing could make me stay. This is no time to discuss it again, but—"

"I can't say now, Paul, I really can't. Don't be angry."

"You love a person or you don't. What's there to think about?"

"Paul, please, try to—"

"All right. Tomorrow. When?"

"If Sarah's—if Sam's cousin gets here—I'll be free all day. Any time."

"I'm tied up in the morning. Chapman's on television, and Horace, Cass, and I have orders to watch. But after lunch—some time after lunch, okay?"

"I'll be waiting."

He smiled tiredly. "So will I."

When Paul entered the small, tasteful room that served as the lobby of the Villa Neapolis, there was no one behind the reception desk. Paul made his way around the counter to the letter slots, found his key, then noticed a patch of white in the deep recess of his slot. He felt inside and withdrew the envelope. It bore his name in script, the handwriting slanted in a style that seemed familiar.

Puzzled, Paul returned to the lobby, tearing open the envelope as he did so. He extracted the letter, unfolded it, noticed that the sheet was the motel stationery, then glanced down at the signature. Slowly, he began to read, and then quickly read to the end.

Having finished, he realized that the hand that held the letter was trembling. The numbness that had formed in his intestines now opened, like an umbrella, through his whole system.

"Oh, Mr. Radford—"

He glanced over his shoulder and saw that the night clerk, with the facial characteristics of a Jivaro shrunken head and the aspect of an old jockey, had returned.

"I was just telling the reporters—they're all in the bar waiting—that Dr. Chapman's still out with the police. I'm sure sorry about it, Mr. Radford. It must be a bad blow. That Mr. Miller was sure a fine gentleman. But people who don't know those mountain roads shouldn't be driving them. Bet there's at least three accidents like that every few months up there. They ought to do something about it. I guess you must feel pretty shaken up."

"Yes," said Paul.

"Like I said, I'm sorry."

"Thanks," said Paul.

The clerk turned on the patio lights and busied himself with the ledger. Paul moved to the doorway, beneath the overhead lamp, and held up the letter again, and reread it.

DEAR PAUL,

I've just done an insane thing, and I have to pay for it. One of the women I interviewed last week, she got under my skin because she was a sinner, and she had children. I've been watching her. This morning, I met her. I wanted to make love to her, but she wouldn't. She's been sleeping with another man every day. I kept after her. I don't remember details.

343

I forced her to make love. She fell down and died. It was an accident, but fat chance I'd have of proving it. The woman's name is Sarah Goldsmith. I'm taking the Dodge and driving somewhere and going off a bridge or cliff, whatever is easiest. It's the best thing, and I'll be glad. The Grand Master can pay for the car out of my GI insurance. I never liked him, and I don't care if this blows the project to hell, because all this emphasis on sex is no good. Make them cremate me. See you one year soon.

CASS MILLER
June 7th

Paul folded the letter carefully, and then, holding it, he remained standing in the doorway, gazing out at the swimming pool. At first, the full significance of Cass's last testament did not penetrate. His concern was with the fact of Cass dead by suicide. The suddenness of it made the fact unacceptable. Yet the fact existed, verified by the desk clerk. Somewhere in the city, Dr. Chapman had identified a basket of bones and shredded flesh.

In life, he had not cared for Cass, Paul remembered, but now Cass was no more, and of the dead say nothing but good, think nothing but good. It was all part of a civilized game. He thought, You like everyone after they are dead, because you are alive and therefore superior, so you like them in the same way you like the poor, the deformed, the minority, the very old, because you are up and they are down, and fair is fair. Poor, bitter, driven Cass. Then, finally, came the shock of significance. Poor, bitter, driven *Sarah*. Poor *Sam*.

For a moment, he realized, he was the Omnipotent. In one morgue lay Cass Miller. In another, or the same, lay Sarah Goldsmith. And behind the bars of a cell, soon to be as dead as they, a corpulent tradesman named Sam. Yet here, high on a garish hill, stood he, Paul Radford, author, scientist, with the paper in hand that would release to the world of living and superiority, a broken human being doomed to die.

At first, he had not paid attention to the sedan moving up the steep road, and then, as it turned into the guest parking lot, he discerned that it was white and black and a squad car of the Los Angeles police. He watched Dr. Chapman emerge, speaking animatedly, gesturing, and the man behind the wheel remained behind the wheel, but another in the back seat, in plain clothes, emerged to join Dr. Chapman and walk with him toward the patio.

As they came nearer, Paul's fingers tightened on the letter. He issued his last ukase as the Omnipotent: Yes, I, Paul Radford, with the holy paper, do decree that you, Sam Goldsmith, may have the gift of life, and because of this, that you, George G. Chapman, must have the black kerchief of death. An eye for an eye, the relentless Hebraic dictum. Sarah on the kitchen floor to be balanced on the scale by the corpse of Dr. Chapman's report.

They had passed before Paul without seeing him. Dr. Chapman listened as the big-shouldered detective spoke. Paul caught a snatch of it.

". . . since the report on the car shows no internal tampering or defective gear. Yet, those witnesses insist that the car swerved sharply. You're positive that he did not drink?"

"Only socially, socially. He was temperate to an extreme. Take alcohol tests. You'll—"

"Tests of what's left?"

They were out of Paul's vision, but they had apparently halted at the foot of the veranda stairs.

"Well, you'll have to take my word," said Dr. Chapman. "Mr. Miller did not drink."

"Have you any reason to believe that he was despondent?"

"On the contrary. When I saw him last night, he was cheerful. He looked forward to getting back home—to the school, that is."

"Well, it beats me. There were no skid marks, so I can't say if he lost control or was even traveling at excessive speed. I suppose it was an accident."

"I'm positive of that."

"Those are dangerous roads. Sometimes a gopher jumps out or a prairie dog, and your instinct is to avoid it, and there's no apron, no leeway, nowhere to go but down. Well, thanks, Dr. Chapman. Sorry to put you through all this. Part of the job, you understand. Routine. You've been very co-operative."

"I owe it to Mr. Miller."

"Yes. Too bad, but that's that. I'll have the accident report typed up and send over a copy tomorrow."

"Thank you, sir."

Paul remained immobile, watching the detective slowly pass before him again, retracing his steps toward the squad car, studying a pad in his hand. Paul shook himself and stepped into the patio. Dr. Chapman was midway up the wooden stairs. Paul called to him. "Doctor—"

"There you are, Paul." He came rapidly down the stairs

again. "I've been trying to get hold of you. You've heard, haven't you?"

Paul nodded. "Yes. Cass told me."

"What?"

"It wasn't an accident."

He handed the letter to Dr. Chapman, who accepted it without looking at it, his eyes still trying to read the expression on Paul's face. Unhurriedly, he opened Cass's note, scanned it, and then, just as Paul had done, he reread it slowly. When he raised his head to Paul, his face was gray.

"I don't believe it," he said.

"It's true," said Paul. "There's a woman named Sarah Goldsmith who was killed this morning. You can check with the police."

"That doesn't mean he did it. He was a mental case. We can all testify to that. He may have heard and—like those compulsive confessions—decided he wanted the notoriety."

"To enjoy after he committed suicide?"

"He didn't commit suicide. He's one of our associates—"

"Doctor, he was well enough to work side by side with us, all these months, and right here. I think the police will accept his confessions as truthful."

Dr. Chapman looked fixedly at Paul, with a certain growing horror. "The police—"

"I'm afraid so. There's another man's life involved. The police are holding Mrs. Goldsmith's husband for the crime Cass committed."

Dr. Chapman nodded dumbly.

"That note will free the man," said Paul.

Dr. Chapman nodded again. "I'll get it to the right—"

Paul reached out and pulled the letter from Dr. Chapman's fingers. "The letter was addressed to me. I think I'd better take care of it."

"What are you going to do, Paul?"

Paul looked off toward the guest parking lot, and Dr. Chapman followed the direction of his gaze. The detective had reached the squad car and was opening the front door. "I'm going to turn it over to them," said Paul.

"Paul, wait—let's not be—let's consider the—"

But Paul had already gone, swiftly, in long strides, hurrying to intercept the squad car. Not once did he look back. He knew that there was a crack in the armor, at last, and he did not want to see it, now or ever.

13

THE ALARM ERUPTED with a brassy scream. Paul Radford's hand fumbled for the clock, clamped over it, pressing down the button and suffocating the reveille.

It was nine-thirty, Sunday morning.

For a while, allowing consciousness to rise, Paul lay motionless on his back. The only evidences of hangover were a thin wire of pressure inside his forehead and a tongue that had been coated with dry gravel. He sat up, unbuttoning his pajama top, and then he remembered the day.

Leaving the bed, he took up the telephone in one hand, removed the receiver with the other, and dialed the desk.

"Good morning," a woman's voice said.

"This is Mr. Radford. Room twenty-seven. Do you have the Sunday papers?"

"Only one left, sir. The other is sold out."

"Can you send it up?"

"Yes, sir."

"Also, tomato juice, two eggs sunnyside up, coffee black."

"Will that be all?"

"Don't forget the paper."

"Very well."

After returning the telephone to the table between the beds, Paul untied the cord of his pajama trousers, let them drop to the floor, lifted one foot free, then, with the other, kicked the trousers upward into his hands. He folded both halves of his pajamas and set them inside his open wardrobe, already packed. He checked the apparel he had hung out for his last day in The Briars. Gray sharkskin suit. Check. Blue dacron shirt and knit tie. Check. Shorts on the chair, socks and shoes on the floor. Check, check. He went into the bathroom to brush his teeth, shave, and shower.

When he had finished the cold shower and begun to dry

himself with the abrasive surface of the white Turkish towel, he finally reviewed the events of the night before.

He had intercepted the two detectives in time, introduced himself, shown them Cass Miller's letter, and replied to a dozen questions. They had been excited about the letter, grateful to Dr. Chapman and himself, and had driven down the hill recklessly to deliver the confession to their chief and, Paul assumed, eventually to the district attorney. Returning to the pool, he realized at once that Dr. Chapman was nowhere in sight. Later, having packed, Paul had learned from the desk clerk that Dr. Chapman had departed in the Ford, leaving word for the press that he would not have a statement until the following day. The series of violent and sad events that had warped the entire day had finally had their effect on Paul, and he had gone off to the Beverly Wilshire bar in Kathleen's car. During a long evening, he had consumed five Scotches and fallen into a conversation with an Englishman on the next stool who had recited the history of Mount Everest, being particularly affecting in the passages pertaining to Andrew Irvine and George Leigh-Mallery. At midnight, Paul had returned to the motel and slept at once.

Now, thoroughly dried, and dressing, Paul wondered if this last day in The Briars were not the last day of Dr. Chapman's entire project. He tried to imagine the consequences of Cass Miller's letter. Certainly Sam Goldsmith would be released by now—to what?—and the press notified. The newspapers, this Sunday morning, would be full of the sensation. He imagined the headlines: "Dr. Chapman Protégé Goes Sex Mad; Slays L.A. Housewife . . . Mother of Two Murdered by Sex Crazed Chapman Associate . . . Chapman Co-Worker Commits Suicide after Killing Woman He Had Interviewed . . . Chapman Sex Expert Strangles Society Matron; Destroys Himself . . . 'She Was a Sinner!' Cries Dr. Chapman Colleague after Garroting Actress."

Paul had no doubt that already the hound dogs of virtue and retribution had been loosed on Dr. Chapman. A telegram from the Zollman Institute, withdrawing. A phone call from the president of Reardon, suspending. A letter from the publisher, canceling. The coded questionnaires of more than three thousand married women would rest, untouched, in the bank safes until the curiosity of another age found them. *A Sex History of the American Married Female* would join the population of creative works stillborn, like Lord Byron's *Memoirs* and Sir Richard Burton's *The Scented Garden*. And millions of women, young and old, unmarried and married, awaiting libration from fear and ignorance, would continue to stagnate in that darker part of the soul. Yet, Paul told himself, other great men had survived lurid scandals. He tried to recollect their names. Henry Ward Beecher for one, yes. But not Shoeless Joe Jackson. Say it ain't so, Joe. No, not Shoeless Joe.

Paul felt sorry for Dr. Chapman, and as sorry for himself, for having been the agent of his mentor's destruction. Judas had done it for money, unforgivable, and all those atomic traitors, Fuchs, the rest, for love and money, unforgivable, but at least he had done it to save an innocent life. You're welcome, Sam Goldsmith.

He was dressed, except for his shoes, when the knocking on the door came. He opened the door, and a bald-headed dining-room waiter entered with the breakfast tray and the thick Sunday newspaper. Paul signed the bill, gave the waiter a half dollar, and closed the door after him.

Alone again, he peeled through the endless sections beneath the colored comics, located the news section, and yanked it free. Drinking his tomato juice, he opened the front page wide on his lap.

The banner headline: President Says Berlin something.

Photograph and caption: Singer Elopes Las Vegas.

Smaller headline: Earthquake Razes Mexican something.

Smaller photograph and caption: Dr. Chapman Associate Dies.

Smaller headline: Sex Historian Miller Killed in Auto Accident.

Quickly, Paul read the half-column story. "Losing control of his rented sedan high on a mountain road in Topanga Canyon, Cass Miller, thirty-two, bachelor authority on sexual behavior and associated with Dr. George G. Chapman in the current Reardon College survey of married woman, plunged one thousand feet to his death. According to police, the accident, the sixth such . . ."

Paul sat back, incredulous. The fact of death was a fact, but all of the rest, a parcel of lies by omission. Not one word was there about Cass's murder of Sarah Goldsmith, not one word of confessed suicide, not one word referring to or quoting from the letter.

Paul scanned the rest of the front page, then the next page, and the next, and continued until page seven, where he found the two-inch story.

Smaller headline: Briars Housewife Found Dead.

Paul read on. Sarah Goldsmith, thirty-five. Kitchen. Broken neck. Police investigating. Husband held for questioning. Sarah Goldsmith. Born in. Member of. Survived by.

Again, no reference to Cass's confession of rape and murder. Again, only the implication of accidental death.

Two strangers had been extinguished in the vast city by sheerest chance. Accidents happen. They happened yesterday. They would happen tomorrow. Two strangers, the first interred on page one, the other on page seven. Relationship, none. Cause and effect, nil. Case closed. Almost closed. Dr. Chapman? Intact. Sam Goldsmith? Interrogated. Cass Miller's confession? What confession?

The letter, Cass's letter, was a fact, Paul decided. No matter who had quashed it, or how, it had been seen by persons official. Certainly they knew Sam Goldsmith was innocent. In the end, they must dismiss him. But would they? What of the coroner's report, the autopsy, the vaginal smear indicating intercourse before death? But no microscope could separate voluntary intercourse from involuntary. Who would be the indicated partner? Sarah's anonymous lover, of course. Sam had come upon them, or upon her as the lover left, and so it would be Sam. But if Cass's confession had been ignored, so, too, might the coroner's report. Or perhaps he could be brought into the conspiracy of silence. How many children did he have? And, if so, Sam would be safe; Sarah's death, an accident.

Paul's mind reeled. He tried to think of direct action. At once, he recalled the detective's name, the one to whom he had entrusted the letter. His name had been Cannady. Paul threw the newspaper aside and went to the telephone. He dialed the operator, and she gave him information, and information gave him The Briar's police department branch number. Paul dialed one-one-one. A sergeant answered, and when Paul asked for Cannady, he was transferred to a lieutenant. No, Cannady wasn't around and wouldn't be for a week. He was in New Mexico on an extradition case. Paul asked for Cannady's partner, the other detective. He was in Encino, and wouldn't check in until evening. Paul tried to explain about the letter, but soon realized that the lieutenant was treating him like a crackpot. Paul asked if Sam Goldsmith was still being held in custody, in the matter of his wife's death. The lieutenant explained that Paul would have to call downtown about that, but information in such matters was usually not given out over the telephone.

After the receiver was back on the hook, Paul tried to consider the various possibilities. At once, he saw clearly what he had refused to see the night before. The crack in the armor.

He asked himself if it were possible, and the probability of it chilled him.

He glanced at the clock. Forty minutes to air time. He had promised to join Horace and Naomi in viewing the television show. After pulling on his shoes and slipping into his suit coat, he hurried to the car Kathleen had loaned him. He decided that he would not miss the guest of honor for anything. Last night, in a matter of life and death, he had played the role of the Omnipotent. But he had been an ineffectual Zeus, with powers limited, after all. Now, he would see the original, the still undefeated and still champion Jehovah, the King of Kings.

❖   ❖   ❖

Borden Bush's weekly half-hour program, "The Hot Seat," originated every Sunday morning from a former legitimate theater, purchased by the network and located two blocks from the giant glass and steel buildings that housed the network itself. The theater had a seating capacity of fifteen hundred, so the network executives had assigned it to Bush, because his show had been exploited to saturation among institutions of learning. On Sunday mornings, the auditorium was jammed full with teachers, older students, and their families. The network regarded the show as prestige and the papered house as good will.

This Sunday, as usual, every seat in the theater was occupied. The one difference was that there were also spectators standing along the walls and in the rear. The drawing power of the guest of honor, Dr. Chapman, was setting a new record. This Sunday, too, as usual, Borden Bush found it necessary to defy the instruction on his bottle of Donnatal and take another pill, the second within the hour, in an effort to moor his stomach.

At thirty-four, Borden Bush, tan, thin, frenetic, possessed a Peabody and an Emmy, but was prouder still of a skin rash and ulcer, both of which he wore like campaign ribbons. On the strength of having been a distant cousin to a network vice-president, of having done a thesis on communications, of having directed a book review show that no one had ever seen, and of having told a columnist on *Variety* that he had read Seutonius in his search for story springboards, he had been

handed "The Hot Seat" two years before and had made it a
social requisite among television snobs and university under
graduates. Now, having washed down his white pill, he waited
unhappily for the discomforting moment ahead.

As producer of one hundred and seven of these egghead
shows, he was used to temperament. He had learned early,
and had always said afterward, that this program had taught
him one thing—that the big names of the academic world
possessed twice the temperament of any thespian, diva, or
dancer alive. Now, here again, was Dr. George G. Chapman,
a case in point. Borden Bush had regarded Chapman, from the
first, a box-office plus and a personality minus. He had seemed
to project about as much irascibility as an elderly sheep and
had even been agreeable to the network censorship memo
demanding that the word *coitus* not be spoken on the air.
Therefore, his sudden thunderclap of temperament, an hour
before, had been doubly unexpected and had thrown the entire production staff into a frenzy of telephone calls. But now
that difficulty was settled, and there was only the last disagreeable task left.

There was a knocking on the door, and Borden realized
that it had been going on for some seconds.

"Come in!" he shouted.

Sheila, his secretary, was holding the door open. "Dr. Victor
Jonas is here, Mr. Bush."

"Show him in."

Borden leaped to his feet and came quickly around the desk
as Dr. Jonas, carrying his thin leather portfolio of notes and
statistics, appeared in the doorway and entered the room.

"Dr. Jonas!" exclaimed Borden, pumping his visitor's hand.

Dr. Jonas smiled uncertainly. "How are you? Forgive me,
if I'm somewhat breathless. That climb—"

"I've fought them two years for an elevator. . . . That'll be
all for now, Sheila. . . . Two years, but no, you can't put it
on the screen, so it's a waste of money. Here, sit down, right
here." He succeeded in shoving Dr. Jonas into the chair across
from his desk. "Cigar?"

"No, thanks."

Borden Bush returned behind the fortification of his desk,
hands jittering. "Used to be some singing queen's dressing
room up here—that's why the tall, steep stairs—all back-
stages have them." He waved his hand at the room. "We've
done a nice job, don't you think?"

Dr. Jonas observed the room. It was painted a restful pale

352

green, with indirect lighting, and the office furniture was all shining walnut and pale yellow leather. On the walls, matted in narrow black frames, were advertisements of past programs. A glass-front book case, partially filled, held orange television almanacs, Kahlil Gibran's *The Prophet*, Mildred Cram's *Forever*, Walter Benton's *This Is My Beloved*, and *Who's Who in America*.

"Attractive," said Dr. Jonas.

"Doctor, we're almost on the air, so I won't waste your time or mine," said Borden Bush with a briskness that belied his stomach's embarrassment. "I don't like to tell you what I have to tell you. It's never happened before. But here goes—I'm afraid we can't use you on the show today."

Dr. Jonas said nothing for a moment. A feeling that had already been inside him, prepared for this, absorbed it now. "I'm sorry to hear that," he said quietly. He took out his corn cob and filled it.

"Something came up."

"You mean, Dr. Chapman came up?"

The wind was out of Borden's sails, and the sheets went limp. "Something like that. How'd you guess?"

"Dr. Chapman's afraid of me. I was puzzled, from the start, that he would allow me to be included on a panel of interrogators."

"That's just it," said Borden, relaxing a little. "He didn't know. We never inform our guests who the panelists will be until they arrive in the studio. That's so they can't anticipate questions. It makes for spontaneity."

"What happened when you showed him my name?"

"Bam. Went up like Krakatoa. Said he wouldn't appear on any platform with you—you were out gunning for him, et cetera, et cetera. Said either you went, or he went. I don't mind telling you, I was stunned. Well, I'm sure you can be realistic about this. It's just like pictures. He's the star. Everyone else is little people. I tried to get you at home, but—"

"Did you tell my wife?"

"No."

"Too bad. She was having friends in to watch me. What did you do about a replacement?"

"Oh, we've got a couple of garrulous old hacks, stand-bys at the local schools. I caught one at home, an anthropology associate—he'd do this just to get Chapman's autograph. I *am* sorry, Dr. Jonas. You will be paid, of course. Maybe we can use you another time, on another show."

"I'll be quite busy. We're opening a clinic—"

"Maybe we can plug it," said Borden Bush.

"I'll leave that to you." He rose and extended his hand.

Borden Brush grasped the hand with his right hand, covering both with his left hand, and encouraging his eyes to moisten slightly, a physiological talent that had given him a widespread reputation for sincerity.

"You're aces, Doctor," he said.

After Dr. Jonas had closed the door behind him, he slowly descended the precarious, winding staircase, holding the railing all the way down. Once on the lower landing, backstage, he surveyed the chaotic preparations. He studied the masses of cabling, coiled like sleeping pythons, and the unwieldy cameras on rollers and tracks, and the monitor sets, and so many people in shirt sleeves hastening about, seeming to do nothing.

Thinking of several glimpses he'd had behind the scenes, he wondered why it was that show business was the one business where so many hurried so frantically amid such disorder to accomplish so much less than was accomplished in the Pentagon, Johns Hopkins, General Motors, the United Nations, where activity was relatively quiet and unhurried. The answer, he decided, was that most personnel in show business did not come to their positions, originally, out of dedicated and careful apprenticeship, and, in contrast to those in other fields who did, were mightily overpaid and overpublicized, and therefore had an exaggerated sense of self-importance. They hurried because they believed the myth, created by their own hands in print, that if they didn't, the earth would stand still, and everyone would fall off. To an outsider, the gaudy flea circus, unable to relate its true proportionate size to outside worlds, was pathetic, and somehow, Dr. Chapman had allied himself with this circus, and that was the worst part of him.

Dr. Jonas could observe the stage now, and a small portion of the sea of faces beyond the footlights. Two cameras were being rolled into position. Someone was vigorously dusting the panelists' table. Dr. Jonas turned to leave, and then he saw, near a flat depicting a forest, the bulky figure made familiar by hundreds of periodicals, newspapers, newsreels, and telecasts. Without rancor, he watched the enemy: the broad, smiling countenance Indian red with make-up, as an elderly woman dabbed a Kleenex against the forehead and cheeks.

When the elderly woman left, Dr. Jonas replaced her. "George Chapman?"

The bulk was all affability. "That's right."

"I'm Victor Jonas." He did not offer his hand.

The broad face, darkening, hid nothing. "*Well*," he said. The tone was clearly that of estate gamekeeper, rifle under the arm, to the poacher.

Dr. Jonas touched his leather portfolio. "I had looked forward to questioning you—"

"Questioning me? You mean, trying to execute me. You'd like nothing better in public."

"You're quite wrong there," Dr. Jonas said mildly. "I don't have the cruelty to—well, to use a television stage as arena for the showdown between our philosophies. I never intended that this be the place to expose the fallacies in your approach. My paper to the Zollman Foundation will be the proper medium for that. No, what I had hoped was, as one scientist to another—"

Dr. Chapman snorted his interruption. "Scientist? You still have the effrontery to call yourself scientist? I'm glad you're here now. I'm glad to tell you what I think, to your face. You're an academic hitchhiker, Jonas, offering nothing, taking the free ride on the accomplishment of others—like that small thing that clings to sharks, to feed—the barnacles that cling to the hulls of vessels—"

Although Dr. Jonas had determined, from the moment of confrontation, to maintain an even temper and not snap angrily if incited, he now found himself involuntarily reddening. "Are you often accustomed to such outbursts, Dr. Chapman?"

"You have one career and one career only," Dr. Chapman continued, "and that's to destroy me."

"Why on earth should I want to do that, as a mere act of destruction? I've never set eyes on you before, and, besides—"

"You're hungry and ambitious, that's why," said Dr. Chapman. "As long as my theories are proved, accepted, there's no place for you. You're like . . . like a horse and buggy manufacturer in 1895, when Duryea came along—"

Momentarily, Dr. Jonas' good humor was restored. He had a witticism at tongue's tip. "You mean—"

But Dr. Chapman, bludgeoning forward, overrode him. ". . . fighting to maintain the old, outmoded ways, fighting for your existence. If you can discredit me by any means—like sneaking into this program or playing footsies behind my back with the Zollman crowd—you'll do so. In order for you to live, I've got to die. You want to be able to step over my carcass to grab yourself a Zollman grant—oxygen for your little quack clinic on the beach—"

Dr. Chapman had run out of breath, and now Dr. Jonas threw himself recklessly into the conversation. "Yes," he said sharply, "I want to destroy you—"

"There!"

". . . but not as you imagine, for self-advancement. Surely your legmen have reported that I already have full support for my clinic and my ideas. I need no more." He had the desire to wound this righteous, condescending adversary. "Understand this, Chapman, the voracious hunger for success that seems to have warped your scientific faculties—it hasn't possessed me, not yet. At the risk of being pompous, I'm telling you all I want is truth—truth, dammit, no more, no less, and I won't apologize for the word. To me, your ideas are not truth but a lie—no, not a lie but a half-truth that you persist in peddling as the full truth, the only truth. It's because I feel you've abandoned all efforts at patient inquiry, unspectacular investigation, trial and error—you can admit to no error, you've lost the humility and objectivity to confess a wrong, to try another way, to revise or improve your methods—because I feel you are performing this way—have to perform this way, because you've gone to the public too soon—because of that I am intent on fighting you. Yes, I shall fight you, and every pretender like you who disguises himself as pure scientist instead of showing himself as the promoter that he is. The mask you wear is Einstein, but behind it I see Barnum and Tex Rickard—"

Dr. Chapman's hands had bunched hard, and his massive head trembled on his neck like one afflicted by St. Vitus's dance. "If I didn't know you were purposely baiting me," he said in a furious undertone, "wanting me to strike you, so that you can get your name in the papers, drag me down to your hooligan level, I'd hit you. I still may."

"I see," said Dr. Jonas. "That would be further evidence of your cool detachment, I suppose? Is that what you advocate to settle differences of scientific opinion—first barring public discussion of your survey, then threatening to slug your critic? I'm not surprised."

"I repeat, you're neither scientist nor critic—you're a hooligan and fool, Jonas. You can't even manage your own little back yard. What have you done out here in California? Talked to a few impoverished Mexicans and slut wives of truck drivers, and then bleated about marriage counseling as the

356

upreme answer? Is that your idea of sexual enlightenment, of improving the species? A fat chance you'll have to convince anyone. I've come two thousand miles out here, to accomplish n two weeks the job you failed to accomplish in two years—en years."

"You've accomplished nothing. You've done infinite mischief."

"I have, have I?"

"Yes, you have. And I'm not guessing. I've had the opportunity to consult with several of the married women you and your associates have interviewed. In one case, a young woman —one of the volunteers you interviewed—was dangerously stimulated, became involved with an entire group of men, with results you can imagine. I'm not blaming this entirely on you —yet, I have every reason to believe that the excitement engendered by your questions, with no attendant warmth of—"

"Don't sermonize me! If that's the sort of *Police Gazette* tripe you're intending to peddle to Zollman—"

"I'm peddling nothing that is not corroborated by careful counter-testing. No, I have no real evidence to prove that your interview technique is harmful in itself. I have only a suspicion, backed by a few isolated cases. But you're giving me an idea, Chapman, I'll tell you that. It may be something worth going into one day—an examination of the harm left in the wake of your samplings. But for the moment, I'm satisfied to know that the net result of your work—"

Dr. Jonas was suddenly aware that the two of them had now become three. The third party was Borden Bush, who, descending the circular staircase, had seen them bitterly embattled and had arrived to break it up.

"Well, well, gentlemen," he interrupted too loudly, nervously washing dry hands, "I see you've met and had your private question and answer session off camera." Firmly, he took Dr. Chapman's rigid arm. "Better take your place, Dr. Chapman. Only five minutes more. We want to do a warm-up. And I want you to glance at the new intro—we're explaining the panel substitution, since the network earlier advertised Dr. Jonas' name on several station breaks—yes—and then, I thought, well, a sentimental word about Cass Miller would be in order."

Borden Bush had Dr. Chapman's attention at last, and he began to lead the larger man toward the stage.

"Good luck," Dr. Jonas called after them, not without irony.

Dr. Chapman looked back over his shoulder. "You go to hell," he said.

◇　◇　◇

It was shortly after three o'clock when Paul Radford hurried into The Briars' Women's Association building and made his way up the stairs, two at a time.

Striding down the empty, stretching corridor, the totem beat of his heels reverberating against the barren plaster walls, Paul carried his outrage high and visible, so that those who wore cracked armor could see it plainly and take to their battlements.

Since early morning, since page one and page seven, the necessity for the tournament of truth had been growing upon him. Actually, he surmised, the necessity for it had been born the evening before, by the swimming pool, with the brief exchange over a dead man's letter. Yet, the exact form the challenge now took had been shaped over the breakfast tray.

He remembered the shock of the opening announcement on Borden Bush's "The Hot Seat." He had been seated beside Horace and a drowsy Naomi, and he remembered the bewilderment he had felt, he and Horace both, at the moderator's suave statement that Dr. Victor Jonas, psychologist, had withdrawn from the show and that a last-minute substitution had been made.

After the sugary half-hour program, a brief portion like a mutual-admiration society in conclave, the remainder a winning monologue by Dr. Chapman, Paul had jumped to his feet and, the applause of the television studio audience still loud in his ears, he had gone into Naomi's kitchen to telephone Dr. Jonas. His call had been answered by Peggy Jonas, who also confessed mystification at her husband's non-appearance. "I can't understand it," she had said. "He was up half the night preparing questions to ask Dr. Chapman." Paul had left Naomi's telephone number with Peggy Jonas, and then, pacing, turning over the possibilities in his mind, he had waited and waited, until finally Victor Jonas had called him back. Then it was that Paul had heard the details of the cancellation. Then it was that the outrage had developed into a formidable weapon.

Too agitated and impatient to eat lunch, Paul had sought to track down Dr. Chapman by telephone, ringing the motel and the Association building, and then each again and again.

At last, after two-thirty, Benita Selby had replied from the phone in the conference room of the Association building. Yes, she had said, Dr. Chapman and she had just returned from the broadcast and the luncheon given afterward by the network and motion-picture producers. Yes, she had promised, they would be cleaning up last-minute work in the building for at least another hour.

Now, arriving at the conference room door, a hundred thoughts wheeling through his brain, Paul halted, inhaled, and raised his hand to knock. Then, instead, he reached down for the knob, turned it, and strode inside.

Dr. Chapman was not alone. He was in the act of dictating to Benita Selby, who sat across from him, her pencil gliding steadily across the shorthand pad on her crossed knee.

". . . was truly a martyr to science and scientific advancement," Dr. Chapman was dictating. "For fourteen months, he gave unsparingly—"

Dr. Chapman acknowledged Paul's arrival with a nod. "Just completing the press release. Be done in a moment, Paul."

Woodenly, Paul crossed to a metal folding chair nearby and sat on its edge.

Dr. Chapman pointed at Benita's pad. "The last, again."

Benita lifted the pad and read, "Saddened by the untimely death of his devoted associate, Dr. Chapman today issued the following statement to the nation: 'Cass Miller was truly a martyr to science and scientific advancement—' "

"Benita, make that, 'to science and the *pressures* of scientific advancement.' Go on."

She poked at her pad, then resumed reading from it. " 'For fourteen months, he gave unsparingly . . .' " She allowed the last to hang in the air.

Dr. Chapman pursed his lips, regarded the light fixture above, and smoothly took up the continuity. ". . . of his mind and body, toiling, not eight-hour days, but ten- and twelve-hour days and nights, so eager was he to see my pioneer work in sexual behavior brought to a successful conclusion. But Cass Miller's martyrdom will not have been in vain. The forthcoming volume to which he contributed so large a part, *A Sex History of the American Married Female*, scheduled for publication next spring, will be dedicated to the memory of Cass Miller. And because of his share in it, I feel sure, all humankind will be the healthier and happier. Services for Mr. Miller are being conducted today in the College Chapel at Reardon, Wisconsin, where colleagues and friends will mourn him. His remains were shipped this morning from Los Angeles to Roswell, New Mexico, where his only surviving relative, his beloved mother, Mrs. R. M. Johnson, resides."

Dr. Chapman looked to Paul for approval, but Paul dropped his gaze to the floor. Paul had been remembering how Cass had admired Rainer Maria Rilke and spoken several times of the poet's soul-sickness. Paul thought of something that Rilke had once written in a letter. He was aware of Dr. Chapman's eyes still upon him, and he could recollect two lines of Rilke's letter: "All the great men have let their lives get overgrown, like an old path. . . . Their life is stunted like an organ they no longer use."

"That does it, Benita," Dr. Chapman was saying. "That winds us up. Make six copies and send them Red Arrow to the wire services and papers on the list. Better get right on it. They've been nagging all day."

Benita, gripping pad and pencil like a penitent possessed of holy relics, dashed out of the sacred grotto to spread His word.

Dr. Chapman pulled his chair in Paul's direction, the legs rasping on the floor. "Grim business," he said. "Glad to have it done." He shook his head. "Poor devil." He allowed a decent moment of reverence to pass, as a transition to the world of the living. He sighed. "Well, now," he said, laying his palms together. "Well, Paul—you saw the show, I hope?"

"I saw it."

"What'd you think?"

"The usual."

"Now, what's that supposed to mean?"

"Nothing more or less. You gave them a lot of platitudes, titillated them with a few flashy sex references, and said nothing particularly new or useful."

Dr. Chapman's eyes narrowed, but he remained calm since he had been expecting Paul to demand an explanation about the letter. He decided that there was yet no reason to be offended. "It's a family program. It goes to all ages, all homes. What would you expect me to do?"

"Are you asking me?"

"Yes."

"For one thing, I'd expect a man of your stature not to insist that the network set you up with a panel of sycophant dummies. Those three asses. You could have lifted any one of them up, bent him over, and he would have squeaked 'Bravo, bravo,' like a rubber doll mouthing 'Mama.' You needed an eligible challenger, not a tanktown setup. Why did you kick Dr. Jonas off the show?"

Dr. Chapman bristled. This was unexpected. "Who said I did?"

"Dr. Jonas said it. To me. And I believe him."

"Jonas? You've been talking to that charlatan?"

"You're the one who sent me to him first, with your little bribe. Certainly I called him. When I heard the announcement on the air, I couldn't believe my ears. They made it sound like he'd chickened out. I had to be sure. So I called him. And I made him tell me, too."

"You know how we feel about him."

"Not *we*, Doctor. You, alone."

Dr. Chapman narrowed his eyes again. His high-pitched voice settled a key lower. "I don't have to defend my actions to you, Paul. That man's a paid destroyer. Worse, he's mad for power. He wants my mantle. If he were a bona fide scientist—interested in truth—that would be different. I'd have welcomed him. But to have my potential assassin foisted upon me without my knowledge, on *my* show—do you think I'm mad?"

"I think you like success more than science. I think you're afraid of losing the limelight. And, in the matter of Jonas or anyone else who honestly disagrees with you, I think you're fast becoming paranoiac."

"That's damn reckless talk—from one who knows my work —and disappointing—from one whom I had hoped to make my successor. You're not drunk, are you? If you are, perhaps it will be easier to forgive you."

Paul sat erect. "I've never been more sober. Liquor could never make me speak like this—to you. Disenchantment might."

"We're all overtired, Paul."

"I'm not. And you don't seem to be. You still seem to have had enough energy left over from yesterday to fire Victor Jonas, and apparently yesterday you had enough energy to transform Cass Miller from rapist and killer into martyr of science. That's impressive alchemy. How do you do it?"

Dr. Chapman remained silent a moment, studying his hands on the table. "Yes, I've been expecting to hear from you— after you'd read the morning papers." He looked up, but not at Paul. "If you think you can be reasonable for a while, I'll discuss it with you. You see, I think in the end it comes down to a matter of proper perspective. You look at a problem up close, too close, and that's all you see, for you see nothing beyond. But step away from it, far enough away, so that your own being isn't involved, and you get a fuller view of the situation and can judge it and what's behind it and around it. Now, take the matter of Cass's letter—you saw only that someone was being held for questioning or arrested, and the letter might save him, and so, emotionally, you ran off to prove the man was being unjustly held, and to devil with the greater consequences. I, on the other hand, kept my head. Perhaps because I was trained as a scientist. You, unfortuately, were not. You behaved as an author, a layman, a romantic. I don't blame you for this. But you were a victim of your background. You see, Paul, I believe that in approaching a crisis of the moment, the true scientist has much in common with the Catholic churchman. Both of us know we have been in business a long, long time and will continue to be in business. We look down on the earthlings through the telescope of history, and we see that every year, decade, generation, age, repeats its critical moments constantly, over and over again. If we became permanently embattled in each and every one, we would lose ourselves to foolish detail, forget the ultimate goals—"

"You are now speaking of survival, not justice," said Paul quietly. "Is that it, Doctor? Let an innocent go hang, he's too small in that telescope of yours, he's a speck, so that you and your grand survey are spared?"

"All right. I'll bring this down to the petty platform on which you insistently wish to engage me. Yes, I'll concede it, the necessity to transform Cass Miller from murderer and rapist to martyr of science. Because I saw that the thoughtless masses would react even as you are reacting. After reading a confession made by an unsettled mind, they would judge us emotionally, without patience for the pertinent facts. But what are the facts? Technically, Cass did not murder that woman. The coroner says she died of a fall. There is no evidence that she was struck. Technically, she was anything but a woman of sterling character. By her own admission, she was unfaithful to her husband and preparing to walk out on her children."

"And you feel that justifies rape?"

"Nothing of the sort. I merely state the facts. As to the rape part, suppose the letter you had so generously passed on to the police had been published with accompanying headlines today? How would it have served the poor woman, the memory of her, to her children and relatives alive? How would

362

they ever have been able to know that it had been rape and not—"

"What kind of rotten insinuation is that?" Paul demanded.

"I've stated her record of infidelity, Paul. Benita's checked the questionnaires, and it was Cass who interviewed her. Perhaps she invited Cass—"

"Cass would have crowed about it in his post-mortem note. Instead, he wrote in abject shame and guilt."

"At any rate, we'll never know. Furthermore, at present, only the deceased woman's husband and a handful of others know that she was engaged in an extramarital affair and prepared to abandon her family. Had the letter been published, the sordid sensation would have branded her children for life. Had you thought of that?"

"I thought of one thing, Doctor. And your sophistries don't make me think differently now. I thought of Sam Goldsmith in the gas chamber, and the children as orphans, unless someone acted with honesty on their behalf."

Dr. Chapman ignored this. "But the even more damaging consequence of the letter was in exposing a member of our team to the public as a maniac who had committed suicide. How the press and readers would have gloated over this. How they would have crucified us. Because of one bad egg, we would have all been rejected forever. Can you imagine, if our enemies had got hold of this—Dr. Jonas—"

"Dr. Jonas knows."

"Knows?" Dr. Chapman echoed, rising to his feet. "What are you saying?"

"Before I came here, I told him the whole thing."

"You stupid fool!"

"I think you're the one who's behaving foolishly, Dr. Chapman. I know Jonas. You don't. He reacted in an objective manner. He even said that there could be some justification in suppressing Cass's letter—because of the ultimate harm it would do, to the family, to your project—if Sam Goldsmith could be saved some other way, if there were no risk to it. He felt that if your project is to be destroyed, it should be destroyed by scientific refutation, intellectually, and not by reason of scandal."

Dr. Chapman remained standing, flushed. "So now we're dealing with Jesus."

"I didn't agree with Jonas, either. I still won't let an innocent bystander be sacrificed to your ego."

"He wouldn't have been sacrificed," Dr. Chapman said

363

angrily. "The district attorney did not burn the letter until he had evidence, this noon, that Goldsmith was indeed innocent."

Paul felt an emotion of relief. "You mean he's free?"

"Of course. He was in Pomona at some damn business meeting or other and finally located witnesses to prove his alibi. Now you have your innocent bystander. There's been no sacrificial lamb. It turns out I'm no tyrant after all. What do you say to that?"

He sat down, more or less controlled, his arms folded across his chest.

"I say nothing's changed," said Paul quietly. "This man is free. I'm glad. But the fact of you, as I've seen you all this day, is the same fact. You are not free, in my eyes. You were prepared to do anything to preserve your work, your future—"

"Not true. No evidence."

"I'm satisfied with the evidence. Somehow, you did manage to subvert truth before it was made public. You did this *before* it was known that Goldsmith was innocent. I don't know what would have happened had he proved no alibi. Would you have finally relented and allowed the letter to be published? I don't know. I don't want to know any more. Maybe even you don't know. But I tell myself, This man whom I have admired for so long, he doesn't care for people as people. I tell myself, maybe that is the weakness in our work, our approach—that it doesn't treat people as warmblooded human beings but as numerals in charts, that this approach, a product of your own neurotic personality, is not the whole truth, and I am a victim of it as much as you—and people who will try to live by these *un*human facts—"

There was a persistent knocking on the door. Dr. Chapman, the color high on his cheeks, considered the door without reply. After a moment, the knob turned, and the door squeaked open tentatively.

It was Benita Selby.

"I'm sorry," she said to Dr. Chapman, "but Emil Ackerman is on the phone—"

"Not now," said Dr. Chapman brusquely. "Later—I'll call him later."

"He only wants to know what time Sidney should meet you at the train."

Dr. Chapman avoided Paul's sharp glance. "Six forty-five tonight," he said to Benita. "I'll give him the details later."

After Benita had shut the door, the two men sat in silence.

Dr. Chapman studied his fingernails, and Paul packed tobacco into his pipe.

"I was about to inform you of that," Dr. Chapman said. "We had to have an immediate replacement for Cass," he added.

Paul put the match to his pipe, then shook it out and dropped it. "Well, at least it answers the question I wasn't going to bother to ask. I'd wondered how, in a democracy, one suppresses an important document after it's been delivered to the law. Now I understand. You find a man who owns the district attorney or the chief of police, and you make a deal with this man. So it *was* Ackerman. I shouldn't be surprised. You once said he was in the business of being paid back. Now you've settled your debt."

"The practice is not uncommon, Paul, even among savants of highest virtue."

"I'm sure you're right about that. I've read a little in history. Presidents and monarchs have stooped to low deals. Philosophers, too. And men of science. But one always has hopes that somewhere there is someone——"

"Paul, you're behaving like an uncompromising child toward an erring parent. This immature inflexibility doesn't suit you. We're adults. I'm saving years of labor in the past, our present, our future—everything—by the most harmless horse trade. For a politician's help, I agree to take on his nephew for a year or two. After all, the boy *is* a sociology major——"

"He's a snot-nosed voyeur. You said it yourself. You said you'd give up your work before debasing it by employing that unhealthy——"

"Hold on now. Things change. You know me better than that. I'd never give him a key assignment."

"The hell you won't. If you don't feed him females, he'll go running to Boss Tweed."

"Never. Trust me on this Paul. Never." He paused. "Look, what's done is done, and after a while you'll see it's for the over-all good. I think you've let your emotions dominate you entirely. By tomorrow, you'll—well, both of us—we'll look at all this in a different light. We've talked too much, puffed the whole disagreement out of proportion. I'd suggest you go and pack, and after a day on the train——"

"There'll be no day on the train."

"I can't believe you'd be so irrational."

"It's not a matter of rational or irrational. It's come down to blind faith, at last. And I've lost my faith in you—in you

365

and your whole approach. There are too many ghosts now—Sam Goldsmith, Dr. Jonas, Sidney Ackerman. But they're the least of it. Perhaps it comes down to so simple a factor as language. I mean, the language of our once common faith, which is love. You speak of love in numbers—so much this, so much that—and the suspicion is slowly growing on me, stronger and stronger, that mere numbers will not penetrate the screen we raise between ourselves and our subjects, or between our subjects' heads and their hearts. I'm beginning to understand, I think I understand, that human beings are hardly numbers at all, that no numbers can add up devotion, tenderness, trust, pity, sacrifice, intimacy. I think love wants another tongue. What it is or will be, I don't know yet, but I'm prepared to seek it."

"I look at you, Paul, but it's Dr. Jonas' voice I hear."

"Yes and no. I think I found the way myself. He gave me a hand, but I'm still my own man. You see, I don't know what Jonas is for. I know what he's against, but I don't know what he advocates. But I do know what I believe and advocate. I believe that the dissection of love's quality will bring me closer to truth than any study of love's quantity. That's the essence of it. Because of this, I believe that every romantic in history, often fumbling, often foolish, was closer to this truth than you. I believe every medieval wandering troubadour, every passionate Abélard, every pitiful Keats, every Shakespeare with his Juliet, and Tolstoy with his Anna Karenina, was closer to the full meaning of love than are you with your charts on orgasm and masturbation."

Dr. Chapman shook his head. "No, absolutely no. Believe that idiocy and *you* are the one who compounds ignorance with ignorance. I'm as aware as you of history. It offers more than you suggest. There is more to learn of sexual behavior—or love, if you prefer—from the *fact* of Shakespeare's second-best bed, from the *fact* of Byron's falling upon a chambermaid in Calais before he'd had time to unpack, from the *fact* of Abélard's love letters being written after he was castrated, from the *fact* of Madame de Pompadour's hating the sex act and dieting on truffles and celery to give her more ardor, from the *fact* of Boswell's having intercourse thirteen times between Paris and Dover with Rousseau's mistress, Thérésa Le Vasseur—there is more to learn from that than your inaccurate nonsense poems and novels and so-called love letters."

"I won't argue with you any further," said Paul. "Quantity is always more sensational than quality. You will have your audience, but no longer will I help you entertain it—or defraud it."

"Walk out then. Quit. Run to Jonas and spill our secrets. But if you do, I promise you, hear this, Paul—*I promise you*—I'll see that you will be branded for what you are, a traitor and a nuisance. You'll never work in academic circles again. Because I'll ruin you."

Paul nodded slowly. "Yes, I think you might. But I rather expect you'll ruin yourself, first. Somehow, I think I'll survive you. I think Dr. Jonas will survive you. And our concept of love—as something more than an unfeeling act of animalism—I think that will survive you, too." He rose to his feet. "Goodbye, Doctor."

Dr. Chapman remained in the chair. "Paul, think carefully—carefully—because if you walk out that door now, like this, without reconsidering, without apology, I'll never let you walk back through it again."

"Goodbye, Doctor."

Paul had reached the door. The mechanical part of the decision was, finally, the easiest part. He opened the door, stepped through it, shut it. He strode down the corridor, down the steps, and outside.

For a moment he stood on the pavement, studying the novelty shop beside the post office across the street. There was a placard in the window. He had not seen it before. It read: "Before you act—thimk!"

He remembered something that he had once read, long ago, and he was not surprised. Sigmund Freud had written, or said, that on the day a son lost his father, he became a man at last, on that day and not before. It was sad, he reflected, that the great gain could only be accomplished through the great loss. Well, today he had seen a parent die. *Requiescat in pace.* Amen.

How many miles he had walked, or how many hours, he did not know. There had been a seemingly endless panorama of chunky date palm trees and thick eucalyptus and Chinese elms, and begonias and roses and birds of paradise. There had been manicured lawns populated by tall men in swimming trunks, and long-legged women in shorts, and children in sunsuits and denims.

Not once in his aimless wandering had he again thought of Dr. Chapman. All that was important to be said, he had said, and now the tiny satans had been exorcised, and he made his way without burden. The future he did not search at all. The past, the more distant past, he evoked constantly. But for the most, his mind was as directionless as his legs, churning memories, happy, unhappy, without significance or conclusion.

Now, for the first time in an endless breadth of time, he was aware of the cotton clouds floating in the gray-blue sky and aware that the bright disk of sun showed only its rim above the irregular heads of the jacaranda trees.

When he arrived at the street on which Kathleen Ballard lived, his sensory perceptions sharpened. He was more knowledgeable now of the avenue beneath his shoes, and the fresh green things, and the houses beyond.

He thought of The Briars as The Briars, a place unknown to him before, where now so dramatic an upheaval had shaken his life, and the lives of Horace and Cass, and perhaps the women, the women too, he supposed.

Lazily, he tried to fathom the meaning of this kind of suburban community in America, in the world, a suburb that was a limb of the urban whole, and yet distinct and separate, and he wondered how representative it was of the sexual mores of this time and age. There could be no capsule answer, of course, except that supplied by Dr. Chapman. And now, at last, he thought of Dr. Chapman and The Briars.

Dr. Chapman's eventual report on this community's sexual mores, or one aspect of its mores, this printed report, would represent a minute segment, although the most widely publicized and known, of The Briars' standing and meaning in its own time. Perhaps, for one hundred years, the report would be passed along from one generation to the next, in the mammoth relay race of evolution, but each time being carried a shorter distance and by fewer couriers. For, gradually, the report on American women in general, and in The Briars specifically, would be less applicable to new times, conditions, morals. Through the decades, it would have a diminishing number of readers and eventually become quaint and unidentifiable, until one day only scholars would consult it as historical source material, and what the scholars digested, culled, rewrote, would be all that remained of Dr. Chapman or The Briars.

How, then, could the distant future ever know this community now, alive on this placid Sunday? Suddenly, with a stab of intellectual pain, the helpless pain of a frustration that must be lived with, Paul realized how haphazard and warped was all history, all knowledge. If he, this day, walking through a street that would one day become a fourth layer of ruins beneath a hump of dirt, could not clarify a picture of life in The Briars—what then could the scholars of the future, the students, his heirs, in not a hundred years but in five thousand years, make of it?

He tried to project this street five thousand years into the future. By then, based on nature's past performance, The Briars, all of Los Angeles, no doubt, would have been buried again and again and again under explosives, floods, fires, earthquakes, with new cities built on old cities, and then crumbling, disintegrating, continually so, until some defeat had left it a vast mound of earth covered by grass or water.

And then, one day, five thousand years hence, an archaeologist—perhaps a nonconformist, outlawed by his colleagues for his absurd conjecture that once there had been a city in this place, once in the twentieth century A.D.—would come with his copies of ancient fragments, with his belief in myth and legend, and direct the diggers. Months would pass, maybe years, and down, down beneath the layers of silt, they would discover their first telltale remnants of an ancient race.

What would have survived the dust? What fossilized pieces would outlast Dr. Chapman and give their own history of this street in The Briars? A mud-caked enamel slab? Would this archaeologist of ten centuries later know the door of a freezer? A remarkable fin of hard substance? Would this archaeologist deduce it had belonged to an extinct beast, or somehow learn it had been the arrogant rear end of a four-wheeled vehicle known as Cadillac? A fancy bottle crusted with the loam of eternity, a portion of its label still legible? Would the cypher experts ever know the word on the label read *bourbon*? A small, gold-plated, faceless idol? Would the experts understand that it was one of the long dead religions, between Judaism and Mormon, or relate it some way to the folk play of the ancient time, when men awarded the idols in prolific number to mimics who permitted their images to be thrown in crude reproduction on a screen of cloth? A skeleton of a young person, probably female, no more than sixty-seven, buried in a time when life was that brief? Would they know that she had once lived in beauty, possessed of a dark and enigmatic soul, and that she had given her sex history to an investigator associated with Dr. Chapman (referred to in the Lake Michigan Scrolls), and that her sex history had been a deceit?

Would this be The Briars in five thousand years? An enamel slab, a fin, a bottle, a statuette, a skeleton? Yes, Paul realized, this might be The Briars. The archaeologist's discoveries would be heralded widely, and the hoary civilization and place reconstructed on countless papers, a place and people of frail women, pagan idols, dead languages, and monster vehicles.

Paul scanned the street and wanted to reject the fantasy. It could not happen here, to this place so alive. To accept so total an extinction, made life pointless and impossible. Yet, his harder heart knew that it had always happened, and would happen again. Thus, the inexorable years made of all history a lie. How ever again to believe that the Egypt, Greece, Troy, Pompeii, of antiquity were what the historian supposed them to be from his faint twentieth-century conjectures?

What did all this mean, after all? It meant, thought Paul, that The Briars existed truly but once. Now, on this day, at this time, in this place. The Briars that Dr. Chapman would record, or the one that he saw, for he and Dr. Chapman were no longer one, was all the reality that remained or that mattered. This was the gift to accept and appreciate: the living particles of time in this living place, chosen for him by some Fate, to be used and not squandered before the inevitable oblivion, before the erosion of never-stopping tomorrows, before the fossils formed, and the diggers came, and the lies began.

Behind him, he had buried the past. Ahead, he could see no future recognizable. Momentarily, he was landless, stateless, and, with no desired haven, the journey ahead would be unendurable.

Resolutely, Paul Radford entered Kathleen's driveway.

She had been so sure that he had given her up, because it was nightfall, and the train was to leave at seven, and he had not called, and he had not come.

While she fed Deirdre in the kitchen, he recounted the events of the critical day past. The child, sensing the importance of it, feeling the security of his presence, ate silently, listening, not understanding, but enjoying it. Kathleen moved about the kitchen, more tense than he had known her to be, and he spoke briefly but fully of Cass's letter, of the newspapers, of the television program, of Dr. Jonas, of Sidney Ackerman, of Dr. George G. Chapman. He reported his actions, but not his emotions. The essence of the day was enough for now. They both understood this. If there should be other days, there would be time for the detail.

Once, she asked, "What are you going to do?"

"I don't know. You mean, my work?"

"Yes."

370

"I don't know."

"You could go back to books."

"I don't want to run."

"Then you should see Dr. Jonas."

"I might. As for what else I do—it depends."

"On me?"

"On you."

She had gone on with the dishes and pans, and since neither wanted to eat, because there was still too much unsaid, she had asked for a drink. While she carried Deirdre off to bed, he had gone to the bar and prepared double Scotches with water.

Now they were two, locked in by the night. She stood with drink in one hand and cigarette in the other, before the wide picture window that faced out on the patio and the enclosed garden, and she said nothing. Patiently, he remained on the sofa, respectful of her isolated silence, and he drank and watched her. Remembering the first time he had seen the lovely child face, the short dark bob, the Oriental eyes, the tiny nose, the cherry-red lips, in the wallet, in the doorway returning the wallet, he felt again the same surge of passion and desire. Her lithe body, high-breasted and narrowing to long, curved hips and thighs, drew close to each projection and concavity the golden silk dress.

He rose and came behind her, encircling the soft breasts with his arms. He kissed her raven hair, and the warm ear shell, and her cheek. "Kathleen," he whispered, "marry me."

She revolved slowly, ever so slowly, her breasts pressing inward and releasing fully inside his arms, until she faced him. Her red lips were unsmiling.

"Paul, I love you."

"Then—"

"But I can't marry you, because I'm afraid."

"But you love me."

"That's it, darling, don't you see? I always knew I'd marry again, for Deirdre at least, for loneliness, for social conformity, but I also knew it would never be someone I loved. With a man who didn't matter, a friend—well, it would be a bargain understood in advance. I would be wife and wifely, and even a bed companion. But if it had to be more, I knew I could not do it. I knew I could never marry for love, because too much more would be expected of me. I would expect too much more of myself. And, Paul, try to understand this— I'm inadequate, incapable; I can't give real love."

371

"How do you know?"

"Because I know." She closed her eyes, lips compressed, and shook her head. "Or maybe I don't know. But I can't chance it. If I failed again, it would be the worst kind of hell. And I haven't the strength to face that. You see, it's because I love you so—"

"Exactly what are you trying to tell me, Kathleen?"

"What I intended to tell you yesterday morning, when I came to your office."

"What, Kathleen?"

"The truth."

She disengaged herself from him. He waited, very still. She took his hand and, wordlessly, led him back to the sofa. He sat down. She sat beside him.

"Paul, when you interviewed me for Dr. Chapman that Thursday afternoon—"

"Yes."

"I lied. I lied and lied."

"Yes," he said again. "I know."

She stared at him incredulously. "You knew I lied?"

He nodded. "It's part of our training."

"And still you . . . you wanted to love me?"

"Of course. One thing has nothing to do with the other."

"But it has, Paul." She hesitated. "I only lied about the married part."

"That's right."

"And still—"

"I love you, Kathleen."

"But you won't, Paul! That's the whole point of it. That's what I went to tell you yesterday. I wanted to have it done and over with and forget it. I wanted you to know about my marriage, and I tried to tell you, and I'm going to now."

"I don't want to know, Kathleen."

"You *have* to know! Paul, I came to ask you a favor yesterday. I'm going to ask it—"

He waited apprehensively.

"Interview me again."

"What?"

"You know the questions by heart. Ask them again. The ones about marriage—marital intercourse—the ones I lied about. Ask them again, and let me tell the truth this time."

"But it's— look, Kathleen, that kind of ordeal isn't necessary."

"You've got to do it. There's nothing more to say unless

372

you do it." She rose and removed herself to the farthest end of the sofa and looked at him. "Go ahead."

"I can't see what'll be gained—"

"You'll see. Go ahead. No screen. The truth this time. I'm scared sick—"

"No—"

"Please, Paul!"

He found his pipe and filled it. Her eyes did not leave him. The pipe was lighted, and he saw her eyes.

"All right," he said. "You were married three years?"

"Yes."

"What was the frequency of coitus with your . . . your husband?"

"The first six months, twice a week, then once a week. The last two years, once a month."

"Once a month?"

"Yes, Paul."

"Sex play before coitus?"

"Almost none. Sometimes a minute—sometimes."

It was curious, he thought, how soon the inadequacy of the Chapman method had demonstrated itself. Here was a statistic, a numeral. A minute, she had said, sometimes. But the fact had no life, and therefore less truth. Hell, he thought, I'm not bound to Chapman any longer. The question is not what *he* must know, but rather what *I* must know to help her.

He resumed his examination, abandoning the formula of the questionnaire in order to seek not numbers but an understanding of her. He solicited Boynton's attitudes toward petting, and then her own, and, although high-strung, she replied to each inquiry without evasion.

"Did you ever take the initiative?" he was asking.

"No."

"Why not?"

"Because—I don't know why not."

"Let's go on."

Mercilessly, but with increasing aversion, he probed her libidinal history. Her answers continued, dulled by pain, and when, again, he tried to halt, she demanded that he continue.

"All right," he said. "Did you attain physical satisfaction always, almost always, sometimes, rarely, or never?"

"Never."

"Were you most often clothed, partially clothed, or in the nude?"

"Partially clothed."

"Why?"

"I didn't like him to see me naked. I didn't like to see him either."

"Was it always that way?"

"I don't know. I don't remember."

"What time of day did you usually—"

"After midnight, when he was drunk enough."

"Was the act ever physically painful to you?"

"Sometimes, yes. He could be rough."

"But generally he didn't hurt you?"

"No, generally he didn't."

Paul watched her a moment. "What characteristics in men do you find most sexually repellent?"

"Men or Boynton?"

"Men."

"Do you mean physical?"

"Anything."

"I don't like fat men," she said, "or the super-Nordic type." She thought about it. "No, that's not what matters, really. I don't like brutality, vulgarity—"

"What do you like, Kathleen—what do you find sexually attractive in a male?"

"Intelligence, empathy, a kind of gentleness."

"An effeminate man?"

"God, no—I mean, mature authority in a man, strength—a solid, grown man, not a thoughtless acrobat. I want all the things in a man my husband never had."

"Did he have anything at all for you, Kathleen?"

"What do you mean?"

"Did he—well, let me get back to the Chapman questions. You never had an orgasm with him. But otherwise—" He paused, then continued. "To what degree did you enjoy the sex act with your husband—very much, somewhat, not very much, not at all?"

"I hated it. I hated every damn minute."

Her hand trembled as she pushed the cigarette into the tray, and then fumbled for another.

"Go on," she said, "go on."

"No, Kathleen," he said. "This is foolishness. You're the one who must go on. I don't need statistics. Just tell me what really happened, how you felt—that's all that counts—how you felt."

She stared at the tea table, drawing steadily on the cigarette. "He came from Korea, this hero—handsomest man on earth—

everyone wanted him, and he wanted me. I was flattered silly."
She remembered a moment, and then began again. "We
eloped. It was in all the newspapers. I'd never been with another man before him. He'd had a hundred women, but never
a love affair, I'm sure. He'd had prostitutes, call girls, camp
followers, and, well, just easy girls who were worshipful and
wanted it on the record." She faltered. "I'm trying to explain
him. I don't know. From the first night, he did what he
wanted for himself, and that was all. I didn't know what to
do, or what was expected of me. And I never had a chance to
react. I never reacted. To what? There was no love—only
intercourse. He wasn't inadequate or anything like that. I was
the one who was inadequate. I came to despise the time and
avoid it. He called me cold, frigid." She looked up. "Do you
know French?"

"Slightly."

"He had a stock of expressions picked up in bordellos.
Femme de glace, he called me once—woman of ice." She bit
her lip. "He kept calling me frigid. He never stopped."

"Why did he call you that?"

"Because I was frigid, I guess," she said helplessly. "I guess
I was. How could I know? At first, I thought it was his fault.
But I wasn't sure. And he was always sure. And so, finally, I
decided that it was my fault. That was after he had died—
no, even before, yes, even before, I was beginning to believe
it was me. I never felt anything, Paul, and I couldn't give anything. I don't mean orgasm. Forget orgasm. I mean, passion,
excitement, tenderness, desire—oh, love, just plain love.
Eventually, he stopped coming home nights at a stretch. When
he was home, I was stiff, I avoided him, I pretended I was
tired or ill. Once a month maybe, he'd take me, or I'd let
him, when he was drunk, and I was drugged with sleeping
pills."

"Did you try to do anything about it?"

"What do you mean?"

"Seek help?"

"Yes, one month I went to an analyst I'd heard the women
discuss. I saw him a dozen times, I think. We just talked. He
was always speaking of beautiful women who were inhibited
by narcissism—women so much in love with themselves that
they had no love left for anyone else—but that wasn't me,
because I never felt beautiful, not even when I was younger.
Also, he quoted Stekel at me—unconscious punishment of a
man who disappointed—well, maybe unconscious, but I tried

375

consciously in the beginning to give something to Boynton. Then the analyst thought possibly it went back to the time when I was six. The neighbor girl and I always played with our dolls, and one day my mother caught us touching each other—you know—and I was punished. I guess I was always nervous about sexual behavior after that. I remembered, when I was twelve, I think, being ashamed of my breasts, walking hunched—anyway, there was no help from the analyst; he was too formal and unsympathetic, like Boynton in a way, and so I didn't go back—just lived on and on in the ice palace."

"And you still think you're frigid?"

"The night I first met you—just before—a friend of Boynton's who had been courting me came over and, well, I'd had the interview in my head and was upset about lying and wanted desperately to be normal, so I decided to give him what he wanted, hoping it might be different. I wanted him to take me. I led him on. But at the last moment I just froze. It was involuntary. I couldn't help it. I stopped him. He was furious." She paused. "And you. When I thought you were trying to pet—you saw—I froze again. I couldn't control myself. I was afraid. I'm still afraid. You say marriage, and I say, how?"

Paul rubbed the briar of his pipe across the back of his hand. "Kathleen, have you ever had another man?"

"No."

"How do you know it's all you then? How can you be sure you're—well, as you put it, frigid?"

"Because I'm afraid of the act, I don't enjoy it, I'm not stimulated, it leaves me cold."

"Have you wanted to sleep with me?"

"Yes," she said immediately.

"That's a rather warm emotion. That's not cold."

"Oh, yes, when we're apart, and it doesn't count. But if I knew it were to happen—"

"You can't be certain how you'd finally feel. Actually, except in the case of a pelvic disorder, there's no such thing as frigidity."

"Please, Paul. I've read those ridiculous books."

"Nevertheless, it's true. Perhaps thirty-five to forty per cent of all women get little pleasure from intercourse—anesthesia of the vagina, the analysts call it, and it's not uncommon— and the reasons vary from guilt to fear of pregnancy to some distant psychic trauma. But in every instance, it is not an inherent coldness the woman suffers, something that can't be overcome, but rather an emotional block that can be worked loose to free the natural warmth down deep inside."

"You think it's an emotional block?"

"With you? Possibly. But possibly not. It may have much less to do with you than you think. It could have been your husband, you know. Too often, it is the man's lack of technique, his poor judgment, his insensitivity, his neuroses, that make the woman unresponsive." Paul laid down his pipe and looked at her anxious face. "You told me yourself," he went on, "that you were shy and timid from the start. Had your husband understood this, then or later, and catered to it, you might have gradually begun to respond. But he couldn't help you because he was ignorant, too. He mistook experience for knowledge, but experience, like common sense, can be a pack of stupid misinformation. And so, to bed. You found him sexually distasteful at once. Emotionally you closed up shop and threw away the key. But, believe me, because ardor and desire are asleep inside you does not mean that they don't exist. They're there, alive, waiting to be freed. But no man, no matter how cherished, can do it without your help. Such prodigies do not exist. I think if you understand how much I love you, how much I love you and want you and need you—there's no question in my mind that you'll find the capacity to love me back."

"But if I don't—can't?"

"You will, Kathleen." He smiled. "End of interview." He held out his arms. "Come here."

She went into his arms.

"Now," he said, "will you marry me?"

Her head was in the safe corner of his shoulder. She turned it upward. "I'll let you answer for me—after you've slept with me."

"You want me to make love to you first?"

"I want us to make love together."

"Why, Kathleen? So I can audition you—have a preview?"

She closed her eyes, and he kissed her hard, almost angrily, and then, his heart wildly pounding, with persistent tenderness. Her breasts strained against his chest, and her body arched high in his arms, and her free hand caressed his face.

Briefly, he held her off, and found speech difficult. While he could, he wanted to have her understand. "Kathleen, I love you. But I've learned something, too—sex is only one part of love."

"I want that part now."

"Why?"

"Because I want you now. I want your sex—and your love—and you."

"All right," he said softly. "Now, darling, right now."

⟡ ⟡ ⟡

Naked and together on her bed, they were joined.

It was still not love, she decided, and never would be. She had not enjoyed a moment of it, and because of this, she knew that he could feel no differently. She had meant to pretend, to at least do that, but this was too important for a lie, and now her heart was heavier than the weight of him above her.

Femme de glace, she had warned him. And now he knew for himself.

Long minutes before—how many? five? ten?—he had crowned the countless kisses and caresses by entering her. She had wanted him and welcomed him with her mind, but her open thighs had been as rigid and lifeless as planks of wood. Yet, somehow, the desired and dreaded penetration had been effected, mechanically and with hurt, and ever since, she had laid stiffened by fear, knowing that each thrust and withdrawal pushed them further apart.

The guarded awareness of her hateful brain, the unyielding flatness of her shameful nudity, kept captive all response and repelled all rapture.

I told you, I told you, she wanted to scream in mortification. I'm infirm below the neck, infirm and petrified, I'm no good. Why didn't you believe me? Why must it end this way?

Her eyes were closed to shut out all embarrassment, but from behind the lids, she imagined the stranger whom she loved and yet could not love because he was a man. She was conscious of each movement of his lean, muscular frame, of his lips and hands and loins, of the piercing of her flesh. Why, oh, why did she belong to that branch of living things that mated in this ridiculous, complex way? How did flora procreate, and fish, and birds? Weren't there some living things that were fertilized by pollen and others that reproduced by splitting themselves into halves? Somewhere she had read—heard—of more sensible means—the tapeworm that possessed both male and female organs and mated with itself; and the oyster, yes, silly oyster, changing from female to male and back again. But this—this exacting complexity—forcing one ignified being to accept a foreign body inside its own? The oolishness of it!

She opened her eyes and stared up at the face she loved, nd saw its love for her, and was sorry for what she was and was not. "I'm sorry, Paul," she whispered. She wanted to say nore, but his lips stopped her, and the lingering kiss and touch f his marvelous fingers on her breasts sent a wave of warmth lowly through her. And for miracuolus seconds, because he was so precious, her white body became pliant and malleable. 'or the first time this night, although she hardly realized it, hat part of him so deep inside her seemed less intrusive and nore pleasurable.

Embracing him, she closed her eyes again and turned her ace sideways on the pillow. She ceased to deliberate, allowng her flesh to relish this new contentment. Almost without nowing it, as an act quite apart from her intent, she had re-axed her thighs. A physical transformation, quite uncontrolable, seemed to possess her—the brown nipples of her breasts had swollen to points, and her womb had started to throb, and n her entire body a fierce genii took shape, a form unknown, lust unknown, now known. Mindless she was, briefly—and hen, suddenly angry at her helplessness and the indecency of t, she opened her eyes and forced her mind to check and re-ress this unseemly reaction.

She tried objectively to see herself, to see this act of sexual ntercourse. Always, before, she had thought Constance Chat-erley's melting beneath the ardor of the mustached game-keeper an absurdity of fiction. How could any man release a woman from bondage to her inhibited past? And by means uch as this?

And yet, now, clinging to her lover, the old doubt seemed ess certain. Objectivity seemed to slide away. Because now, now, his love was so full inside her, parting and rending her flesh from its old inertia, heating her skin so recently cold, arousing her limbs with his consummating desire, lifting her passivity to the turmoil and rage of rapture and lust.

For a frantic moment, as in the old, old way, she tried to keep her identity, her aloof identity, to prevent losing it to the other individuality, prevent absorption into the other flesh. Desperately, she tried to curb the rising excitement and re-place it with the habit of safe fondness and esteem. Ridicule this unnatural thing, she told herself, this unoyster thing, mock this ancient coupling, mock the awkwardness of the position, with limbs so ludicrous, mock the act itself, this unaesthetic muscular exhaling and inhaling, see the constricted breathless face above divested of all nobility and friendship—fight it, fight it, reach for the smooth used weapons of retreat and resistance, find them, grip them, fight it, fight it.

But grope as she would, there were no weapons, and she was helpless and alone with this wild engagement, and she was weak, weak, and all at once she did not care, and was almost happy. For now, more and more, conscious thought and control slipped away from her. Against her broken will, hating what was happening and loving it, she found her enemy body an ally with the one above.

Gradually, and at last, it was easier not to think than to think. It was easier to feel, and to allow her wandering mind finally to betray her and join her inflamed torso and surrender to the one above. Yet, in defeat there was a special victory, for the conqueror offered her more than she had ever known love to possess, not timid tenderness alone, not mere security, not simply art, but savage, joyous sensuality.

And suddenly the remote identity was gone and she wished only to be blended into the oneness of him. That instant, fused by passion, she let go of something held so many years—let go her separateness—and joined him without reservation. Crying out, she gave herself totally, gasping words she had never spoken aloud, demanding that he take her, take her, remove her from this unendurable rack of pained pleasure.

Momentarily emerging from the animal agony of suspension, one human fear flashed through her head, and with it her heart seemed to stop. What if there would not be another time like this, and another and another? How could she live a day without this? Without her beloved? What if he awakened her for this wondrous night only, and then left her a corpse, shattered for an eternity of years? Oh, couldn't he see? She had come alive. She had crossed the barrier. She was his own. She had loved him before this night, but it had not been her entire life, but now she could not live without him.

She opened her eyes, meaning to ask him, but found that she had no voice except in her womb, and so with that, wildly, shamelessly, proudly, she told him her need. And he answered in her womb, and then with his lips whispering against her eyelids and parted mouth.

The past had dissolved, and there was left the present she could trust, and so she abandoned herself fully to carnal love. Thus impaled, champion over pride and fear, she clawed his shoulders, urging him closer, closer, closer, begging for re-ease, caring for nothing but to be emptied of herself and all that had coursed into her loins and had risen dammed to the bursting point.

"Don't stop," she heard herself cry out, "don't stop—don't—"

Pitched to a frenzy by her chant, his love-giving became a ferocity matched by her own primitive love-taking.

Distantly, she heard him. "Kathleen—"

And herself. "Yes—oh, yes—"

Oh, Paul, she groaned.

And Paul—Paul—Paul—

Oh, Paul.

. . . thank God, Paul forever, forever.

❖ ❖ ❖

When she awakened in the night, a vessel so wondrously drained, so peaceful with self and all the world, she was neither startled nor surprised to find her mate asleep beside her. She caressed his consumed naked body with her eyes, and gently she rubbed her neck on his arm heavy with slumber, and blissfully she luxuriated in the gift of an immortality of living years ahead.

Moonlight had invaded the room, and touched them both, and heightened the sense of eternity. Quietly, Kathleen slipped off the bed and padded in nudity through the moonlight, like a goddess that had made her offering and received the ultimate blessing.

At the window, she parted the drapes slightly and lifted her gaze to the serene blue sky, observing how the multitude of stars, in crystal clarity, blinked their approval and paraded in celebration. Silently, she thanked them for miraculous life, as once she had on a Christmas Eve in childhood.

She thought, Old earth, I love you, love you.

When she returned to the bed, he was waiting. She went into his arms, joyful for their all-pervading intimacy.

She wanted to tell him about this, and against his chest she spoke, and he kissed her sweetly, and then he spoke. They talked bit by bit like this, softly, surely, occasionally, of what had been and what would be and what they were, and, after a while, they slept again. . . .

14

JUNE HAD GIVEN way to July, and summer to autumn, and with the coming of Christmas, the days in The Briars were short and the nights festive. Winter brought its intermittent rains and winds, and soon it was spring. Now the first yellow warbler came to The Briars, and then the busy finches and the needle-billed hummingbirds beating their wings over cups of gold on the vine, and the Monterey pines wore their green hoods more brightly and the magnolia trees opened their puffs of white, and the dusty gray sight-seeing buses appeared in great number again, and in this new and burgeoning springtime, Kathleen Radford gave the *bon voyage* luncheon for Teresa Harnish.

Dr. Jonas had the car pool this mild morning, and Kathleen waited at home until he had picked Paul up for the short ride to the clinic before she changed into her best maternity dress. Later, at noon, in the auditorium of the Association, she personally greeted with a smile each of the arriving forty guests. Grace Waterton displayed a post card from Naomi Van Duesen in Michigan. Naomi was leaving the sanitarium soon, to move into the bungalow at Reardon that Horace had bought. Ursula Palmer excitedly announced the opening of her husband's third branch firm, and proudly passed around a brochure that she had written. Mary McManus, seeming older than when she lived in The Briars, appeared with photographs of her infant son, and was grateful to one and all that they had not forgotten her, though she now had a house in the valley. Bertha Kalish had put on weight, and spoke of Sam Goldsmith's children as if they were her own, and when someone asked when there would be a wedding, she blushed deeply.

Once assembled, the women, most of them anyway, began eagerly to discuss the recently published book, *A Sex History of the American Married Female.*

Dr. Chapman's six-hundred-page report had been made public five weeks before, and within two weeks it had replaced James Scoville's *A Man Called Boy* at the top of the nation's nonfiction best-seller lists. On this spring day, coast to coast, Dr. Chapman's volume led the nonfiction lists of the New York *Times*, New York *Herald Tribune*, *Time* magazine, *Publisher's Weekly*, and *Retail Bookseller*. In five weeks, it had sold 170,000 copies, and the bookshop in The Village Green had placed its third reorder. Dr. Chapman's photograph was everywhere, and this morning a Broadway columnist had printed the rumor that Dr. Chapman was forsaking Reardon College for an academy of his own to be financed by the Zollman Foundation, and the Zollman board members had said that they had no comment but that an announcement relative to Dr. Chapman would be shortly forthcoming.

In the small group of women clustered about Teresa Harnish, all listened sympathetically to Ursula Palmer's complaint about Dr. Chapman. Ursula had just finished reading Dr. Chapman's book, and she was objecting now to the graph that reported specifically on twenty-seven high-income suburban communities, each listed by name, and The Briars among them.

"You'll find it in the appendix," Ursula was saying. "He states baldly that in communities like this, and he means ours, too, over twenty-nine per cent of the married women up to thirty-two years old are having, or have had, extramarital relationships, and thirty-eight per cent—mind you, thirty-eight per cent—have committed infidelity by the age of forty-five. Now, what do you think of that?"

"I'll tell you what I think," said Teresa Harnish. "That dreadful book should be classified as fiction, not nonfiction, that's what I think."

And almost everyone in the group solemnly agreed.